8-Bit Syndicate

April Orion

To those who refuse to be victims.

Contents

Prologue

Wren - Five Years Ago

The worst nightmares never start in the dark. The truly horrifying ones are built over time. Block by block, day by day - they grow until your subconscious decides to show you the final product. What a lot of people don't realize, is the same logic can be applied to terrible situations.

To be fair, I've never had a life other people should envy.

We've wanted for everything: money, food, space...luck. You name it, we lack it. My nightmare began when my mom died a little over a year ago. Then, dad's auto body shop started to lose business. That was when dad hit the bottle. Hard.

My paternal grandmother, Grams, moved in with us to help out. It's not like there's anything she can do. No matter how many times I've poured the bottles down the drain he finds another source. It's not a decision we can make for him. I know that and Grams knows that, but that doesn't mean we stop trying. So, there you have it. I'm thirteen years old, my family is in shambles, and I'm trying to run my dad's business for him.

That's my nightmare. That's my reality.

"The writing was on the wall, but no one bothered to read it." Dad's voice startles me. I thought he had fallen asleep in his recliner like he does every night with the remote in one hand and a bottle of bourbon in the other: his holy trinity. I'm doing my homework at our kitchen table with my best friend, Miles. I'm not sure why we bother. We both know we'll be working for the Syndicate in a few years.

"Everyone talked about globalization. Companies outsourcing production to low-cost countries to fatten their bottom lines. No one thought about what would happen when those workers demand better wages, benefits, and more safety precautions. They had to find other ways to cut costs. It started with automation in factories replacing dozens of human workers with a single machine. Then there was a truck driver shortage. No one wanted the long hours or time away from their families. So, what did they do?" He turns in his chair to look at us.

"Automate it?" I ask, halfheartedly. I don't want to encourage his alcohol-fueled soapbox. Miles sets his pen in the center of his textbook and crosses his arms. He knows it makes me uncomfortable when Dad is like this.

"Smart kid. A brewery was the first company to make an autonomous shipment in the country. Not that I'm surprised. The entire field of statistics was created to brew a better Guinness. Never underestimate mankind's quest for a perfect draft." He raises the bottle in an exaggerated toast before taking another swig. A few drops dribble off his chin and onto his shirt.

"There were riots. Protests driven by mass unemployment that ultimately went nowhere. People hardly noticed when Axton AI undercut their competitors until there was no one left. It's amazing what you can accomplish in this country with a strong legal team and a bottomless lobbying fund." He sets the empty bottle on the table.

"I guess we're all victims of the past, held prisoner by the decisions other people make for us. You can spend hours and thousands of dollars on therapy, medication, or alcohol to cope. A cheaper solution is to stop caring. Don't forget that, Wren."

"Sure, Dad," I say. He leans his head against the back of the recliner. Before long, soft snores fill the room. I pick up my pencil and try to focus on the page, but the words all bleed together.

"He's wrong, you know," says Miles. He brushes his shaggy blond hair out of his eyes. "I care about you and you care about me. As long as we look out for each other, you don't have to worry about anything."

I was naive enough to believe him.

Chapter 1

Ash

I've always been a stranger in my own home. The black sheep. The outcast. The son who could never quite measure up, so at some point I stopped trying. When life gives you lemons, you throw them out and buy some damn oranges if that's what you want.

I loathe people who have a passive approach to life.

Unfortunately, everyone who will be at the party tonight falls in that category. The Council hosts a celebration the night before Ascent Day to grease palms and rub elbows with the most influential people in the city. The Ascent Day happens once a year. Any citizen aged eighteen to twenty-five can buy a single-entry lottery ticket. Winners get the privilege of bidding on available jobs in the elite sectors. It's the Council's way of doling out a limited number of legal, well-paying jobs.

The celebration is a lavish event, so I'm stuck wearing a black tuxedo pressed to perfection with a starched white shirt. My black hair, generally unruly, has been combed into submission. Two attendants circle me like vultures descending on carrion while adding a few final touches to the look - a bow tie here, a shoeshine there. These shoes have never been worn outside of the house, so I don't know how they could have gotten scuffed enough to require the extra attention.

"Is this really necessary?" I grumble. The question is rhetorical. My opinion is completely irrelevant.

"Absolutely! It's not every day the director invites high society into his home," gushes a young woman with orange lipstick. She was recruited last Ascent Day as an attendant to my family, so this will be her first major celebration serving the elites. I try to remember that as she tightens my bow tie to the point of mild asphyxiation.

"Fancy suits and bad company are better descriptions," I mutter.

"Can you go get me a pair of cuff links?" My second attendant, an older man with blond hair, stops the girl before she can continue blabbering.

"Sure, Don!" I watch in the mirror as she practically skips to the door.

If I tried to be that cheerful, I'm pretty sure it would kill me.

Don loosens my bow tie. "Jenny is a nice girl, but she can be a bit much. I'll work with her on it."

"I'm not home often enough for it to matter." I say 'home' like it leaves a sour taste in my mouth. This may be my childhood bedroom, but the Axton mansion has never once felt like home. The walls are a rich cream color leading up to vaulted ceilings outlined in white crown molding. There's a mahogany four-poster bed pushed up against one wall with a painting of my stepfather hanging beside it.

When I lived here, I hid the portrait under my bed. I guess the maids found it and put it back up after I left. It was creepy. For one, his eyes tracked me like a sadistic Mona Lisa. Not to mention, I was a teenager in this room. Who wants a life-size painting of a parent watching that life stage? Nope. Hard pass on that.

Byron Axton is a man with many titles, the first of which should be World Class Douche. He's the CEO of Axton AI, the largest robotics manufacturer in the country. He's the director of the Council, the leader of our governing body. He's also my stepfather.

Portraits of the director are hung in all government buildings as a sign of deference and respect. Technically, the Axton family mansion qualifies as a government building. It's strange the man feels the need to hang his picture in every room of his own house.

See what I mean? World. Class. Douche.

"You know, it wouldn't kill you to visit every once in a while," says Don, interrupting my thoughts.

I wince. Don practically raised me after my mother passed away when I was fourteen. She was a nurse at a hospital downtown. Mom had a severe immunodeficiency disorder. I never found out exactly what it was because she never talked about it. Maybe she felt like if she pretended it didn't exist, then it would go away.

It didn't stop her from getting her nursing degree. She told me she wanted to help others just like the nurses had helped her. When she married Byron, she continued working even though she didn't have to. My mom is the reason the Ascent Day lottery exists. She pitched the idea to the Council to give every citizen an equal opportunity at a better life.

She believed in underdogs and second chances.

The Syndicate rewarded her with a bullet through her skull.

"Found them!" Jenny bursts through the doors with a level of enthusiasm that doesn't fit the occasion. She's holding the cuff links like she's showing off her little league trophy to a proud parent. Don rolls his eyes in the mirror with a knowing smile while Jenny busily secures them on my wrists.

"Last, but not least," says Don. He slides a thick gold band on my right ring finger. It has a coat of arms cast into it with the letter "A" prominently displayed on the face. It's one of those old rings people used to create wax seals on envelopes. Byron insists we wear them for all important occasions. As a result, mine sits in a box in my bedside drawer where it is extricated once a year for the Ascent Day festivities. For a man who built his career on technological advancements and industrial automation, Byron has an uncharacteristic appreciation for antiquity.

"I guess there's no more stalling," I say.

"Same time next year?" Don asks, only half joking. The man knows how to aim for the heart.

"I wouldn't miss it for the world."

Seeing Don, that is. If I never had to go to another Ascent Day celebration, I would die happy.

I leave Don and Jenny behind, opening the double doors to the hallway. The walls are lined with a bold red wallpaper imprinted with a gold floral pattern. Not that much of the pattern is visible. Both sides of the hall are covered in portraits showcasing generations of the Axton family going back to a time when seal rings were a relevant accessory. The final portrait is one of my stepbrother, Jace. The portraits stare at me as if passing silent judgment on the outsider, telling me I don't belong here.

As if I need the reminder.

I escape the hall and descend the grand staircase into the main foyer where the guests are starting to congregate. The women are wearing long dresses with sequins in bold colors, their hair dyed to match. They sport heels that cannot possibly be comfortable to walk in and long earrings that look so heavy I'm surprised they can keep their heads up. The men are dressed in black tuxes, similar to mine. Most of them wear expensive watches, as if they need to keep track of every minute wasted.

Small serving bots navigate through the crowd with trays ladened with appetizers and drinks. The squat contraptions look like a cross between a cocktail table and a RC car. I snatch a glass of champagne from a passing tray and make my way across the room.

I need some liquid patience to get through tonight.

"Hey, handsome." Elle slides through a gap in the crowd, a living picture of elegance through simplicity. She's wearing a dusty blue dress that floats to the floor and her light blond hair is tied back in a loose braid.

Elle and I joined the Enforcers around the same time, but she advanced much faster. The Enforcers are a private security organization empowered by the Council to uphold their laws. They are better equipped and more feared than the state-funded police.

Elle is the youngest person to hold an Enforcer leadership position. She leads easily because she sees everything with a clarity that eludes most. She's by the book, strong, and a self-declared badass. Not that anyone would argue with that description.

Let me be clear, I don't care about the Council. What I do care about is wiping out the Syndicate, the criminal organization responsible for my mom's murder. Joining the Enforcers was a calculated move to bring me one step closer to that goal.

Elle asked me once why I didn't try to work my way up the chain of command. The answer is simple: I don't need to. As a squad leader, I have my own team and I get to lead raids on Syndicate strongholds. I can influence command's decisions regarding which targets we hit without being bound to a desk job. Revenge carried out by someone else just isn't as satisfying. I will personally bring down the Syndicate or die trying.

"Hey, gorgeous," I reciprocate.

Elle pulls me in for a hug and stands on her tiptoes so she can whisper in my ear.

"Pretend like I'm hitting on you. Mother is trying to set me up with Jace again." Elle rolls her eyes and steals my glass of champagne.

"Wait, you're not hitting on me?" I ask dryly. "Do you call all of the men in your life 'handsome'?"

"Only the rich ones." She finishes my drink and shrugs, setting the empty glass on a passing serving tray.

"I can always count on you to boost my ego."

"Don't worry, baby!" Liam slaps my back and joins our conversation. "You'll always be my number one." He gives me an exaggerated wink that elicits a laugh from Elle.

Liam is balancing an appetizer plate on his forearm, but still tries to give me a double finger gun to drive his point home. I swear he comes to these events exclusively for the food. His bow tie is already undone, hanging loosely around his neck. I can't say I blame him. I feel like I'm being strangled slowly even after Don loosened it. Elle and Liam are the closest thing I have to friends. While Elle has her sights set on Enforcer leadership, Liam works with our undercover operatives. He used to be a field agent, but a bullet in the leg ended his career.

Elle's parents have been trying to set up a match between her and Jace Axton for years. Jace is the designated successor and will inherit a controlling portion of shares in Axton AI, as well as his father's position as head of the Council. While Jace is a bit of a peacock with a power complex, Elle has an ulterior motive for wanting to avoid him and the entire male dating population in general. I watch as she discreetly makes eye contact with a woman across the room and smiles.

Elle and I have been a part of this world long enough to know the rules. Do not express interest in anything or anyone. If you care about something, hide your feelings so no one can be leveraged against you. Better yet, don't care at all.

"Incoming," I say, nodding towards Elle's mom making her way through the crowd.

"Let's go hang out in the courtyard." She loops her arm through mine and tugs me towards the French doors lining the wall of the foyer. The other guests step out of the way, creating a makeshift path. Most of them lower their voices, watching

Elle as she passes. She's practically a celebrity among the elites. I'm just the director's charity case. Elle stops abruptly on the threshold. I bump into her, my hands going to her waist to stop us from falling forward.

"Sorry," I say, taking a step back.

Jace is leaning against the fountain with a cigar hanging out of his mouth. He's talking to Penny Bronxton. The two of them represent the next generation of power in this country. Their parents built Axton AI from the ground up. The company specializes in robotics manufacturing everything from the cocktail bots servicing this party to the chip implant I have in my arm. Penny tosses her brunette mane over her shoulder and lets out a shrill laugh.

I don't know why. Jace isn't funny. She touches his arm and leans in to whisper something in his ear. I grimace.

The girl is about as interesting as a teaspoon and a complete princess.

She couldn't be more perfect for him.

Elle tries to steer us back into the foyer, but it's too late. Jace gestures for us to join him.

"Is there an Enforcer meeting I wasn't invited to?" Jace asks. He shoos Penny away with a bored flick of his wrist. She huffs and stomps off like a toddler preparing for a meltdown. Jace is dressed in the uniform of an Enforcer general with the gold epaulets and red ceremonial sash standing out against the sea of black tuxedos. He's a few inches shorter than me and carries some extra weight around his center from living the high life. His dark hair is combed over, forced into an unnatural shape by an entire can of hairspray.

I have the urge to strike a match to see how fast it goes up in flames.

Jace has been groomed from birth to inherit Axton AI and the director's seat on the Council. It shows. He wears an aura of self-importance like a second skin. The Enforcer general uniform is a prime example. It takes most people decades to move up in the ranks. It took Jace five minutes to have his assistant fetch him one.

Jace isn't an Enforcer, but that doesn't keep him from attending all of the leadership meetings. It's not like anyone is going to stop him. No one tells the director or his son they can't do something. Sometimes I think the only reason Jace is so involved with the enforcers is to annoy me. He knows how important my job is to me.

"Without our fearless leader? Never." Liam somehow fails to sound sarcastic, a feat I'm not sure I could manage.

"Want a drag?" Jace asks, offering me the cigar. My mouth starts watering.

"No, I'm good." I pull a pack of cinnamon chewing gum out of my pocket and pop one in my mouth. Jace knows I quit.

"Your loss." He takes a long draw and blows the smoke in my face. Dick.

"Elle, why don't we get out of here and give them something to gossip about?" Jace says, giving her a smarmy smile that turns my stomach. It's a game Jace and I have played since day one. Jace thinks Elle and I are together ergo Jace wants Elle.

"Why would I do that?" Elle crinkles her nose like it's the most disgusting thing she's heard all night. Jace's face turns an impressive shade of red, almost matching his sash. Pissing off Jace isn't only a poor career move, it can be downright lethal. Elle is aware of the unfortunate accidents that befall his enemies, but it's not in her nature to be a pushover. She realizes her mistake and quickly masks her disgust. "I'm here with Ash."

Elle slides her arm around my hips and smacks a kiss on my cheek. She might as well have ordered the coffin and buried me herself. Not that I can blame her. As much as Jace and I argue, Elle knows he has never attacked me directly. He wouldn't dare.

That would require having balls.

Besides, the director gets pissed when Jace and I fight. Neither one of us wants to sit through that lecture. Jace taps his chin in exaggerated contemplation, his lips curling up in a Cheshire grin. It's not a good look for him.

"I wonder if Elle will still be so loyal after father's announcement tonight?"

"What would that be?" I ask.

Jace leans towards me to whisper, but he says it loud enough for everyone to hear. "You're getting married."

I quirk an eyebrow. Now I know Jace is messing with me.

"Are you sure he wasn't talking about you? You're the oldest."

As if he needs the reminder.

"And you're the charity case. Father has to arrange the perfect match for me. In the meantime, he can use you for...less desirable but strategic matches." He delivers the news with complete indifference, like he's negotiating for something at a market. Elle's fingernails dig into my hip. Even Liam, the most easy-going person in our group, looks like he's about to start throwing punches.

"So, who's the lucky girl?" I ask, attempting to match his indifference.

"Penny Bronxton."

I groan and know it's a mistake as soon as the sound leaves my mouth. You don't cut your hand before swimming with the sharks. Reacting to Jace's taunt was the equivalent of chopping my arm off, ringing the dinner bell, and diving in headfirst.

"Why don't you marry her?" I ask. "You're an Axton and you were flirting with her two minutes ago."

"Not my type," Jace shrugs. Luckily, Don interrupts us before I can throttle him.

"What do you want?" Jace barks before Don can open his mouth.

"The director requests your presence in the ballroom," says Don. To his credit, Don keeps his tone level and respectful. You have to admire the man's professionalism.

"That's our cue." Jace drops his cigar, not bothering to grind it out. "Congratulations, little brother." He makes the endearment sound like an insult.

"Jerk," Elle mutters when Jace is out of earshot.

"I second that," Liam says, stepping on the cigar. "So, what's the plan?"

My friends look to me for instruction, but I don't think there's a way out of this. The director and I have navigated our relationship with cordial indifference since mom died. I would have expected him to at least speak to me about an arranged marriage. I guess that's too much to ask. This puts the brakes on everything. I doubt the director will let me continue my campaign against the Syndicate in the near future. He'll want me to do the obligatory interviews and photo shoots that accompany a high-ranking elite wedding.

What a colossal waste of my time.

"Let's get this over with," I sneer. Liam and Elle follow me back into the foyer. We're swept towards the ballroom with the rest of the crowd. I hear a few people gasp as they walk through the doors.

The Axton ballroom was built to intimidate. Four crystal chandeliers hang from a gilded ceiling decorated with frescoes that wouldn't be out of place in a European cathedral. The floor is polished marble. The walls are lined with mirrors that make the room appear even larger than it is. A stage has been erected in the middle of the room and most of the guests have already taken their seats. When we reach the back row of chairs, Elle taps my arm to get my attention and gestures for me to lean down so she can whisper in my ear.

"Are you sure?" I ask, alarmed. She nods once before choosing an aisle seat near the back with Liam. The director is already climbing the stairs onto the stage accompanied by

Jace. I jog down the center aisle and jump up on the platform. The director purses his lips, but he's not going to reprimand me for my classless entrance or my tardiness.

That's a conversation for behind closed doors.

When Byron Axton takes the podium, the room falls silent. Unlike Jace, he doesn't need a uniform to command respect. The director is a short man. He has graying black hair and a close-cropped salt and pepper beard. He looks down his aristocratic nose in a move that oozes high class. His tuxedo is accented by a blood-red pocket square and matching tie, the only splash of color he allows himself in an otherwise colorless life.

"It is my pleasure to welcome you into my home to celebrate Ascent Day!" The crowd breaks into applause. "Fifteen years ago, I was elected director. I promised the people of our great nation security, equality, and safety."

Byron Axton is an entrepreneur turned politician. His platform focused on investing in automation today to compete in the markets of tomorrow. He cited studies that demonstrated the effectiveness of robots in the workforce and the proclivity of companies to capitalize on those efficiencies, making human workers obsolete. Instead of waiting for the inevitable, Byron argued that our country could lead by example.

He advocated for affordable retraining programs and accessible stimulus packages for displaced workers, pitched the idea of universal basic income in a society where fewer jobs would exist, and touted the safety statistics of replacing human workers in fields with high mortality rates. As it turned out, most people would rather bury their heads in the sand than admit a problem exists. Byron became the leper on the campaign trail and was quietly forgotten.

A few years later, he was back in the headlines. Byron's company, Axton AI, became the change he warned the world against. Axton AI autonomous trucks took over the transportation industry eliminating jobs for millions of drivers. Their software replaced restaurant workers, and warehouse associates before branching into white-collar roles traditionally held by college graduates.

The government tried to keep the working class afloat. They authorized stimulus packages until they went bankrupt and foreign aid dried up. Byron Axton didn't take control of the country through an election. He didn't have to. There was simply no one left to stand in his way. Byron created the Council, a replacement governing body consisting of private industry head honchos and politicians from the previous administration. He appointed himself director. In fifteen years, he hasn't had a single challenger.

"Axton AI bots have eliminated dangerous jobs and mind-numbing tasks. They have helped us to build a new and better society. A more resilient society. Ascent Day is our annual reminder that humans and machines can work in tandem without one replacing the other. We need engineers, scientists, and enforcers. Many professions require human ingenuity and creativity."

I have to stop myself from rolling my eyes. The Ascent Day lottery was mom's idea. Byron saw it as a peace offering to gain approval amongst low-skilled workers. He marketed it as a way to create jobs and start to rebuild the broken economy. In reality, the Ascent was the equivalent of slapping duct tape on a bullet wound. The lottery isn't as randomized as people would like to think. Elites always get the first pick. If you have the right family name, you have a job if you want it. If you don't have the name, then money will do. I guess in some ways it's similar to the college admission scandals before the higher education bubble burst. Rich parents paving the way for their children with cash.

The Ascent didn't fix anything. It just drove a bigger wedge between the upper and lower classes. Axton AI created an automated workforce that pulled the drain plug out of the job pool without a transition plan. It was this tension that led to Byron being shot during a televised speech that a protest group called the Syndicate later took credit for.

At the time, the Syndicate was a group of protesters pushing back against the social inequality driven by Axton AI and the invasion of privacy they attributed to identification chip implants. Byron was rushed to the hospital and, during his recovery, he met and fell in love with my mom. They were married and we traded our studio apartment for a mansion. I took the Axton name at my mom's request and Jace became my stepbrother. When Mom was killed by Syndicate protesters looting the hospital, Byron did what he does best: he set out to solve the problem.

This time, the problem was dismantling the Syndicate. The underfunded police force couldn't keep up, so Byron created the Enforcers. He wanted his own private security team dedicated to deterring the rioters. It worked, for a while.

Then the Syndicate evolved. They quietly rebuilt in low-income neighborhoods. They gained followers and power. They set up marketplaces and organized trade and communication for the poor, grunt sectors. They created new industries trafficking illegal drugs, alcohol, and other contraband. By the time I was old enough to enlist with the enforcers, the Syndicate's roots ran too deep to be pulled out easily.

"My sons stand beside me tonight: Jace and Asher Axton."

I refrain from groaning. I despise my full name. The alliteration makes me sound like a dick-sucking, scrappy sidekick. You know - the one that has a bunch of quippy one-liners the audience gets bored with, so the writers kill off the character after the first season?

Jace, the prodigal son, beams at my stepfather as he delves into his extensive accomplishments. I force my expression to remain neutral even though I want to roll my eyes. I don't know what I did to deserve annual, front row tickets to this shit show. Byron drones on about the success of Ascent Day, eliciting more cheering from the crowd.

"While I don't want to detract from the importance of the Ascent, I have an announcement to make."

I take a deep breath and do something I have never done before: I interrupt Byron.

"Actually, I have something to say first." The crowd sucks in a collective breath. Byron glowers at me, but I can't back down now. I step forward and grab the microphone off the podium before he can react. Jace looks like he's ready to arrest me himself. I wink at him knowing it will piss him off. He scowls.

"Elle, baby, you out there?" I say, even though I know exactly where she's sitting. Elle glances around in faux surprise and gestures to herself as if to say, 'Oh, do you mean me?'"

I press my lips together to contain my smile. Elle is about as demure as a rottweiler, but she knows how to play an audience. She slides out into the center aisle and skips towards me. I jump off the platform and meet her halfway. The crowd gasps. Axton's never mingle. They always stand aloof and apart. They certainly don't get on their knees.

One knee to be specific.

I take Elle's hand in mine while speaking into the microphone. "Elle, I met you four years ago today when we joined the enforcers together. My life has never been the same. It seems fitting that I do this on the anniversary of the day we enlisted." I slide the seal ring off my finger and hold it out to her. "You're the best friend and life partner a guy could ask for. Will you marry me?"

"Of course, you dummy!" Elle squeals as I slide the ring on her finger. It's way too big. What can I say? It's not like I had a lot of time to prepare. I gather her into a bone-crushing hug as the crowd bursts into applause.

"Call me baby again and I'll end you," Elle murmurs against my neck.

"I owe you big time."
"Yes," she says. "You do."

Chapter 2

Wren

My neighborhood could easily be the backdrop for your average cable crime drama. Seedy characters on street corners? Check. Lack of general maintenance and greenery? Double check. A general feeling of despair? You got it.

I weave my motorcycle around potholes navigating an obstacle course built by neglect. Abandoned buildings line the road, bearing down on me like angry gray beasts: the burnt-out shells of progress. Once vibrant storefronts feature shoddy electrical wiring and boarded-up windows, a nod to a golden age swallowed by economic depression.

I park under the familiar red and gold awning of a takeout restaurant, killing the engine. A graffiti artist decided to impart some sage wisdom by modifying the name. Instead of reading "The Golden Duck" it now has a four-letter expletive in front of it. Classy.

Not that anyone will ever complain.

Most of the businesses in my neighborhood went under years ago. I push open the glass door covered in a paper mâché layer of outdated fliers. The takeout menus above the counter are still illuminated, but half of the inserts are too faded to read or missing entirely. Makeshift aisles are installed where the chairs and tables used to be. Each row features a variety of goods fighting for space: food, medical supplies, repair parts, clothes, and tools. Everything is piled on the shelves in organized chaos.

Otto, the store owner, perks up when I enter. He's in his seventies with a growing bald spot, wireframe glasses, and a hooked nose. He's wearing his trademark polo with too many buttons undone showcasing an uncomfortable amount of chest hair.

Otto looks like someone's grandpa...if that grandpa was a retired mobster.

He sets his tablet aside and his hand disappears below the counter where I know he has a weapon stashed. He hasn't survived this long by being an easy target.

"It's just me." I hold up my hands and wiggle my fingers. He grunts in acknowledgment and returns to reading his tablet. I have no idea how Otto became the last man standing on the block. I have a feeling I don't want to. If the Council and the Syndicate couldn't shut him down, he must be doing something right. At the very least, you have to admire his entrepreneurial spirit. I shuffle down the first aisle to find some canned goods.

It's all beans. Lima beans. Pinto beans. Black beans.

God, I hate beans.

If I never eat another legume in my life, you won't hear me complaining. But they're high in protein and, more importantly, cheap. I grab two cans to tide us over, hoping Otto will stock something else tomorrow. The small flat screen mounted on the wall lights up with a banner that reads "Ascent Day" accompanied by the familiar Council jingle. A news anchor with raven hair and a crimson dress smiles into the camera. A cookie-cutter person for a cookie-cutter story.

"Don't forget to buy your Ascent Day tickets! The drawing will be broadcast live tomorrow morning." She starts listing off the cities and job openings available across the country with annual salary information.

I turned eighteen today, so this will be the first Ascent drawing I'm eligible for. Not that it matters. I can't afford a ticket. If you win, you get the opportunity to bid on one of the few legal, well-paying jobs up for grabs. Legal is the keyword. The maintenance business I run with my best friend, Miles, is strictly unpermitted and highly illicit. It's not like we have another choice.

I like food. I also like having an apartment. Both cost money.

There is a clip playing of a dark-haired man and a woman in a blue dress. The reporter is recapping some drama that went down at the annual Ascent Day ball, but I'm not paying attention. I set my purchases on the counter.

"Cash?" Otto asks, glancing at me over his tablet. I don't know why he bothers asking. He knows the answer. In this neighborhood, we buy and sell goods using Syndicate credits. In simple terms, the Syndicate is a criminal organization built around a shadow economy. It provides an alternative job market for people without an education or the right family connections. When automation technologies swept through the country, the elite families took the remaining jobs and the rest of us were left fighting over scraps.

Otto is running a permitted business that can accept legal currency, but he blurs the lines to buffer his bottom line. It's almost impossible to get a business permit unless you're an elite. I have no idea how Otto managed it. For most of us, the Syndicate is the only option.

I shake my head and tap the 8-Bit app on my phone. The familiar start menu pops up featuring a collection of vintage video games ranging from Space Invaders to Super Mario Bros. I know if I click on any of the games they will work perfectly, but that's not why anyone uses this app.

Ignoring the icons, I select the gold coin in the upper right-hand corner to navigate to the marketplace. I log in with my password. A prompt appears asking for permission to scan the area for my Axton AI chip implant as a form of two-factor authentication.

Creepy? Maybe. But you can't pay for anything or go anywhere without one. People will put up with an alarming number of personal security violations for the sake of convenience. When the transaction clears, the screen switches over to a snapshot of my profile picture and account balance.

I resemble my mom with my olive skin and soft round face, but I have my dad's green eyes. My curly brown hair is escaping from my ponytail at all sorts of strange angles. It was not one of my better hair days. Then again, my hair expectations are the equivalent of throwing a Maine Coon in a dryer and expecting it to look sleek when it comes out.

So yeah, that's what we're working with.

I watch the credits in my account trickle down until it stops dangerously close to zero. I'll be lucky to make rent this month. Scooping the cans off the counter, I give Otto a two-finger salute and hip bump the door open. I shove the cans in my backpack and roll Indy out of the parking space to drive to work.

Indy is my motorbike. She runs well despite her appearance. Indy was originally black, but after years of neglect, she has more rust than anything else. Thankfully, I was able to keep her at the shop while I scavenged parts over a few months.

I started running my dad's auto body shop four years ago after he died. Jimmy's Auto is named after my grandfather, James Parker, and passed down to my father who shared his name. The building is nothing fancy. It's a cinder block rectangle with a hole punched in the side for a garage door. When the neighborhood went downhill, we started replacing the glass with plywood and went on with our lives. Miles and I don't bother to market our business. We don't have to. We're one of the only repair shops in the city that isn't permitted or run by the Council. Our customers aren't exactly upstanding citizens which means a derelict structure no one looks too closely at transforms from a red flag into a selling point.

Axton AI brought autonomous vehicles to the mass market about a decade ago. I'm probably one of the few people in my generation who bothered to learn how to drive. The Axton AI Pod, the first vehicle of its kind, was the same price as the average economy car, fully electric, and statistically safer. Axton AI acquired a rideshare company and launched AVA - short for autonomous vehicle application. AVA is web-based. It can be accessed from your phone or a variety of public viewing screens. It's only compatible with Axton AI Pods.

They were both the best thing for the world and the worst thing for Dad's business. With less frequent crashes, auto body work wasn't in high demand. When Axton AI vehicles break down, they are repaired at Axton AI shops where Axton AI technicians can work on more advanced computer problems that traditional auto body shops are ill-equipped to handle. Axton AI was able to provide its service at a price so low it rivaled public transportation. Over a decade, the urban population transitioned away from owning personal vehicles to using AVA.

Well, at least the law-abiding citizens did.

That's where my business comes in. It turns out, there's a healthy market for well-maintained vintage cars that can't easily be tracked. I complete the mechanical repairs and Miles handles the technology side. We're happiest when we stay in our lanes. We make enough to pay rent, so I guess we're doing something right.

I brake and jump the curb into an alleyway a few blocks from Jimmy's Auto. I park behind an overflowing dumpster, pocket the keys, and throw a few trash bags over Indy for added security. If anyone is willing to wade through garbage and knows how to hotwire a ride, they earned it. I walk the remaining two blocks at a brisk pace wearing my signature don't-mess-with-me expression. No one has ever accused me of being too approachable and that's exactly how I like it. Circling the shop, I unlock the three locks on the back door.

Yes, three. And, no, that's not overkill.

The door swings open before catching on the security chain. I curse and slam the door shut again before banging on it a few times with a closed fist.

"Go away or I'll shoot your dick off," Miles yells. Charming.

"It's me. Open the door."

I hear the rattle of the chain being removed and then the door swings open. I raise my eyebrows at my best friend and business partner, Miles O'Reilly. He wears his blond hair tied back in a bun to keep it out of his eyes and his scruff is trending more towards a beard than I-forgot-to-shave-today. His chest and arms fill out his faded t-shirt, making me stare a moment longer than I should.

"What if I was a customer?" I push past him into the shop. "Also, what's with the beard? You look like a hipster gang-banger."

He doesn't. It's annoyingly attractive.

Yes, I have a crush on my childhood best friend. Am I going to tell him? Nope. I have zero desire to potentially screw up our friendship. Nothing is worth that.

"You and I both know our customers don't care, Chickadee." My real name is Wren. I made the mistake of telling Miles the first day we met and he has never once stopped his ridiculous onslaught of avian-related nicknames. I should have made something up, like the fake name you give a barista to identify your coffee order when your real name is too common or too complicated. It would have saved me years of teasing.

"So, you like the beard?" He asks, his blue eyes lighting up with mischief.

"Normal people pick nicknames that are shorter than the person's real name," I say, choosing to ignore his question.

"We run an underground repair shop for the mob. We don't do normal."

I narrow my eyes. "Stop poking holes in my flawed logic."

Jimmy's Auto looks exactly like it did four years ago when I started running it. I have yet to put my personal touch on the place. A neon sign advertising Dad's favorite beer hangs above a small corner office basking the shop in an eerie red glow. The office is a complete disaster. There are invoices and fast-food containers from restaurants that closed a long time ago littering the desk and floor.

I haven't had the heart to clear it out. As a result, Miles's workspace occupies a corner of the shop. He set up two monitors on a folding table stacked on top of old repair manuals to make the desk more ergonomic. The shop itself is organized. Every tool has a place. When things break, they are replaced or repaired immediately...or when I have enough credits.

It's the only part of my life that's put together.

I drop my bag on Miles' computer chair and fish out the two cans of beans. I toss one behind me. Miles catches it effortlessly, frowning when he reads the label.

"Beans again?"

"It's the only thing Otto is stocking."

"Remind me to have a word with the old man."

I snort. "Like that'll ever happen."

"What, you don't think I'd do it?"

"I don't think, I *know*. You'd have to be stupid to piss off the only food provider in a thirty-mile radius and, while you're mechanically challenged, I don't think you're an idiot."

Miles places a hand over his heart and fake swoons. "That's the nicest thing you've ever said to me."

I hide my smirk and get to work. I'm trying to replace the brake lines on a pickup truck. "Trying" is the keyword. My lift crapped out two days ago and I haven't been able to fix it yet. I can't find the parts to repair it. I could buy them from

Axton AI, but I don't want anyone looking into the purchase. I'm stuck until I can find someone on the 8-Bit app selling what I need.

As a result, I get to manhandle pre-bent, stainless-steel tubes through awkwardly small spaces while I get showered with rust. It's super fun. After my failed fifth attempt to get the final brake line in place, I let out a slew of curse words.

"Sounds like someone is having a good time," Miles chuckles. I use my feet to propel the crawler out from under the truck. I glare at him upside down. Miles peers over his monitor, his fingers moving across the keys effortlessly.

"Trade places with me or shut it," I grumble, rolling back under the truck.

"Not a chance."

"Didn't think so."

We both know my threat is empty and that trading places with Miles isn't an option. Miles isn't stupid. He's a genius when it comes to computers, but he's somehow less mechanically inclined now than when I met him.

I grunt and try once again to bridge the distance between the final brake line and the ABS control module. At a high level, it checks the brake system to make sure the right pressure is applied to each wheel to keep your car from locking up or skidding out.

Kind of important.

What it actually means is I have to manhandle a tiny steel brake line tipped with a bolt into a small hole above my head. My curly brown hair is escaping from my ponytail in a frizzy halo. I let out a puff of air to move it to the side.

Why is the last one always the hardest?

After more swearing, I finally manage to get the bolt seated and tightened. I slide out from under the truck and use the inside of my shirt to wipe the rust from my face. I stand, stretching my hands over my head until my back pops. It's one of the most satisfying feelings in the world.

Boom. Boom. Boom.

Three rapid knocks make me freeze mid-stretch. Without looking up from the computer, Miles grabs a sawed-off shotgun from under his desk and hands it to me. I snatch it from him and quietly make my way to the back door. My heart is beating double time as I slowly open the flap covering the peephole. I relax as soon as I recognize the man outside. Lowering the shotgun, I unlock and open the door.

I'm instantly met with the foul odor of a hard day's work combined with the faint aroma of garbage juice. You know, the rancid cocktail that brews at the bottom of a dumpster that was never meant for human eyes or noses? Garbage juice.

My client is a middle-aged Syndicate lackey with greasy black hair and a mustache to match. He's wearing a beat-up gray jumpsuit with stains on the knees and a phone protruding from the breast pocket. I've worked for him on a few occasions, but have never had reason to ask for a name. He doesn't know mine either. As far as we're both concerned, the other person doesn't exist. There's safety in anonymity.

The man pushes past me. Rude much?

I hand the gun back to Miles. The man stands with his arms crossed staring at Princess. Princess is what I call his truck because she's high maintenance and is picky about when she starts. My customers may not have names, but their cars certainly do. The man looks over Princess nodding like he has x-ray vision and can see the repairs I made under the vehicle. Eventually, he decides to stop gawking and approaches Miles.

"What do I owe you?" He asks. Miles glances up from the screen, appearing annoyed at the interruption.

"I don't know, why don't you ask your mechanic?" The man glances at me with feigned surprise as if seeing me for the first time. I bite the inside of my cheek to keep myself from saying something I'll regret.

He knows who worked on his car. This isn't his first time in our shop.

I'm a mechanic *and* I'm a woman. The two aren't mutually exclusive. Shocking, I know.

Insert eye roll here.

"What do I owe you, sweetheart?" He pulls out his phone and looks at me expectantly. There's nothing I hate more than being called "sweetheart" or "honey", especially by people I don't know. It's a level of condescending I'm not in the mood to deal with, but I bite back my retort. Getting paid is more important than principle. I pull out my phone and navigate to the 8-Bit app. The man taps the screen for a few seconds before slipping the phone back into his pocket. Fifty credits appear in my account.

Fifty. Freaking. Credits.

"You're short," I snarl. Sensing trouble, he reaches under his coat. I didn't notice a weapon when he walked in, but it's possible I missed something.

"Do you think you can draw faster than I can shoot?" Miles asks in a bored tone. He leans back in his chair wearing a cold smile. The shotgun is aimed at the man's chest. Miles can be truly terrifying when he wants to be. It's something I have always respected him for. The man frowns, grinding his jaw. I watch the internal battle play out between pride and self-preservation.

"You should go," I say, nudging him towards the right decision.

The man hesitates, but ultimately decides we're not worth it. He retreats to his vehicle. I open the garage door and toss him the keys. He fumbles them and drops them twice before he manages to get in the truck. Miles keeps his weapon trained on him until the garage door closes then sets his gun next to his keyboard.

"Well, that was dramatic. 'Do you think you can draw faster than I can shoot?' Really?"

Miles snickers. "I heard it on an old western. Seemed like a good time to try it out. He was so intimidated he practically ran away."

"I'm pretty sure that was because of the gun, not your crappy one-liner."

"You don't know that." Miles laughs. He picks up an envelope laying on his desk, weighing it in his hand for a moment before offering it to me. "I got you something. It's for your birthday."

I groan. "You know I don't celebrate that." Birthdays were always my mom's thing. We never had a lot of money, but she would always go out of her way to make me a chocolate cake on my birthday. She was a terrible cook. One year there was even a partially cooked egg chunk in the middle, but it's the thought that counts, right? My dad did his best after she died, but my birthday was never the same. After a while, we stopped acknowledging them altogether. It was easier that way.

"Trust me. You'll want this one." His previous joking tone is gone, replaced by a seriousness I don't often see from my best friend. My curiosity wins out. I take the envelope and slide my finger under the opening, breaking the seal. There's a single slip of red, iridescent paper inside.

"Is this real?" I whisper, gliding my fingers over the Ascent Day bid number at the top of the lottery ticket.

"Happy Birthday, Chickadee. Don't forget about the rest of us when you win." Miles winks. I continue to stare at the lottery ticket in disbelief.

"Thank you."

Miles smiles, his eyes landing on my lips. Is he leaning closer? Maybe I'm just imagining it. No, he's definitely leaning closer.

"I..." I start, but my voice dies in my throat when the red light mounted beside Miles' computer flickers to life. The screen mounted on the back wall illuminates with security footage showing our perimeter. Figures dressed in white tactical gear and black boots are swarming the outside of the shop.

"Enforcers," I whisper in horror. Miles grabs his computer and sweeps the contents off his desk and into his backpack in one go. I stand frozen in the middle of Dad's shop. I take in the neon beer sign hanging above his office door. The broken lift. The old tool chests with peeling paint. This can't be happening.

"We have to go," says Miles. He grabs the shotgun. "They're going to breach the door."

I take a deep breath to clear my head before going into Dad's office. I installed a removable panel behind the desk a few years ago as a safety precaution, but I never thought we would have to use it. I've always been so careful. The Syndicate loves my work and they protect my shop accordingly. What went wrong? Did someone turn us in?

I pry the board away from the wall and set it aside. Our escape route is a rough hole knocked through the wall of the building with a sledgehammer. It's not elegant. It won't fool the enforcers for long, but it doesn't have to. There's a six-inch gap between the back of Jimmy's Auto and an abandoned factory. It was easy to cut a hole through both to create an emergency exit.

Miles doesn't hesitate before ducking through the opening. I hang back and take one last look, committing this chapter of my life to memory. I'm not generally a sentimental person, I can't afford to be, but I still grab Dad's wrench off his desk.

My dad and I didn't have the best relationship. At the end of his life, his blood alcohol content was higher than my grade point average. I pawned off most of his tools the day he died. I'm not heartless. I just didn't have time to grieve. With both my parents gone, it fell to me to take care of the bills. That money paid for his burial, put food on our table, and kept a roof over our heads until we could get the shop up and running. Despite his many flaws, my dad taught me everything

I know about repairing cars. He gave me the tools I needed to earn my way in the world. It only seemed right to keep one of his.

I duck through the hole after Miles. If I had to guess, I think the building housed a fabrication shop. There are overhead cranes and large presses meant for moving and shaping metal. Anything valuable was looted a long time ago, but the relics lining the shop floor provide plenty of cover as Miles and I sprint the length of the building. A distinct hum fills the air.

This is bad.

The soft ping of tranquilizer darts hitting the pavement pushes me to run faster.

The humming grows louder.

This is really bad.

Miles dives behind a machine and disappears into the darkness. I throw myself after him, crashing into his chest. He wraps his arm around me and pulls me to the ground so we're lying on our stomachs. Three quad-copters glide into view. They hover about five feet above the floor, the gentle humming sound generated by their four propellers. The machines continue past our hiding place without pausing. I'm surprised they don't have infrared cameras. After a few more breaths, the humming fades away.

I let out a breath I didn't realize I was holding.

Miles pulls me up and takes off at a brisk jog. I take a moment to collect the full tranquilizer darts, slipping a few into my pocket before following him. It makes me feel better to have some sort of weapon, even though Miles' shotgun will be far more effective against attackers.

The screech of metal echoes behind me and I hear shouts. I glance over my shoulder, refusing to slow my pace. Enforcers filter down the aisle behind us in white cargo pants, heavy combat boots, and white tactical vests. Miles holds his backpack strap with his left hand and grabs my hand with his right, pulling me along so fast my feet barely make contact with the floor. An enforcer runs into the aisle ahead of us. I can see the door that leads to the alley.

Ten feet to freedom.

Five feet.

We're going to make it.

Then, the alley door bursts open and more enforcers flood our escape route. I spin around, frantically searching for another way out.

There isn't one. We're surrounded.

The soldier in the front steps forward with his rifle poised to shoot. He's wearing the enforcer uniform - heavy canvas pants, tactical vest, and black combat boots. The Council emblem pinned to his chest is different than the others. It must identify him as the leader. His straight black hair is buzzed short on the sides and transitions into a tousled, longer cut on the top. The man can't be much older than I am, maybe nineteen or twenty at most. His eyes are so brown they're almost black. They lock onto mine, posing a silent interrogation made more menacing by dark eyebrows and a strong jaw.

"Drop the gun," he orders.

Miles squeezes my hand. "I'm sorry, Wren."

Wren. Not Chickadee.

If anything tells me we're in trouble, that's it.

Chapter 3

Ash

You can't rely on people, but you can rely on their instinct for self-preservation.

We received an anonymous tip that led to the arrest of a Syndicate drug runner. He was driving an ancient black truck outfitted with an illegal transponder that would allow him to cross the city border freely. We've captured a few runners like him in the past. The Syndicate employs them to transport goods and people between outfits.

The Council ordered the construction of border walls surrounding metropolitan areas when the Syndicate evolved from local protests into something more sinister. They built checkpoints along major highways and bridges to cut down on illegal goods moving around the country. Now, any citizen who wants to travel outside of city limits has to obtain a permit from the government.

I convinced the runner we would limit his sentence if he gave up the person who installed the contraband. He pointed me to Jimmy's Auto. All records list the business as being abandoned four years ago when the owner, James Parker, died. Obviously, we were wrong. After trading my tuxedo for enforcer combat gear, I took a unit to investigate.

"Drop the gun," I order.

The Syndicate mechanics were prepared - I'll give them that. They saw us coming and almost managed to escape through a makeshift exit hacked through the back wall. The woman glares at me, but reluctantly complies. The first thing I notice is her eyes. They're a startling green, the same color as grass after a rainstorm. I didn't know human eyes could be that shade. Her curly brown hair is escaping her ponytail in frazzled ringlets that frame her round face. She should be a mess considering the smudge of grease on her cheek and her rust-caked clothes, but she isn't. She has a casual sort of beauty that sneaks up on you, but once you notice it you can't unsee it.

The guy with the man bun continues to aim his gun at my unit. Pathetic.

"Miles!" The woman hisses. "Drop it. They'll kill you."

At least one of them has brains. I can see the exact moment the man, Miles, admits defeat. His shoulders sag and he tosses the gun aside. It clatters against the concrete. I motion for my unit to move in. Elle appears at my side. She secures Miles' wrists in front of him and I do the same for the woman. Tapping the screen on my armband, I initiate a chip scan. Her profile pops up with her picture and her name.

"Wren Parker, right?" I don't know why I phrase it as a question. Our system is rarely wrong.

"I prefer grunt," she mutters.

My lips twitch at the derogatory term. A grunt is an illegal worker. At least, that's what it used to mean. Over time, "grunt" has become synonymous with "poor" or "uncultured." I close out of her profile and lead her outside where a line of black Axton AI Pods are parked along the curb. Civilian Pods are entirely white with translucent windows and cushy leather interiors. Conversely, the enforcer Pods are black with opaque windows. They're built for transporting soldiers and prisoners. Elle is loading the male mechanic into a Pod near the front.

"Miles!" Wren yells. She struggles against my hold. I tighten my grip.

"It's alright," Miles says. He gives Wren a small smile. "I'll take care of it."

I almost laugh. There's nothing he can do. It's foolish to pretend otherwise. Miles and Wren are linked to a Syndicate arrest. If they're lucky, they'll spend the rest of their lives in prison. If they're not, the Council will make an example out of them with a public execution for treason. Elle forces Miles to take a seat in the Pod. She sits beside him and the doors slide closed. I lead Wren towards a different Pod, but she digs in her heels.

"Where he goes, I go."

"It's cute that you think you get a choice."

"You must watch the same crappy movies as Miles," she says.

I'm about to ask her what she's talking about, but Wren stops abruptly and throws her head back. She's a foot shorter than me, so the top of her skull makes contact with my nose.

I actually hear the crunch.

Swearing, I drop Wren's arm and gently prod my nose. My hand comes away red. Wren is running across the street. She has a decent head start, but I'm pissed. It's easy to catch up with her even with my distorted vision and blossoming headache. I loop my arm around her waist, yanking her off her feet. I overcorrect and barely manage to keep us from sprawling on the ground. I practically carry her to the nearest Pod. She's kicking and screaming, drawing the eyes of the other enforcers. Her boot makes contact with my knee and pain radiates up my leg, but I manage to keep my grip.

She's wearing steel toes.

The other enforcers stand by waiting for my orders. They know better than to help me. Out of the corner of my eye, I see a few of them snicker at my predicament. Some of them have the decency to hide their amusement. I make a mental note of those who don't, so I can ensure they get extra laps next time they're training.

Am I being petty? Definitely.

Will it bring me great joy to see them break a sweat? Absolutely.

"Move out," I bark. I don't look behind me to see if they're following my orders. When I get to the Pod, I toss Wren unceremoniously on the floor and climb in after her. The doors glide shut automatically. I take a seat on the bench as the Pod lurches forward. Wren sits up slowly, crossing her legs underneath her. She prods at the back of her head and winces. I smirk.

"Head butts are never a good idea," I say. My voice comes out garbled and nasally. I curse internally. She grins, but it doesn't reach her eyes.

She points to her upper lip. "You got a little something right here."

I swipe the back of my hand across my face. My nose is bleeding. I pull up the neck of my uniform to try to staunch it.

"Where are you taking Miles?"

I give up trying to stop the bleeding and let my ruined uniform settle back against my chest. "Why do you care?"

"Where are you taking him?" Wren repeats. I lean back in my seat, propping my right ankle on my left knee. I lazily balance my rifle on my shin so that it's aimed at Wren. She crosses her arms and scowls.

The Pod interior lights flash to a dull blue and I feel the vehicle rumble to a stop before reversing. Wren's eyes snap to the overhead lights. "What was that?"

Good question. I tap my wristband to pull up AVA. It's similar to the version civilians use, but the enforcers have a higher access level. I open the navigational console that houses the Pod sensor data. What I see doesn't make sense, but I tell her anyway.

"Incoming hostiles." Wren gives me a confused look. I swipe at my console to remove the glazing from the Pod windows so we can see outside. The Pod is headed straight for a group of black-clad figures. They're covered head to toe without a single swatch of skin showing. It's impossible to make out their age, sex, or race, but it's easy to see that they're holding weapons. Keeping my rifle trained on Wren, I tap the display on my forearm to bring up the command panel to see if there are any enforcer personnel in the area. There aren't.

That's when they start firing.

I dive to the floor, pulling Wren down with me just as the front window shatters.

"Call them off," she yells.

I raise my rifle and fire blindly through the window. "I can't. They aren't enforcers."

"Can you at least stop the Pod?"

"I'm locked out. We've been hijacked."

"Can you do anything? Anything at all?" She curses when another volley rips open the bench I was sitting on moments before. "This is the worst arrest ever. Take these cuffs off. I can get us out of this." When I don't respond, she slams a fist against my chest. "Hey, your plan sucks! Lose the cuffs or we're both dead."

There's no way this can end well, I know that, but what do I have to lose? I release her cuffs. Wren throws the restraints on the floor and starts ripping the seat cushions off the bench. She removes a wrench from her cargo pants, going to work on the bolts securing the compartment under the seat.

"What are you doing?" I watch her closely, waiting for her to make a move for my rifle.

"Getting us out of here. If an access panel is breached for any reason while the Pod is moving, it shuts down and alerts the authorities. Axton AI doesn't skimp on safety features." Wren tears the panel off and, as she predicted, the Pod starts to slow. I have to admit, I'm a little bit impressed. I risk a glance out the window. Our armed assailants are only fifty feet away from the Pod now and it's not braking fast enough.

"We're jumping," says Wren.

Before I have time to object, she throws herself out of the Pod and hits the ground running. I follow suit, trying to lay down some cover fire. I see one figure go down, but there are at least five more. I make it to the alley without getting hit just in time to see Wren use her wrench to break a glass door. The top panel shatters.

Wren reaches in and unlocks the door, pulling it open. "We need to get off the street."

"You know, that's breaking and entering." I lean around the corner and take out another masked figure. His friends dive for cover, buying us a few precious seconds. I follow Wren inside, my boots crunching on the broken glass.

"Yeah, whatever. You can arrest me twice if we survive this."

The building looks like it used to be a convenience store, but the shelves are cleared off and a layer of dust has settled on them. This place has been abandoned for a while. Wren races to a door behind the counter. She tries the handle, but it's locked. She curses and throws her shoulder into it. It doesn't give.

I hear our pursuers getting closer.

"Move," I say.

Wren steps to the side and I throw my full weight against the door. It flies open, sending me crashing to the floor. Wren hops over me and sprints down the hall.

"Thanks for holding them off," she calls over her shoulder.

Savage.

I hear the crunch of broken glass and I know our assailants are already inside. I scramble to my feet and take off after Wren.

Right. Left. Right. Right.

Wren weaves her way through hallways lined with numbered doors. She tries each handle as she goes, but they're all locked. Finally, one opens. She ducks inside and I follow her. She closes the door behind me and presses a finger to her lips. You know, because I was planning to announce our hiding place to the homicidal maniacs following us.

She looks through the peephole. Footsteps thunder down the hall outside. I can hear them talking. I hold my breath, worried that any sound could alert them to our presence. The apartment features a rotted couch and a trashed kitchen. All of the light fixtures are broken and graffiti decorates the walls. There's a cracked picture frame laying on the carpet a few feet from the front door. It looks like a couple and a small child. They're all smiling. We're silent for a few minutes after the footsteps have faded.

Wren steps away from the peephole. "How about a deal, enforcer?"

"I don't negotiate with criminals."

"Those were Syndicate brawlers. They won't just give up. They'll keep searching the area until they find us."

"How do you know they're with the Syndicate?"

"I recognized one of their voices. Look, I'm the best mechanic the Syndicate has...allegedly." She adds when I quirk an eyebrow. "They probably saw the auto shop get hit and are here to make sure I don't get arrested. I can tell them you work for me, so they won't kill you. In return, you let me go and erase my record."

Like there's any way I would ever agree to that.

If Wren is as important as she seems to think she is, why would I give the Syndicate back one of their most valuable assets? I remember the way Wren manipulated the Pod and got us to safety. If I were in this situation alone, I would already be dead. I can always renege on our deal later. Right now, I need her help.

"Deal," I say.

Wren eyes me suspiciously, but she extends her hand. "What's your name anyway?"

"I prefer pansy," I say, shaking her hand and mimicking her earlier response. Her lips twitch up, her eyes flicking to the pansy insignia pinned on my chest - the symbol of the Council.

The Council selected the pansy to pay homage to Francois Quesnay, the French Physiocrat who coined the term *laissez-faire*. The Council protects private industry first and foremost, so I suppose it's fitting they picked the flower featured on Quesnay's coat of arms for their symbol. The insignia is the reason most grunts refer to the enforcers and other Council sympathizers as "pansies." To be fair, the Council probably should have run it by a marketing firm before they rolled with it. They practically served up the nickname in a slow-pitch softball tournament. It was an easy home run.

"It's Ash," I add. I don't know why I tell her my name, but for some reason I want her to know.

"Is that short for something? Ashley? Ashton?"

"It's just Ash."

"Okay," Wren says, drawing the word out into multiple syllables. I've never had anyone speak to me the way this grunt does. My entire adult life I've held a position that demanded respect. Honestly, it's refreshing to meet someone who doesn't treat me differently because of the Axton name.

"Well...Ash," she tries out my name. She eyes my white jacket and tactical vest with disdain. "Unless you want to get shot, you should lose the enforcer uniform. Or don't. Whatever."

I grip the velcro straps securing the vest for a moment. I know it's stupid to care about my uniform when we're running for our lives, but there's some part of me that balks at leaving it behind. I rip the velcro apart.

The sound is like a gunshot in the silence. We both wince. I listen for footsteps, but I don't hear anything. I tug the vest off and unzip the white jacket revealing my black t-shirt underneath. Wren gives me a once-over and frowns. She squats and tugs my pant legs out of my boots.

"You still look too neat. How is that possible?" She grabs the hem of my shirt and yanks it out of my waistband before running her fingers through my hair to mess it up.

I swat her hands away. "Do you mind?" I snap.

"No," scowls Wren. "If you look too clean, they'll never buy that you're a mechanic. You'd blend better if we could remove the giant stick from your ass, but that would take longer than we have."

"Hilarious," I say flatly.

Wren ignores me, cracking the door to check that we're clear before opening it all the way. She takes the lead, winding through the building and outside. I see our abandoned Pod idling in the middle of the street. Wren circled back on our path. I'm guessing our pursuers are still somewhere behind us. Smart move.

Glancing over her shoulder to make sure I'm following, Wren jogs across the street and disappears down an alleyway. She tosses trash bags out of the way to reveal an old black motorcycle. Motorcycle is a loose description. A rust bucket held together by duct tape and prayers is more accurate.

"You coming or what?" She asks.

"There's no way I'm getting on that thing. It looks like it's going to fall apart."

Wren glares at me, then pets the side of her bike. "He didn't mean it, Indy. Ignore the rude man."

"Indy? You named that piece of junk?"

Wren advances on me until she's nearly chest to chest. I would feel intimidated if I didn't have a foot and a hundred pounds on her. "I'll have you know; Indy was put together by the best mechanic in the city." She points her thumb at her chest. "Me. She's fast and reliable. If you can't respect her, then you don't deserve a ride." She swings her leg over the bike and kick starts it.

I've never ridden a motorcycle before. I never even learned how to drive. I have never needed to with the easy access to Pods downtown. Wren revs the engine and quirks an eyebrow. I guess I don't have a choice. I sit behind her and rest my hands on her hips. I'm barely settled before she guns it. Suppressing a yelp, I wrap my arms around her waist and slam my eyes shut. This thing is terrifying. I feel like we're driving at supersonic speeds, but I know this rust bucket can't possibly be going that fast.

"Hold on," Wren yells. I force my eyes open, but the wind makes them well up with tears almost instantly. I can just make out the Syndicate goons running down the street behind us. They must have realized we circled back.

"Nah, I thought I'd let go," I grit out, tightening my hold on her waist. Bullets hit the pavement around us, but Wren speeds up until we're out of range. Suddenly, a truck skids across the intersection and parks, blocking our escape. A man stands in the bed with a semi-automatic weapon trained on us. I didn't even know Syndicate members had access to equipment like that. Wren brakes hard, bringing the bike up on its front wheel. The back wheel comes down with a teeth-rattling crash. The gunman makes a cutting motion across his throat and Wren kills the engine. A metallic taste fills my mouth. I must have bitten my tongue.

"Hey guys, how's it going?" asks Wren. She sounds like she's meeting a group of friends for brunch. The black-clad figures jog towards us. We're so screwed.

"Why did you run?" asks the Syndicate thug.

"I don't know," Wren taps her fingers against her chin in mock contemplation. "Maybe because you were chasing me?"

"We were sent to make sure you weren't arrested. Who's the guy?" The man nods at me.

"He's new at the shop."

"What happened to his face?" he asks.

Wren shrugs. "We had a run-in with some enforcers, but we got away."

The masked figures draw to a stop behind us. The gunman holds up a hand to stop them. He stares at us as if he can see straight through Wren's lie, but I do my part and hold his gaze. Finally, he spits on the asphalt and shakes his head.

"You should have updated your file."

"Yeah, yeah, I'll get around to it eventually," says Wren. "Were you able to get Miles?"

"No, we got here too late."

"Oh." I hear the disappointment in her voice, but all I feel is relief. It means Elle and the rest of my team got away safely. "Well, thank you guys!"

Wren starts to walk the bike forward.

"Not so fast. You owe us 300 credits."

She stops rolling. "For what?"

"Your protection fees."

"I already paid those."

"You didn't add the new employee to your file." The man shrugs. "You can either pay or I shoot the newbie."

"Go for it," Wren mutters so only I can hear. I squeeze her hip to let her know I'm not amused. She takes out her phone and taps the screen. I can't see what she's looking at. The man standing in the truck bed does the same.

He nods at the screen, as if confirming her payment, then pockets the device. "Ya'll have a good day."

Wren grumbles something that sounds a lot like "yeah, screw you too." The wind roars in my ears as Wren picks up speed. We pass boarded-up businesses and a group of kids playing street hockey. Someone tosses a bucket of trash out of a third-story window. How quaint.

Earlier this evening, I was wearing a tuxedo and sipping champagne. I can't believe we're still in the same city, let alone the same universe. Wren keeps going until the buildings begin to look less sketchy, then she parks the bike when we're still a few miles from downtown. She kills the engine.

A lady walking a poodle gives us some major side-eye. She tugs on the dog's leash and picks up her pace. I can't say I blame her. With my blood-encrusted shirt and face, I feel like I belong on the set of a slasher movie. She probably expects us to rob her.

"You can let go now," Wren says. I glance down at my arms and realize they're still wrapped firmly around her waist.

"Sorry." I scramble to get off the bike, nearly face planting in the process. Real smooth.

"I would say it has been a pleasure, but it hasn't." She offers me her hand. I stare at it blankly. "This is where we part ways." She says each word slowly as if I'm too stupid to live.

"You're still under arrest."

"We had a deal," Wren scowls. "I save your life, you let me go. Besides, I lost 300 credits saving your sorry ass."

"If we're counting, I saved your life first when they started shooting at the Pod. We're even."

"That first time doesn't even count! I was already on the floor."

"I have multiple witnesses that put you at an illegal business and I scanned your chip. You made your choice when you joined the Syndicate. You don't get to walk away now." Her face falls when she realizes I'm not going to give.

"I should have known better than to trust a pansy. Can I at least get a coffee first?" Wren sighs, getting off the bike. She puts her hands in her front pockets, appearing resigned to her fate.

"What?"

"Coffee. If I have to put up with you, I need caffeine."

I can't believe this.

"No." I grab her elbow. "We're finding a Pod and I'm taking you in."

"Then you're responsible for any deaths that occur as a result of my caffeine deficit." She shrugs. I rake a hand through my hair. I can't believe I'm entertaining this.

"Fine. I think there's a coffee shop around the corner." Wren beams. I step forward to lead the way. I realize my mistake a second too late. There's a sharp, stabbing pain in the back of my neck just under my hairline.

"What the..." My vision swims and my legs give out, driving me to my knees. "What did you do to me?" I'm vaguely aware that I'm slurring my words. My tongue feels heavy in my mouth. Wren twirls an empty tranquilizer dart cartridge between her fingers like a poker chip before tossing it on the pavement beside me.

"When you wake up with a migraine, just remember I wasn't the one who went back on my word," she says.

Wren gets back on Indy and starts the engine. I watch her drive away, my vision fading fast. I try to yell at the lady with the poodle, but she's already too far away to hear me. There aren't many pedestrians at this hour. I'm not sure if I'm disappointed at the lack of help or grateful no one can see me this way.

I manage to drag myself further onto the sidewalk and prop myself up against the building. My eyes settle on the window across the street. It's the coffee shop I thought was around the corner. The owner flips on the digital display in the window indicating he's open for business. His eyes widen when he notices me. He locks the door before taking out his phone to call for help.

I could go for a coffee right now.

It's the last thought I have before my vision fades to black.

Chapter 4

Wren

I don't remember the last ten blocks. I keep glancing over my shoulder, half expecting Ash to come barreling after me. It was shitty to leave him in the street. I own that, but what could I have done differently? He was going to arrest me and then there would be no one left to take care of my family or bust Miles out. I pull into the alley and stash the bike, then take the five flights of stairs up to my apartment at a breakneck pace.

Maybe if I run fast enough, I can leave all my problems on the ground.

Surprise, surprise, it doesn't work. My life is still a raging dumpster fire.

When I reach the fifth floor, my legs are burning and I'm panting. I've taken the stairs at least twice a day my entire life, but never at that speed. The elevator has been out of service for as long as I can remember. Yellow caution tape is draped across the doors on each floor. I'm not sure why the landlord bothered. More often than not, tenants roll back the doors to use the elevator shaft as a trash shoot. I punt a few empty food cartons into the opening to keep them from stinking up our hallway. I'm sure our first-floor neighbors will appreciate the air freshener.

I grab the spare key from the top of the door frame and let myself in. The lights are off and the bedroom door is closed. My family is already asleep. I shuffle out of my boots and set dad's wrench on the shelf beside the door, almost losing my balance when a furry head butts against my thighs.

"Hey there, Max." I smile, petting his head. Max is a German Shepherd. He's missing part of his left ear and walks with a limp. He was Mom's dog. They worked together on the police force until they both responded to the call that took Max's health and Mom's life. The force had no use for Max after the incident, so he came to live with us.

Mom was part of the old police force that patrolled the city before the enforcers took over. I don't think it exists anymore. At least, not in the way it did before. The Council cut their funds and responsibilities until nothing was left but their name. A few officers, like my mom, stuck around on principle. She died breaking up a riot when Syndicate protesters stormed a political meeting downtown and shot the director.

I was young, only twelve at the time. I don't think Dad ever recovered. Soon after her death, the Syndicate approached him about working for them. He refused, at first, but relented after a few broken ribs and threats. I think that's what killed him in the end. Not losing mom, but losing our family legacy to the people that took her from us.

Why do I work for the Syndicate if they cost my family everything?

It's simple. Ideology doesn't put food on the table.

I take a quick shower and grab a loose t-shirt and sweatpants from under the sink. After a few late nights at the shop, I started keeping clean clothes in the bathroom. It's better than going into the bedroom and waking everyone up. I ball up my soiled clothes and stuff them back under the sink. I'll deal with them later.

The sun is starting to peep through the ragged curtains hanging over the kitchen window, illuminating the peeling floral wallpaper. We only have three chairs at our table, the fourth stands lopsided against the wall with a broken leg. I secured the top of the chair to the wall with a screw, creating a makeshift stand for our small flat screen. A refrigerator, sink, and counter line the wall across from the front door. I flop onto our sunken couch. It groans under my weight and a broken spring presses into my lower back. Max jumps up on my legs. The apartment is cold, so I don't mind. I pet his head until he settles down.

I try to sleep. I really put in my best effort, but I can't stop thinking about Miles. Eventually, I give up and open the 8-Bit app. I scroll through the Syndicate job postings. My phone screen is a spiderweb of cracks, but it still works. There are a few requests that fit my expertise. Setting up a security camera system in a bar. Installing a new water heater. The jobs are all small, which means less pay. It looks like I'm skipping a few meals this week. I sigh. It could always be worse. The bedroom door opens with a squeak.

"Wren, can you get the coffee started?" Grams mumbles. Her real name is Roberta Parker, but everyone I know calls her Grams. She's just under five feet tall with a personality the size of a Syndicate brawler. Her wiry gray hair is pulled back into a low bun. She's wearing a gold locket around her neck where she keeps a picture of our family. It's the last photo we have of all of us together: Grams, my parents, Miles' family, and me. We're not related to the O'Reilly's by blood, but we're family in all the ways that count. I've never seen her take it off.

Ariel, our resident two-year-old whirlwind, is sitting on Grams' foot with her arms wrapped around her leg. She looks like a princess with her pink nightgown, a halo of brown ringlets, and a contagious smile. Grams tries to walk into the living room, dragging Ariel with her. She freezes when she sees me. I don't know what tips her off: my expression or the dark circles under my eyes from a sleepless night.

"What's wrong?" she asks. I shake my head, glancing at Ariel. Grams gets the idea. She takes Ariel into the bathroom and starts filling the tub. I head to the kitchen where Max is already waiting at the refrigerator expectantly.

"Sorry, boy," I say. "I don't have anything for you." Max whines and lays on the floor with his head resting on his paws. His eyes slay me. "You don't play fair, do you?" He rolls on his back and his tongue flops out.

I grab the carafe from the coffee pot and start filling it. A pool of water trickles from under the cabinet, soaking my socks. Cursing, I grab the pliers I have sitting on the counter for this purpose. We've had a bad coupling for almost a year now. I've always intended to fix it, but never had the time or money to bother. I tighten it down and finish filling the carafe. The water stops running in the bathroom and soon after Grams comes outside. She leaves the door open so she can keep one eye on Ariel and the other on me.

"Spill." She crosses her arms.

I grab a coffee filter and shake some grounds in it before I respond. "Long story short, enforcers raided Dad's shop. They arrested Miles."

Grams inhales sharply. "Are you okay?"

"No, but I don't have time not to be."

"Oh, sugar," Grams uncrosses her arms and pulls me into a tight hug. She smells like peach bar soap.

"I'm going to get him back."

"We can ask around about hiring a lawyer."

"With what money?" I laugh, but there's no humor in it. There's a quick knock at the door before Miles' dad, Don, enters with Robbie beside him. Robbie is Miles' twelve-year-old brother. He has the same blond hair, dimple on the left side of his mouth, and a smattering of freckles across his nose as his older sibling. Sometime in the last year,

Robbie shot up in height. He's lanky and awkward, having not quite grown into his body yet. He smiles when he sees me and my heart shatters. I don't want to have this conversation.

Pulling away from Grams', I force a smile.

Don looks like he might be more tired than I am. He has deep bags under his eyes and his shoulders are hunched. He drags his feet with each step as if the effort of lifting them is too much. Don works for an elite family downtown. Every year around Ascent Day, he picks up double shifts to cover all of the festivities surrounding the event. I wouldn't be surprised if he fell asleep standing up.

Grams squeezes my arm. "I'm going to go get Ariel out of the tub, you two make yourselves at home." Grams leaves, giving me privacy to speak with Miles' family.

"I've got to head out early. Ascent Day festivities are never-ending this week," says Don, unaware that I'm about to bring his world crumbling down. "Can Robbie stay here for a few hours?"

"Sure," I say.

"I don't need a babysitter," Robbie grumbles. He's probably right. Robbie is a great kid with a ton of energy, but he needs somewhere to direct it. He has asked Miles and me more than once if he can work at the shop. We both told him no. There's no way we would allow him to get involved with the Syndicate before he has to. I want to protect his innocence for as long as I can.

"Grams could use your help with Ariel, if you're up for it," I say. Robbie's face lights up.

"I can do that," Robbie says. Don perceives that as the end of the conversation and turns to leave.

"Wait, there's something I need to tell you. Both of you," I add when Robbie looks up curiously.

"Make it quick, I can't be late," Don grumbles.

"Look," I say, swallowing. "I've never been good with words, so I'm just going to come out and say it. Miles was arrested this morning. Enforcers raided Jimmy's Auto. I got away, obviously, but I couldn't stop them from taking Miles. I'm sorry."

Robbie sinks into a seat at the kitchen table. He runs his hands through his hair, appearing utterly destroyed. Don stares listlessly out the window. I'm not even sure he heard what I said. "I have to go," he repeats in a monotone. "I'm going to be late."

My mouth drops open.

"That's it?" I growl. "I tell you your oldest son was arrested and you just walk away? What's wrong with you! You work for an elite family. Can't you ask them for a pardon? Plead your case?"

Don shrugs and keeps walking. "I won't risk my job over this. Miles made his choice. And, in case you didn't notice, I have another mouth to feed." He shoots a glance at Robbie as if he's just another piece of baggage and not the center of his world.

Unbelievable.

Don closes the door behind him. Everything that has happened since this morning comes to a head. Losing Dad's shop. Losing my best friend. Dealing with a cocky enforcer. Watching Don's indifference. I scream and slam my fist into the drywall. It punches through, leaving a fist-sized hole to the right of the window. Robbie wraps his arms around my waist, pinning my arms to my sides before I can do more damage.

"I'm sorry about my dad. He fights with Miles a lot about working for the Syndicate. I guess, in his mind, this is Miles getting what he deserves."

I sniffle, wiping the tears from my eyes before they can fall. "I'm going to get him back."

"I'll help you," Robbie says, resting his chin on my head. Since when did he get so much taller than me?

"No." I step back. "This is on me. I don't want you involved."

"He's my brother."

"And as my best friend's brother, I don't want you anywhere near this situation. Miles wouldn't either."

Ariel runs into the kitchen and body slams my legs. Despite everything, it brings a smile to my lips. I swoop her up and pepper her face with kisses causing more giggles.

"Hi, baby girl."

"I'm not a baby," Ariel pouts.

"No, you most certainly are not. Could a baby decide which cartoon she wants to watch?" I ask. Ariel beams. I set her down and she starts tossing the living room searching for the remote.

"Besides," I return my attention to Robbie. "I need you to keep an eye on Ariel and Grams while I figure this out. Can you do that?"

Robbie frowns, instantly turning serious. "Sure."

"Thank you." Grams helps Ariel turn on the TV.

A Council broadcast appears on the screen. "Get your tickets ready! We'll announce the Ascent Day winners live after this break."

"Where toons?" Ariel asks. She clicks the button to change the channel, but they are all airing the same broadcast.

"The cartoons will be on in a minute. We just have to wait for this to finish," I explain, sitting beside Ariel.

Hold on a second.

I pat my pockets until I find the wrinkled piece of paper Miles' gave me. I can't believe I still have the lottery ticket. I run it along the edge of the end table to flatten it out.

"Woah, is that real?" Robbie sits down beside me, running his fingers over the iridescent red paper.

"It is."

"Waste of money if you ask me," says Grams.

"Miles got it for my birthday. I know there's no chance of winning, but I feel like I owe it to him to check."

The commercial break ends and the news anchor starts her announcements. Our city has twenty allocations today.

It's different for every city based on the local needs and the number fluctuates every Ascent Day. I stare at the screen as the first five numbers are posted. Then fifteen. Then nineteen. All busts.

"And last but not least, we have fifty-eight, twenty-eight-"

My breath hitches.

"Eighty-nine and seventy-two. If you have a winning ticket, please join us at the Academy to place your bid. Congratulations and best of luck next year!"

Ariel reaches for the remote and I let her take it. I'm only half-conscious of my movements at this point. I'm still staring at the slip of paper in front of me.

58 28 89 72

"Damn," whistles Robbie, leaning over my shoulder.

Then our world explodes.

The front door is blown off its' hinges. Ariel screams. I leap off the couch, ready to put the first intruder on the ground. Before I can do any damage, someone hits me so hard it sends me to my hands and knees. My ears are ringing and I see an entire galaxy of stars. It takes me a moment to realize I was pistol-whipped. When my vision clears, I see five enforcers in my apartment aiming their weapons at my family.

The man leading the squad isn't what I expect. He holds his gun like it's his first time. His dark hair is combed over and perfectly coiffed. I have to assume hairspray is involved because natural waves don't look like that. He smiles at me, but it does little to calm me down. It's the type of smile you see in toothpaste commercials – never in real life. It's unsettling.

The only way I identify him as the group leader is by the Council insignia on his chest. It's the same one Ash wore. I ease myself up into a seated position. Robbie has Grams and Ariel behind him in the kitchen. He's doing his best to shield them in a corner with a glare that could level armies.

"I'll come with you. Leave my family out of this," I say. The leader scowls, kicking my arms out from under me. I crumple to the ground for a second time.

A male enforcer with close-cropped brown hair steps in front of me and faces down the leader. "Jace, what the hell? She was down!"

"Move, grunt, or I'll shoot you too," the enforcer leader, Jace, says. It takes me a moment to realize he's calling the other enforcer a grunt. That's...interesting.

The male enforcer ignores Jace. He turns around and squats beside me, offering his hand. "That would require knowing how to," he mutters. I cough to conceal a laugh. Well, damn. I accept his hand and he helps me to my feet. I sway a little, my head throbbing, but the enforcer steadies me.

"Cuff her," Jace orders. The man looks like he wants to object, but decides against it. He unclasps the cuffs from his belt.

"That isn't necessary," says Grams. She steps out from behind Robbie. I thought she was trying to pacify Ariel, but I was wrong. She's holding her phone in one hand and the winning lottery ticket in the other.

She didn't.

"You can't arrest a lottery winner," Grams says.

Oh, she definitely did!

Grams must have registered my ticket online while the enforcers were distracted. The Ascent Day lottery is the biggest publicized event the Council has. If this Jace guy is smart, he won't risk the wrath of the director by arresting a winner. The male enforcer who helped me up is the first to act. He scans my chip implant and smirks when my profile pops up with the gold "Winner" banner.

"She isn't lying." Jace grabs the man's arm and yanks it towards him, pulling him off balance. His expression turns murderous.

Grams steps forward before he can say anything. "I want to give this to my granddaughter. For good luck." She raises her hands slowly and undoes the clasp of her locket. I go to her, wrapping my arms around her waist.

What's Jace going to do, shoot me? I doubt it.

"Thank you," I whisper. Grams loops the chain over my head and secures the clasp. Ariel is hiding behind Robbie's legs, staring at me with wide eyes. I blow her a kiss. She hides her face in Robbie's pant leg.

"Keep them safe," I tell Robbie. He gives me a single nod.

Jace grabs my arm and hauls me towards the door. His hold is strong, bruising even. I suppress the urge to deck him. I don't want to test how much leniency my newfound status grants me. A few of our neighbors poke their heads out to see what the commotion is all about. As soon as they see the enforcer uniforms, the doors close and I hear the snick of deadbolts sliding into place. Jace manhandles me down the stairwell. My feet are bare. I try to avoid the garbage and broken glass. He leads me outside to a waiting Pod and slams me against the metal exterior so forcefully it steals my breath. My back arches, conforming to the shape of the Pod.

Jace gets in my face. "I don't know how you pulled this off, grunt, but I'll bury you."

"Good luck with that," I mutter.

Jace slams a fist into the metal by my head. The loud boom makes me blanch.

So much for playing it cool.

"Sir, do you want me to escort her to the Academy?" Asks the enforcer who helped me up. Jace backs away a few steps and straightens his uniform.

"Get her out of here." He shoulders past the enforcer and gets into another Pod. The friendly enforcer swipes his wrist against the Pod door to open it. I get in and scoot over to the far window. He sits beside me. Two more enforcers take the bench across from us. The Pod door closes and I feel it move away from the curb, but I can't see out the windows.

"I'm Liam, by the way," he says. I glance at him. Liam has warm, hazel eyes. He's a big dude, taking up his seat and half of mine with his broad shoulders, but I don't feel intimidated.

"Thanks," I say.

"I'm sorry Jace treated you like that. He had no right."

"He's an Axton," says the enforcer across from me. "He can do whatever he wants."

"Jace is an Axton?" I feel the color drain from my face. "I didn't know the Axton's went on enforcer raids."

"They don't," says Liam. A wrinkle appears on his forehead. "Most of them, anyway."

So, what changed? And, more importantly, how did he find me? Ash pulled up my profile when he arrested me, but it's not like the enforcers have my address on file. I used a fake address when I got my Council-required chip implant. Something doesn't add up. I glance at Liam and contemplate asking him. That's when I notice the white adhesive square just below his hairline.

I've seen those patches before.

There was an anti-drug campaign in our neighborhood a few years ago. It was run by a bunch of elites looking for an excuse to post their good deeds on social media, so it never got much traction. They were focused on helping surge addicts. From what I know, surge is a highly addictive synthetic concoction laced with a smattering of self-loathing and a promise of a good time. Council volunteers handed out the patches and told us they could be used to wean people off the drug. I wonder what drove Liam, an enforcer who appears to have his life together, to take a street drug? I'm not about to ask.

The decrepit warehouses and trash-filled streets are gradually replaced with windowed skyscrapers, clean sidewalks, and well-dressed pedestrians. Digital billboards adorn the buildings selling products I have never heard of before. The models have beautiful smiles and perfect skin. The storefronts lining the walkway advertise red lipstick, ten-dollar lattes, and ripped jeans that cost more than I make in a year.

We turn a corner and the Academy comes into view. It's the tallest building in the city, a giant mirror reflecting the skyline back at us. Arched steel beams cross over the entrance like bangles decorating the arm of our most important branch of government. Elaborate landscaping, marble stonework, and fountains line the immaculate square fenced in by crowd control bots. The machines are built to intimidate with clear, plexiglass shields that stand almost as tall as I am, menacing red lights, and armored bases. They link together, expanding and contracting to accommodate the size of the crowd like a giant snake preparing to strangle its' prey.

Drones swarm the Pods in front of us, taking pictures of those lucky enough to hold a winning lottery ticket. The dull buzz of the quad-copters sends adrenaline shooting through my veins activating my flight response.

This was a mistake.

Before I can jump out of a moving vehicle for the second time in twenty-four hours, the Pod glides to a stop. Liam steps out and waits for me to join him. I want to drag my feet. I want to run away.

I want to be anywhere else, but my best friend needs me.

So, I get out of the Pod and try to look as respectable as a person wearing sweatpants and no shoes can. The flashes from the cameras are blinding. People shout questions at me, but I can't make out their words. Liam stands beside me, blocking the crowd with his body as he leads me inside. The automatic doors swish open with a burst of cold air. I don't remember the last time I felt air conditioning. It reminds me of a morgue. My skin breaks out in goosebumps and I reflexively cross my arms over my chest.

A secretary sits at a desk with two enforcers standing on either side of her in full tactical gear. She's dressed in a suit with a sleek bun and diamond earrings. I'm surprised the Academy keeps a secretary when a bot would be more efficient. The woman gives us an undisguised look of disgust.

A bot would have also been more welcoming.

Behind the secretary, an expansive waterfall pours from the second story into a pool on the ground floor. Pieces of glass hang from the ceiling, a chandelier of broken shards. The foyer is open for at least ten stories with enforcers and elites hanging over the railings. Their cheers fill the space, echoing off the walls.

"There will be an announcement in a bit," says Liam. "Good luck." He gives me a small smile, his tone genuine.

"Thanks," I say. Liam leaves to join a group of enforcers mingling off to the side. For the first time, I notice a slight hitch in his step. He's favoring his right leg. The crowd consists of representatives from the different companies that sponsored Ascent Day jobs, as well as elite patrons. All of them are dressed up except the enforcers who are wearing their uniforms.

I guess power is like a little black dress, it wears well at any occasion.

Human servers and bots glide through the crowd with glassware. I have never felt more out of place. My eyes go to the ceiling where the chandelier hangs, the pieces of glass each reflecting a different part of the crowd. I'm so absorbed in analyzing the reflections that I walk into someone.

"Hey, watch it!" The woman I almost knocked over is wearing an oversized green shirt that makes her appear even more petite than she already is. Her black hair is buzzed short on the sides, tapering up into a faux hawk of wild curls that are tighter than my own. She has a silver barbell through the top of her left ear with simple black studs in her earlobes. Her ripped blue jeans and chunky boots aren't standard issue and, judging by her crossed arms, neither is her attitude.

"Sorry about that," I say.

"Cool, a fellow grunt!" Her scowl morphs into a grin, taking me by surprise.

"What gave me away?" I ask.

"You mean, aside from the bare feet and sweats?" she laughs. My cheeks warm. "None of these rich pricks even notice that gaudy chandelier. I'm Glitch, by the way."

"Glitch...is that your real name?"

"Of course not," she snorts. She offers me her hand. "Take it or leave it, that's the only answer you're getting."

I give her a genuine smile. "I'm Wren."

"What job are you bidding on?" Glitch asks me the first question I should have asked myself when I won the lottery. The truth is, I haven't had a chance to think about it.

"Uhm, what are the options?"

"You didn't pay attention to the listings? They were listed on the broadcast right before the winners were announced."

"In my defense, I didn't expect to win!"

"I didn't either," chuckles Glitch.

"Then why are you giving me a hard time?"

"Because I like to watch people squirm."

She points to a display projected on the wall with all of the job postings. I scan the list. There are openings for medical staff, engineers, designers, and...the enforcers. I don't have the money to hire a lawyer right now or the time to earn it.

"I'm going to bid on the enforcers," I say. It's the only way I can get close enough to Miles to bust him out.

"No, you're not." I whirl around. Raven hair, haunting charcoal eyes, and the pissed-off expression of someone who took a nap on concrete greet me.

This day just keeps getting better and better.

Chapter 5

Ash

"Ash don't go too far. Director Axton will be ready to leave any minute."

Don stands on the threshold framed by French doors that lead into the foyer of the Axton mansion. His hands fidget in front of him as if he's unsure of what to do with them. He looks at me with a pained expression, opens his mouth as if to say something, and closes it again with a sigh.

What can he say?

My mom's funeral is today.

I walk through the courtyard. Tall brick walls with evenly-spaced windows surround the gardens protecting our Eden from the outside world. The flower beds are immaculate, tended to daily by an army of servants. The only thing out of place are the dog kennels tucked in the corner. Byron had them constructed when he raised Great Danes. That was before mom and I moved in, so I never saw the animals. He wanted to give them a safe place to be outside. The enclosures are plain compared to the rest of the courtyard, a chain link box built for utility rather than appearance.

My hand absentmindedly leads the way clutching a small model airplane that soars above flower beds, maneuvers through the bushes, and skims along the water in the fountains. It's childish, but my mom and I built the model together. Today, more than ever, I need to feel close to her.

My foot catches on something and my body hits the ground with a bone-rattling crash. The plane soars from my fingers, disappearing into a bed of poppies. Jace leers down at me. I try to hold back tears. Despite my best efforts, they pour down my cheeks in traitorous rivulets.

"Aww, the little baby is crying," he laughs. "Father says crying is a sign of weakness."

I frown. Wiping my tears, I stand up and face Jace.

"Mom says...said," I choke on my words. "That crying means we care about something and caring makes us strong."

"Your mom didn't know what she was talking about," Jace scowls. I try to walk around him to look for the plane, but Jace shoves me so that I fall again. In the last year, he has grown a few inches taller than me. It makes it hard to fight back. Not that I ever would. Fighting with Jace makes Byron yell more than usual.

"Let me go look for my plane," I huff. "Please?"

It comes out more like a question than I mean it to.

"No."

I try to stand up, but Jace shoves me again. I throw out a fist that catches him on the jaw. Jace shrieks, clutching his face.

"Asher!" Byron's voice booms. I skirt around Jace and run straight into the field of poppies. I know I can't avoid him for long, but I will be grounded from the courtyard for hitting Jace. I have to find my plane now or risk losing it forever.

I wade through the flowers searching desperately, but there are too many leaves. I feel the tears welling up in my eyes again. I plop down, disappearing into the sea of red. There is a chirp and a small rustle to my right. A mouse scampers into view, so light it barely moves the leaves around it.

"Where did you come from?" I murmur. It's close enough to touch, so I extend my hand. The mouse darts out of reach.

Mesmerized, I repeat the action, but the mouse continues to dart through the branches with ease. Finally, it stops to sniff at something silver laying on the ground. My plane!

The mouse looks up at me, ticking its head to the side curiously.

A shadow appears over the flowers. "When I say come, you run." I scramble to my feet. Byron is standing at the end of a path of trampled flowers.

"I'm sorry, I had to find my plane," I say. "Mom helped me build it." I don't know why I tell him that. Maybe I think it will help him to understand me better - to be more lenient. Byron frowns at the toy on the ground before bringing his boot down on it, crushing the toy and the mouse in one go. I stare at its mangled body in disbelief.

"I told you not to get too attached to things, Asher, it makes you weak," he mumbles. "Why can't you be more like Jace?" I don't respond. My eyes are glued to the wreckage of the plane and the thimble of blood covering poppies with hearts black enough to rival Bryon's. If I didn't care about my plane, that mouse would still be alive. I killed it. Jace was right, caring is a weakness. Caring kills.

The courtyard tips upside down as my world tilts on its axis. I fall into the night sky, swallowed by darkness.

***

A steady rocking brings me back to consciousness like a lighthouse beckoning to a lost sailor...who got hammered with Davy Jones. I groan.

"Look who finally decided to rejoin the land of the living." I open my eyes slowly. Elle is leaning back in a chair with her boots kicked up on my bed. She stops nudging my shoulder with her foot when I glare at her. Shrugging, she takes a sip of coffee from her mug. Scratch that, my mug. We're in my compartment.

That's when it starts coming back to me.

The arrest. The attack. The dart.

I really did go down with my ship. I grab Elle's mug and chug half the contents in one go.

"Get your own," she scowls at me.

"Technically, it's my coffee. You're in my compartment." She snatches the mug back, hitting my nose in the process. I see God for a second and my eyes water. I gently run my fingers over my face. My face is swollen and there are bandages taped across the bridge of my nose.

Elle winces. "Sorry. I had the medical team take a look at your nose while you were out. It's broken."

I prop myself up against the headboard. The back of my neck burns. I trail my fingers along the skin and I can feel a sensitive, raised bump. "That's from a tranquilizer dart. The kind we load the drones with." Elle reaches into the bag of chips on her lap and tosses a handful into her mouth. I take in the empty food containers littering the end table. She has clearly been here a while.

"Make yourself at home," I grumble, but I can't help the feeling of warmth that spreads over me. Elle stayed through the night to make sure I didn't have any side effects from the tranquilizer. Side effects are rare, but not unheard of. She's a better friend than I deserve.

"How long was I out?"

"About six hours. The last time I saw you, you were loading that mechanic in a Pod bound for the Academy. Care to explain?"

"Apparently 'that mechanic' is really important to the Syndicate. Some guys in masks hijacked our Pod."

"I didn't know the Syndicate had that capability."

"Neither did I," I say. I tell Elle about escaping from the Pod, our mad dash through the convenience store, and our final confrontation with the Syndicate thugs.

"Why didn't they kill you? Obviously, I'm glad they didn't, but it was risky to let you walk," says Elle.

"I made a deal with Wren. If she passed me off as her employee, I would wipe her record."

Elle smirks. "Wren?"

"The mechanic," I growl.

"That explains the missing uniform," says Elle. "What happened?"

"She paid off the Syndicate and we got out of there. Then I tried to arrest her."

"Wait," Elle holds up a hand to stop me. "You reneged on your deal?"

"She's a Syndicate mechanic. Of course, I did!"

Elle tosses a handful of chips in her mouth from the bag sitting on her lap. "Still, not cool. Is that why she knocked you out?"

"I don't want to talk about it," I grumble.

Elle chuckles. "I'm beginning to like this girl."

I ignore her, rolling out of bed and grabbing a new mug from my small kitchen. The compartments for squad leaders are larger than the recruit dormitories and more furnished. Each unit has a twin bed, an enclosed bathroom, and a modest desk with a swivel chair.

I spent the night in my fatigues. I feel grimy and sore. I need caffeine, a shower, and food.

Preferably in that order.

"The director is pissed," says Elle, her voice turning serious.

"*Byron* is always pissed. What's new?" I refuse to call my stepfather by his title. It gives him power over me he doesn't deserve and I don't want him to have. Elle rolls her eyes. She's always up for a bit of rebellion, but you won't see her disrespecting Byron. She knows how to choose her battles.

It's different when I push back against the director and the Council. I can get away with it. She can't.

I pour a cup of coffee and dump in a packet of creamer to achieve a consistency one step above battery acid. Coffee has always been my coping mechanism. As my tolerance for bullshit erodes throughout the day, it keeps me from going nuclear.

"I didn't think there was anything I could do to get a reaction from the old man. I was beginning to think he'd given up on me entirely," I say.

"He talked to my mom after your announcement to see if she knew about our engagement plans."

I freeze. "What did she say?"

Elle chuckles. "She rolled with it. I think she has half the wedding planned already."

"What can I say? I'm a catch."

"Sure, when you consider the size of the pond." Elle balls up a discarded chip bag and sends it sailing at my head. It floats to the floor, falling short by a few feet. "You need to be careful."

I shrug. "It's not like Byron can execute me for being annoying."

"No, but he can kick you out of the enforcers."

"He can't."

"He can and he will. You need to cool it or you'll lose your shot at taking down the Syndicate."

"I'm sorry, I don't take unsolicited advice before 10 a.m."

"Ha ha," Elle rolls her eyes. "Axton owns the Council. Maybe not officially, but you and I both know his voice is the only one that matters." I grit my teeth. She has a point. As if speaking his name summoned the demon, my phone vibrates in my pocket. It's a calendar invite from Byron's secretary requesting our attendance at the bid ceremony in fifteen minutes. I sigh and shove it into my pocket.

Elle must have gotten the same notification, because she swipes at her armband and removes her feet from the bed. "I'll see you downstairs." She pauses at the door. "Just be careful, please?" I stare at the door for a few beats after she closes it.

In the shower, I peel the medical tape off my nose. There's no way I'm going to the bid ceremony with that on. I change and find another patch to slap on my arm to alleviate my pending headache before leaving my compartment. The leadership floor is empty. The hall is lined with doors at equally spaced intervals like an apartment complex or a hotel. All enforcers on active duty are required to live full-time in the complex – a rule instigated by the Council to reduce Syndicate influence. I suppose it worked. The enforcers have never had anyone defect. There have been a few arrests and executions over the years, but no one has switched sides successfully. I take the elevator to the atrium. When the doors open, I stop short when I recognize a figure with curly hair.

You've got to be kidding me.

Wren has her back to me. She's talking to some edgy chick I don't recognize. At some point, she changed into a pair of baggy sweatpants and a t-shirt. Her feet are bare. It's like she jumped out of bed and decided to come downtown without getting dressed. The elites give her a wide berth and I almost laugh. She couldn't stick out more if she tried. I approach with caution.

What? The woman managed to escape a raid, knock out a trained enforcer unit leader, and win the lottery in twenty-four hours. There's no way I'm underestimating her again.

"I'm going to bid on the enforcers," Wren says.

"No, you're not." The words leave me before I can stop them. Wren turns around. Her lips part in shock, her eyes traveling from my shoes up to my face as if she doesn't believe I'm here. I raise an eyebrow. "Enjoying the view?"

Wren blushes. "No."

"Liar." I counter. Wren scowls, her blush deepening.

"Excuse me," she apologizes to her friend. "I need some fresh air. His ego is displacing all the oxygen." She skips around me and bolts. Her friend smiles at me.

"Can you pause your argument long enough for me to get some popcorn?"

"Shut it, goth Barbie."

She smiles, offering me her hand. "I'm Glitch."

"I didn't ask." I sidestep her and jog to catch up with Wren. What kind of idiotic name is Glitch anyways?

"Stop running away," I say.

"Why, having trouble keeping up after your nap?" Wren smiles sweetly, then picks up her pace.

"I need to talk to you."

"No."

"Yo, Ash. Got a minute?" Liam calls.

"Not right now," I reply, waving him off. Liam gives me a confused look as I grab Wren's arm and duck into a hallway lined by deserted conference rooms. Wren swings her wrist to break my grip, the move surprisingly well-executed. "What is your deal?"

"My deal?" I laugh incredulously. "You broke my nose! You knocked me out and left me in the street. I'm allowed to be pissed, sweetheart." Wren shoves me into the wall, the action taking me off guard. She balls the fabric of my shirt in her fist and gets right in my face. Or tries to. She has to look up to meet my eyes.

"Yeah, that was a dick move. I'll admit it, but that doesn't make it alright for you to drag me across a room full of people. That was disrespectful and unnecessary. I didn't want to talk to you before and I definitely don't want to talk to you now. Oh, and one more thing. Call me sweetheart again and I'll stab you while you're sleeping."

She's so close her breath is mingling with my own. The rage crackles in her eyes like the embers of a dying fire. Why not throw some gas on it? I chuckle and lean in until my lips brush the shell of her ear. She shivers.

"So, you think about me sleeping?" I whisper. I see the exact moment Wren realizes how close she is. She drops my shirt and backs up a few steps, then throws up her hands in frustration. I smirk. She's fun to mess with it.

"Why are you the way you are?" she asks.

"Most people find me charming."

"Most people are idiots," she shoots back.

"You're not bidding on the enforcers."

"Try to stop me, I dare you."

"I won't," I say.

She looks surprised. "You're giving up?"

"I can keep arguing with you if you want. You seem to get off on it."

Wren turns and takes a few steps away. "Goodbye, Ash."

I snag her hand before she can get too far, interlacing my fingers with hers. "Let's make a deal."

"Are you sure? The last deal didn't end well for you." She gives me a look that could freeze the sun and tugs her hand away, but she doesn't leave. That's got to count for something, right?

"I think you want to join the enforcers to help Mason."

"Miles." Wren corrects.

"Close enough."

Wren narrows her eyes. "I don't need your help." She glances down the hallway towards the atrium as if searching for someone to rescue her from this conversation. Too bad for her no one would dare interrupt us.

"Are you sure about that? He could be anywhere. The enforcers have dozens of locations where they keep suspects awaiting trial. It could take months to find him without my help."

She crosses her arms. "You're an asshole."

"Only if you stand in my way. Here's my offer. I'll secure a pardon for your friend. In return, I want you to help me take down the Syndicate."

Wren tenses. "You know I can't do that."

"Why not?"

"They'll go after my family."

"We can protect them," I say.

Wren snorts. "That's wishful thinking. I don't get why you want my help anyway."

"You're the 'best mechanic the Syndicate has,'" I say, repeating her words from last night.

"Allegedly," Wren interjects.

"Whatever. I've always colored inside the lines. I know how to survive among the elites, because I know what the rules are. Those don't apply to this situation. You grew up in that world. You know how criminals think."

"I'll take that as a compliment," Wren grumbles.

"It wasn't."

"You're terrible at asking for help."

"I don't get it, are you trying to protect them or something? What do you owe the Syndicate anyways?" I ask.

"I'm not protecting anybody. I love complaining about the Syndicate as much as the next grunt, but when it comes down to it, I can't survive without them. You get roughed up for failing to pay protection fees every once in a while? Too bad. The Syndicate isn't perfect, but it gave us a way to breathe when the Council watched us drown."

"Besides," Wren huffs. "I'm flattered that you think I have the power to take down the entire Syndicate. I'd be lucky to set up even one of the crews."

"Crew?"

"Wait, you don't know what a crew is?" Wren appears genuinely surprised. "The enforcers are more behind than I thought."

"Then why don't you enlighten me," I growl.

"Well, the Syndicate has a boss and then there are different leaders for each part of the business." Wren taps her chin thoughtfully. "I might be able to help you take down the crew leader that manages the distribution of surge."

My fists clench at my sides. How did she know to play that card? I've never touched surge, but it nearly destroyed Liam's life. I won't settle until the entire Syndicate is dismantled, but taking surge off the streets isn't a bad place to start.

"Okay," I relent. I don't like to be outplayed, but every interaction with Wren has left me feeling one step behind. I extend my hand.

Wren ignores it. "If you go back on your word, I'll make sure the Syndicate finds out who you are. That's a promise."

She walks away. I drop my hand and take a few quick strides to catch up to her. As soon as we round the corner, I make eye contact with Byron and curse. Wren's eyes shoot to mine. He's talking with Carl Bronxton, his business partner and Penny's father. Byron is wearing the same black suit and starched white shirt he always wears. The only difference is the blue tie. He gives me a mildly displeased look like he ordered a steak at his favorite restaurant and the waiter delivered a salad instead.

Mr. Bronxton is worse at hiding his distaste. He purses his lips and smooths an invisible wrinkle from his pants. I can't say I blame him. With the way I stood up his daughter, I'm sure I fueled the elite gossip chain for years to come. Unlike my father, Mr. Bronxton has a patterned shirt on under his suit and a tie that clashes horribly with the fabric. I know it's some trendy fashion statement, Elle told me as much, but that doesn't mean I'm on board with looking like an idiot. Apparently, Bronxton is all too comfortable with the idea.

"Asher." Byron excuses himself from his conversation and strides toward me. He glances at his watch before giving me a pointed look. "It's nice of you to join us."

"I was catching up on my beauty sleep." He knows damn well why I was late.

"I need a word with my son." He eyes Wren with disdain. Wren's jaw is practically on the floor. She obviously knows who Byron is. It makes sense. He's one of the most important people in the country and, as such, is on the Council broadcasts pretty frequently.

"Your son," Wren emphasizes each word slowly. She gives me a look that says she's reconsidering our deal. "Sure thing...*Asher*." She gives me a final murderous glare before melting into the crowd.

"It would be nice if you could keep up appearances for at least a day following your engagement. It's the respectful thing to do. While we're on the subject, you should have told me about your plans ahead of time."

"I agree. It would have been nice to know about my arranged marriage before you announced it to a room of reporters," I seethe. "Penny Bronxton? Seriously?"

Byron glances around until he locates Mr. Bronxton standing safely out of earshot. Then he returns his glare to me, the unbridled anger breaking through his carefully constructed facade.

"Penny Bronxton is a perfect match. She's from a respected family..."

She's wealthy.

"...she's going to inherit her father's shares in Axton AI..."

She has something Byron wants.

Byron drones on, but I continue to read between the lines. It's the same story I've been listening to since mom died. I'm a disappointment, a failure, and an embarrassment to the Axton name. Part of me is glad she didn't live long enough to see the man she loved turn into this. Of course, Byron Axton never speaks ill of anyone. Not to their face. That would be beneath him. He has to cloak his true feelings under a layer of passive-aggressive comments for his superiority complex to remain firmly in place.

"You can't honestly tell me you're interested in that enforcer girl," he finishes.

You know what? Fuck it. I dig the hole deeper.

"Her name is Elle. I can decide who I want to marry. I know myself better than you do." I cross my arms and stare at him.

"Whom," he corrects. "Your mother would be disappointed in you. If I find out this engagement is a sham and you embarrassed me for no reason, I will recommend your demotion to the Council."

I bite my cheek so hard I draw blood. I've toed the line with Byron for years. I piss off Jace like it's an Olympic sport, but this is the first time I've crossed the line. Suddenly, winning the gold seems more like a death sentence than an achievement. The enforcers are my lifeline. It's the one thing that hasn't been tarnished by Byron or Jace. I worked hard and earned my title. It's the only place I've ever belonged and he's threatening to take it away from me. I should have expected it.

I embarrassed Byron Axton. No one does that and walks away unscathed.

"Understood." I choke out. Byron returns to the party, closing the door on what little relationship we had left. I don't know how long I stand there in my own world. Elle nudges my arm.

"Hey, you in there?" she asks. I smile weakly.

"What happened? I saw you speaking with the director." I spot a camera focused on us from across the room. I pull her against me, brushing her hair away from her ear.

"He threatened to have me removed from the enforcers," I whisper. "He guessed that our engagement was a sham and told me if I embarrassed him that was it."

She grimaces. "Do you believe him? I mean, do you think he would go through with it? The Council respects you. You're well-liked and the enforcers would promote you quickly if you gave them the opportunity. Do you think they would throw all that away just because he asks them to?"

I think about it for a moment.

"Byron is a lot of things - a liar isn't one of them. He omits details when it suits him and is a master manipulator, but he always tells the truth. Yeah, I believe him." I rake my hand through my hair. "What do we do?"

Elle tugs my hand from my hair and clasps her fingers with mine.

"First of all, you stop playing with your hair. You won't have any left for the wedding. I'm not sure I can marry a bald dude," she snickers. I smile. "I think we let this play out. We can have a long engagement. There's no reason we have to break it off right now. We monitor the situation and respond accordingly. Nothing has changed."

I squeeze her hand. "Thank you."

She gets on her tiptoes and presses a chaste kiss to my lips, resting her forehead against mine. I realize she's angled us in such a way that the camera and Byron have an unobstructed view.

"We'll get through this," she murmurs. I wrap my arms around her waist, holding her against my chest. Byron got it wrong. Elle isn't just "some girl." She's my best friend, she's smart, and she knows how to play a role as well as I do. We'll be the prize marionettes the puppeteer parades around - the golden couple of the elites.

They don't need to know we cut our strings a long time ago.

Chapter 6

Wren

This is the last place I thought I would ever end up. I cross my hands behind my head and point my toes, attempting to take up the full length of my new bunk. The enforcer recruits were assigned a compartment with a roommate after the bid ceremony. It isn't a large space. It shares more similarities with a prison cell than an apartment. The bunks are positioned against one wall with the top bed, my bed, being so close to the ceiling I can't sit up all the way. A closet and small desk with a single chair occupies the opposite wall. There are no decorations, no windows, and no-frills.

I feel positively spoiled.

What can I say? I'm used to sleeping on a lumpy couch with a spring poking into my back, so getting my own bed is absolute heaven. Glitch's soft snores filter up from the bunk below. She rolls in her sleep causing the metal bed frame to creak. I was surprised when she bid on the enforcers. I didn't peg her as the law-abiding type. After the bid ceremony, Glitch simply declared we would be rooming together and I didn't fight it. Not that I wanted to. After listening to the two elite recruits next door complain about the quality of the mattresses, I consider myself lucky.

I spent most of the bid ceremony in a blackout rage after learning Ash is the director's son. Asher Axton. Seriously? Try saying that ten times fast. I get why the guy insisted I use his nickname. Not only is the tool bag related to the director, a fact he conveniently left out when we were discussing our deal, but he's also engaged. From eavesdropping, I gathered her name is Elle. She also poops rainbows and walks on water.

Fine, I made that second part up, but it's a good summary of what the other elites say about her. She's their golden girl, an elite-born being targeted for enforcer leadership. Apparently, she and Ash have been friends for years. He proposed at the Ascent Day ball the same evening they raided my shop. It took me a minute to place the beautiful blond as the enforcer who arrested Miles. Talk about an irritating power couple.

I shouldn't care. I *don't* care. What I do care about is being lied to.

On one hand, I'm certain having the Axton family name means Ash has the pull to negotiate Miles' release. On the other hand, if Ash is killed by the Syndicate, I'll probably be arrested. I have no idea how I'm going to find the surge crew. I was talking out of my ass when I dangled that carrot in our negotiation. It was a lucky guess. I saw the surge patch on Liam's arm and Liam seemed to know Ash. I needed something I could trade for Miles' release. Now that I think about it, I'm not so sure setting up the surge crew is realistic.

A few years ago, I had a surge crew member stop at Jimmy's Auto. He told me they were looking for a full-time mechanic to fix up vehicles for their runners. From what I understand, the runners move product between cities and within city borders undetected. Miles and I always avoided declaring loyalty to a single crew. We stayed safely in the middle, working with everyone while remaining neutral. It's the safest way to do business. I turned down his offer. The guy didn't seem offended, so I could probably find the transaction on the 8-Bit app and contact him to see if the offer still stands. I scrub the heels of my hands into my eyes.

What am I doing?

I'm planning to infiltrate a Syndicate crew with an enforcer partner who hasn't spent a day outside of the elite sectors. One wrong move and our cover is blown. I think of Ash with his soldier's posture, pressed clothes, and upper-class vocabulary. You wouldn't have to look too closely to find something out of place. Even if I was willing to risk myself, could I put my family in danger? I trail my fingers over the golden locket around my neck. The Syndicate doesn't take betrayal lightly. The list of problems continues to grow the more I think about it, each scenario cycling through my head making it impossible to rest. I startle when a pillow lands on my face.

"It's a beautiful day to be alive!" Glitch crows. I bat the pillow away to reveal Glitch beaming up at me.

"Do you have to be so...cheerful?"

Glitch cackles. She climbs down the ladder and opens the door. "There's no other way to be. Hurry up, roll call is in five minutes." She disappears into the hall, closing the door behind her.

I nearly miss the ladder getting out of the bunk, but manage to recover my footing at the last minute. I tug on a black shirt and white canvas pants. They're a little too large, but not terrible. I tuck the shirt in haphazardly, trying to remember what Ash's uniform looked like. I do my best to lace up the shiny black boots. They pinch my toes and need to be broken in. I rock back and forth on my feet trying to stretch them out. I wish Jace had given me a chance to grab my boots.

The hall is lined with recruits. Last night, the enforcer doling out compartment assignments explained that all new recruits in our region are trained at the Academy. That means the people who won the lottery in nearby cities were transported here overnight. Half of them look like they're asleep on their feet. Someone yells something unintelligible. I assume it's a command to get moving, because the crowd converges on the stairwell. I allow myself to be swept along. We climb three flights of stairs before exiting into a very large, very empty room. There are a few locked cages against the wall. I can't make out what's inside. The rest of the room is blank. It's as if they took an entire floor of the skyscraper and cleared out the interior walls and blacked out the windows.

"Pipe down." A voice booms above the confused chatter from the recruits. A man with a bald head stands at the edge of our group. His hands are clasped behind his back, his posture so rigid it makes me wonder if he's even capable of slouching. The guy has the token expression of someone who has seen the world and doesn't care for it. I feel like I could ask him to wrestle a crocodile while fighting an army of riot bots with one hand tied behind his back and he wouldn't blink. He waits for everyone to stop talking before he continues.

"I'm Commander Harper and I'm in charge of training recruits here at the Academy. Get into groups of five. Each group will be assigned to a senior enforcer for your training and aptitude test." We all stare at him. He scowls. "That means move!"

Glitch grabs my hand and pulls me to the side. "Hey, you!" She points at a tall, lanky kid with red hair and a narrow nose dotted with freckles. He looks startled when Glitch stalks towards him. "You're on our team." He opens his mouth to say something, but seems to think better of it. "So are you." She tells the two elite girls who roomed next to us. One of them crosses her arms.

"You don't get to order us around, grunt," she says.

"She can't, but I can." Ash saunters over to our group looking as refreshed as ever. His clothes are wrinkle-free and he has just enough scruff on his jaw to say "this was intentional" rather than "I woke up late." I have the sudden urge to throat punch him.

I'm not a violent person.

Okay, fine, that's a lie. But they say the first step is recognizing you have a problem, right?

My problem is I spent the entire night fretting about how to infiltrate the Syndicate and this prick rolls in looking like he got eight hours. So yeah, I think a throat punch is warranted. The two elite girls giggle making no attempt to hide their obvious interest in Ash. Kill me now. Ash leads our team to one of the racks and presses his forearm against a scanner to unlock it.

"This room is a virtual reality arena. Each of you will get a backpack, headset, and weapon that will let you see and interact with the course." He starts handing gear out. Glitch squeals with excitement when Ash gives her a headset.

"I've always wanted to try this!" she whispers. I'm almost surprised when she doesn't jump up and down with excitement. My knowledge of VR technology is limited to what I've seen on TV. Axton AI sells personal devices, like the headsets Ash is handing out, for enjoying VR at home. There are also businesses downtown that offer more inclusive experiences, like emulating the sound and smell of sitting on a beach. I'm not sure what to expect today, but a "virtual reality arena" doesn't sound like the kind of place you go to relax.

Ash hands me a backpack, headset, and a rifle that vaguely resembles the enforcer weapons. It feels heavy and foreign in my hands. The guy with red hair takes the next set from him. He frowns, before leveling the weapon at Ash's chest.

"Are you sure you want to do that?" Ash quirks an eyebrow, appearing more amused than concerned.

"Don't be an idiot," Glitch hisses. "It doesn't shoot real-"

He pulls the trigger. It clicks loudly and I flinch. Ash stares down at the recruit, a deadly glint in his eyes. He takes a few steps forward and knocks the gun to the side so it jerks his wrist at the wrong angle. The recruit yelps and clutches his hand.

"What's your name, grunt?" He doesn't respond. Ash grabs his arm and hauls him over to the equipment rack scanner. He forces the recruit's forearm against the display until it lights up. "Roy Bishop. Next time I ask you a question, don't hesitate." Ash shoves Roy back towards us. His shoulder crashes into Glitch.

"Drawing a weapon, any weapon, on another enforcer is an offense that will land you and your family in prison," growls Ash.

"Is there a problem?" Commander Harper chooses this moment to check in with our team. Roy stiffens next to me. I focus on my shoes. I can't watch this. Roy doesn't deserve to die because of his stupidity. They'll throw him in jail, broadcast his execution, and-

"No problem, sir," Ash says coolly, interrupting my internal spiral of worst-case scenarios. My eyes shoot up, boring into the back of Ash's head. The commander frowns, clearly not believing him.

"Alright, you're up first."

"Yes, sir." As soon as the commander is out of earshot, Ash rounds on Roy.

"Do that again and I'll have you arrested. Are we clear?"

"Yeah, sure," Roy grumbles.

"Yes, sir," Ash corrects. He shows us how to put on the gear. The headset feels strange. It completely covers my eyes and is secured in place by straps on the top and sides. I push it onto my forehead so I can see. The backpack is fairly lightweight and connects to the headset. The weapon itself is a decent replica of the enforcer rifle Ash was carrying during the raid on my dad's shop. It feels foreign in my hands. The only weapon I have ever used is Miles' shotgun. My aim is one notch above mediocre, so I've got that going for me.

Ash leads our team to the edge of the room. The other team is lining up against the opposite wall. I watch Commander Harper direct the rest of the recruits out a side door I didn't notice before. There are maybe fifty recruits in total. I wonder where he's taking them.

"Our game will be broadcast for the commander and the other recruits to watch," says Ash, reading my mind. "Removing your headset or earpieces is considered cheating and you will be disqualified. The goal is to reach the other side of the room. There's a button on the wall the other team is defending."

"Where is it?" asks Roy.

"It's not a physical button, but you'll be able to see and interact with it in the game."

"It's kind of like capture the flag," says Glitch, looking over the rifle in awe.

"Right," Ash nods. "The first team to hit their opponent's button wins. The game is used to evaluate your strengths and weaknesses. It tells the commander and the other instructors what you need to work on." Ash picks up a band attached to the bookbag and straps it onto his wrist. "Last thing. If someone on the other team hits you, you'll get a shock from this wristband. It's not strong enough to knock you out, but it's enough to get your attention. Just stay on the ground until the game is over."

The others hold their wristbands away from their bodies as if they are poisonous snakes getting ready to strike. I feel about as enthusiastic as they do, but I strap on the wristband anyways. "Alright, headsets on everyone."

I pull the visor over my eyes and put the earpieces in. A white loading screen with a countdown on it greets me. It ticks down to zero and the white fades away. I find myself standing in a room with the rest of my team. The characters are all the same height and weight, normalized to make it impossible to distinguish one person from another. There are three doors on the opposite wall and the button Ash was talking about is positioned behind us. It's big, red, and anything but discreet. I raise my hands in front of me. They're clad in black gloves, but when I rub my fingers together the material isn't there. Obviously. It's still a weird sensation.

"There's no safety on these weapons. You just aim and fire. Try not to get hit," says Ash. The figure to my left moves forward to take the lead. I notice there's a green diamond floating above his head. It has to be Ash. He takes the doorway on the left. The other figures follow him. They also have green diamonds floating above them. It must be our team marker.

"We should split up. Two people to each door," says Glitch. "We're more likely to make it to the other side that way."

"Good idea," says Ash.

"I'm with Ash!" One of the elites squeals, reminding me how annoying the Ash fan club is.

"Yo, Wren. Want to partner up?" Glitch asks.

"Sure thing," I say. That leaves Roy and the other elite on a team. Ash takes the door on the left, so I decide to go with the middle. I look down at my hands covered in gloves. They're a bit larger than my actual hands. I reach for the handle. Have you ever opened a door with no weight and no substance? It's trippy.

"This is so freaking cool," says Glitch beside me. I have to agree. The scene is surprisingly familiar. We're standing in an open-air marketplace set up on the bottom level of a double-decker bridge. It used to carry two levels of traffic across the river, but has long fallen out of use. Vendors line the streets in makeshift stalls assembled from cardboard boxes and scrap wood. None of the stalls have awnings or coverings. They don't need them. The upper level of the bridge protects their wares from the elements. I've heard of places like this, but I have never been to one in real life. They are in a different sector of the city than where I live. I assume it's a decent replica, but something feels...off. For one, there are no people. The market is completely deserted and the stalls are entirely too neat, the wares perfectly polished and lined up.

"This looks like a grunt marketplace built by someone who has never been to a grunt marketplace," murmurs Glitch.

"It's creepy," I agree. I tighten my grip on the rifle. "We should go." It becomes obvious pretty quickly that there is a set path through the marketplace. The visor lights up red when we veer off track and the wristband vibrates in warning. Logically, I know we're in the same square room in the Academy, but it doesn't feel that way. The earpieces play sounds that match the visual around us, like the wind ruffling a stack of papers on a counter. Underneath it all, there's some kind of white noise that blocks out the real-world noise.

A figure sprints into the open. I don't think, I just raise the rifle and fire. The avatar lets out a yelp and collapses on the floor. It convulses a few times before lying still. A red diamond floats above the body. I guess that's how we tell who the bad guys are.

"Nice shot!" Glitch cheers.

"We should stay quiet. There might be another one," I murmur. Glitch gives me an exaggerated nod. It's hard to read body language and facial expressions when the other person is a digital blob. We should have practiced some hand signals ahead of time. I feel like we were set up for failure. The bridge dead ends in a road giving us the option to turn right or left. I shrug and start left. The entire setting shifts.

"Woah," Glitch startles. I whirl around, but there's only a wall behind us. There's no way to get back to the bridge. We're standing in an office space of some kind. There are glazed glass offices to the left and a cubicle farm to the right. We make a couple of turns through the maze and continue down a hall with faded floral paintings and motivational posters plastered every two feet. I'm pretty sure this is what the road to hell looks like. I try the door handles as we come to them, but none of them turn in my hand. I guess that means we keep going.

"Hey!" Someone calls behind us, making me jump. I manage to pause with my finger on the trigger when I see the green diamond. Unfortunately, Glitch doesn't do the same. The avatar falls to the ground convulsing. The avatar curses, writhing on the floor.

"Roy?" Glitch recognizes his voice and lowers her rifle. Her body freezes and she falls to her knees a second later. "Ouch! That stings."

"What's going on?" I ask.

"I got disqualified for shooting a teammate," says Glitch.

"Karma," says Roy.

"Hey, I wasn't the jackass sneaking up on two armed players. You should keep going," says Glitch.

"You sure?" I ask.

"Yeah, get out of here." Glitch waves me off.

"Where is your partner?" I ask Roy.

"She's out, but we took down a member of the other team."

That's two down and four to go. "Thanks," I say. I know this is just a game, but it feels wrong to leave them behind. The faster I get to the other side of the room, the faster I can check on Glitch.

I try the next door down and it opens. This time, I don't have to wait long. An avatar with a green diamond above its head is grappling with an opposing team member. Their weapons are nowhere in sight. The enemy manages to gain the upper hand, flipping my team member onto their back and pinning their hips to the ground. I fire, taking out the enemy avatar before they punch my teammate.

"I had it under control." I recognize Ash's voice.

"I think what you meant to say is 'thank you.'" Ash crawls under the stall counter to retrieve his weapon before getting to his feet. For the first time, I take in the new environment and realize I'm back in the open-air marketplace on the bridge. "This is where I started."

"You took the middle door," says Ash. It's not a question, more a statement.

"And you took the first door. What does that have to do with anything? And what happened to your number one fan?"

"She got hit when we got to the office. Did you go through the office too?"

"Yeah," I say in surprise. Ash looks at the avatar sprawled on the floor. He gestures for me to follow him and jogs a few stalls down before ducking behind some crates stacked haphazardly. I sit beside him.

"The game is built around four maps. Two of them are the room we started in and our opponent's starting point. This market is map three and the office is map four. The two center maps are randomly generated each game so players who have been through the simulation before don't have an advantage. There has to be another door in either this map or the office map that takes us to the other team's starting point."

"How many players did you eliminate? We took out two. With your partner gone, we're the only players left on our team."

"I took out one more player. That leaves them with three," says Ash.

"Those aren't terrible odds," I say.

"That's funny, I didn't think you were a glass-half-full type."

"I don't need to be an optimist to know I'm going to win."

"Wow, you're so humble," says Ash.

"I'm definitely the best at it."

"Do you always have to have the last word?" he asks.

"Yes," I say.

Ash sighs. "Can you show me which door you took on this map, so we can narrow down the door options?"

"Sure." I poke my head around the corner to make sure the coast is clear. Jogging across the bridge, I stop at the fork in the road. "We went left."

"We went right," says Ash.

"So where…" I trail off when my eyes land on the door straight ahead. I didn't notice it the first time through, because it blended in so well with the rest of the surroundings. Could it be that simple? Ash follows my gaze.

"Your call," he says.

"Since when do you let me take the lead?"

"Hey, this is your evaluation. I'm just along for the ride." Ash puts up his hands and steps back. I narrow my eyes at him, but I know he can't see the action through the visor.

"You're using me as a human shield. You want me to go first just in case the other team is waiting for us."

"Dang, you figured out my evil plan." I can hear the yawn in his voice. The bastard is a little too relaxed. I sigh and lift the rifle preparing to open the door. Ash places a hand on my shoulder, startling me. It's strange to see the digital hand, but feel his touch.

"Stay low. They'll be expecting you on eye level. When we breach, I'll go left and you go right. Deal?"

"I hate that word," I grumble.

"Do you want to win or not?" he asks.

"Fine."

Ash motions for me to stand aside and kicks in the door. I rush into the room, following his advice to stay low. There are three players spread out across a room that is a mirror image of where we started the simulation. I take out the player on the right and Ash fires on the left. The player in the middle is too fast. I try to get out of the way, but I know it's a lost cause. I brace myself for the shock.

"Go for the button," Ash yells, diving in front of me. He shoots as he falls, taking out the final player and clearing the way to the finish line like some over-dramatic action hero. Ash hits the ground and convulses. Did he just...?

Yep. He took a fake bullet for me.

I walk to the button placed on the wall and press it. The visor turns white and a message pops up asking me to remove it. When I tug off the visor, I look around. I'm standing on the opposite side of the room from where I started. The other players are getting to their feet. They're spread fairly evenly throughout the room. I watch Roy help Glitch to her feet. Commander Harper appears with twelve more recruits. His arms are crossed behind his back and he's wearing a stern expression. I wonder if the man knows how to smile.

"What's your name, recruit?" I glance around before I realize he's talking to me.

"Wren Parker." He quirks an eyebrow. "Sir," I add. He nods.

"Nice job, Parker. Pass your gear onto the next person and join the others in the viewing room." He walks to the next cluster of recruits with his hands clasped behind his back.

Ash gets up and offers me his fist for a fist bump. "Good game, grunt."

"Why did you do that?" I cross my arms. Ash stares at me.

"Do what?"

"You know what. You took the hit so I could press the button."

Ash shrugs, giving me a lopsided smile. "You were closer than I was. You need to win if you want the commander to approve you for a mission. Don't worry, I wouldn't take a real bullet for you. You're not worth it."

"And they say chivalry is dead." I tug off my gear and hand it to the closest recruit before making my way to the viewing room.

"You know," says Ash. "You're not half bad at this. You would make a decent enforcer." I don't know which is worse. That Ash doesn't deliver the statement with sarcasm or that he sounds hopeful.

"Careful, pansy," I say. "That almost sounded like a compliment."

Chapter 7

Ash

"Are you imagining a face on that bag?" asks Glitch. She's halfway through a set of push-ups, but manages to get the words out between breaths. Wren slams a fist into the center of a punching bag, rocketing an uppercut into an imaginary assailant's stomach. She's a lot stronger than she looks. A potential attacker could easily underestimate her, making a potential weakness a strength. My recruits keep talking, ignorant to the fact that I can hear everything they're saying.

"Probably Ash's," says Roy. Wren steps back from the heavy bag to give Roy space. He throws a roundhouse kick that lands with a hollow thump. Roy is a promising recruit. I just wish he would learn to stop running his mouth. "If he makes us run another mile, I swear-"

"That you'll thank me later?" I cut him off, deciding to put him out of his misery before he digs himself a bigger hole. Roy is so startled he misses the bag completely with his next punch, throwing him off balance. He ends up half hugging the bag, his face flushed red. I bite back a smile. Wren's eyes flick to mine before refocusing on her target. She throws another punch.

I step up to the bag, perpendicular to her. "If you turn your hips when you punch, you'll be able to hit harder." I stand with my feet shoulder-width apart with my left foot forward. I show her a right cross in slow motion, emphasizing how my right hip pivots with the strike. I follow it up with a second cross at normal speed. Wren mimics my form. She smiles when the resulting punch is more powerful.

"Good," I say, continuing down the line to help the next person.

After bid day, I volunteered to train the new recruits. I had to call in some favors to make sure Wren was on my team, but if I want a newbie authorized for an undercover mission with the Syndicate she has to be perfect. Commander Harper isn't easy to impress. That's why I covered Wren during our game in the VR arena so she could win. She has to stand out if this is going to work. I don't trust anyone else to train her to meet the commander's standards.

So, I've been pushing my team hard since the first exam. For twelve hours a day, they learn the basics of hand-to-hand combat, practice with firearms, and run a minimum of five miles. When they're not working out, I'm instructing them on the enforcer techniques, rules, and protocols they will be tested on before their placement exams. I discreetly watch Wren throwing punch after punch into the bag. She is easily the most focused person I've ever worked with.

After bid day, Liam told Elle and me about the raid Jace led on Wren's apartment. Part of Liam's job includes approving personnel requests for all operations. I had to go through Liam when I planned to hit Jimmy's Auto. Liam saw a last-minute order come through with Jace listed as unit leader and tried to call me, but I was still unconscious and Elle didn't want to leave me alone. Liam's leg injury has kept him from active duty for two years, but he signed up for Jace's squad anyway.

I'm glad he did. From the way Liam described it, Jace threatened Wren's family at gunpoint before dragging her outside. No one deserves that kind of treatment, not even a Syndicate mechanic. I still have no idea why Jace ordered the raid or how he found out where Wren lived. Jace isn't a hands-on leader. He would rather rule his kingdom from the comfort of the Axton mansion. Something doesn't add up. Elle pokes her head into the training room and waves, indicating it's time to go.

"Recruits!" I say. The chatter takes a moment to die down. "Today, you will be going on your first patrol. We'll pair you with a senior enforcer to show you the ropes. Follow me." I leave the room with my recruits trailing behind me like ducklings.

We take the stairs to the underground parking garage. Where the Academy atrium is beautiful and welcoming to guests, the space where we keep the enforcer Pods and tactical gear is dull and utilitarian. It's dimly lit and damp. A dozen black Pods line the curb with racks of weapons sitting open beside them. Elle is standing by the equipment racks with a tablet pairing up recruits from other teams with more experienced enforcers.

"You're in van six," she says as I approach. She gives me a mischievous grin that makes me hesitate. "Move along, you're holding up the line." She shoos me away.

Okay, that was weird.

I shrug on a bulletproof vest and grab one of the rifles, checking to make sure it's loaded with tranquilizer darts. The Pods we're using today aren't standard. They're a larger version built to hold both enforcers and crowd control bots. I get in the Pod with the flashing six displayed on the side. Inside, a row of crowd control bots lines each wall with two seats sandwiched between them.

I take the seat farthest from the door and rest my rifle across my thighs, tapping my foot impatiently. I prefer to spend as little time couped up in a vehicle with the bots as possible. I know they're equipped with cameras that are supposed to be turned off during transport, but I can't shake the feeling that someone is watching my every move. Wren steps into the Pod and scowls when she sees me. Of course, Elle, the eternal meddler, would pair me with her. When she found out Wren won the lottery, she thought it was hilarious. She's not done tormenting me.

Wren plops down next to me. "Why did they have to pair me with you?" She grumbles.

"Good morning, sunshine," I say.

"Is it?"

"It wouldn't kill you to be polite."

"Wouldn't want to risk it."

"Is this how it's going to be the whole time we're working together?" I ask. I wouldn't mind. Arguing with Wren is something I've started looking forward to. She knows who I am, but it hasn't changed the way she interacts with me. She isn't fake-nice or a kiss-ass like some of my colleagues or the other recruits. If anything, I respect her for it.

Wren gives me a fake smile. "I'm sorry, that was rude. Did you enjoy your breakfast? Baby chinchilla marinated in the tears of your enemies?"

"I prefer baby hamsters with a side of crushed hopes and dreams," I say, hiding a smile. Wren huffs and sinks further into her seat.

She's cute when she's frustrated.

The Pod doors slide closed, cutting off the light from outside. The low runners kick on, bathing us in an eerie glow. I feel a slight lurch as we start moving.

"Have you heard anything about Miles?" she asks.

I asked Liam to find out where her friend is being held. As soon as he finds Miles, Liam is to transfer him to the holding cells at the Academy. Even if I knew where her friend was, I wouldn't tell her. I don't trust her. She would probably try to bust him out herself and, when she inevitably failed, I would have to spin some story to cover her ass.

"It took you thirty seconds to ask."

"Can I at least see him?"

"No, you haven't delivered on your side of the bargain yet."

Wren scowls. "Have you gotten the commander to approve an operation yet?"

"If your patrol goes well, I'll talk to him when we get back. You should be far enough along with training for him to consider our request."

I don't add that the commander has been particularly impressed with her progress. The worst thing she could be in this situation is cocky. I know Wren has worked with the Syndicate before, but never with the intention of double-crossing them. It's my job to make sure she is as prepared as possible before we put ourselves in a dangerous situation.

"What's with the bots?" asks Wren.

"They're mainly for crowd control, but today we're using them as scouts. See that one closest to the door?" The bot I point out is bulkier than the rest with a larger platform housing more electronics. The size difference isn't noticeable unless you know what you're looking for. "That's the leader. It's the only bot we can communicate with. We use our wristbands to give the lead bot instructions. The lead bot then relays the orders to the other bots in the unit."

Wren studies the machinery curiously. I can practically see her breaking it down in her mind.

"Huh, so you don't control them independently of one another. It's more like one bot with a bunch of different arms."

"Right."

"Hey," Wren turns in her seat to face me. It's an awkward motion considering how close we're sitting. "I'm sorry about your nose."

She broke it about three weeks ago, so the pain and swelling are pretty much gone. The bridge of my nose is now slightly crooked, probably because I refused to keep it taped. Even with the permanent change, I couldn't bring myself to stay mad at Wren. I should have anticipated her attack, because if our roles were reversed I would have done the same thing.

"Just don't make it a habit," I say. I decide to ask a question that has been weighing on me for a few weeks now. "Why Indy?"

"What?"

"Your motorcycle," I clarify. "Why did you name it Indy?"

"'Her,'" corrects Wren, "not 'it.' I'm surprised you remember that."

"I've found that near-death experiences help with recall."

Wren laughs. "Fair enough. My motorcycle is an Indian Scout, so I call her Indy for short."

I frown. "You named her Indy, because of a brand?"

"I had a few things on my mind while I was rebuilding her. I didn't have time to be creative with her name!"

I let out an exaggerated sigh. "I expected more from you."

Wren scowls and punches my arm a little harder than jokingly, making me snicker. I have to remind myself that Wren and I are supposed to be enemies. When I talk to her, it's easy to forget that we have opposing goals and the only reason we're here now is because we made a deal. It's one of the many reasons I need to get our mission approved as soon as possible. I don't have time for distractions.

The bots come to life, a green light illuminating the base of each machine.

"You have arrived." A voice emits from the overhead speakers. Wren starts to get up, but I touch her arm gently to stop her.

"Wait for the bots to exit first. They protect the entrance and scan the area for hostiles." As if on cue, the Pod door opens and a small ramp extends. The crowd control bots roll down the ramp and form a semicircle around the door. The console secured to my wrist lights up with a report from the lead bot indicating the area is clear.

"Won't the bots cause a panic?" Wren asks.

"People are getting used to them. The Council has approved more bot patrols in marketplaces over the last few months to cut down on Syndicate activity. They'll scout ahead and blend in with the crowd."

"Nothing like normalizing big brother," she mutters dryly. I guess it is strange that the Council is authorizing more bot patrols in grunt neighborhoods. The primary objective for the enforcers is to uphold Council laws and to protect Axton AI assets. As terrible as it sounds, they generally don't care about grunts unless the Syndicate is involved. There haven't been any reports of increased Syndicate activity in this area to warrant the additional patrols. I make a mental note to ask about it when we get back to the Academy.

I follow the last bot out of the van with my rifle raised and do a sweep before gesturing for Wren to follow me. Tents line the street on both sides with vendors hocking everything from mobile phones to canned goods. It's similar to the marketplace the VR assessment draws information from, but more vibrant.

Plywood signs with spray paint indicate what each stall is selling. The street is bustling with people. The sound of a thousand negotiations occurring simultaneously is overwhelming. I swipe a pattern on my wristband and the bots fan out through the pedestrians ahead of us. They roll slowly, parting the crowd like lepers. People appear generally uncomfortable with their presence, but they aren't running in terror. I guess their need to buy necessities outweighs their unease.

"The two most important things to remember when you're on patrol are to stay with your partner and to keep the bots in sight," I say. "There's safety in numbers. Call for backup if you need it. Don't try to be a hero." I scan the stalls, searching for potential threats. Senior enforcers would have made certain this area was clear before authorizing a training patrol, so I'm not expecting any surprises.

"What exactly are we looking for?" asks Wren. She sounds nervous, but she's holding her rifle in her arms like I taught her. Her training is kicking in even if the situation feels foreign.

"Nothing in particular. The goal for today is to teach the recruits the basics. I don't expect to arrest anyone if that's what you're worried about." The other pedestrians give us a wide berth. They duck into storefronts or walk past us at a brisk pace with distrustful glares.

"It's strange to be on the other side of that look," says Wren. Her expression falls.

"You get used to it."

"Don't pretend to know how I feel, pansy."

"I'm not pretending," I say, stepping around a couple arguing in the middle of the street. "I lived in an apartment two blocks from here until I was thirteen." I don't know why I tell her that. It's not something I share freely. Liam and Elle are the only people outside of my family that know the details about where I grew up. The other elites have a vague idea, but they also have short memories. I'm one of them now. My past doesn't matter.

Wren's eyebrows shoot into her hairline. "But you're the director's son, that doesn't track." I'm glad she kept her voice low. I have no desire to fight off a hoard of angry grunts who disagree with Byron's politics. That's not my burden to carry.

"Stepson," I say.

"Same difference."

"Big difference. We got lucky. Mom married up and we moved out. We cut ties with everyone in the old neighborhood. Most of our friends either wanted something from us or didn't trust us after the move. So yeah, I have some idea of what it feels like to be a stranger in your own home."

Wren is quiet for a moment. She readjusts her grip on her rifle. "You talk like a walking dictionary. You don't carry yourself like a grunt, you don't dress like one, and you embrace the elite lifestyle like you were born into it. It's hard to believe you feel like you don't belong."

"Sometimes the easiest way to get what you want is to conform. If you play the part long enough, other people start to believe it even if you don't. It makes them less likely to stand in your way."

"Sounds lonely," says Wren. Her eyes drift along the stalls lining the road before they land on mine. It's not a pitying look, simply understanding. Like she knows what it's like to play a role that isn't the lead in your own life.

I don't get a chance to respond. The bots pick up speed, zipping through the crowd and drawing cries of alarm from pedestrians. I frown and tap the receiver on my wrist to see what's going on. I notice a woman with spiky blond hair leaning against a brick wall under a weather-beaten awning out of the corner of my eye. She's wearing a torn canvas jacket with patches on the arms and breast pocket.

The building looks like some kind of bar. The front window is barred, but the glass is cracked beneath it, spider-webbing out from a point near the center. The awning was red at one point but has faded to a pastel pink making the illegible gold font more gaudy than elegant. The concrete step leading to the front door sits at a slant as if the whole building is sinking on its foundation. Or maybe it's just the devil summoning his servants back to the underworld and the building is responding. The woman glances at us before disappearing inside. Before I can figure out what's bothering me about the situation, my wristband lights up with an alarm.

"I'm getting a warning from the lead bot. It's under attack," I explain, breaking into a jog.

Wren matches my pace. A few heads turn our way, but as soon as the bystanders recognize our uniforms they return their eyes to the ground. I stop at the corner of an alley when my wristband shows that we've reached the location of the distress signal. I press my back against the wall and peer around the corner.

There's a man at the end of the alleyway slamming a baseball bat into the lead crowd control bot over and over again. It's bouncing off the shield and doing little damage, but it doesn't matter. Assaulting an Axton AI bot is grounds for detainment.

"Cover me," I say. Wren nods and raises her rifle. Thankfully, she works well under pressure.

I step away from the building. "Drop the bat." The man ignores my warning and continues hitting the bot. He doesn't even acknowledge me. Does he have a death wish? I take a few metered steps forward.

"Sir, you need to stop or I will authorize the bot to shock you." The man pauses, panting from exertion. He drops the bat, letting it clatter to the ground at his feet. "Hands where I can see them," I instruct. The man does as he's told. I circle behind him and check to make sure Wren is still in position. She hasn't moved, so I remove the handcuffs from my belt and swing my rifle over my shoulder. It's held in place by my chest strap.

"You're under arrest for destroying Council property. You have the right-"

"Ash," says Wren. My eyes snap up. The woman I saw under the red awning a few moments ago has a revolver pressed to Wren's head. Her forearm is wrapped around Wren's neck in a chokehold. I see a blur of movement just in time to avoid a bat to the head. I knife my hand into the man's throat. He chokes and collapses on the ground. I level my rifle at Wren's captor, but I know it's futile. We walked into a trap.

"Drop your weapon or I'll kill her," says the woman. Two more men appear behind her. This is just fantastic.

"Are you sure you want to do this?" I say. "The charges for assaulting a-"

"Last warning," she cuts me off. She wraps her arm tighter around Wren's neck. Wren's eyes bulge and she claws at the woman's arm, but her lips are starting to turn blue. I mutter a curse before slowly removing the rifle strap and setting it on the ground. The two men stride forward and secure my wrists in front of me with a zip tie. I try to maintain some space between my hands to keep the tie loose, but a swift elbow to the ribs puts a stop to that. The restraint is cinched painfully tight.

"Get them off the street. Take their wristbands and bring the bot inside," says the woman. One of the men removes my wristband. It doesn't matter. When we fail to report back to the Academy, the bots assigned to my patrol will be deactivated and they'll send out a search party. We just have to stall them long enough for help to arrive.

Wren and I are led into the bar with the torn red awning. A flickering neon sign in the front window advertises a local beer I've never heard of. Inside, red suede couches line the walls with girls draped across them like decorative throw pillows. There are a few male patrons in various stages of inebriation flirting with them. Music is pumping through the speakers, sending vibrations through my chest. A haze of cigarette smoke hangs in the air making my mouth water. I wish I could reach for my chewing gum without getting shot. I wonder if anything has changed in this bar since it was built a few decades ago. It's like these people run their own Hotel California where no one ever leaves the neighborhood and nothing changes.

Except for me.

Our captors lead us to a door behind the bar that opens into a short hallway with four doors. I'm not sure where they're taking us or if they're going to lock us up. If we want to escape, now is the time. I lurch to the side, crashing my shoulder into one of the men and sending him into a wall. He cries out when I drive a knee into his stomach. I loop my arms around the other man's neck and pull tight. The first man recovers and sends a few punches into my ribs. When that doesn't stop me, I feel a sharp pain in my lower back. Wren yells something unintelligible. My body convulses and I lose control of my legs, collapsing onto the floor.

The bastard tased me.

The muscle spasms eventually subside leaving me weak and subdued. Strong hands grab me under the armpits and pull me down the hall. The heels of my boots click as they catch on the small dips between tiles. The bot rolls along behind us. Someone must be using my wristband to control it. I notice they've already spray-painted over the camera lens. These guys knew exactly what they were doing. Losing the camera will make it harder for the enforcers to find us, but the tracker is harder to disable.

They drag me through the second door on the right and drop me. I manage to twist my body so my head doesn't hit the floor. Wren is shoved down beside me. I crunch up into a sitting position and stifle a groan. We're in an office of some sort. There's a desk in the middle of the room with a computer that looks older than I am and a precarious stack of paperwork. Who uses paper anymore? The answer is simple: someone who doesn't want a digital fingerprint. If I needed another clue that this bar isn't above board, that's it.

A young boy is standing on a ladder in the corner installing a security camera. He can't be much older than thirteen. He has unkempt, blond hair that sticks out at every angle and a smattering of freckles on his nose. He looks at us in surprise.

"Change of plans, mechanic. I need you to remove the tracking device from this bot," says the woman.

The young boy climbs down the ladder. "That isn't the job we agreed on." He sounds nervous confronting his boss, his eyes darting between us and the woman.

"It is if you want to get paid." She tosses my wristband to the boy underhand. He fumbles the catch and has to scoop it off the ground. "If you have questions, use that to zap the pansies. It should make them more agreeable." The woman and her guards leave, closing the door behind them. I hear a lock click.

"Wren?" The boy speaks softly, taking a few tentative steps toward us. Does she know him? The woman said he was a mechanic and he knows who she is. Wren's face is a torrent of emotions I can't quite decipher. Her shoulders slump, her hands falling limply at her sides.

"Robbie," she croaks. "What did you do?"

Chapter 8

Wren

When you go to bed at night, you close your eyes believing the world will look the same when you wake up. Sure, dreams come and go, but ultimately you can differentiate between a nightmare and a living hell. At the moment, I can't tell the difference. More importantly, I don't want to. I'm relieved this situation could all be part of my imagination - a twisted piece of masticated art created by my subconscious to torment me.

If only I were that lucky.

"A few days after you left, a couple of brawlers showed up. I tried to stop them, but it's not like we could lock the door. It was still broken from when the enforcers kicked it in. They wanted more credits. I told them we didn't have any, but they tossed the apartment anyways. When they didn't find anything, they threatened to lift our protection order. I told them I would work off the debt and they agreed," says Robbie. He delivers his explanation quickly, barely pausing to breathe. He looks worried, like I'm going to give him a verbal beat down for his actions.

"Wait, as in *Syndicate* brawlers?" Ash asks. If I'm being honest, I completely forgot he was here. I was so thrown off by seeing Robbie I managed to block out his presence entirely.

Robbie looks at his feet. "Yeah, I'm sorry I couldn't do more to protect Grams and Ariel."

I study Miles' younger brother. He gave up everything to help my family and he's sorry he couldn't do more for them? He's too good for this world. I crawl to Robbie's tool bag, my tool bag, and start looking for a screwdriver to remove the fasteners on the bot.

"I'm so sorry, this is all my fault."

"It was my choice," says Robbie. "I'm not a worthless little kid anymore, you know."

"Don't you get it?" I snap. I give up searching and upend the bag on the floor. "Once you enlist with the Syndicate, you're in for life. Miles and I did everything in our power to keep you away from that and you ended up working for them anyway!" My voice cracks. I find the screwdriver I need and go to work on the panel at the base of the bot.

Robbie sighs. "Do you want me to untie the enforcer?"

"Yeah, sure," I say. Robbie cuts the zip tie securing Ash's hands. Ash rubs his wrists where the plastic bit into his skin. He looks pretty out of it from being zapped. Can't say I blame him.

"Are you alright?" I ask.

"I think so. Who is he?" Ash points at Robbie.

"Robbie O'Reilly." Robbie throws his shoulders back and stands a bit taller under Ash's scrutiny.

"As in, related to Miles O'Reilly?" Ash asks, connecting the dots faster than a fried human brain should be able to.

"Yeah, he's my big brother," says Robbie.

"That's...interesting," says Ash. He seems to notice what I'm working on for the first time. "What are you doing?"

"Removing the tracking device," I say.

"We can't give the Syndicate an untraceable bot!" He tries to intervene, but I bat his hands away.

"If we don't, they kill Robbie."

"He can come with us!"

"I can't," says Robbie. "If I bail on this job, the Syndicate will lift their protection order on Wren's family. They'll be killed before we can get there."

There's the conundrum. I can't ask Robbie to put himself at risk for Grams and Ariel, but what other choice do I have? Right now, all three of them are alive and well. This is the best-case scenario. Crushing guilt lodges in my chest as Robbie starts picking up the tools I dumped on the floor. This isn't the life a kid should have. Especially not one as bright and kind as he is.

"New plan," I say. "Once I remove the tracker, Ash and I will get out of here and go to the apartment. Robbie will meet us there when he's done installing the cameras." I finish loosening the final screw and tug the panel off.

"And I repeat, we will not be leaving an untraceable lead bot with the Syndicate," says Ash. "They can hack it to control the group. Do you want them to have access to an entire squad of crowd control bots?"

"No, but we don't have a choice." I unplug the tracker and sigh. "Look Ash, I'm not asking you to stop fighting your war against the Syndicate. I'm asking you to lose this battle to save two lives."

I watch the internal struggle play out across Ash's features. I hate asking for help, but I still have to fight my way out of a Syndicate bar before I can help Grams and Ariel. Having a trained enforcer at my side would make escaping a lot easier.

Ash groans and presses the heels of his hands into his eyes. "Fine." My lips part in shock. I didn't expect him to agree, but I'm thankful he did. He glances at Robbie. I guess the pansy has a heart after all.

"Thank you," I say. I smile at Ash. He clears his throat, uncomfortable with the whole situation. We take a few minutes to come up with a plan. When we're ready, Robbie knocks on the door.

"Hey, guard! I removed the tracker. Want to let me out?"

I hear some grumbling on the other side before the deadbolt disengages and the door opens. Before the guard is fully in the room, Ash lunges and wraps an arm around his neck. The guard struggles, but Ash keeps his hold until the guard's eyes roll back in his head and his body starts to go limp. Ash lowers him to the floor. I watch his chest until I see it rise and fall with his breath. Ash's attack was practiced and cold. Sure, I've seen him fight at the Academy, but that was just training. It's different in real life. More brutal.

"If anyone asks, we overpowered you and escaped." I hug Robbie. "Be safe."

"Always am," says Robbie.

"Then be safer."

Ash grabs the gun from the waistband of the unconscious guard and checks the clip before snapping it back into place. "You ready?"

No.

But I nod anyway. Ash toes open the door, leading with the gun. He peeks around the corner before stepping out into the hall. The music is blasting, masking any noise Ash might have made taking out the guard. I see customers milling around on the other side of the bar, but none of them have noticed us yet. We run to the end of the hall. Ash slams into the crash bar on the exit door just as Robbie sounds the alarm. Someone yells behind us, but I don't look.

Ash takes the lead. He runs around the back of the building, taking the corner so quickly he nearly wipes out. I do my best to match his pace. I thought I was in shape, but my breathing is heavy and I'm falling behind. Ash leads us back into the marketplace. We make it two blocks before a vase sitting on the counter of the stand in front of us explodes. Shop owners and customers scream and dive for cover.

Ash curses and stops short. He pivots and fires behind me. "Get behind that counter," he says, inclining his chin to indicate a booth on our left. I run past him and dive over the counter of the food stall, hitting the ground hard. The stall owner screams at me, but I'm not paying attention. I don't even breathe until Ash lands on the ground beside me.

"You good?" he asks.

"Yeah."

Ash stays low, bent nearly in half when he opens the flimsy door at the back of the stand. I follow his lead. It opens to a tent with patrons cowering under folding tables, their meals sitting forgotten. A few of them let out surprised shouts. Ash ignores them, blowing through the tent and out the back. There's a metro station with stairs leading down to an underground platform. We take the steps two at a time. Thankfully, the station is empty. Ash jumps onto the tracks, avoiding the third rail. I follow him down, his hands going to my waist to help me.

We take up a brisk jog. The dim running lights at the base of the tunnel are barely enough to illuminate the tracks to keep us from tripping. We keep our pace for what feels like hours. Realistically, I know it can't be more than twenty minutes.

"I'm impressed, pansy," I say. It's the truth. If I needed to verify Ash's claim that he lived in this neighborhood, he proved it during our escape. He knew how to navigate the market, which food stall had a back exit, and where the metro station was. He's the reason we got away safely.

"That was an ambush," says Ash, ignoring my compliment. "They knew where we would be patrolling and how to detain the lead bot."

"Do you think they worked with someone at the Academy?" Ash is quiet for a moment. It dawns on me that I'm probably the lead suspect. "What, you think it was me? I haven't said anything! Why would I risk my chance to rescue Miles?"

"I know," Ash sighs. "It has to be someone with access to the patrol plans. Did you recognize anyone at the bar besides Robbie?"

I think back to the woman in the canvas jacket, the customers, and the thugs who detained us. None of them looked familiar. "No."

"I need to send a unit to recover the bots. I'll talk to Elle and Liam about the mole when we get back to the Academy. We'll have to keep it quiet. I don't want to tip off the informant."

"I'll meet you back at the Academy. My family is my priority."

"I'm coming with you," says Ash.

"But you just said you have to take care of the hacked bot."

"I'll call Elle when we get up top to let her know what's going on. I promised I would help you and I meant it."

Ash sounds offended that I wasn't counting on him, but he went back on his word once and I have no doubt he would do it again if it suits him. My hand goes to the locket around my neck. It's tucked under my shirt and out of sight. I just hope the Syndicate bought Robbie's story.

We walk for another ten minutes before we come to another station. There are a couple of passengers sitting on the benches, but they look half asleep. No one says anything when Ash and I exit the tunnel and climb up on the platform. I'm not sure they even notice. When we get topside, I realize I have no clue where we are. The buildings are old but well maintained. I don't think we're in a wealthy sector, but it's nicer than the area we just left. If I had to guess, we're in one of the outer elite communities.

If you took an aerial snapshot of the capital, the Academy and big technology companies would be located in the center. The wealthiest elites live closest to the center of the circle. The further you live from the center, the less money you have. Eventually, it switches over to the grunt sectors. The poorest citizens live in the outer ring that butts up against the border walls designating the boundaries of the capital. Any travel beyond the walls requires a permit.

I've never been outside of the capital, so I don't know if it's the same in other cities. I know my parents took me to visit relatives in the country, but I was too young to remember. The border walls went up before I was old enough to go to school. We didn't travel after the walls went up. We couldn't afford to. Even when my grandparents passed away, we couldn't scrape together enough to go to the funeral. Permits are expensive and the application process is extremely selective. Everything and everyone I care about is within the capital city limits. I've never had a reason to leave.

Ash calls someone, I'm assuming Elle, and explains what happened with the bot. He leaves out the part about Robbie. "I'll be back later tonight. I have some personal business to take care of," he says.

What a shady way to end a call with your fiancée.

"Elle is going to send a unit to the bar. I'll schedule a Pod to take us to your apartment." Ash opens AVA and glances at me. "What's your address?"

Habit makes me pause, but what does it matter? I have to move my family today. Worst-case scenario, the enforcers have an old address on file. I give it to him.

Ash taps his phone screen. "The Pod will be here in ten minutes. There aren't very many running in this sector."

"Because the people living here probably can't afford them," I say. "The first time I rode in a Pod was when you arrested me."

"Seriously?" Ash frowns. "I guess I've been with the Axton's for so long I've forgotten what normal is." The admission surprises me. He puts his thumbs in his pockets and rocks on his heels, his face flushing under my gaze. Is he...embarrassed? I didn't think it was possible for the cocky enforcer. "Want to grab a coffee?"

I follow Ash's gaze to a coffee shop on the corner.

"I don't have any money," I say.

"I'll spot you." He must sense my hesitation. "I know you're worried about your family, but the Pod is ten minutes away whether we spend it standing here or getting a coffee. I think we could both use a minute to pull ourselves together."

He's right. My hands are shaking, the fading adrenaline leaving me drained. It just feels wrong to be doing something as mundane as getting coffee when the Syndicate could be headed to my apartment.

"I'll pay you back when I get my first enforcer paycheck," I say.

"I'll hold you to it." Ash winks. He tucks the guard's gun in his waistband and pulls his shirt over it. He opens the door for me. The coffee shop is an old-fashioned place that still has plush couches and physical books to entice visitors to cozy up and stay a little longer. There's only one other patron nestled in an armchair scrolling on a tablet. Soft music plays in the background and the heavenly aroma of freshly brewed coffee greets us.

"Afternoon, folks. What'll it be?" The man behind the counter doesn't bat an eye at our enforcer uniforms. It's strange compared to the reaction of the people in the market. Where they avoided eye contact and walked faster, this man appears completely at ease.

"What do you want?" It takes a beat for me to realize Ash's question is directed at me. I scan the menu, but all of the drinks have four-word names. I've been in coffee shops before, but they've never had this many options. It's overwhelming. Ash starts listing off the options, trying to help but stops when I continue to look confused.

"Just plain coffee?" he asks with a chuckle.

"Yes, please," I say with relief. "Regular coffee with cream."

"Don't all mechanics drink their coffee black?" Ash asks.

"That's a stereotype."

Ash quirks an eyebrow.

"Okay, fine," I laugh. "It's an accurate stereotype, but I'd rather be mocked for my coffee choice than drink something disgusting to save face."

"Fair enough. We'll take two," says Ash. The cashier enters our order and Ash scans his chip to pay for it.

"I'll have those ready in a minute." The cashier smiles at Ash and goes to work brewing the coffee. I choose a booth near the window so we can watch for the Pod.

"I thought all enforcers drink black coffee?" I ask, watching a group of kids cross the street. One of them is dribbling a basketball down the sidewalk. They're laughing and shoving each other playfully. I wonder what it would have been like to grow up somewhere like this. Where you can play outside without worrying about your safety.

"Only if they want to look more macho. I just choked out a guy and escaped from a Syndicate bar. I don't need any help in that category." Ash winks.

I snort. "I think you should let other people tell you you're macho. When you say it, you sound like a dick."

"Point taken," Ash laughs.

"Does Axton AI sell a robot that makes coffee?" It's not something I thought about before, but the cashier seems to be doing everything manually. Maybe it's because this particular shop can't afford the machine. Maybe it's just part of the nostalgic branding.

"They do, but having a robotic barista is like buying a fancy bottle of wine with a screw top. It ruins the experience."

I give him a pointed look. "I think that might be the most pretentious thing you've ever said."

"I'll blame it on the Axtons." Ash smiles.

"Why do you talk about the Axtons like you aren't one of them? You always say 'they' or 'the Axtons' instead of 'us.' What gives?" I know it's a personal question, but I'm curious.

Ash leans back in his seat. He's quiet for a moment as if deciding how to answer. "I guess it's because I never felt like I had a place with the Axtons. Jace, my stepbrother, is Byron's successor. He will inherit the director seat on the Council and a controlling number of shares in Axton AI. I'm just a reminder of everything he lost when mom died."

It's a bleak outlook, but I have no doubt Ash believes every word he's saying. I can't believe Jace is going to be director. Of course, I knew that was the case. Everyone in the city knows, but all I can think about is when Jace busted into my apartment. Ariel's screams. The way he kicked me when I was down. Someone like that shouldn't be in charge of anything, let alone an entire country.

"I'm sorry that you lost your mom," I say.

"It was a long time ago," says Ash.

"Doesn't make it any easier."

"I'm sorry you lost your parents," says Ash. He gives me an apologetic smile. "I read your file."

"Yeah." I should be upset about the invasion of privacy, but I'm not.

He looks out the window. "Mom was killed in a Syndicate raid on the hospital where she worked. That's why I joined the enforcers. My goal is to make sure no one else loses someone because of the Syndicate." Ash interlocks his fingers and rests them on the table, a sad expression taking over his features. "Can I tell you something that doesn't leave this conversation?"

I nod, unsure of where this is going.

"Elle and I aren't a real couple," he keeps his voice low, barely above a whisper.

"What do you mean?"

"We faked our engagement. Byron...the director surprised me with an arranged marriage proposal at the Ascent Day celebration. Elle bailed me out."

I focus on Ash's clasped hands, unsure of what to say. "Why are you telling me this?" I finally whisper.

"I just wanted you to know." Ash shrugs, a small smile playing at the corners of his lips. "I trust you."

"You don't even know me."

"Maybe. I know you're the type of person who puts herself in danger to save a friend. I know you have a mean right cross, you're capable under pressure, and you're smart. You don't seem like the type of person who would run back to the Academy and tell everyone my secret."

I'm not sure how to respond to Ash. I can feel his eyes on me, but I can't bring myself to meet them. I hear the truth in his words. He believes what he's telling me. The only problem? I don't return his trust. I can't. I'm not sure I ever can.

"Why couldn't you just tell the director you weren't interested? That seems a lot simpler than faking an engagement-"

"Coffee for the happy couple," the cashier places two mugs on the table. I wince, unsure of how much he overheard.

"Not a couple," I say.

"Thanks," Ash says at the same time. The cashier gives us a curious look before returning to his place behind the counter. I take a sip. The coffee tastes like everything right and good in this world.

"He wouldn't have accepted that answer," says Ash, answering my question from before we were interrupted.

"He can't force you to marry someone against your will."

"No, but he can make sure it's in my best interest to agree."

"What does that mean?"

"He could have me discharged from the enforcers. He could have Elle or Liam arrested. Honestly, that might be a better option for him considering I don't care what he does to me." Ash takes a sip of coffee and sets his mug down. "Byron takes everything you care about and uses it to manipulate you. He doesn't fight fair. He fights to win. What saved me was proposing in front of a crowd on a live broadcast. The only thing Byron won't sacrifice to win is his reputation."

I study Ash, seeing him in a new light. I try to imagine what my life would have been like if I were in his position. Surrounded by enemies. Losing my mom, my one ally, and being forced to adapt to a world where every statement and situation is loaded with double meaning. Forming alliances with friends to protect myself, knowing those same alliances could be used against me. It sounds exhausting.

A notification pops up on Ash's phone from AVA. "The Pod is here."

We pound the rest of our coffee and head outside. I've never ridden in a civilian Pod before. It's different from the enforcer vehicles. This Pod was built for comfort with a wrap-around booth covered in black leather and a table in the center, lush carpet, and dim lighting. The windows aren't tinted, so I can watch the buildings and the people go by. Part of me wishes I could enjoy the experience without the overwhelming dread hanging over us like a dark cloud. Ash stays quiet during the ride. I don't know if he is as uneasy as I am or if he senses I don't want to talk. Either way, I'm grateful I don't have to pretend to be interested in a conversation I can't focus on.

The Pod stops in front of my apartment. The street is quiet. There aren't any unfamiliar cars parked out front or any sign that the Syndicate has been here. Ash tugs the Syndicate guard's gun out of his waistband.

"I'll order another ride when we're ready to leave. I don't want the Syndicate to know we're here," says Ash.

He taps his phone screen and the Pod pulls away. It's a good idea. If anyone is watching, I don't want them to get suspicious. I lead Ash up the stairwell to our floor. He doesn't say anything about the garbage in the stairwell or the faint smell of mildew. Now that I think about it, this is the first time I've brought an outsider home. When we get to the landing, Ash throws out an arm. He checks to make sure the hall is clear before we step out in the open.

It's a nice gesture, but unnecessary.

I'm fully capable of taking care of myself. I'm so used to it, that I've forgotten what it feels like to have someone in your corner. That's when the guilt sets in. I think of Miles, probably locked away in some enforcer prison awaiting judgment. I had a partner once and I couldn't protect him. Now, Grams and Ariel are in danger. I can't protect anyone. I've never felt so inadequate.

I walk the length of the hallway and stop in front of my unit. The door is back on its hinges and a new lock has been installed. I'll have to thank Robbie when he gets here. I knock. I hear movement inside and the click of the deadbolt disengaging. The door swings open and a flash of movement sends me jumping back.

Ash raises his gun, but I quickly slam his hand down. Grams is standing just inside the apartment wielding a broken broom handle like it's Excalibur. She's wearing a light pink housecoat with flowers on it, baggy pants, and bare feet. Max growls and pushes between her legs to face the intruders. When he recognizes me, he jumps up and puts his paws on my chest, trying to lick my face.

I laugh. "Hi, Max."

"Wren?" Grams asks, her eyes wide.

"I'm sorry I scared you," I say. She hugs me around Max, nearly stabbing Ash with the broken handle she still has in her hands. He takes a few steps back and sticks the gun into his waistband, covering it with his shirt. The action draws Grams' attention.

"It's okay, sugar. Who's your friend?" Grams pulls away. She looks at Ash with suspicion, her eyes going to the outline of the weapon concealed under his shirt. Her grip tightens around the broom handle.

"I'm Ash," he says, offering his hand. Grams looks at me.

"He's a friend," I say. Grams frowns but accepts his hand.

"I'm Roberta Parker. My friends and family call me Grams. I'll let you know when you fall into that category." She pumps his hand once before releasing it and swings the door wide. "No sense making a scene in the hall. Come on." She leaves the door open and walks into the apartment. Out of the corner of my eye, I see Ash shake his hand out.

"Lady has an iron grip," he grumbles.

"I also have eyes in the back of my head and can hear a pin drop from a mile away," Grams calls from inside. Ash pales and I burst out laughing. It's refreshing to see the hardened enforcer scared by an old lady in her loungewear.

He's human after all.

The apartment is exactly as I left it. The same faded curtains, the same old furniture. It's strange in some ways. I've changed so much in the last month I guess I expected my childhood home to evolve with me.

Ariel is sitting on the couch watching cartoons, oblivious to what Grams was doing to protect our home from invaders. As soon as she sees me walk through the door she leaps off the back of the couch with her arms outstretched, expecting me to catch her. I grab her under the arms and twirl her around.

"I missed you, baby girl!" I pepper her face with kisses.

Ariel giggles. "I miss you too mommy!"

Chapter 9

Ash

"She's yours?" I ask. Wren turns around, resting the little girl on her hip.

"Yeah," she says, giving me a wary smile. I'm intruding on a personal moment with her family in a uniform that busted down their door a month ago.

I get it.

The little girl squirms until Wren gets the message and sets her down. She toddles over to me, staring up in awe. She's a miniature version of Wren with startling green eyes and a wild mess of brown curls. I look at Wren for permission before squatting down so I'm at her daughter's level.

"I'm Ash, what's your name?" I ask.

"I Ariel!"

"I *am* Ariel," Wren corrects.

"No, you not." Ariel frowns. "I Ariel. You mommy. Can we watch toons?"

Wren gives me an exasperated look, but her lips twitch up in a smile. "Sure, we can watch them."

"Don't take this the wrong way," says Ms. Parker. "I love seeing you, but aren't you supposed to be training with the enforcers?" She eyes our white uniforms with a disgust that makes me feel two inches tall. Wren sighs. I can tell she wants to spend time with Ariel and pretend like today didn't happen, but she won't because she's not the kind of person that ignores her problems.

"I can sit with her while you talk to Ms. Parker," I say. I use her preferred name, because quite frankly the woman scares me. There's no doubt in my mind she could put even Commander Harper on edge.

"Are you sure?" Wren asks.

"Yay! Let's go!" says Ariel. She grabs my hand and tugs me towards the couch, but I don't let her move me.

"We'll sit on the couch where you can see us," I say. Wren nods, but her shoulders are still tense. She doesn't trust me and that hurts more than it should. I have no one but myself to blame. The first time we met I made a deal with her and immediately went back on my word. It was a terrible first impression. I know it'll be hard to come back from that, but the more I get to know Wren the more I want her to trust me.

Like I'm beginning to trust her.

I have no idea why I shared the bit about my fake engagement. Wren could sink my career and what little relationship with Byron I have by sharing my secret. Somehow, I know she won't. I read her file. I know that her mom died trying to break up a Syndicate riot when Wren was twelve. I know her dad drank himself to death when she was fourteen. She hasn't had it easy. After invading her privacy without her permission, I felt like I needed to share something with her.

Ariel gets impatient. She drops my hand and runs around the couch, taking the corner so quickly that she flops on the carpet before scrambling up on the cushions. Max jumps up beside her, resting his head on her lap. I take the seat next to them. Max perks up and gives me some serious side-eye. Thankfully, he decides I'm not a threat and lays back down.

"Why didn't you tell me about Robbie?" Wren asks her grandmother, keeping her voice so low I have to strain to hear it over the cartoon.

"I was waiting for you to call first. I didn't want to risk reaching out to you and having someone listen in," says Ms. Parker.

Wren recaps what happened during our patrol, starting with the stolen bot and ending with leaving Robbie behind. "He's going to meet us here once he finishes the job. I need you to pack a bag. I'm moving you, Ariel, and Robbie to a new apartment tonight," Wren says.

"You can't be serious," scoffs Grams. "If Jimmy and I moved every time someone threatened us, it would be a weekly event."

"I can't ask Robbie to keep working for the Syndicate on my behalf. He's twelve!" Says Wren, raising her voice. It's followed by silence. "I'm sorry, I shouldn't have yelled at you."

"No, you're right," says Ms. Parker. "That isn't fair to Robbie, especially without Miles around to protect him. We need to talk to Don. If we aren't safe here, then he isn't either."

"Does he know about Robbie's involvement with the Syndicate?" Wren asks.

"No."

"I'll talk to him. In the meantime, pack a bag," says Wren. I watch Ms. Parker walk down a hall I assume leads to the bedroom. Wren taps me on the shoulder. I lean my head back so I'm looking at her upside down. "Come on, we need to talk to Robbie's dad."

"No," says Ariel. She flops over, making Max move his head or risk being squished. "Ash wants to watch toons with me."

Wren sighs, her shoulders sagging. The dark circles under her eyes are somehow more prominent now than when we got here. She looks drained. "I can hold the fort for a few minutes," I say.

"Are you sure?" Wren sounds skeptical.

I shrug. "What can I say? I have a thing for cartoons."

"Ash is staying," says Ariel. She crosses her arms and glares at her mom. I chuckle. The girl is two going on twenty.

"Okay then...I need to talk to Robbie's dad. He lives three units over, so it'll only take a minute," says Wren. She looks torn with one foot pointed at the door and the other firmly planted by us. I know this is a big step for her, so I decide to make it a little easier. I stand up, angling myself so Ariel can't see what I'm doing. I pull the gun out of my waistband and hand it to Wren.

"Take it. The safety is on." Wren grabs the gun and tucks it in her waistband, tugging the enforcer uniform over it. The thick material easily hides the outline. "Now, I'm at the mercy of Ms. Parker and her broom. I don't know about you, but I'd put my money on her in a fair fight."

Despite her unease, Wren smiles. "I would too. No offense." She looks like she wants to say something more, but decides against it. "Two minutes and I'll be back."

"Okay." I take my seat on the couch. Wren hesitates for a moment longer before I hear the apartment door open and close.

"Which dinosaur are you?" Ariel asks after a while.

"Huh?" I'm completely lost in my thoughts, distracted by my conversation with Wren.

"Which dinosaur are you?" Ariel repeats. I return my eyes to the screen and, for the first time, realize the cartoon has a bunch of talking dinosaurs in it.

"T-Rex?" It's literally the only dinosaur I can think of. What? It's not like dinosaurs come up a lot at the Academy.

"But T-Rex is the bad guy." Ariel scrunches her nose. "Are you a bad guy?"

"No, I don't think so," I say. "Which dinosaur are you?"

"Brontosaurus," says Ariel. She stumbles over the word a little bit, but it blows my mind she knows it at all. "They have super long necks and can see the whole world." She raises her arms wide above her head, almost knocking me in the face in the process.

"Which dinosaur should I be since I'm not a T-Rex?" I ask.

Ariel thinks about it for a minute. "Triceratops."

It takes me a beat to remember which one a Triceratops is.

"They have big heads they crash into stuff with," says Ariel.

Well, okay then. I laugh. If I needed proof Ariel is related to Wren, her response is it.

"What are you two laughing about?" Wren asks. I didn't hear her come in. Ariel jumps off the couch and runs to meet her. I turn on the couch so I can rest my arms on the back cushion. Ariel body slams her legs, nearly knocking Wren off her feet.

"If I were a dinosaur, Ariel thinks I would be a Triceratops, because 'they have big heads they use to crash into stuff,'" I repeat. Wren stares at me for a moment before she bursts out laughing. She scoops up her daughter.

"I mean, she's not wrong." Wren wipes a tear from her eye, she's laughing so hard. A man I recognize walks through the open doorway behind her.

"Don?" I ask in disbelief.

Don freezes. "Ash?"

"Wait, you know him?" Wren asks, looking between us.

"Don works at the Axton mansion," I say. I need a moment to process that the Don I know is standing in Wren's living room. I knew he had kids of his own, but he didn't talk about them much at work. Some people need that separation between their work and home life, so I never pried. I never would have guessed Robbie and Don were connected.

"Hey, Dad," Robbie steps around Don and into the apartment. He's carrying the duffel bag he had at the bar over his shoulder. He looks tired but unharmed.

"Thank God you're alright," says Wren. She hugs him around Ariel, crushing her between them. Grams drags a suitcase into the living room. When she sees Robbie, she drops the bag and joins the group hug. My breath lodges in my throat.

This is her family. This is what a family is supposed to look like.

It's easy to forget that my dysfunctional relationship with Byron and Jace isn't standard. Normal families love. They do crazy things for each other like join the Syndicate, enlist in the enforcers, or marry the director.

I've had a privileged life. No one can dispute that. My world has been filled with lavish parties, servants, fast cars, and designer clothes for almost a decade. I've had women throw themselves at me because of my last name and avoided arrest as a rebellious teenager because of who Byron is.

Somehow it never felt real.

My existence has always been a caricature of Jace's – the same lifestyle with some characteristics drawn out of proportion. In Wren's universe, the artist doesn't exist. She lives an unairbrushed and unfiltered reality that is better defined by the things she doesn't have. It's messy and beautiful. It's something I wish I had.

"Where are we going?" Grams asks, when the group hug breaks apart. Wren puts Ariel down.

"I'm not sure, I just know we can't stay here. I need to get back to Jimmy's Auto. I can tell the Syndicate the shop is back up and running and they can come to me for the protection fees. I just need to buy us some time to get the word out."

That's when the light bulb clicks on.

"What if we use that as our cover story?" I ask. Wren looks at me. "I get command to approve our assignment. You and I go back to work at Jimmy's Auto. You told the brawlers I worked for you. No one would suspect a thing."

Wren thinks it over for a moment. "That makes sense, but where can my family stay in the meantime? I can tell the Syndicate today the shop will be up and running, but that doesn't mean anything if I can't leave the Academy without being arrested for abandoning my training. I have to get them out of here for a few days while we figure things out."

I don't even hesitate. "They can stay at my apartment."

"Don't you live at the Academy?" Wren asks.

"Most of the time." I get off the couch to stand with the group. "But I have an apartment hardly anyone knows about. I didn't trust Byron not to mess with my position in the enforcers, so I bought this place as a backup and kept it off books."

"And you would just offer up your place to a bunch of strangers?" asks Wren.

I shake my head. "Not a bunch of strangers. I know you. Don practically raised me. He made living with the Axton's bearable. I owe him. I'll give your family a place to stay, in the meantime, our deal still stands. I'll get everything sorted out when we get back to the Academy."

"Thank you, sir," says Don. He bows his head in a gesture of respect that makes me uncomfortable. Wren presses her lips together. I can tell she doesn't want to say yes, but she doesn't have a better option.

"Okay," Wren grits out. I call a Pod while everyone is finishing packing. The app sends a push notification to make sure I didn't type in the address by mistake. I doubt anyone in this building has ever ordered a Pod. Wren is bustling around trying to get everyone ready. Don and Robbie stand off to the side arguing. Don isn't happy with his son for joining the Syndicate and dragging him into this.

"You're no better than your older brother, when this is over I want you out of my house," snaps Don. I've never heard him so angry.

"Hold on," I say, approaching them. Don's face flushes. Robbie appears defeated, his shoulders slumped like he's supporting the weight of the world on them. No kid should look like that. "Robbie took the Syndicate job to protect Ms.

Parker and Ariel. You can't kick him out for trying to do the right thing."

Don stares at me. "Are you, of all people, defending someone who works for the Syndicate?" I wince because that's exactly what I'm doing.

"Robbie doesn't deserve that," I repeat, but the fight has gone out of my words. Don glares at me, but my phone pings, notifying me the Pod has arrived.

"Pod is here," I announce.

Wren picks up Ariel and tries to do an awkward half squat to grab the bag.

"I've got it," I say. I take the suitcase from her and grab a second one from Ms. Parker. Robbie opens the door and leads our progression towards the stairs. Max sits in the middle of the apartment pouting. "Come on, Max," I say. His ears perk up and he trots behind us, his tail flicking happily now that he's included.

"Thank you," says Wren.

"You weren't going to leave him here," I say. I saw the way Max cuddled with Ariel and was prepared to fight me when I sat down. I'm not going to take a protector away from Wren and her family when they have enemies coming at them from all directions. It would be cruel.

"No," Wren gives me a small smile, "but I'm glad you're on board. It makes my life easier." We pile into the Pod. It's a tight fit with five people, a dog, and all of our luggage. Ariel sits on Wren's lap to save space. Five minutes into our journey, Max jumps on my lap so he can be closer to Ariel and Wren. He fumbles around, his paws crushing my balls. I mutter a few curse words under my breath. He isn't exactly dainty. Finally, he settles down.

"He likes you," says Wren. She pets Max's head and he licks her hand.

"I think he likes me the same way he likes the couch," I say. Wren snickers.

It's dark outside by the time the Pod pulls into the underground parking garage. I tried to be strategic when I chose my apartment. It's in the elite sectors, but far enough from downtown that the vetting process for new tenants is nonexistent. It has few amenities and old-school locks - a far cry from the flashy apartments downtown that are set up for facial recognition technology and drone delivery services. The property management company advertised the building as "a retro-minimalist's dream." Whatever that means. I didn't want to have to jump through a bunch of hoops, because each step would make it easier for my real identity to be discovered.

The apartment is registered to Trevor Lewis. The real Trevor died five years ago. Liam took over the identity and created a profile for me just as he would an undercover operative. Identification credentials registered with the Council, tax returns for a fake job at an architectural firm downtown, bank statements - you name it. It passed the sniff test and I signed the lease. It's the best insurance I've ever bought.

Max takes the hint and gets off my lap when I start to stand up. I unload the bags in a pile beside the Pod. Wren scoots across the bench, trying not to wake Ariel. She nodded off during the drive, falling asleep with her head resting on Wren's shoulder.

"I'll get the bags," I whisper.

"Thank you," Wren mouths. The parking garage is blissfully empty. I punch in the building access code on the keypad next to the elevator. When it arrives, everyone gets on and I hit the button for the eightieth floor. Max whines when it starts moving.

"It's okay, boy," says Robbie. He pets Max's head with one hand. His other hand is clutching the railing with white knuckles. "I haven't been on an elevator before either."

The elevator stops on my floor and the doors slide open. The hallway is decorated simply with white tile, white walls, and black and white photographs hanging on the walls of generic, pre-Council cityscapes. The space couldn't be more bland if it tried.

When I get to my unit, I run my hand along the top of the door frame until I find my spare key. I've found in a world where automation is king, common sense is often lacking. Most elite apartments have switched over to chip implement scanners, but that's not an option for me. My chip implant is keyed to my real identity. Liam could have created a key card with a false identity, but I didn't think it was worth the risk. The building security system could easily pick up my real implant, rendering the cover identity useless.

"Seriously?" Wren asks, raising an eyebrow at my hiding place.

"What? No one has found it yet. Besides, this is a safe house. If I'm coming here, chances are I won't be able to pick up a key from the Academy. After you," I say, allowing the group to file into my apartment.

I turn on the lights and close the door behind us, sliding the deadbolt in place. It's highly unlikely anyone from the Syndicate would be able to gain access to this building, let alone the eightieth floor, but I feel like I should take every precaution.

The foyer opens into a living room with floor-to-ceiling windows showcasing a jaw-dropping view of the capital. The windows are one-way glass, so there's no way for surveillance drones to see inside, and it eliminates the need for curtains. There's a white leather couch with a matching armchair, a marble-top coffee table with slim black legs, and a natural gas fireplace. I don't have anything hanging on my walls or any knickknacks on my counters or shelves. All of the furniture came with the apartment. I didn't pick anything out myself.

My kitchen is on the right. It's all stainless-steel appliances and granite countertops.

Robbie lets loose a gasp. He runs into the living room and flops down on the couch, kicking his feet up on the coffee table. Max runs after him, leaping up on the couch and settling down beside him. Robbie crosses his hands behind his head, sinking into the cushions. "I could get used to this."

Don scowls. He shoves his son's feet down and pushes Max off the couch. "No feet or dogs on the furniture."

"It's fine," I say. "Make yourselves at home." Don looks at me in disbelief. Robbie just smirks at his dad and puts his feet back on the coffee table.

Wren walks into the apartment as if in a daze, drawn to the floor-to-ceiling windows. Ariel is still asleep in her arms. Ms. Parker stands beside her. I approach them hesitantly. "The bedroom and bathroom are down the hall. There are a couple of air mattresses in the closet for everyone else. I'll talk to Don before we leave to see if he can pick up groceries. There should be some dry goods in the kitchen, but I haven't been here in a while."

Wren touches my arm gently.

"Thank you," she says. "I'm going to put Ariel to bed. I'll be right back." I watch Wren disappear into the bedroom.

"So you're an Axton," says Ms. Parker, startling me. Her eyes scan me from my boots to my hair, the look on her face telling me she's not all that impressed.

"Yes, ma'am," I say. I could give her the same answer I gave Wren. That I'm an Axton in name only. That I've never really belonged with them. To Ms. Parker, I'm not sure it matters.

"I don't know what Wren is planning other than it has something to do with helping Miles. Sometimes I wish he had never given her that lottery ticket, but I know she would have found another way. I'm not asking Wren to stop chasing after Miles. She's the most stubborn person I know. Gets it from her grandfather. Asking her to stop doing something is the equivalent of telling her to double down. Point is, you care about her. You wouldn't let us stay here if you didn't. When people like us get involved with people like you, it never ends well for us. I don't know what she is to you or what kind of deal you two made, but if you care even a little bit then make sure Wren comes back to us. She's more fragile than she lets on. Been through enough for one lifetime already."

Her eyes bore into mine. I want to argue with her. To tell her she has nothing to worry about when it comes to Wren's safety, but that would be a lie. We're planning to approach the Syndicate with the explicit purpose of deceiving them. The safest thing for Wren would be to scrap our plan, but she won't because she's in this for Miles. She's willing to risk everything to protect him because he's a part of her family as much as Ms. Parker or Ariel.

"I'll look out for her," I say. I shouldn't promise her anything. I know that, but something has shifted in my relationship with Wren. A month ago, I wouldn't have blinked at going back on my word and keeping Miles locked up after Wren finished helping me. I can't do that to her. Not after getting to know her, meeting her family, and learning about her connection to Don.

"Ariel is asleep. Are you ready to go?" Wren asks.

"Sure, if you are," I say. Wren pulls the gun out of her waistband. "I want you to take this." She hands it to Ms. Parker.

"This building has decent security..." I trail off when Ms. Parker takes the gun. She drops the clip to check how many rounds are left, puts it back, and takes the safety off with practiced ease that makes both our jaws drop.

"How did you...?" asks Wren. Ms. Parker gives her a small smile.

"I grew up on a farm and started the auto shop with your grandfather. We both know it's not in the best area. Let's just say I picked up a thing or two over the years."

Wren hugs her. "Be safe. Try to keep Robbie out of trouble." I book a Pod while Wren says goodbye to Don and Robbie and we make our way to the elevator. I scan my chip and press the button for the parking garage.

"What were you and Grams talking about? It looked pretty intense," says Wren.

"She's worried," I say. "She asked me to keep an eye out for you."

Wren's features soften. "I haven't spent this much time away from home since Ariel was born."

"You miss them."

"Yeah," sighs Wren. She leans against the back wall of the elevator. "I don't think I'll feel right until all of this is over. Thanks for watching Ariel, by the way."

"No problem. I'll have to refresh my dinosaur knowledge for next time."

Next time. What am I saying? Like Wren would willingly allow me around her family again.

"I'm sure she would appreciate that," says Wren.

We're silent during the ride home, trapped in our thoughts of what's to come. I direct the Pod to drop us off at the back entrance in the parking deck. I have zero desire to walk through the atrium after we went missing on patrol. I'm sure Elle has notified everyone that we're alive, but people will still talk. I need a few minutes to myself before the questions start. We get out of the Pod and it rolls away.

"Hey," says Wren. She taps my arm to get my attention. "Thank you for letting them stay at your apartment. You didn't have to do that." She stands on her toes and gives me a quick peck on the cheek. She pulls away quickly, her face turning pink. I'm not sure who is more surprised, Wren or me.

"No problem," I stammer. My skin tingles where her lips made contact. Her eyes are a torrent of emotion and thoughts I can't begin to read. I clear my throat. "It's tradition for the recruits to celebrate after their first patrol. Commander

Harper should be free since classes let out early. I'll talk to him about authorizing our mission."

Wren clears her throat. "Let me know what he says."

She practically runs for the stairwell. I watch her go; my feet frozen in place.

There are two primary reasons why I'm well and truly screwed.

One, I let Robbie, a known Syndicate mechanic into my safe house when I should have arrested him.

Two, I care about Wren.

I could lie and say it's because I promised an old woman to protect her granddaughter, but I'm not that altruistic. Wren is the stick of dynamite that causes an avalanche. She's loud, blunt, and a total pain in my ass. That should be enough to send me packing, but I find myself wanting a hell of a lot more than a kiss on the cheek.

Chapter 10

Wren

"**T**here you are!" Glitch opens the door to our shared compartment. "What are you doing?"

Trying not to freak out about Robbie joining the Syndicate or trying to process the fact that I kissed Ash would both be acceptable answers.

"Staring at a brick wall trying to figure out the meaning of life," I say instead, because avoidance is a healthy coping mechanism.

"You find any answers?"

"Nope, but I feel like twenty more minutes of this will get me closer."

Glitch plops down on the mattress beside me. "What happened to you guys? Roy and I volunteered to join the search party. Everyone was worried when you didn't report back after patrol."

"We were attacked by the Syndicate. They were trying to steal a bot."

"For real?" She raises an eyebrow. "That's so exciting! My patrol was super boring. We just walked around downtown for a bit and came back. Talk about a letdown. Anyways, we need to get ready to go."

"Go where?" I ask.

"All of the recruits are going out to celebrate their first patrol." I vaguely recall Ash saying something similar, but it didn't register as something I would be attending. I don't feel like I belong with the other recruits. I'm using my position to rescue Miles, nothing more. When he's released, I'll be leaving Glitch and the other enforcers behind. It makes me feel like a phony.

"I think I'd rather stay in," I say. Glitch stops short. She puts her hands on my shoulders and shakes me.

"What is wrong with you? Our first night off in a month and you're going to sit in our compartment by yourself? Not on my watch!" She grabs my hand and tugs me to my feet, handing me my shower caddy.

"You're going to shower because dry shampoo can only do so much. I'll meet you back here in a few minutes." Glitch pitches a towel at my head. I catch it before it hits me in the face, draping it over my shoulder. I guess that settles it. I go to the bathroom and take a shower, rinsing away the grime from the day. My mind wanders back to the expression on Ash's face when I kissed his cheek. I could have sworn there was something there - a spark of interest that could turn into something more.

I won't let it.

I close my eyes and let the water pour over my neck and shoulders like a warm embrace. I promise myself I'm not going to think about Ash for the rest of the night.

Then, I proceed to break that promise two times before my shower is over.

I shut the water off with a frustrated sigh. I try to reason with myself, but it's no use. As much as I want to hate Ash, the more I get to know him the harder it is to hold his actions against him. I put on the fresh t-shirt and a pair of jeans I brought with me. Piling my dirty clothes on top of my shower caddy, I return to my compartment.

"This better be an epic-" My voice dies in my throat when I see Jace laying on the lower bunk tossing a black stress ball against the wall. Glitch is nowhere in sight. The ball bounces off the wall and he catches it creating a dull thump, thump, thump pattern that's half the speed of my heartbeat.

"What are you doing here?" My voice wavers.

"Is that any way to speak to an officer?" Jace admonishes. He catches the ball with a solid thump and frowns.

"I wasn't aware you were an officer," I say, managing to get my tone under control. I set the shower caddy and my dirty clothes on top of the desk.

Pro tip: It's easier to be intimidating when you're not holding your underwear.

Jace stands up and approaches me, his civil mask falling away to reveal the monster beneath. There's nothing regal about his posture. He's not a lion stalking his prey. He's a hyena – cackling and mocking me with a power play meant to instill fear.

"What do you want?" I ask, my nerves overriding my bravado. Jace doesn't stop until he looms over me.

"To know what you and Ash are planning." He flashes a saccharine smile that makes me uneasy. When he trails his hands up my body, I'm hit with a barrage of images I've repressed so well over the years.

The memory of rough hands, an unwanted touch.

It never ceases to amaze me the way trauma comes back to bite you in the ass. You can deal with it, move on, and be fine for years. But fine is a relative term. Am I really okay when something as small as a taste, a smell, a touch, or a setting can transport me back to that moment as if no time has passed?

"Please stop," I whimper, hating how weak I sound.

Jace grabs my jaw and slams his mouth against mine. I shove him away with both hands.

"I said, stop."

Jace ignores me.

I knee him in the balls.

Jace howls and staggers backward. I throw open the door, nearly colliding with Glitch.

"Let's go." I grab her arm and race down the hall.

"You didn't even change," Glitch cries. I hear the door crash open behind me followed by heavy footsteps.

"You don't get to walk away from me. Do you know who I am?" I turn on him, all of my previous pent-up rage bowling over my common sense.

I shrug. "You're not an enforcer, so I don't see why it matters."

Glitch inhales sharply. I know I shouldn't talk back to Jace. He has the power to make my life miserable and the personality to enjoy it.

Sue me, I've had a long day. I turn my back to him and continue walking away.

"I said stop," he yells. The irony isn't lost on me when I keep walking. People are starting to crowd around us, interested in how this plays out. A hand wraps around my wrist, jerking me back. I keep my elbow low and close to my body. As I pivot, I swing my arm in a lever-action to weaken his grasp just like Ash taught us in training. Jace's hand breaks free.

I sucker punch him.

It isn't elegant. It probably hurt me as much as it hurt him, but it's worth it when he swears and clutches his jaw. I take up my fight stance - left foot forward, right foot back, readying myself for him to come at me again. Glitch stands beside me, mirroring my stance. I'm surprised. I expected her to take off rather than confront a senior officer.

"That's enough!" Elle shoves through the crowd to stand between us. "Jace, what is this?"

"Get out of the way, I'm teaching this recruit a lesson."

"From where I'm standing, it looks like this recruit is kicking your ass." A few laughs erupt from our audience turning

Jace's ears crimson. "Get out of here before you embarrass yourself."

Jace looks like he wants to argue, but reconsiders when Elle shifts her feet into a fighting stance.

"Whatever, you're not worth my time," he says. He storms down the hall.

"Show's over, get lost," shouts Elle. The recruits scatter like a pack of spilled M&M's, disappearing down the stairwells and popping back into their compartments. The hallway falls eerily silent.

"That was awesome!" Glitch exclaims.

"That was stupid," corrects Elle. "Do you have a death wish?"

"It's not my fault Jace was in my compartment."

"He broke into your compartment?" Elle sounds shocked. The scowl reappears on her face, but this time I know it isn't directed at us. "I'll deal with this. For now, you and your friend should go out with the other recruits."

"It's a tradition we will most certainly be honoring," says Glitch. She grabs my arm and tugs me down the hall before I can complain. I sigh, tightening my ponytail. After the day I've had, I want nothing more than to sink into a mini coma in my bed.

"What was that about?" Glitch asks, keeping her voice low.

"Nothing," I say, trying to shut down her line of questioning. I could tell her about the deal I made with Ash and how Miles is probably rotting away in an enforcer prison, but I can't. That would imply I'm capable of trusting other people.

You're beginning to trust Ash. The little voice in my head pipes up. I grit my teeth and shut it down.

"Hey, Wren?"

"Yeah?"

"I don't need to know the details. I won't ask you any questions. Just know, if you ever need a friend, I'm here to listen." I swallow.

Well...damn. Now I feel like a dick.

Glitch knocks on a door at the end of the hall.

"Who is it?" Roy's voice comes from inside.

"Madame Rousseau's escort service," says Glitch in a faux seductive voice. Roy throws open the door, rolling his eyes. He's wearing loose athletic shorts and a white undershirt. His hair is still damp from the shower. He looks checked out for the night.

"What, no pizza delivery this time?"

"It could be an escort service that brings pizza." Glitch pushes past him into his compartment.

"Please come in." He says sarcastically, sweeping his arm in an exaggerated welcome gesture. I snort.

"Wait, on second thought that's genius!" Glitch completely ignores Roy's comment, lost in planning her new business venture. She dumps the contents of a book bag I didn't notice she was carrying on Roy's bedspread. I see a pile of clothes and make-up.

"What are you doing?"

"Nope, this is a we activity," she gestures to the three of us with a circular motion. "We are going to Intrepid. It's tradition."

"What's Intrepid?" Roy asks.

"What's Intrepid?" Glitch parrots incredulously. She looks from Roy to me. I shake my head. I have no idea what she's talking about. "It's only the hottest nightclub in the city."

"I've never been to a club before," says Roy, slowly warming to the idea.

"No time like the present," crows Glitch. She throws a mesh shirt at Roy and a pair of jeans. "Put these on. We need to blend."

"A black fishnet shirt is considered blending?" Roy laughs. "Gotta love the pansies."

"Where did you find that?" I ask.

"A girl has to be prepared," shrugs Glitch. She tosses me a slinky black dress with more holes than fabric. "Put this on. Roy, turn around."

"I'm not wearing this," I say.

"Wren, don't be a party pooper. This isn't something you would normally wear. I get it, but that's also the point. Let's go have some fun!"

"I think you need to return this dress. They forgot the other half," I grumble. I glance behind me to make sure Roy's back is still turned. I shimmy out of my jeans and pull the dress over my head. It fits me like a glove. Glitch is slightly shorter than me so the dress barely covers my butt. I'm instantly self-conscious.

"This isn't going to work."

"But it fits you so well," Glitch pouts. In the end, we compromise. I end up wearing some jeans with Glitch's combat boots. She knots my t-shirt in the front to expose part of my midriff to make it more "club-like." Her words, not mine.

"Sit on the bed, let me do your makeup."

"Has anyone told you you're kind of bossy?" I ask.

"It's one of my best virtues," she beams. Roy snorts. I sit on the edge of Roy's bed, but something hard presses against the back of my thighs. I hop up, unsure of what I sat on. Glitch reaches under the comforter and pulls out a camera. "What is this?" She sits up and gives Roy a curious look. He blushes.

"I smuggled it into the Academy." Glitch powers it up and starts flipping through the pictures. Roy looks uncomfortable, but doesn't stop her. I sit beside Glitch so I can peer over her shoulder. There are pictures of people and places in the city – stunning images in black and white showing still lives. A street artist spray painting a brick wall. A vendor stall in the marketplace with the owner showcasing his baubles. As Glitch continues to skim backward, she comes across a portrait of a little boy hugging a dog and pauses. He has the most beautiful smile. Roy captured him mid-laugh, his eyes alight.

"Who is this?" Glitch asks. She turns the camera around to show Roy. His jaw tightens and I see the sorrow behind his eyes.

"That was my little brother."

"I'm sorry," says Glitch, acknowledging the past tense. She powers down the camera and pulls Roy into a hug. "I didn't mean to bring up bad memories." He doesn't say anything for a moment. When Glitch pulls away, he tugs on the back of his neck.

"That was the last picture I took of someone I know," Roy says softly. "He died shortly after in an enforcer raid. It was one of those wrong place, wrong time deals. I refuse to take pictures of loved ones now. You never know when the next picture will be their last. I know it doesn't make sense, but I feel like if I take pictures of people I know, I'm doing them a disservice. People grow and change. Portraits don't. Sometimes we don't always want a reminder of who we used to be."

For the first time since I met her, Glitch seems at a loss for words. She picks up the camera and snaps a picture of Roy. He glances up, startled by the flash. She turns the camera towards me and takes another picture.

"What are you doing?" Roy asks.

"We're going to go out tonight. We're taking pictures and we're going to have a good time. At the end of the day, we're coming back here. Nothing bad is going to happen. I promise." She presses the camera to his chest until his hands rise to take it. Roy stares at her, his lips parted in shock.

Glitch tells me to sit down and starts applying powders to my face and eyelids. She puts something on my eyelashes that causes my eyes to water and asks me to purse my lips while she smears lipstick on them. The lipstick is the only thing I recognize in the entire pile.

"Almost done, let's get rid of this." Glitch pulls the hair tie out of my hair. "Now, bend over and whip your head back.

It helps add some volume." She does a whipping motion with her hair. Her mohawk doesn't move at all, making the move somewhat hilarious. I mimic her anyways. It makes me a little dizzy, but when I stand upright Glitch is beaming.

Roy is wearing the mesh shirt Glitch gave him and light-washed jeans. He's so pale his bare chest practically glows through the material. Roy was skinny when we started training, but he's since started to fill out. He's beginning to look more like an enforcer than a grunt. He blushes when he realizes I'm watching him watch Glitch. She's busy putting on her makeup, oblivious. We take the elevator down to the atrium, but when we get outside no Pods are waiting for us.

"I guess we waited too long to leave," Roy says.

"Oh well," I shrug. "I guess that means we have to go back to the room."

"You're not getting out of this that easily," says Glitch. She pulls a phone out of her clutch and orders a Pod. I stare at the device in shock. It's a brand new model with no cracks in the screen. The kind only elites can afford.

"Wait, are you secretly a pansy?" asks Roy suspiciously, noticing the same thing I did. Glitch guffaws.

"Nope, I bought this on the black market."

Not likely, but I decide not to press. I've had enough surprises for one day. I promise myself I'm not going to ask questions I don't want to know the answer to tonight. A Pod pulls up to the curb and a panel on the passenger side starts blinking. Glitch taps her phone to the panel. It turns green and the doors slide open.

"Welcome, Natasha!" A voice intones through the overhead speaker. "Please let me know if there is anything I can do to make your ride more enjoyable." We get in and the doors slide closed.

"Who's Natasha?" asks Roy.

"That's my nickname. Play some music!" says Glitch. I vaguely wonder if Natasha is her real name, but I doubt it.

"What type of music are you in the mood for?" asks the Pod's virtual personal assistant.

"Party music."

"Playing party music." The music starts playing so loudly it vibrates the seats.

"Open sunroof," says Glitch.

"Opening sunroof. Please stay seated at all times to ensure safety."

"Yeah, yeah," mutters Glitch. The ceiling rolls back allowing the cool night air to flow in. Glitch climbs on top of the table until all that's visible are her legs. She shouts the lyrics into the night, her arms spread wide. I shoot a look at Roy and laugh.

Say what you want, the girl knows how to have a good time.

The ride to Intrepid only takes ten minutes. We pull up in front of a short building sandwiched between two bars. There's a line weaving down the sidewalk and a beefy bouncer is standing guard.

"So, what's the plan for getting in, Natasha?" I ask. Glitch smirks. She saunters up to the bouncer, ignoring the line. Roy and I hang back shuffling our feet nervously. The bodyguard smiles at something she says. He steps aside and Glitch waves us over. I'm not even surprised.

"How did you do that?" asks Roy in awe.

"Let's just say I know a guy," yells Glitch over the pumping music. She's a mystery wrapped in five feet of attitude and I couldn't be more grateful. The music is loud, blaring a mixture of EDM and techno. Multi-colored strobe lights are illuminating a crowded dance floor. I'm suddenly grateful Glitch was in charge of our wardrobe choices. The three of us are dressed on the conservative side and that's saying something.

A DJ with an orange mohawk is on the stage bopping his head up and down with sound-canceling headphones held to one ear. The bartenders are handing out flights of shots in test tubes. The second-story balconies feature cocktail tables and booths crammed with people. I'm starting to feel a little claustrophobic. My chest is tightening, my breaths coming in short, constricted pants.

Oh good, here comes my second panic attack of the evening.

"You look nervous," shouts Glitch. "I'll get us something to drink. Give me a minute." She shoves her way through the crowd and disappears. I'm starting to get light-headed. Bodies are pressing against me, boxing me in. Roy says something to me, but I can't hear him over the music.

"What?" I yell.

"I said, 'are you okay'?" Roy raises his voice.

"I don't do well with crowds," I yell back. To my surprise, Roy shoves the two guys who are attempting to grind on me away and steps closer to shield me from the crowd.

"Thank you," I yell. He nods.

Glitch reappears with three test tubes. She hands one to me and Roy.

"What should we toast to?" she asks.

"Surviving," I say.

"Nah, that's boring," Glitch scoffs. "Let's celebrate the look on Jace's face when you sucker-punched him. Now that's something worth toasting."

"You hit Jace?" Roy asks. He looks around frantically like he expects Jace to appear.

"It was awesome," Glitch cackles. She raises her tube. Roy and I mimic her with a shared look of skepticism and apprehension. "Here's to bad choices and good friends."

I tip the shot back. It tastes a lot like a pixie stick. I grimace. The song changes.

"Oh, this is my favorite! Come on, we have to dance."

"I don't dance," I mutter. Glitch grabs a couple more test tubes from a passing serving bot.

"Two more of these and you will. Let's go!" She shoves them into my hands and takes off, dragging Roy behind her.

I know I shouldn't drink any more. I'm in a room surrounded by enforcers, but I'm done being responsible.

"Here's to being someone else tonight," I say.

I tip both shots down my throat, one right after the other and follow my friends onto the dance floor. The shots hit me right away and I realize I haven't eaten since this morning. I find myself moving with the crowd. I'm sure I look like a seizing cat on the dance floor, but I don't care. I'm dancing on a weeknight with my friends. This is what normal people my age are supposed to be doing.

"Wren?" The voice is right in my ear. If I wasn't so high on the music and alcohol, I would probably have jumped a foot in the air. But I recognize that voice. I lean back against Ash's rock-hard chest and feel his hands go automatically to my hips, swaying with the music. He smells like cologne, his trademark cinnamon gum, and heaven.

"What took you so long?" I ask giddily.

Giddily? Drunk me is bubblier than sober me. Noted.

"What are you doing?" Ash spins me so we're face to face. He showered and changed since we parted ways. He's wearing a fitted black dress shirt with black pants. The monochrome works for him.

He looks...good. Drunk me can admit that.

"Dancing with my friends."

"You're drunk," Ash scowls. I have the sudden urge to kiss his frown away. Instead, I roll my eyes giving him a 'well duh' look.

"So are you, you smell like a whiskey vending machine." I jab a finger into his chest. He doesn't. I just want a reason to touch him. I miss my mark by a few inches but that's beside the point. "First Elle kicks me out of the Academy and now you're criticsiz...criquing....telling me what I should and shouldn't do."

"What do you mean Elle kicked you out of the Academy?"

I give an exaggerated one-shoulder shrug. "Jace was in my compartment when I got back. He came on to me. I told him no, but he was pushy. I ended up punching him in the hall. Elle broke up the fight. I was winning in case you were wondering."

"Jace forced himself on you?"

"It's okay," I hiccup. "I took care of it."

"No, it's not, Wren." Ash scrubs his hands over his face, a murderous look in his eyes. "You shouldn't have to put up with that."

"I can take care of myself. Besides," I say. "I don't trust you."

I know I made a mistake saying those words as soon as they come out. It's not even the truth, but I'm on edge and my defense mechanism has always been to push people away.

"Come with me," he interlocks his fingers with mine and leads me through the crowd. Glitch is on her way back from the bar with another round of drinks. Ash says something to her, but I can't make out what. She nods and winks at me before returning to Roy. Ash leads me to the bar where he grabs a handle of hard liquor and asks the bartender for a bottle of water. He scans his chip to pay.

"How do we get up to the roof?" he asks. The bartender looks at him like he's crazy until her wristband lights up with a generous tip. After that, she can't tell him fast enough.

Ash leads me behind the bar and up four flights of stairs to a metal security door. He pushes it open and puts a brick in front of it to keep us from being locked out. Cigarette butts are littering the ground and a few empty beer bottles. The bar is shorter than the buildings surrounding it, the skyscrapers looming over it like vigilant guards against the night. The music drifts up from below, but it's much quieter than before.

Ash sits with his back propped up against the brick ledge. He motions for me to join him, handing me the bottle of water. "You need to sober up and I need a drink. Let's meet somewhere in the middle."

"Fine," I pout, opening the bottle and plopping down next to him. I take a few long drinks not realizing how dehydrated I was until the water hits my throat. I wipe my lips with the back of my hand and put the cap back on.

"I talked to the commander when we got back to the Academy," says Ash. "He agreed to the undercover mission."

"That's great!" I exclaim. Ash takes a drink. He winces, holding out the bottle to read the label before setting it aside.

"What do I have to do to earn your trust? I won't sign off on this mission unless I know we can work together," Ash says. I've never heard him so serious. I sigh and lean my head back against the cold brick wall. It feels nice after the suffocating heat of the club.

"You can stop lying for one," I say.

"I've never lied to you."

"Lying by omission counts."

"Give me an example," says Ash.

"You didn't tell me you were an Axton before we made our deal," I say.

"Would it have made a difference?"

"Yes."

Ash stares at me for so long it makes me blush. "Does it really matter? If I'm going to be honest with you, then you need to be honest with yourself. Would knowing my last name have made you choose differently?"

I study him for a moment and take another sip of water. He has me there. "I guess not. I would have done anything to save Miles. *Will* do anything to save him. But it would have been nice not to be blindsided."

"Who is Miles to you?" Ash asks. "I'm genuinely curious."

"I told you, he's my best friend."

"But there's more to it than that, isn't there?" Ash presses.

I cross my arms. "I don't owe you an explanation."

"How about a trade, then? A truth for a truth or a lie for a lie."

"If you said 'let's make a deal,' I would have punched you in the dick."

Ash bursts out laughing. It's a full belly laugh that erases the lines around his eyes and ages him backward. Ash isn't handsome in the traditional sense. He's all sharp edges and harsh lines, beautiful and lethal like shards of glass or a burning building. His nose is slightly crooked where I broke it, but it gives him a rakish, devil-may-care look that works for him. He's devastating and I hate myself for noticing.

Because in the end, beautiful monsters are still monsters.

Chapter 11

Ash

"**I**s Miles Ariel's father?" I ask, because apparently, I'm a masochist. Wren pauses, the water bottle hovering at her lips.

"What?" she snorts, taking a sip before screwing the cap back on the bottle. "No."

She pulls her knees into her chest, wrapping her arms around them. I've never seen an elite wear jeans to Intrepid, but that's the thing about Wren. She approaches life with a boldness that demands respect. Her hair, normally tied back, is let loose. It frames her face in a stunning halo of curls.

"Miles and I have been inseparable since his family moved across the hall when we were five. We've been through a lot together. Miles' mom walking out on them. Losing my parents. I don't think I would have been able to get Jimmy's Auto running without him. He helped me when I was pregnant with Ariel. He's just always been there for me."

"Huh," I say, taking another pull from the bottle. It's disgusting, like drinking lighter fluid.

"What's that supposed to mean?" Wren asks, her forehead wrinkling.

Don't say it. Don't say it. Don't say it.

"Nothing. I guess I thought you and Miles were together."

And I said it.

"Nope," Wren says, popping the 'p.' She frowns and takes another sip from her water bottle.

"Do you want to be?" I ask, more quietly. Wren flushes.

"That's two questions. It's my turn to play the interrogator," Wren says.

"So, that's a yes."

Wren rolls her eyes. "Has anyone told you you're persistent?"

"Every day," I say.

"It's annoying."

"Ask your question, grunt."

Wren laughs. "Who is Elle to you? You must be pretty close if she is willing to fake an engagement to help you out."

I roll the bottle back and forth on the ground, watching the amber liquid slosh around inside.

"She's my Miles. When I moved into the Axton mansion, the other elites were brutal. Elle has always been popular and respected. I guess she decided to take pity on me. We started hanging out and everyone stopped giving me crap. Without her, I'm not sure I would have been able to make a life for myself among the elites."

"So you're not *together.*"

"We went on a few dates in high school, but I think that was more because everyone expected us to end up as a couple rather than mutual attraction. We both knew it wasn't going to work out. Nothing is going on between Elle and me up to and including our engagement. I'm not her type. Elle would be more interested in dating you, than dating me. My turn."

"No," says Wren. "I still get one more question."

"You asked how Elle fits into my life and if we're together. That's two questions in case you forgot how to count."

"I didn't ask if you were together. I made a statement and you interpreted it as a question. So, I get one more."

I huff, but a smile tugs at the corners of my lips. "Fine. Fire away."

Wren thinks about it for a moment. "What are your plans after you take down the Syndicate?"

"What do you mean?'

Wren shrugs. "You talk about eliminating the Syndicate all the time, but what happens next? If the Syndicate disappeared tomorrow, what would you do?"

I take another sip. "I think busting up the Syndicate will keep me busy for a while."

Wren frowns. "You're missing the point of the question."

"The rules were a truth for a truth or a lie for a lie. I'll fight to take down the Syndicate until my last breath. Nothing else matters. That's my truth. My turn."

I didn't mean to come across as blunt as I did. I can't think about what I'll do after I eliminate the Syndicate. If I'm being honest with myself, I don't think I'll live long enough to see it. I'm at peace with that. It's not something I'm going to tell Wren, or anyone for that matter. Elle and Liam would probably lock me in my compartment with a horde of therapists if they heard me say anything to that degree. They already think I have an unhealthy obsession with my job. I don't need to give them another reason to worry about me. Wren finishes off her water. She crushes the plastic and puts the lid back on, setting it beside her.

"You don't have to answer this if you don't want to," I say, finally deciding on a question. "I read your file. There were some emergency room records involving your dad. It wasn't hard to connect the dots."

"What's the question?" Wren asks, her voice cold. I can practically see her building up her walls.

"Do you ever worry that you'll be like him when it comes to alcohol?" I put up my hands when Wren crosses her arms. "I'm not judging. Let me give you some context so you don't think I'm being a prick by asking that question."

"Too late," she growls.

"Give me a chance to explain?" I ask. Wren stares at me for a moment, then nods.

"I started smoking to piss off Byron. It was a crappy reason, I know that, but Byron became unbearable after mom died. He corrected everything I wore, said, and did in an attempt to shape me into someone he would be proud to call a son. I tried to appease him until I realized it was a grand exercise in futility."

I haven't explained this to anyone. Sure, Liam and Elle are aware of my struggles with smoking, but they never knew why I started in the first place. I think they assumed it was an addiction I brought with me from before I met them that got worse over time.

"Enjoying the occasional cigar is considered a high-class habit that's socially acceptable. According to Byron, cigarettes are for bums. When I gave up on trying to earn his approval, I bought my first pack and smoked the entire thing over a few hours in the courtyard of the Axton mansion. It made me cough. I vomited from the nicotine because I wasn't used to it and way overdid it. I didn't particularly enjoy the experience, but nothing says stick-it-to-the-man like petty rebellion.

"Byron was livid. Don maybe even more so. Byron threatened to throw me out, but I knew nothing would come of it. He cares too much about appearances to risk the scandal it would have caused and I made it clear I wouldn't go quietly. After a year-long pissing match, I joined the enforcers and we limited our interactions to the obligatory Ascent Day activities. That's when I decided to quit.

"The cravings were stronger than I anticipated. I caved two or three times before I consulted the guardian of all knowledge: the internet. The first recommendation was to build a routine. So, I kept my compartment immaculate and managed my schedule. I aimed for perfection because I knew one step in the wrong direction could send me hurdling back to the bottom. The second recommendation was to set a goal for myself. That was easy - take down the Syndicate."

"I'm not sure that's what the article author had in mind," says Wren.

"Probably not, but it was the best goal I could think of."

"That explains the cinnamon chewing gum," says Wren. I glance at her in surprise.

"You noticed that?"

She shrugs like it's no big deal. "How does this story relate to your question?"

"My point is, I thought I was in control when I started smoking. Turns out, I wasn't. I'm not lecturing you. I'm just curious if my relationship with cigarettes is like your relationship with alcohol. Do you drink because you have something to prove to yourself?"

Wren considers my question, the anger and defensiveness disappearing from her expression.

"Yes and no," she sighs. "I rarely drink. It makes me cautious. I'm aware of the risks, but I'm not going to cut it out of my life completely. It's not that I have something to prove to myself. I just don't want to give alcohol power over me like it had over dad. It probably doesn't make sense to you, but that's how I feel. If I can drink a reasonable amount occasionally and I don't lose control, then there's no reason to be afraid of it, right? It can't hurt me in the same way it hurt my dad, because I don't give it the power to do that. You know? Now, I'm just rambling and you probably think I'm crazy."

"No, it makes sense, actually," says Ash. He raises an eyebrow. "Any particular reason you decided to drink tonight?"

"What are you, my mom?" I snort at my lame joke.

Ash winces. "I didn't mean for it to come out like that." He looks sincerely apologetic.

"Tonight was an exception," I shrug, deciding to let him off the hook. "I don't do so well with crowds and, with everything going on with Robbie and Miles, I needed to put reality on pause for a few hours to maintain my sanity. That doesn't mean I forget about my dad's struggles.

"Dad had a lot of other stuff going on at the time that kind of snowballed. He lost my mom and the shop was going under. He wouldn't switch over to serving the Syndicate and our regular clients were disappearing. We were broke. The bills kept piling up. I think he felt like he didn't have anyone to lean on. I'm not making excuses for his addiction. I'm just saying that I understand it in a messed up way. I wish I could have been a better support system for him, so he didn't have to find it at the bottom of a bottle."

"You were a kid," whispers Ash.

"I know, but I still feel like I could have done more." Wren shakes her head. "Talk about a buzzkill, sorry."

"No, it's alright. I asked the buzz kill question, so that's on me."

Wren's stomach growls loudly, breaking the somber tone our conversation has taken on. She laughs.

"I haven't eaten anything since this morning," she admits.

"Do you want to get pizza?" I ask.

"Right now?"

"Yeah."

"Um...sure."

I stand up and offer Wren my hand. She takes it. Her hand is freezing.

"You should have told me you were cold."

"I didn't notice it," Wren shrugs. "Can Glitch and Roy come too? I came here with them, so I don't feel right ditching."

"Sure."

I don't make it a habit to take my recruits out to dinner, but Wren has become the exception to so many rules I've lost count. Might as well make one more. I leave the liquor bottle on the roof and we make our way downstairs. The music is blasting and the dance floor is more crowded than when we left. I spot Glitch and Roy dancing in the middle of the crowd. Glitch has her arms around his neck. They look pretty into each other. I doubt they would notice if Wren skipped out, but I push my way through to extend the offer anyways.

"We're going to get pizza, do you guys want to come?" Wren yells. Glitch glances at Roy. He shrugs, leaving the decision up to her. She says something to Wren that I can't hear over the music. Wren nods before pulling away. She stands on her toes to talk in my ear. She trips a bit, falling against me. I put a hand on her waist to steady her.

"Sorry," she says. "They're going to stay. We can leave."

Wren leads the way to the exit. I see Elle leaning against the bar talking with a group of enforcer squad leaders. She raises an eyebrow, giving me a questioning look when she sees my hand in Wren's. She mouths "be careful." She's probably right. If Byron hears about me leaving a nightclub with one of my recruits, he's going to throw a fit. Especially, when he finds out she's a grunt.

Let him. It's none of his business.

I'm not doing anything wrong. If Byron wants to keep tabs on me, that's his choice. I'm not going to live every day of my life asking myself "What would Byron do?" There's no way.

"There's a decent pizza place a few blocks from here. Are you okay to walk?" I ask when we get outside where it's quieter.

"Yeah," says Wren. She leans into my side wrapping her arm around my waist, shivering. I put my arm around her shoulders pulling her against me. It's oddly...normal. Like we're a couple who finished a night out dancing and are picking up a pizza on the way home. Labels don't exist in this moment.

Pansy. Grunt. Enforcer. Syndicate.

None of it matters. Tonight, I'm just a guy taking a girl he kind of likes to get a slice of pizza.

If only it were that simple.

"So, how did you find this place?" asks Wren.

"Drunk exploring," I say.

"For real?"

"It's true," I chuckle, recalling the night. "Elle and I found it when we were celebrating our first patrol at Intrepid. Elle wanted pizza, so we found a place within walking distance. She puked in that alley." I point to the alley we just passed. "I'm surprised the owner didn't kick us out. We were a mess."

"That's hard to imagine," Wren laughs. "You and Elle both seem to have your lives together."

I could see how she would think that. She has only seen Elle at Council functions or the Academy.

"Elle and I are similar like that. We're both good at playing the game, keeping our professional appearance up for everyone except for a select few."

"I don't know how you can change your personality like that. I only have one setting. What you see is what you get. There aren't two versions of me," says Wren.

"Bullshit."

Wren pulls away so she can meet my eyes. "What?"

"You heard me. I'm sure you speak to your customers differently than you speak to your family," I say.

"Of course."

"Then there are at least two versions of you. There are probably a hundred other versions if you start making a list. That's why it's impossible to know someone completely. You only see and get to know the version they want you to see and get to know."

"That's... profound for someone who was drinking out of a bottle not ten minutes ago," says Wren.

I laugh. Wren glances up at me thoughtfully. "So, how do you know what the default is? Ash Axton version 1.0. What's that guy like?"

That's a good question. When you break down my life into all the roles I've played, what's left? I don't know if I can tell you which one is a persona and which one is simply...me.

"I don't know," I say, honestly.

Wren smiles. "Well, I'd like to be around when you figure it out."

"I'd like that too," I say, pressing a kiss into her hair because it feels right.

"Are you going to tell Byron about your engagement?" Wren asks.

"I'll have to eventually," I groan. "I can't expect Elle to keep up the charade forever. That isn't fair to her."

"Just tell him the truth. The worst that can happen is you two fight. He might even respect you for standing up to him."

"I've tried talking to him before," I say.

"Recently?"

"Actually," I pause. "I think the last time I talked to Byron for longer than five minutes was when I was a kid."

"Now, you're an enforcer squad leader with your own title, connections, and friends. He might be more willing to listen."

I can't fault her for being optimistic. I was too, once. After getting shut down one too many times, I know better. I've avoided speaking with Bryon for years. Of course, there are the obligatory social gatherings and the rare occasions he corners me after a Council meeting, but those moments are in public. They're either being broadcast on the Council news channel or there are other people around. We're always on our best behavior, because we're being observed. So, naturally, we don't talk about anything that matters.

Now that I think about it, I wonder if Byron sprung the engagement with Penny Bronxton on me because he didn't get the chance to ask me ahead of time. It's not like I return his calls or make an effort to schedule a family dinner.

The pizza place comes into view and I put my thoughts on hold. It's an absolute dive complete with a flickering neon sign and a logo that's outdated by a few decades. They sell pizza by the slice and nothing else. I think Intrepid is the only thing that has kept this place running.

"So this is the best pizza place in the city?" Wren asks.

I snort. "Nope, their pizza is absolute garbage. It tastes like cardboard and is the consistency of leather."

"You're really selling this place. Why are we here?"

"Because you're drunk and it's within walking distance of Intrepid. It's tradition."

"I'm not that drunk," says Wren. She trips on a crack in the sidewalk and nearly face plants. I grab her arm to stop her from falling, giving her a pointed look. She bursts out laughing.

"That wasn't because I'm drunk. I'm just clumsy."

"Uh-huh."

She opens the door to the pizza place, grinning like an idiot. Inside, it smells like warm cheesy goodness. You can almost feel the grease settling on your skin. Wren and I order two slices each. She picks a red vinyl booth in the corner. The seats are kind of sticky and I don't trust that the table has been cleaned, but it's part of the charm. It's relatively quiet. There are few other customers in party attire, but it's still early. The rush won't be for a few more hours. Thankfully, I don't recognize anyone and they don't seem to recognize me. I fold the pizza in half and take a giant bite. It hits all the right spots.

Wren moans, her eyes fluttering shut. "This is the best thing I've ever tasted in my life."

"Now, I know you're drunk."

"Shut up," she rolls her eyes and shovels more pizza into her mouth. The bell above the door rings, drawing my attention.

"Just what I needed," I groan. Wren looks over her shoulder. Jace walks inside with his arm slung around Penny Bronxton's waist. She purses her lips when she sees us and taps Jace's arm to point us out. He saunters over to our table.

Great. Just fantastic.

"Didn't know you were going out little bro," says Jace.

"I'm not your bro," I growl.

"Penny, go grab us some pizza. We're having dinner with Asher." He waves her off. She looks annoyed, but doesn't say anything. I wonder why she sticks around when Jace treats her like trash.

"It's Ash," I say. Jace knows I prefer the shortened version of my name. He ignores me and starts to sit by Wren.

Nope. No way am I going to let that happen after what Wren told me.

"You should sit by Penny," I say, getting up and offering him my side of the booth. He doesn't push it. I take the seat beside Wren. Jace settles into the booth across from me. He slings his arm over the back of the seat.

"Does Elle know you're seeing other people?" he asks.

"It's none of your business," I say.

"Maybe I make it my business and tell her." Jace's eyes light up. My fists clench under the table. Penny arrives with two slices of pizza in hand. She sets both of them in front of Jace and sits next to him. She didn't get anything for herself. She looks Wren up and down, crinkling her nose.

"What's the grunt doing here?" Penny asks.

"Her name is Wren. Find some respect," I growl. Penny rolls her eyes. She takes a nail file out of her purse and starts filing her nails at the table. Wren hasn't touched her pizza since Jace sat down. Her face is pale, her body tense.

"Hey, let's get out of here," I tell her. Wren nods. I scoot out of the booth and Wren slides out after me. I pick up her uneaten slice of pizza and we head for the door.

"Whore," Jace coughs. Penny laughs. I stop walking.

"What did you just say?" I ask.

"Ash, it's fine. Let's just go," says Wren. I hand Wren the slice of pizza and turn around, putting myself between her and Jace.

"No, it's not fine. He doesn't get to treat people like garbage and get away with it."

"I said she's a whore." Jace stands up and strides over to me, taunting me. "She came on to me earlier. I bet she didn't tell you that. Now, she's here with you. It makes me think she's a gold digger...just like your grunt mother. I'm just looking out for you, little bro."

I clock him in the face.

Penny screams.

I don't even know if I made the conscious decision to do it, I just snapped. Jace howls, doubling over clutching his nose. I haul him up by the front of his shirt, slamming him down on top of the table. My knuckles sting and there's blood dripping from them, staining his white shirt red.

"If you ever so much as think about Wren again, I will end you. Understood?" Jace clutches at my hand, trying to get me to release him. I slam his head into the table again to make sure I've got his undivided attention.

"You will not speak to her. You will not look at her. You will not so much as breathe in her direction. You got that?"

"Yes," he grates out. I release him and he goes limp. Penny is cowering in the corner of the booth like if she can press against the wall hard enough she'll melt into it. The second I threw Jace on the table, she scrambled out of the way. She didn't even bother trying to stop me. Wren's hands wrap around my arm and she tugs me towards the door. I let her, following her outside. I order a Pod to take us back to the Academy. I take a few deep breaths, trying to calm my racing heart.

"I'm sorry about that. Jace is a garbage human," I say.

"Yeah, he is," Wren whispers.

"I haven't hit Jace since I was probably fourteen." I scrub a hand over my face already dreading the conversation with Byron this will spur.

Wren bites her lip. She looks worried. I stop and put my hands on her shoulders.

"Hey, what's wrong? Are you okay?" I ask. She won't meet my eyes.

"He was lying. You know that, right? I didn't hit on him. I don't want you to think I'm some sort of hussy," says Wren, quietly.

"Hussy? What is this, the 1960s?"

"You know what I mean."

"I believe you. If anyone is a...hussy...it's Penny Bronxton." Wren gives me a confused look. "The girl that came in with Jace. Her dad is Byron's business partner at Axton AI. She's the one Byron was going to announce my marriage with at the Ascent Day celebration."

"You were supposed to marry her?" Wren asks incredulously, glancing behind us like Penny's walking on the street. "Next time I see Elle, I'm personally thanking her for bailing you out."

I chuckle. "Yeah, I owe her big time for that."

Wren smiles. She finishes the pizza in the Pod on our way back to the Academy. When we get to the elevator, I hit the button for the enforcer leadership compartments. Wren reaches out to press the button for her floor, but I stop her.

"You're staying with me," I say.

Her eyes widen. "I can't-"

"I'm worried about Jace retaliating. I'll talk to Liam tomorrow about additional security for your compartment. We'll be leaving for Jimmy's Auto in a couple of days anyway, but I still want to make sure you have a safe place to stay."

Wren studies me as if looking for the dishonesty in my words. Does she think that little of me? That I would try something when she's one, drunk, and two, in a vulnerable state?

Jace did.

Yeah, I could see how she would think my entire family is rotten. Jace isn't exactly a gleaming endorsement of chivalry or morality.

"I'll take the couch, you can have the bed," I add, wondering if that's her hold up. "Text Glitch to make sure she has somewhere else to stay as well. If not, she can stay at my place."

"Okay," Wren agrees slowly. She takes out her phone, presumably to text Glitch. The elevator stops on my floor. Everyone is either asleep or still out partying. Thankfully, the hall is empty. I open my door and flip on the lights.

"I only have the set of sheets that are on the bed, sorry," I say. It's not like I have guests staying in my compartment. I grab one of the pillows off the bed and toss it onto the couch. Wren is still standing in the middle of the room. She has her arms crossed like she doesn't know what to do with them. I open my dresser and pull out a pair of sweats. I clear my throat to get her attention and offer her the sweats.

"The bathroom is through that door. You can use these if you don't want to wear jeans to bed." Wren uncrosses her arms and takes the sweats from me.

"Thanks," she says quietly. She turns to go into the bathroom and walks straight into the wall. I bite back a smile. She blushes and disappears inside. After a few minutes, I hear water running. I take the opportunity to trade out my pants and shirt for something more comfortable then lay down on the couch. It's not too bad. My feet are propped up on the armrest, but I can definitely sleep like this.

A few minutes later, Wren emerges from the bathroom. She must have washed her face, her makeup gone. She's wearing my sweatpants. The top is rolled multiple times, but she's still swimming in them.

She looks adorable.

"Glitch texted me back. She has somewhere else to stay."

"That's good." I'm glad Wren agreed to stay here. If she refused, I probably would have slept in front of her door like a guard dog to make sure Jace didn't try anything. That's how far gone I am for the stubborn Syndicate mechanic. Wren lays her jeans on the bedside table and gets under the sheets. I reach above my head to flip off the lights. I hear her rolling around in bed, getting comfortable. I relax into the couch, closing my eyes.

"Goodnight, Wren," I mumble, already half asleep.

"Goodnight, Ash," Wren whispers.

Chapter 12

Ash

The bed creaks when Wren rolls over with a groan. She rubs her eyes, peering at me over the covers. When she realizes where she is, she bolts upright.

"Good morning," I say, turning off the stove. I split the scrambled eggs in half and dump them on two plates.

"What are you doing?" Wren swings her legs over the side of the bed and approaches the kitchen. Her hair is in wild disarray, her clothes rumpled from sleep.

"Making breakfast."

"Why?"

"Because you drank a lot last night. I don't want you to throw up." She rubs her temples with a groan. I hand her a glass of water with a couple of ibuprofen.

"Thanks," she mutters, downing the pills with a sip of water. I set the plates out on the counter with two forks and two cups of coffee. I don't have a kitchen table, just two barstools and a counter. It's not like we host a lot of meals in our compartments. Wren takes a bite of her eggs. Her eyes light up.

"These are great. I didn't know you could cook."

"Don't be too impressed, you're looking at the extent of it." I smile. Wren eats in silence, slowly coming to life as she drinks her coffee. There's a knock at the door.

"Ash, you in there?" Liam calls.

"Yeah, give me a second," I say. Wren's eyes widen in panic. "It's okay," I tell her. "It's Liam." She lets out a breath. I open the door and Liam stalks inside. He looks pissed.

"What were you thinking?" Liam growls. It's strange to see the most easy-going person I know go nuclear. I wonder if he heard about me punching Jace? I expect Elle to chew me out, but not Liam. He's not the kind of person to judge anyone for their decisions.

"What are you talking about?" I ask, deciding to play dumb.

"I know Commander Harper sanctioned a covert mission to take down the surge crew. He's targeting you and Wren for it. I won't approve it."

So that's what this is about.

Liam crosses his arms and scowls. As the operations lead, Liam has the authority to nix any undercover assignment he deems too risky. I should have seen this coming.

"Liam, you know this is the best chance we have ever had at stopping the distribution of surge. I can't drop it. Let me do this for you." Liam looks like he's about to take a swing at me, but then he notices Wren.

"What is she doing here?" he asks.

"Jace broke into her compartment. I didn't want her to stay there until I could ask you about additional security," I explain.

Liam addresses Wren, the anger disappearing from his voice. "Yeah, I'll take care of that first thing this morning."

"Thank you," says Wren. Liam sighs.

"Do you know what the Syndicate does to enforcer moles?" he asks, the fight draining out of him. "They lock you in a cell with no windows and no lights. They beat you and torture you for information and, when that doesn't work, they pump you full of surge until you're hooked. Then, they take it away and let your body go through withdrawal." Liam lowers his fists, his shoulders hunched. "They give you a few more doses and let you go through withdrawal again. And again. And again. Until you can't feel or think about anything but the pain."

I step around Wren and place my hands on Liam's shoulders. His breath is coming out in short bursts as the demons that haunt him take over. "We won't get caught."

"No, you won't," says Liam. "You're not doing this for me, Ash. You're doing this, because you have a vendetta against the Syndicate that's going to get you killed. I'm blocking the mission."

"You can't do that," gasps Wren.

"Look, I know Ash has some kind of bargain with you. It's not worth it. Find another way. I'll take care of securing your compartment. You don't need to worry about Jace." He leaves, shutting the door behind him.

When we rescued Liam from the Syndicate, he had been a prisoner for almost three months. He had a broken right femur, enough bruises to conceal his natural skin tone, and an unchecked surge addiction. It took him a week to keep solid food down and a month to start talking again. He still relies on the adhesive patches to keep his hands from trembling.

Maybe Liam is right. I'm not doing this for him. My motives are more selfish than that.

I'm doing it so I don't have to watch another friend hit rock bottom.

"I'll fix this," I say. Wren frowns, setting her coffee down.

"I can't believe I'm saying this, but Liam might be right. This is too dangerous."

"We had a deal," I say. "Do you want me to release Miles or not?"

As soon as the words leave my lips, I know it was the wrong thing to say. Wren freezes.

"You selfish bastard," she seethes. "Liam is right. You don't care about anything or anyone outside of taking down the Syndicate. You told me you were afraid of having personal relationships because Byron can use them against you. Well, guess what? You're doing the same thing by trading Miles' freedom for my help. You're no better than he is."

Her words are the equivalent of sinking a knife in my chest and twisting the blade.

"I'll uphold my side of our deal, but the second things get sketchy I'm out." Wren storms past me in much the same manner as Liam. She throws the door open and pauses, giving me a sad smile. "You want to know what the worst part is? I was starting to see you as a real person, Ash. You dropped your enforcer mask and showed me a guy I could relate to, but I think I got it wrong. That guy sitting beside me on a nightclub roof? That's the illusion. I think you've been driven by revenge for so long you don't know who you are without it." Wren leaves. She's still wearing my sweatpants, her jeans laying forgotten on the bedside table. I don't go after her. What would I say? She's right. I know she is, but I don't have a choice. I need her help and using Miles is the only way I'll get it.

I shower and change into my uniform. There's a Council meeting this morning. I'll talk to Byron and convince him to override Liam's authority to authorize the mission. The Council gathers in a meeting room on the top floor of the Academy where the high-ranking members have their offices.

The executive suites are unlike anything else in the building. The entire floor consists of real leather furniture, mahogany paneling, crystal chandeliers, and floor-to-ceiling windows. It's a nod to the elitist lifestyle and everything it stands for. I bypass the Council members chatting in the hall to take my seat at the rectangular table that sits in the middle of the conference room. It's an ugly obsidian slab that's so large I wouldn't be surprised if the walls were constructed after it was put in place.

The usual crew shuffles in: the head of the big hospital downtown, our public transit director, and a handful of others. Carl Bronxton sits near the end of the table looking prim without a hair out of place. It isn't an impressive feat considering he's well on his way to going bald. He meets my eyes and scowls. I wonder what I did to piss him off this week. Elle takes the seat next to me.

"Do we have a problem?" Elle asks me.

"We have lots of problems. You'll have to be more specific."

"Leaving Intrepid with a recruit. Hitting Jace." I don't miss the way she calls Wren my recruit. I wince. She's right. Technically, I'm Wren's commanding officer.

"Are people gossiping?" I ask.

"What do you think, genius?"

"I'm sorry," I say. Our arrangement may be fake, but I know what it would have looked like to everyone else. That I'm messing around behind Elle's back. I have to end this. "I'll talk to Byron today and tell him the truth."

"You can't do that, he'll kick you out of the Academy," she sighs. "You can tell him after you take out the surge crew. Until then just...be smart, please?" She studies me, her blue eyes searching mine. It strikes me for the first time that Elle isn't worried about her reputation. She's worried about me. About what Byron will do when I tell him I lied. About my reputation if rumors start circulating about me being involved with a recruit.

"I'll do better."

She nods. "I found that Miles guy you were looking for," she whispers. "He was being held at a black site."

"What?" I yelp and cover it with a cough. Most enforcer prisoners are held in the lower levels of the Academy, especially those awaiting trial. Black sites are designated for prisoners that require interrogation or are classified as extremely dangerous. "Any idea why?"

"No, but I'll do some more digging and let you know what I find. In the meantime, I'm calling in some favors to get him transferred to the Academy."

"I owe you one."

"You owe me two or three if we're keeping score." Elle frowns when Jace strolls into the room. He has a nasty black eye. "I had to break up a fight between Jace and Wren yesterday."

"I know. That's why I was with her at the club. He broke into her compartment and made a pass at her. I asked Liam about more security."

"Jesus, what an asshole. Is that why you hit him?"

"Something like that."

"Good," snarls Elle, surprising me. I expected her to give me a hard time for antagonizing Jace, not endorse it. Jace takes the seat at the head of the table – the director's seat. The chatter dies out.

"Where is the director?" I ask, attempting to keep the malice out of my tone. Jace's fingers sink into the leather armrests, molding to his hands.

"The director asked that I start the meeting without him. He'll be joining us shortly."

Elle frowns. There are some whispers around the room, but Jace silences them with a sharp look. Byron lives for Council meetings. I have never known him to be a minute late. A quick look at my phone tells me there are still five minutes before the meeting is due to start. What is Jace's play?

Mr. Bronxton clears his throat. "Very well, as many of you know, the enforcers have been working closely with Axton AI security to update monitoring systems across the city. The initial results are promising. We have been able to cut human patrols by fifty percent in the trial sectors. If we continue at this rate, we will no longer need to recruit enforcers through the Ascent Day lottery. I'm seeking approval to expand bot production to implement a city-wide rollout by the end of this year."

"Wait a minute," I say, leaning forward. "Are you suggesting we remove the enforcer bids from the Ascent?"

"That's exactly what he's suggesting," says Jace. "We have to train recruits. We don't have to train machines. If one is more efficient than the other, it seems like an obvious choice." My mind flashes to Robbie and our run-in at the Syndicate bar. If we had put bots in that situation, they would have killed him. Machines don't care about circumstances. They don't understand context.

"You can't do that," I blurt out. Jace glowers.

"Last time I checked, I'm the designated successor. I can do whatever I want."

I cross my arms and lean back in my chair. "You mean you can do whatever you want so long as the Council agrees."

"And why wouldn't they?" Jace scoffs looking thoroughly annoyed. "The data speaks to the competency of Axton bots. The analysis is irrefutable. Why would we recruit grunts and send them to their childhood neighborhoods to arrest friends and family? There's a clear conflict of interest there. Humans make mistakes. Machines don't."

There are a few murmurs of agreement throughout the room. "This is crazy." I stand up. "What I'm hearing is you want to take the human element out of policing. Machines are great tools, but cannot make ethical decisions."

"We can code ethics into them. Add constraints," Mr. Bronxton interjects.

"But who will be the person to code it? You?" I snort. "Creating a police force consisting of members encoded with the same ethics is the same as the Council declaring martial law over grunt neighborhoods. You can't honestly think that's the best thing for everyone." I pause on the last word, letting the Council soak in my meaning. If they agree to what Jace is proposing, they will have written off the grunts entirely. The doors fly open and Byron strides in, flanked by two guards. He has a deep scowl etched on his face that further defines the crow's feet around his eyes.

"What is the meaning of this?" Byron asks.

"Jace and Mr. Bronxton suggested that we remove the enforcer bids from Ascent Day," I explain curtly. I feel like I'm a little kid again tattling to Byron about Jace's wrongdoings. His expression morphs from annoyance into something resembling curiosity.

"What's the verdict?" Byron asks.

"We haven't called a vote yet," says Jace.

"Then, by all means, don't let me interrupt you," says Byron. He grabs the back of Jace's chair and tugs it hard. Jace topples over. He grabs the edge of the table and steadies himself after a few staggering steps. "You're in my seat." Jace's cheeks tinge pink. Byron sits down and Jace takes the seat across from mine. To my surprise, he doesn't say anything about his son's black eye.

"My mother created the Ascent to give every person an equal chance to succeed. It gives the people a voice in our government by offering them a seat at the table through job allocations. By removing the enforcer bids, over half our citizens lose representation with the law," I say.

"And why shouldn't the citizens responsible for over ninety-five percent of the crime lose representation?" Jace gives me a pointed look. "Grunts generally don't have the best judgment. They're uneducated and incapable of making the right decisions. They bring our society down while failing to contribute to it."

I roll my eyes at the obvious dig on Wren. There was a point in my life when I would have thrown my chair at Jace's head for a comment like that. Now I recognize it for what it is, a diversion tactic. Jace feels threatened so he's lashing out and trying to make me say something I'll regret.

"Enough." Byron holds up his hand to stop us and glares at Jace. An emotion I never thought I would see flickers behind Jace's eyes: Fear. "I want to raise a motion with the Council. All those in favor of stripping Jace Axton's rank as designated successor say 'aye.'"

"Aye," I say without hesitation, standing up to my stepbrother for the first time in my life. The Council members fidget in their seats, not making eye contact with Byron. They glance around, unsure of what to do.

"Aye," says Elle. She isn't cowering like the other members and her voice doesn't waver.

"Aye," another member follows. His eyes dart around the room like he's expecting some sort of trap. Jace is gripping the edge of the table with white knuckles. I'm fairly certain it's the only thing keeping his hands off my neck. The other board members join us.

"The decision is unanimous," says Byron.

"You can't do this," snarls Jace.

"I can and I did." Byron raises an eyebrow. "I would like to call another vote. All those in favor of promoting Asher Axton as my designated successor, say 'aye.'"

He barely finishes his statement before the Council voices their approval. After a few moments of silence, I realize I'm staring at Byron with my mouth hanging open. I close it slowly.

Byron Axton doesn't like me half the time, so why would he nominate me as his successor?

"Then it's decided. The enforcer bids stay in the lottery and I have a new successor."

"That's my birthright!" screams Jace.

"Guards, remove Jace from the room until he can cool off and bring me his pin."

Two guards approach Jace from behind and grab his arms. One of them pulls the successor insignia from Jace's lapel and hands it to Byron. Jace throws the guards off before straightening his suit jacket. He jabs a finger at me on his way out the door.

"You'll regret this," Jace snarls.

For once, I believe him.

"This meeting is adjourned. We'll vote on advanced bot funding next week. Please read Carl's proposal and come prepared." Byron dismisses everyone with a bored flick of his wrist. I see where Jace gets it. He exits the room, leaving us all sitting in stunned silence. I bolt after him.

"Byron-" I stop myself when he turns around with a scowl. "Director, sir. What was that about?" I correct, deciding to play nice.

Byron inclines his head towards his office. I follow him in, the glass frosts automatically to conceal us from anyone standing in the hall. Byron's office has the same floor-to-ceiling windows as the conference room. The walls on either side are crammed with books. He has always preferred reading paper over tablets. There are no personal effects on his desk and no pictures on the walls. This office could belong to anyone in the city.

"What can I do for you, Asher?"

"We haven't had a civil conversation since I was a kid. You don't even like me. Why did you make me your successor?"

Byron walks over to the small bar nestled between two bookcases where crystal decanters hold a variety of amber-colored liquids. He pours two glasses and offers me one. He raises his glass in a silent toast. I mimic him and take a small sip. After last night, I'm not in the mood for more alcohol. Besides, I try to hide my grimace, I hate scotch.

"Ash, just because we fight doesn't mean I dislike you. You challenge me. You do your research and form your own opinion of the world then you go to bat for that belief. If anything, I respect you for it."

I focus on the liquid in my glass, swirling it around. My frown is reflected at me on the polished surface. "You have a strange way of showing it."

Byron chuckles sardonically, taking a long pull from his drink. "What, I didn't spend enough time playing catch with you when you were younger? Grow up."

I slam the glass down on the desk with so much force I'm surprised it doesn't crack. I guess being an irritating, condescending prick runs in the family.

"You want my dissent? So be it. I oppose the continued partnership between Axton AI and the Council. Increasing monitoring in grunt neighborhoods is a gross invasion of privacy. The Syndicate could leverage this to recruit more members. We can't replace human enforcers in grunt sectors. Period. Recruits from those sectors come to us through the Ascent. Why not use them? Send them into those neighborhoods as a positive example of what the enforcers can do when we're not arresting their parents, siblings, or friends."

I'm breathing heavily when I finish my tirade. I feel like I willingly placed my head in a guillotine and I'm waiting for him to drop the blade, but this is one point I can't back down on. Wren and I may have our differences, but innocents like Robbie don't deserve to be aimlessly slaughtered in our war against the Syndicate.

"The partnership with Axton AI is a means to an end. The Syndicate is out of control. The streets are flooded with drugs and we're unable to raid their operations as fast as they install new ones. I'm beginning to suspect they even have eyes and ears inside the Academy," says Byron.

"That's crazy," I mutter.

"You're not that naive," he scoffs, throwing back the last sip of his drink. "It's the only reasonable explanation for how they've avoided us for so long. We'll vote on the funding proposal next week. It will get passed. Once the Syndicate has been eliminated, I intend to remove the bot patrols from the grunt sectors at once. The partnership with Axton AI was never meant to be a long-term solution. After the Syndicate is wiped out, I plan to step down as CEO of Axton AI. It was always my intent for Jace to run my company and for you to run the Council. The two roles are too powerful to be combined."

I cradle my drink against my chest. Byron is going to willingly relinquish power? Yeah, right.

"Why were you trying to marry me off to Penny Bronxton?" I ask.

"Penny will inherit Axton AI once her father passes away and her mother approves of the union. You and Penny would be a second check on Jace's power. I love my son, but he tends to act first and then pretend it was part of a strategy. Besides, you and Penny would have made a lovely couple, but I see your heart is elsewhere. I want to offer you my congratulations on your engagement."

My fingers whiten against my glass.

"I thought you believed caring about anything or anyone makes you weak," I scoff. Byron sets the glass down and circles his desk. He pulls the top drawer open and rummages around before setting a small silver plane on the polished surface. The top is crushed in and the wings are slightly dented. He pushes it so it rolls a few inches. I stare at it in disbelief.

"Do you know why I campaigned to be the director?"

"Because you're egotistical and thought you could solve the world's problems?" I mutter. Byron laughs.

"That may be one reason, but not the biggest. I grew up in a working-class neighborhood with my father. He had a job at a local factory on the assembly line."

I am unable to conceal a snort.

"Something funny?" Byron glares at me.

"The Axton family was rich before you founded Axton AI and became the director. I doubt you even know what a working-class neighborhood looks like."

Byron swirls the liquid in his glass before taking a measured sip.

"That may be true, but I wasn't born an Axton," says Byron. "I was adopted."

I study his face for deception, but he appears to be telling the truth. This is the first time I've heard about Byron's so-called adoption, but that doesn't mean it's untrue. Byron never talked about his childhood. I always assumed it was because it was as miserable as my own.

"I used to walk to the front gates every day after school and wait for his shift to end. One day, the gates opened and he didn't come out," Byron continues.

"What happened to him?"

"He was killed. A dumb accident that could have been avoided. I was absorbed into the foster system where there were other kids with stories just like mine. I promised myself I would do something about it. There were other reasons I wanted to change the narrative. Companies couldn't hire and train enough workers to keep the economy running after the Boomers retired. Integrating robotics and automation into warehouses and factories was something I had thought a lot about over the years. The fact is, stories like mine don't exist today. We live in a better, safer world. The question is, are you going to help me keep it that way?"

Byron offers me his hand.

"No," I say. "I refuse to be your successor. I refuse to be part of a broken system. Find someone else to solve your problems."

Byron pauses, setting his glass down on the polished bar with emphasized control. He stalks towards me, malice glowing in his eyes. This is the man I know. The reason behind the mangled airplane on his desk. The destroyer. The manipulator.

"It's interesting what you can learn when you're in my position. I know you tried to get a mission approved to take down surge distribution and that it was shot down by the head of operations. I could approve it. Although, it would be unconventional to send my successor into a war zone. I don't know if I'm comfortable having you on the enforcers, to begin with."

He retrieves the successor insignia he took from Jace. He places it over my heart and slams it into place with his palm. The pin on the back pierces my skin, holding it in place. I grit my teeth, refusing to make a sound. He drops his hand from my chest. "You will be my successor or I will have you dismissed from the enforcers. Is that clear?"

"Yes, sir," I say. My voice sounds hollow, even to me.

"Then I'll approve your undercover mission. You're dismissed."

I press my palm against the frosted glass door rather than using the handle. I hope it leaves a smudge.

"Oh, and Asher?" I pause with the door half-open.

He tosses me the plane and I catch it instinctively. "Don't make me regret this."

"I won't, sir." It's not even a lie.

Chapter 13

Wren

“I didn’t know anyone could be this bad at driving,” I say. “Congratulations, you lowered the bar!”

I dab the front of my shirt with a wad of shop towels trying to sop up the coffee I spilled. Ash hit the brakes so hard that I emptied the entire cup. No joke, the mug was completely full and now there isn’t a single ounce of liquid inside.

“Sorry,” mutters Ash. He floors it and the car lurches forward so quickly my head almost hits the dash. He does brake more slowly this time, so I guess I’ll count that as a win.

Two days after I stormed out on Ash, an enforcer officer stopped by my compartment to tell me the surge crew mission had been approved. Glitch was pissed. I told her and Roy I would be leaving the Academy on a special assignment, keeping the details as vague as possible. I asked them not to worry about me. Of course, telling someone not to worry is the equivalent of getting drunk and saying “hold my beer” before attempting a gravity-defying stunt.

Everyone knows it’s not going to work.

I put on the clothes I wore to the bid ceremony and met Ash in the lobby. It was the first time I talked to him since leaving his compartment. Okay, so that wasn’t my finest moment, but you can’t say the guy didn’t deserve it. I had mandatory training with him, but I timed it so I got there right before the lessons started and left as soon as they were over. I made sure Glitch and Roy were with me at all times outside of class.

In short, I made a Herculean effort to avoid speaking to Ash.

The next day, I found my jeans sitting outside my compartment. When I picked them up, a handwritten note fell out of the folds. It was an apology from Ash. He said he was sorry for using Miles' imprisonment as a bargaining chip. That I was right and he was being a hypocrite. There was also a signed contract from the Council granting Miles a full pardon upon the completion of our mission. It was a step in the right direction. It makes me want to believe I can trust him, but that's a dangerous notion.

Why? Pick your reason. Multiple choice test, all answers are correct. He's a selfish jerk who only cares about taking down the Syndicate. He talked with Ariel about dinosaurs. He gave me and my family a place to stay when we were in danger. He made me breakfast. At the end of the day, Ash is a pretty decent guy. Half the time I can't decide if I want to punch him or kiss him.

I'm a mess and Ash is a walking contradiction wrapped in an enigma.

"Who drinks coffee out of an open mug in a car anyway?" asks Ash.

"What else would I be drinking it out of?"

"A travel mug! Any cup with a lid."

"I didn't have a problem before you started driving. You ruined a perfectly good pair of pants."

"I think 'perfectly good' is a stretch," says Ash, eying the coffee patch that's already indistinguishable from the other stains on the fabric.

"Yeah, yeah, whatever. Eyes on the road." I wave him off.

Ash smirks. Right now, he doesn't look like the director's son or an enforcer. He looks like a mechanic with his faded blue jeans, black t-shirt, and scuffed boots. I guess it shouldn't be surprising that he blends in considering he grew up in a grunt sector, but it's easy to forget where he comes from when he's at the Academy.

It has been a little over a week since we reopened Jimmy's Auto. We've been staying at my old apartment and running normal business hours at the shop. We've fallen into a routine of sorts. I cook dinner and Ash washes the dishes and vice versa. Ash makes coffee in the morning while I shower.

It's strangely...domestic.

Grams, Ariel, and Robbie are still staying at Ash's apartment. I thought it would be safer to keep them away while Ash and I are actively trying to eliminate the surge crew. There are so many ways this could go wrong. I don't want them in the middle of it. So, in the meantime, I get to teach Ash how to make beans a thousand different ways and he gets to work with me on hand-to-hand combat. Every night we sit on the couch, watch a movie, and talk. About everything - our lives, jobs, and families.

Our hopes, dreams, and fears.

I hate that I can't hate him.

When we were at the Academy, Ash guarded his words and hid his personality behind a persona he created. Here, where there isn't anyone to impress, I feel like I get to see the real him. Ash is quick-witted and sarcastic, something I most definitely appreciate. He's loyal, smart, and caring, but he hides it behind a facade of nonchalance that isn't easy to see through. I wonder what he would be like if he didn't spend half his time and energy maintaining a charade.

Sometimes, it's easy to forget this isn't real.

I sent a message to my old surge crew contact, but I haven't heard back from him yet. I could follow up, but I don't want to spook him. I blew him off the first time he offered me a gig. It would be weird to come off as desperate now. In the meantime, I've been working my way through the backlog of jobs that have piled up since I left for the Academy.

Ash brakes again and I put some serious strain on the seat belt.

"Seriously?" I yelp. I give up on the stain, tossing the paper towels on the floor.

"Why is the pedal so sensitive?"

"It's a freaking Corolla, not a sports car. It's definitely a you problem."

Ash grits his teeth. "Remind me why we're doing this again?

"Because a mechanic who doesn't know how to drive is suspicious."

Ash pulls into the parking lot at Jimmy's Auto and puts the car in park. "I think that's enough for today."

"You only went around the block twice!"

"And it aged me a decade."

I scoff. "Drama queen. I'm going to run to Otto's to get food for tonight. We don't have any appointments booked, but do you mind staying behind just in case?" I don't have to tell Ash I'm worried someone from the surge crew is going to stop by while we're gone. We're both anxious to hear back from my contact. Our entire deal hinges on a few words exchanged with a stranger over a year ago. I try not to think about that too much. My nerves can't handle it.

"Sure," says Ash. We get out of the car and swap sides. Ash disappears inside the shop. I have to move the seat forward so I can reach the pedals. Ash complains about it every time I make him practice, because he bangs his knees on the steering wheel when he gets in the car.

It's not my fault he's a tall human.

I back out of the parking space and take the familiar route to Otto's store. I probably shouldn't be using a client's car to teach Ash how to drive, but Indy is the only vehicle I own. Given how his past few lessons have gone, it's going to be a while before I let him on my bike.

Despite his horrendous driving skills, Ash has been surprisingly helpful to have around. He doesn't know anything about cars, but he's a fast learner. I only have to explain something once and he runs with it. If I were looking to hire another employee, Ash wouldn't be the worst choice. He even got the enforcers to release Miles' computer so we could use his files.

Miles is a complete slob with the sole exception of his computer. He keeps excellent records and has a folder on his desktop with frequently used programs. So far, I've been able to help every client who has walked through the door with a technology issue despite my minimal expertise. I just hope nothing crazy comes up in the meantime. I park along the curb in front of Otto's shop, facing the wrong direction. It's not like anyone is going to ticket me. I grab my bag and go inside.

"Shoot me and you won't get paid," I say, not slowing my pace.

"Did your shop get raided again?" Otto calls. I head for the back aisle and start shoveling food cans into the bag.

God-awful legumes.

"Nope," I say. "Got anything other than beans?"

"Nothing I'm willing to part with," he chuckles. "How's that new mechanic working out for you?" I brought Ash to Otto's store on day one to stock up on supplies. I made the mistake of allowing him to go through the door first. I think Otto might have scared him more than Grams.

"You're talkative today," I grumble.

Otto shrugs. "The news has been slow lately. Not much worth reading about." He flicks his finger sending the screen on his tablet scrolling like a roulette machine.

I dump the cans on the counter. "Haven't fired him yet, so I guess that's something."

"Guess so."

Otto rings up my purchases. I notice a display with cinnamon chewing gum beside the register. I grab a pack and toss it on top of the pile. "That too." He gives me a curious look while he scans it. I pay through the 8-Bit app and slide everything into my bag.

When Ash checked out with me last time, I didn't think about it when I pulled up the app. He confronted me afterward. Apparently, the enforcers know about 8-Bit, but they haven't been able to hack into it. They've never gotten past the game storefront. I knew the app was secure, but I didn't think it had the clout to stand up to enforcer resources. I couldn't help but feel an unwarranted sense of pride.

New users have to submit an online application followed by an in-person meeting to verify their identity with a chip scan. When Ash signed up, he kept his first name the same, but changed his last name to 'Laghari.' I thought it was an identity the ops team came up with. A few days later he told me it was his birth name. His name before he became an Axton. Asher Lagari sounds a lot better than Asher Axton. He should have stuck with it. I told him as much. Ash shrugged it off. He told me "Axton" opens more doors than "Laghari" and left it at that.

We came up with a cover story. So far as the Syndicate is concerned, Ash didn't leave his crappy apartment in the grunt sectors. He took a job at the hospital as a data analyst, but was laid off when they automated his role. Since then, he has been scraping by on savings. This is the first time he has had to work for the Syndicate. The story flows so effortlessly that I have to remind myself that it isn't the truth. It's like Ash and I came to the same fork in a road where Ash went right and I veered left. Now, our paths are coming together again. I drive back to Jimmy's Auto and take my bag inside.

"I have a surprise for you," I say in a sing-song voice when I open the door.

Ash pokes his head out of Dad's office. "What's up?"

"What are you doing?" I drop my bag.

He holds up a garbage sack. "Thought I could do some cleaning while you were gone and make myself useful...from the look on your face I'm guessing this was the wrong thing to do." He frowns.

I storm across the room, snatching the garbage bag from him. "You have no right."

"Okay," he says, elongating the word into several syllables.

I open the trash bag and dump the contents on the floor at his feet. It's mostly fast-food wrappers and old newspapers. I take a deep breath and let it out slowly, trying to calm down.

"Hey, I'm sorry. I was just trying to do something nice for you after you spent all that time teaching me how to drive." Ash steps to the side so I can look into the office. "I started stacking the papers I thought could be important. I only tossed the real trash. I'm sorry, I overstepped," he says.

I squat down and start sweeping the trash back into the bag. "It's fine. You didn't do anything wrong."

Ash bends over to help me. "Clearly I did. Want to tell me what's going on?"

"That's Dad's office. I haven't touched it since he died."

Ash pauses with a handful of wrappers. "Don't take this the wrong way."

"With an intro like that, how could I?"

Ash continues with his question, unphased by my smart-ass comment. "Why do you call it your 'Dad's office' or your 'Dad's shop'? You've been running the place for two years-"

"Four years," I correct automatically. I continue picking up loose papers and used food containers. It's not that I don't want to answer his question. I just don't know-how. Ash takes the full bag from me and ties it off. I start a new bag. Ash silently studies me, waiting for an answer.

I give him a dry laugh. "You just keep picking and picking until you get an answer, don't you?"

Ash considers my question. "I hate small talk. I don't care about the weather, the latest gossip, or the last show you watched. I especially hate when people ask you how you're doing. Do you think anyone wants an honest answer to that question?" Ash shakes his head. "I could be experiencing a catastrophe of biblical proportions, but do you know what I'd say? I'm fine. Saying anything other than that isn't socially acceptable. It's rude. It's unloading your problems on another person who doesn't care."

Ash gives me a small smile. "When I ask a question, I honestly want to know the answer. I don't mind waiting for you to sort through your thoughts. If you don't want to respond at all, that's alright too. Why do you call it your 'Dad's shop' and not your shop?"

Ash's expression is unyielding, but not intimidating or unkind. He wants to know what I have to say, but he wants it to be my choice. He's giving me the opportunity to open the door to my thoughts or slam it in his face.

Something inside me snaps.

"You want my honest answer? Here it is. I treat this shop like I expect Dad to walk through the door and take over tomorrow. It's not logical, but it feels like the second I make it my own it means I'm letting go. Like I'm giving up on Dad." I finish stuffing the second trash bag and tie it off, setting it aside.

"While I'm at it, you asked if Miles was Ariel's dad? He isn't, but sometimes I wish he was. I was raped when I was sixteen. It was a client who came into the shop while I was alone. He was going to kill me, but Miles showed up and distracted him. I shot him with his own gun." I lay out the facts for Ash, the years whittling down the emotion in my story like the river at the bottom of a canyon. "I regret a lot of things, but ending his life has never been one of them. Maybe that makes me a monster. I don't know. I guess if there is a God I'll be judged for it in the afterlife. Until then, I'm not going to lose sleep over it.

"When I found out I was pregnant, it took a long time to come to terms with the fact that the worst thing that ever happened to me gave me the best thing that ever did. Ariel is my whole world and, as much as it sucked, I wouldn't change a thing.

"I hate it when people find out about Ariel, because they treat me like a victim when I'm the strongest person I know. I've had to be and I'm proud of that. I don't want anyone to pity me, because it diminishes all the healing I've done. I'm a survivor. I refuse to let one bad thing that happened to me define my story.

"I've coped, but sometimes I wonder if any of that even matters. How can I be okay when I keep revisiting my trauma over and over again like some messed up rerun I can't shut off. I had two panic attacks the night Jace broke into my compartment. I'm just as messed up now as I was then." I scrub my hands over my face. I'm sure I look like I'm out of my mind, but I couldn't care less. I've kept my emotions locked down for years and the dam has finally burst.

"I'm just so angry and tired and…lost. I'm lost without my best friend. Miles and I shared every major milestone in our lives. Every birthday. Every loss. He was there when I had Ariel. I love him. Not in a romantic way like I once thought. Not even in a normal, 'you're my best friend way.' I love him like it's the only thing my soul is capable of. It's not healthy. It's not reasonable, but he's built into my foundation. When the enforcers took him, my house fell apart and I'm trying to rebuild when pieces are missing.

"Want to know what's ironic?" I laugh, but it's a lilted, wounded sound like an animal that has been hit by a car. "I accused you of wearing a mask, but the truth is I've been wearing one too. I hide my pain from my family, because I don't want them to worry. It took months for Grams and Miles to stop tiptoeing around me. I can't go back to that. How can you have a normal relationship with your family when they treat you like you're made of glass? It's impossible. So, I haven't allowed myself the luxury of breaking down. When everything goes wrong, I'm the moron standing at the edge of the inferno with a squirt bottle to keep the flames in check. So yeah, everything is just peachy. Thanks for asking."

I snatch the cinnamon gum out of my backpack and peg it at Ash's head. "That's for you." It bounces off his chest and falls in his lap. Ash stands up, putting the gum in his pocket. He takes one step towards me then another.

"Thank you," he whispers. I don't know if he's thanking me for sharing my story or for the unexpected gift. Ash uses his thumb to wipe a tear from my cheek. I didn't even realize I was crying. "I'm sorry. I don't want you to think I'm pitying you, because I'm not. You're right. You're the strongest person I know, Wren, but I'm sorry you've had to be. Because that kind of strength only comes from a situation that gave you no other choice."

That's when I lose it. I break into ugly, chest-wracking sobs. I can't remember the last time I cried like this. It's like everything that has happened over the last four years is hitting me at once. Ash wraps his arms around me, holding me against his chest. I'm soaking his shirt with tears, but he doesn't seem to care. My arms go around his waist and Ash rests his chin on my head. He doesn't ask any questions. He doesn't apologize. He simply gives me a safe place to remove my mask until I'm ready to put it on again.

"I don't cry." I sniffle into his t-shirt, wiping my eyes with the back of my hand. It comes away wet, directly contradicting my words.

"It's okay. I do." Ash presses a kiss into my hair. "Promise you won't tell anyone?"

I let out a choked laugh. "Your secret is safe with me." I lean back so I can see his face, his hands falling to my hips. "How are *you*?"

"You don't have to do that."

"I want to. A truth for a truth or a lie for a lie, remember?"

Ash chuckles. "Okay."

I take a few steps away from him until his hands fall from my waist. I don't want to, but I know it's the smart thing to do. I feel something for Ash. I'm not sure what it is. Maybe it's a spark that will fizzle out in a day or maybe it's something more. Maybe I'm just grateful to have a third-party sounding board where I can voice my thoughts without consequence. I don't know, but I'm certain I don't want to find out. At the end of the day, he's still an enforcer and I'm still a Syndicate mechanic with a toddler.

Ash rubs the back of his neck and sighs. "I guess I feel conflicted." He lines up the sockets I have sitting in an open drawer of the tool chest from largest to smallest. "For years, the Syndicate has been the punching bag I directed all my anger towards. Then you came along and screwed everything up by giving that enemy a face." He gives me a lopsided smile that tells me he isn't all that mad about it. "You're not the worst person I've met."

I roll my eyes. "I bet you tell all the pretty girls that."

"Who said you're pretty?" Ash laughs. "Kidding!" He adds when I scowl. He stands the last socket on end. "It's just hard for me to accept the Syndicate that was responsible for mom's death is the same Syndicate that keeps the grunt sectors running. There has to be another way." Ash tucks his hands in his front pockets and rocks back on his heels. "Byron named me his successor."

I stare at him. "I thought Jace was his successor."

"He was until Byron decided to denounce him and nominate me in front of the Council. Speaking of that jackass, I should kill him for what he did to you," Ash growls.

I gently take his arm. "While I appreciate the gesture, I'm more than capable of fighting my own battles."

"I know, but that doesn't mean you should have to." He gives me a look so intense it sends the butterflies in my stomach fluttering.

I clear my throat. "I haven't seen anything on the news about you taking over as successor." When Jace was given the title, they played the broadcast on repeat for weeks. I assume if the title changed hands, the media coverage would be just as intense.

"They're waiting to announce it until after I get back from this mission."

"I'm surprised the director allowed it."

"He didn't. I refused to be his successor. Byron threatened to kick me out of the enforcers. You know, regular father-son bonding stuff. When we get back, they'll make an announcement." He has told me time and time again that his only goal is to take down the Syndicate. I don't know how he can be both the director's successor and an enforcer. I think Ash knows it too. My phone pings with a notification. I scramble to fish it out of my pocket, holding my breath as I read it.

"What is it?" asks Ash.

"It's my surge crew contact. He wants to meet."

Chapter 14

Ash

I hate everything about this situation.

Wren's surge crew contact texted her an address and gave us an hour to meet him there. We didn't have time to prepare. I can't help but feel it was intentional, a calculated move to throw us off our game. If that was the case, then he succeeded. I can't stop the chaos in my stomach or the tightness in my chest.

This feels like a mistake.

Wren parks Indy behind a car sitting on cinder blocks. Well, sort of. The block under the left front wheel is missing, so the car is tilting dangerously to the side. A cinder block sits in the middle of the road, cleaved in two, like someone knocked it out of place with a sledgehammer. We're idling in front of a dingy brick building that succumbed to nature a decade ago. The bushes are so tall they half block the front windows. Green ivy has woven its way up the side of the building reaching the roof. I'm not sure if the mortar is holding the bricks together or the vines. It's hard to tell. The front door is hanging off its hinges and most of the windows on the second story are cracked or missing. Wren kills the engine.

"Are you sure this is the place?" I ask. She takes her sunglasses off, hanging them from her shirt collar. I shove my sunglasses on top of my head. That was the first lesson I learned after riding on Indy. Anything over forty miles per hour requires eye protection or you can't see anything. I'm still not comfortable on Wren's bike, but it's her only transportation. I offered to have a car from the enforcer impound lot brought down. She refused. Wren thought it might draw unwanted attention. She didn't want anyone asking questions.

She checks her phone. "Yeah, 2098 is the house number." There are gold street numbers pinned beside the front door. The nine is crooked and the eight is missing entirely. I scan the neighboring houses to confirm. Unfortunately, the haunted house is definitely our meeting place.

"It's not what I was expecting," I say.

Wren quirks an eyebrow. "What did you think it would look like? A factory with a big production line? A backroom of a bar like some mobster movie?"

I clear my throat. That's exactly what I was expecting, but I don't tell her that.

"Surge is the highest priced synthetic drug on the market. They have to be able to afford better buildings," I grumble.

"Better buildings draw attention," says Wren.

I take the lead, jumping up on the porch to skip the three rotted steps. Not that the porch is in better shape. There are holes in the boards so large you can see the ground below. I try to keep my steps light, but it creaks and moans with every movement. I grit my teeth. By some unknown miracle, I make it to the front door without falling through. I nudge the door open using my boot and yelp when I come face to face with a ghost.

Not a ghost. A man. He stares at me with unseeing eyes, wearing a lazy smile on his face. His appearance is made more grotesque by hollowed cheekbones and sunken eye sockets. He's not wearing a shirt and his skin looks like it has been stretched taut over his bones. I can count every rib. His pants are a few sizes too big, held up by a drawstring knotted tightly around his waist. He wanders away, disappearing from view.

Yeah, this house is giving me a warm and fuzzy feeling.

I pry the broken door open far enough that I can squeeze inside, holding it for Wren to step through behind me. The townhouse could have been beautiful once. I see a whisper of grandeur in the peeling wallpaper and the remnants of a chandelier lying on its side in the corner. There's a stairwell in front of us that looks about as sturdy as the porch. You couldn't pay me enough to try it. To my left is a living room with people sprawled out across a filthy couch and on the floor. They don't seem to notice the filth on the worn carpet or the stench of unwashed bodies. The smell itself is enough to bowl me over. The man who startled me is standing in front of a blank wall with the same dazed expression on his face.

Creepy.

"What is this place?" asks Wren. She's plugging her nose, so her voice comes out nasally and muffled.

"It's a surge den," I say. "People come here to buy the drug and shoot up."

It reminds me of when we rescued Liam from the Syndicate. He had the same empty expression and lackadaisical smile like he was viewing a world only he could see. I clench my fists to stop my hands from shaking. I want to tear this place down brick by brick, but that's not what we came here for. I'm wound so tightly that I'm more likely to throttle Wren's contact before we get a chance to talk to him.

I need to pull it together.

Attacking Wren's contact is the wrong move. He's a single cockroach that strayed too far from the nest. If we're smart about this, we can follow him home and take out the whole infestation. I can do this.

"Trip!" Wren yells. I jump a foot in the air - no joke - and scowl at her.

"What are you doing?"

She shrugs. "Do you want to search this place room by room? Trip!" She yells, again.

"Seriously, that's his name?"

"You can't say the guy doesn't have a sense of humor, even if it is in poor taste," Wren says dryly. The porch creeks behind us.

"Yo, I'm out here. You can stop bothering my customers." The man sounds like his vocal cords have been rubbed over sandpaper.

Wren shoots me a look. I nod and gesture for her to go first. This Trip guy knows her. It's better if she leads the conversation. I know that.

So why do I feel the need to throw her over my shoulder and run for the back door?

I follow Wren outside. Trip is leaning against the brick ledge of the porch. I actually look around to confirm that he was the one speaking. The guy looks around our age. He's wearing a slouchy, gray t-shirt and black skinny jeans with holes in the knees. The white laces on his sneakers stand out in stark contrast to the soiled sides, indicating they have been replaced recently. His hair is a pale blond that's mussed up on one side, like he just rolled out of bed to come this meeting. He has a cocky smirk that makes me instantly dislike him.

This can't be Wren's contact.

"Sorry about that," says Wren. "It's good to see you again." His eyes travel from Wren's boots to her face, lingering longer than they should. I take a step closer to Wren. He needs to back up. Trip gives me an amused look.

"Who's the pretty boy?" He tilts his head towards me.

"He works for me," says Wren.

At the same time, I say, "None of your business."

Wren glares at me, silently telling me to shut up.

"Didn't think you wanted to work with a crew," says Trip. He turns his attention back to Wren.

"My opinion changed," says Wren. "Where's your boss?"

I wince when Trip tenses. "Why the rush? The boss wants a test run. See if you're as good as I said you are."

"Is there a car here you want me to fix? It would be easier to take it to the shop. I don't have any tools with me-"

"No car." Trip swings the book bag off his back. He unzips it and tilts it forward so Wren and I can see inside. It's filled nearly to the brim with capped syringes holding a pinkish liquid.

Surge.

An entire bag of surge.

"The boss wants you to make a drop," says Trip.

"That wasn't what we signed up for," I say, crossing my arms.

Wren gives me a sharp look. "No, it's okay. We'll do it." I try to catch her eyes, but she refuses to look at me. Trip zips up the bag and hands it to her along with a torn slip of paper.

"That's the address. Memorize it then destroy it. The package needs to be there in thirty minutes."

Wren glances at the paper and snorts. "I'm good, Trip, but no one can make that drop in thirty minutes."

He shrugs. "Then don't do it. The boss offered you a job before and you didn't take it. This is you proving you're worth a second chance." Wren and Trip stare at each other as if having a silent conversation. There's nothing about this situation that makes me feel warm and fuzzy inside. This wasn't the plan. We should be calling this off right now. We can find another way.

"Come on," says Wren, grabbing my arm. She tugs me down the stairs. The wood creaks so loudly I'm worried the whole structure is going to collapse. She loops the book bag straps over her arms, tugging them tight so that the bag sits snugly against her chest. I guess we're doing this. I risk a glance back at Trip. He has his forearms propped on the brick ledge watching us with an unreadable expression on his face.

This doesn't add up.

At roughly four-hundred credits a syringe, we're carrying enough surge to buy a few city blocks. Why would they use such a large shipment for a test run? Either Trip is an idiot or there's something else going on.

"Hurry up," says Wren. I sigh. I take a seat behind Wren. She guns it as soon as my arms are around her waist.

"Where are we going?" I yell over the wind.

"A grunt sector on the other side of the city."

"Can we make it in time?"

Wren doesn't respond, she just pushes the bike faster. I guess that means our odds aren't good. After weaving through city streets at a breakneck pace, she banks right and brakes. There's an off-ramp leading below street level with concrete barricades blocking the way. We use our feet to keep the bike balanced while she maneuvers around the blockade. Wren accelerates as soon as we're clear. There are no lights in the tunnel, the only illumination coming from Indy's single headlight. Thankfully, the road is mostly free of debris. In my peripherals, I see bright eyes flash as something scurries across the floor.

Rats maybe? I try not to think about it too much.

It takes me a moment to realize this must be one of the tunnels that were built so drivers could avoid downtown traffic. I remember Byron complaining about them. Pods would lose signal in the tunnels leaving customers stranded or redirected, so the Council closed them off. Traffic isn't much of a problem downtown anyways. All Pods are linked up to the same network with vehicle-to-vehicle communication. I don't know exactly how it works, but at a high level, the Pods can time their approach at intersections to reduce congestion in highly populated areas.

I can see why Wren wanted to take this route. For one, it's probably the most direct path to the grunt sectors on the other side of the city center. Additionally, with the amount of surge we are carrying, it would be beneficial to avoid enforcer patrols. They would arrest us and we would have to waste time explaining who we are. We would miss Trip's deadline. It's better to avoid them altogether.

A red light blinks ahead of us. At first, I thought I imagined it. It was no larger than a pinprick. I'm about to write it off as another rat when it happens again. I lean forward so my lips are right by Wren's ear.

"Slow down," I say, keeping my voice low. "I think there's something up ahead. There's a red light on the right at the edge of the tunnel. Watch for it." She eases up on the throttle allowing the bike to coast.

The light blinks again.

"Hold on," Wren says before slamming on the brakes. Just before she turns the bike, Indy's headlight reveals a row of motorbikes with drivers in white uniforms.

Enforcer uniforms.

Wren turns Indy so hard the bike skids sideways and I smell burning rubber. I follow Wren's lead, leaning into the turn to balance us. As soon as we change directions, she opens the throttle and we rocket back the way we came. I hear the enforcer's bikes roar to life. Their headlamps illuminate the tunnel, casting shadows on the arched walls. Indy is capping out and the enforcers are gaining on us.

We're not going to make it.

In front of us, more headlights flick on revealing more enforcers blocking the tunnel entrance. They must have been waiting for us. If there's any doubt in my mind Trip set us up, this erases it. There's no way the enforcers are stationed here by chance. Someone tipped them off. I run through my options. I could try to explain who we are, but are they going to believe us? We're dressed like grunts in a restricted area of the city carrying illegal substances.

I wouldn't believe me.

Wren decides for us. She speeds up, preparing to run the blockade. There are a few shouts of surprise and the enforcers start firing. The sound is deafening in the enclosed space. My breath hitches when muzzle fire lights up the tunnel like a stop motion film.

They're using live rounds.

I listen in horror as their shots go wide, tearing into the enforcers chasing us. I hear their screams and the screech of crumpling metal as they crash. Who's in charge of this operation? This is an absolute massacre. We're not going to make it through. The closer we get, the easier it will be for the enforcers to aim.

At this point, I don't think turning ourselves in is an option. They don't care if they take us in alive. What happened to innocent until proven guilty? I make a snap decision. Tightening my arms around Wren's waist, I stand up on the footpegs and fall backward off the bike.

I'd like to think I'm the kind of person who has a meaningful flashback when they're about to die. Some montage capturing the essence of my life before hurtling into oblivion. Today, I found out I'm not that kind of guy. My only thought?

Oh good, this is how I die.

I push us free from the bike and then we're tumbling end over end. I do my best to protect my head. Eventually, I come to a stop on my back, the air leaving my lungs in a painful whoosh. I hear the chaos of Indy crashing into the enforcer line. Gnashing metal. People screaming. The broken beams from fallen bikes bounce wildly off the tunnel walls.

I take a few deep breaths. Everything hurts. I gingerly touch my ribs. I don't think anything is broken, but I'll have some epic road rash and a few dozen bruises to remember this moment. Wren groans a few feet away from me. She pushes up to her hands and knees. She's alive. I say a silent prayer of gratitude to any higher power that might be listening. I half crawl, half stumble to Wren.

"Can you walk?" I ask. Wren tries to stand, but her left leg collapses.

"My ankle is messed up."

She looks up at me with wide, terror-filled eyes. I loop one arm under her legs and one around her back, picking her up. My body screams in protest. I take a few shallow breaths and force myself to walk. There's a stairwell at the side of the tunnel, lit up by a stray headlight. It's hard to tell if there's any natural light coming from the opening. It could be boarded up, but right now it's our best option. Luckily, the enforcers are still distracted. We make it to the stairwell without dying, so this is already going better than I could have hoped. I stumble the last few steps into the stairwell and crash land. I barely manage to prevent myself from crushing Wren.

"I can walk," she says. She scrambles to her feet and holds the railing for balance. She takes the first step and nearly face plants.

That's not reassuring.

Ignoring my discomfort, I get up and secure my arm around her waist to provide additional support. We climb the stairs together as fast as we can. It's not pretty. We're a hobbling mess of injuries, but we make it to the top only to find the entrance is boarded up with a sheet of plywood. I curse. I throw my right shoulder into the board. It shutters and I feel it give a little.

"On three," says Wren. She counts down and we throw our weight at it together. The plywood falls forward, squealing as the nails pull loose. I swear when we land in a heap on the sidewalk. I have to blink a few times before my eyes adjust to the sunlight.

"There," says Wren. She points to a side door propped open in an alley to our left. It's a terrible hiding place. It's one of the first places the enforcers will search when they make it topside, but we're in no condition to run. We have to do something before the enforcers get organized and come after us. I'm not sure who's supporting who as Wren and I make our way inside. I knock the brick holding the door open aside so it falls closed.

We're in some sort of backroom filled with nondescript boxes, some of them are open with packing material spilling onto the linoleum. I can smell food cooking and there's music playing from somewhere nearby. There's a door separating us from the front of the building, so we're out of sight for now. I shove a chair under the doorknob. I'm hoping it will slow any employees or enforcers down long enough for us to get out of here before they raise the alarm.

I fish my phone out of my jacket pocket to order a Pod. When I open AVA, I receive a notification that I don't have a card tied to the account. I curse.

"My chip is registered under Laghari. I don't have access to any of my accounts."

"Give me your phone, we can use mine. I got my first enforcers paycheck before we left the Academy." I hand her my phone and Wren enters her details, her fingers gliding over the screen to tap out the address. The light illuminates her face in the dim lighting. She has a cut on her cheek and I can see the tightness in her jaw. She's in pain, but she's trying not to let it show.

"ETA is three minutes," says Wren, giving me back my phone.

"Thank you."

"Don't mention it. I owe you for last time, remember." My mind wanders back to our conversation at the cozy coffee shop.

Another time. Another Pod. Another emergency.

Not for the first time, I wonder what it would be like if Wren and I had met under different circumstances. If I was truly a mechanic, hired on at Jimmy's Auto, to pick up the slack. I wonder what it would be like to have a conversation that wasn't impeded by circumstance.

"Hopefully they didn't send the brightest enforcers after us," mumbles Wren. She slides down against the back wall and sighs.

"They should have been using tranquilizer darts," I grind out, taking a seat beside her.

"Any idea why they weren't?"

I shake my head. "Trip set us up."

"Yup," Wren pops the 'p.'

"Why do you think he did it?"

"Maybe his boss was more offended about Miles and I snubbing his job offer than he let on."

"It just seems like a lot of surge to waste if he knew he was going to burn us."

Wren shrugs the book bag off her shoulders. It's amazing she still has it after our tumble from the bike. She unzips the top and takes out a syringe. Uncapping it, she squirts a little liquid onto her finger. To my horror, she licks it.

"What...?"

Wren spits, then chuckles lifelessly. "It isn't surge. It's water and food coloring." She shoves the bag aside, the contents worthless. I lean my head against the wall and let my eyes fall shut.

"Do you think Trip knows we're enforcers?"

Wren snorts. "I doubt it. The Syndicate likes to make examples out of moles. You saw as much with Liam. If they suspected us, we would know. Sicking the enforcers on us was more of a slap on the wrist." Wren shifts and winces.

"Let me look at your ankle."

"I'm fine."

I roll my eyes and crawl to her feet. Pushing up her pant leg, I slowly rotate the joint and she hisses. It's already swollen to twice its size. "Can you move it?"

Wren rotates her ankle slowly and bites her lip to prevent herself from crying out. "I don't think it's broken, just a bad sprain," she says.

"Either way, you shouldn't walk on it."

"Thanks, Dr. Obvious. I'll wrap it when we get back to the apartment."

Wren could have died.

The thought hits me with the force of a bat to the chest. I'm willing to take risks. I know the work I do is dangerous, but I always thought it was worth the risk. The image of Wren laying on concrete after I pulled her off Indy hits me.

Lifeless.

Dead.

Now, I'm not so sure it's worth it. I couldn't breathe until I saw the rise and fall of her chest.

I'm willing to risk my life to take out the Syndicate, but am I willing to risk hers?

Absolutely not.

The answer comes to me easily. There's no doubt or hesitation as if I've known the answer all along. My grip tightens on my phone. If I could be certain the surge crew isn't watching us, I would reroute the Pod to the Academy. My goal hasn't changed. I still plan to eliminate the Syndicate. I don't have a choice. Byron has been bugging me to make a public announcement regarding my new successor title, but I can't have my face plastered on every screen in the city. Trip isn't a genius, but it wouldn't take more than a single brain cell to connect the dots between me and Wren.

The only way out of this situation is through, but that doesn't mean she has to be tangled up in my mess.

"Hey," Wren nudges my shoulder with hers. "Where did you go just now?"

I shake my head, as if that will bring order to the chaos of swirling emotions and worse case scenarios. "The Pod will be here any minute."

Wren frowns. Her hand goes to her neck, reaching for the locket I've noticed she finds comfort in. It's not there.

"My locket," Wren gasps. She gets frantically to her feet, nearly falling over when her ankle gives out. I get up to help her. A quick scan of the floor tells me what she already knows. It's not here.

"I must have lost it during the accident," she groans, raking her hands through her hair. "It was the last thing I had that was my mother's."

"I'll call Elle as soon as we get in the Pod. She can organize some recruits to look for it."

"You'd do that?"

"Of course."

"Thank you."

Wren wraps her arms around my waist, startling me. It takes me a second to reciprocate her hug. She looks at me like I hung the moon and stars. I don't deserve it.

A few months ago, a Syndicate mechanic set my world on fire.

I never thought I'd be happy to watch it burn.

Chapter 15

Wren

I am a majestic flamingo standing under a waterfall.

Pfft. Right.

More like a wonky pigeon with a broken leg bathing in a city fountain.

My ankle is swollen to twice its normal size. It hurts to put any weight on it, which makes balancing in the shower a harrowing experience. Couple that with a suspected concussion sending waves of dizziness crashing over my brain and I'm amazed I'm still vertical. I close my eyes, allowing the warm water to trickle through my hair and down my back. I keep one hand planted against the wall to orient myself.

By some miracle, we managed to sneak out of the building without the enforcers noticing. I'm not sure if they were completely incompetent or if they simply didn't care enough to look for us. We took the Pod back to the apartment to lick our wounds and regroup. When I open my eyes, the water circling the drain is clear. No more blood. No more dirt. It's as if our wild ride through the tunnels never happened.

Except that it did.

I know crossing the Syndicate is dangerous. It's impossible to work with them for as long as I have without hearing things, but I never thought they would stoop so low as to turn their own people over to their worst enemy. I can't stop thinking about Ash's expression when we were hiding out in the backroom of the restaurant.

Like something inside of him broke.

I can only imagine what he's going through. The enforcers are his haven. They gave him a place to call home when his own became unbearable. It's impossible to reconcile Ash's version of the enforcers with what we saw in the tunnels. That was a massacre.

The shrieks. The crunch of Indy smashing through the enforcer line. The gunfire.

It's a scene I'll never be able to forget. I shiver despite the scalding hot water. This is the first time Ash has found himself on the receiving end of enforcer brutality. It's hard to come to terms with the fact that the organization you've committed your life to serving isn't what you thought it was. For the past few weeks, Ash and I have had enemies coming at us from all directions. Between Trip's betrayal, losing my locket, and crashing Indy it feels like I can't catch a break.

Today was just a few sprinkles on top of the shit cake that is my life.

I flip off the shower and step out of the tub. Unfortunately, I lead with my injured foot and almost faceplant when my ankle collapses. I grab the towel bar to stop my fall, but it pulls loose from the drywall and I hit the ground anyways. I let loose a slew of curse words. There's a quick knock on the door.

"Are you alright?" Ash asks.

"Yeah, I'm fine. Be right out." I lean the towel rack against the wall and get up. Cheap piece of crap. I'll have to repair it later. I scrub myself dry and throw the towel over the top of the shower curtain rod. Sifting through the clothes under the sink, I grab an oversized hoodie and loose-fitting sweat pants. I don't want anything that puts pressure on my ankle. Just thinking about it makes me sick. I look in the mirror. My wet hair is laying limply and there are dark circles under my eyes.

I'm in desperate need of a nap. We both look like garbage, so it's not like it matters. I might as well own it. I open the bathroom door and walk into the living room.

"So, what are we going to..." My voice trails off because it's hard to form full words with your jaw on the floor.

I take it back. Only I look like trash.

Ash looks like God's gift to humankind. He's wearing a pair of blue jeans and nothing else. He has his arm raised, trying to get a better look at the road rash on his back in the reflection on the TV screen. The motion causing him distress.

Does it make me a bad person for ogling him while he's in pain?

Probably.

But shit, he's pretty.

Ash has broad shoulders, a defined chest, and a six-pack - because of course he does. Who the heck has a six-pack? That designation should only be used in reference to beer or donuts as far as I'm concerned, but that doesn't mean I don't look. That I can't appreciate.

He has a tattoo on the left side of his chest. The piece is fairly large, taking up his left pec and part of his shoulder. It looks like a mechanical bird. The body and head are built like a machine with gears, plates, and joints making up its anatomy. I trace my fingers over the feathered wings and a tail that are outstretched simulating flight. There's a single stem rose clutched in its talons.

"Beautiful," I say. Ash shivers under my touch. He captures my wrist, stopping my roaming fingers. His hands are calloused and warm. My eyes snap up. His brown eyes study me with such intensity my skin heats under his gaze. I feel my cheeks flush when I realize I was feeling him up without permission. He probably thinks I'm an absolute creep.

How did I cross the room without noticing my feet were moving?

Sorcery. That's how.

I try to pull my hand away, but he won't let me. Instead, he lifts my hand to his lips, pressing a light kiss on the inside of my wrist.

"You're not so bad yourself." He gives me a sexy, lopsided smile that should be illegal. I tug my hand away and, this time, he lets me.

"I meant it's beautiful. Your tattoo that is," I say, attempting to dig myself out of the crater I created.

Kill me now.

"What does it mean?" I ask, because apparently, I'm a glutton for punishment and queen of the awkward.

Ash groans. "You do realize that's the most stereotypical question you can ask someone when you find out they have a tattoo, right?"

"I'll tell you about mine if you tell me about yours."

"You have ink?" Ash's eyes light up. They roam over my body in a way that tells me he's more than just a little curious. I shrug and give him a conspiratorial smile.

"Like I said, I'll tell you if you tell me."

"Always the negotiator," Ash sighs dramatically, but he's clearly willing to play along. He picks up the black t-shirt he has slung over the TV and tries to put it on. The entire process is painful to watch.

"Here, let me help you." I'm not sure if I'm helping, but it feels wrong to do nothing while he's struggling. I do my best to help him get dressed without irritating his wounds.

"I had a dream like this once, except you were helping me remove clothes, not put them on."

"Maybe I don't like what I see." I shrug, forcing my voice to remain nonchalant.

Ash snorts. "That's a lie."

My face turns beat red.

"Tell me about your tattoo," I order, changing the subject. Ash snickers, sinking into the couch with a groan befitting someone twice his age. I sit next to him and prop my injured foot up on the coffee table to elevate it.

We're a mess.

"I got it when I was eighteen, right after I joined the enforcers," says Ash. "The rose is supposed to represent my mom. The mechanized bird was an impromptu decision. I saw something similar hanging on the wall at the tattoo shop and had the artist adapt it. It reminded me of the system that failed her: beautiful in theory, but twisted into something ugly and tormented."

"That's beautiful," I say, taken aback by his honesty.

He yawns and scrubs a hand over his face like talking about it exhausts him. He gives me a tired smile. "Your turn. Let me guess, butterfly tramp stamp?"

"Screw you," I laugh. "I don't have any tattoos."

Ash's eyes narrow. "You what?"

"I just never found anything I wanted on my body permanently. It's not that I'm against them. I just haven't found the right design for me."

"You little liar." He lunges at me before I have a chance to defend myself and starts tickling my sides until I'm writhing with laughter.

"Stop, I can't breathe. I can't breathe," I manage to get out. Ash stops tickling me, but it takes me a second to catch my breath.

It takes another second for me to realize I'm practically lying across his lap. His face is inches from my own. His hands are still on my sides, his touch turning from teasing to a caress. My eyes flick to his lips and I suddenly have the overwhelming urge to kiss him.

So, I do.

Ash tenses.

I completely misread that situation. I'm an idiot-

Then, he kisses me back. His hand goes into my hair, weaving his fingers through the strands so I can't pull away again. My mind goes blank. There's nothing shy or hesitant about Ash's kiss. It's all-consuming. The type of kiss that short circuits your brain and makes you want more. This is by far the best worst decision I have ever made.

Worst best decision?

Whatever.

I ball my fist in his shirt and tug him closer. Ash takes the hint and flips us so he's on top of me, his forearms braced on either side of my head.

"Does this hurt too much?" I gasp between kisses. Ash trails his mouth from the corner of my mouth to my ear.

"Who cares," he grumbles. I laugh. He runs his lips along my jaw and then peppers wet, open-mouthed kisses down my neck. It feels so good. My hands skate under his shirt and over his back feeling the cords of muscle contract as he moves. I want more.

Scratch that. I need more.

Then, my phone rings.

Ash groans. "Don't you dare answer that." He tries to kiss me again, but I push at his chest. Ash sighs, rolling to the side to give me space. I grab my phone from the coffee table.

"It's Grams," I say, giving him an apologetic look.

"Answer it," says Ash.

"It's a video call."

Ash sits up with a wince and scoots to the far side of the couch while I try to make my hair look like we weren't just making out on the couch. I'm classy like that. I hit the button to answer the call when I deem us somewhat presentable.

"Hey Grams!" I say, my voice coming out a bit too high-pitched. Grams eyebrows raise. I cough. "Sorry, I think I'm coming down with something."

Real smooth, Wren.

"What are you up to?" she asks, pointedly.

Nothing. Nothing at all.

"We just got back to the apartment," I say, clearing my throat. I try not to wince at how guilty I sound.

I give Ash an apologetic look. He mouths "it's okay" and gives me a small smile.

"Come here," says Grams to someone off-camera. "Say hello to your mom."

I watch as Ariel's nose takes up the entire screen, her breath fogging the camera. "Hi, mommy!"

I laugh. "Hi, sweet pea." Grams re-situates them so Ariel is sitting on her lap with the phone far enough away that I can see both of them. Ariel has her curly hair pulled in a high bun that's sitting crooked on top of her head. I swear she's grown a few inches since the last time I saw her. I know it has only been a couple of weeks, but that's a lifetime for a little kid. My eyes well with tears. I can't believe I've been away from her for so long. The feeling of choking, overwhelming guilt gnaws at my insides.

Guilt for risking our family. Guilt for kissing Ash when I should be doing everything to speed up our mission so I can get back to Ariel.

"Did you know there are fifty floors in Mr. Ash's house? It's ginormous," exclaims Ariel, throwing her arms wide. She almost knocks Grams in the face with her hand.

"That's so cool," I say, willing my tears to disappear. I don't want Ariel to see me cry. She's obviously having a great time at Ash's place. For her, this is probably a mini vacation. There's no need to upset her with my wallowing.

"Where is Mr. Ash?" Ariel asks. I tilt the phone so she can see Ash sitting next to me. He waves at her. "Mr. Ash!" Ariel crows, waving back enthusiastically.

"You can just call me Ash," he says.

"Okay...Mr. Ash, I got the coolest new dinosaur. Wanna see?"

"I'd love to," says Ash, matching her enthusiasm and melting my heart a little more. Ariel runs off-screen.

"She has been crazy about that stuffed animal since Ms. Mable gave it to her," says Grams.

"Who's Miss Mable?" I ask.

"Her tutor," says Grams.

"Tutor?"

"I asked Don to find a tutor for Ariel and Robbie since they can't go to school right now. Don't worry, he would have vetted them to make sure they were qualified and discreet," says Ash. "Don must have told her that Ariel likes dinosaurs. Sorry, I should have said something. I didn't know Don had found anyone yet."

"Wow, that was...thoughtful," I say, meaning it. Ash shrugs like it's no big deal.

"I suppose he's not too bad, for a pansy," says Grams. Her lips twitch and I know she's suppressing a smile. Ash snorts. Despite her words, she seems to be warming up to him. Ariel jumps on Grams' lap with a stuffed purple T-Rex that's almost as big as she is.

"Miss Mable said I could pick out a dinosaur if I did good on my lessons. I asked for a T-Rex, because I know it's your favorite. Now you can come play with me!"

"I would love that," Ash says, his voice cracking. I glance back and forth between the screen and Ash. He has an unreadable expression on his face. Does talking to Ariel make him uncomfortable? My stomach sinks. I hope that isn't the case. I don't know what this thing is between us, but if he isn't comfortable around my daughter then this ends here.

I choose Ariel. Every time. No exceptions.

Why does it matter? The small voice in my mind whispers. At the end of the day, this arrangement with Ash is temporary. When he gets what he wants, he'll grab a Pod back to the Academy and I'll never see him again. The thought disappoints me more than I care to admit. Sure, I was kissing the man a moment ago, but kissing is one thing. Thinking about how Ash fits in with the rest of my family? That's not something I should be thinking about.

So long as Ash is holding Miles over my head, we can never be equals. If we aren't equals, then we can't have any kind of meaningful relationship. I can't forget that.

I clear my throat. "Say goodbye to Ash. I need to talk with Grams for a bit," I say. I don't like where my mind is headed. I need some one on one time with my family to put things into perspective.

"Bye!" Ariel yells. She waves at the camera and pushes off Grams' lap, taking the stuffed T-Rex with her.

"I'll talk with Grams in the bedroom so you can relax," I tell Ash. He nods, but he doesn't meet my eyes. I go into the bedroom, closing the door behind me. I sit on the bed, stacking a couple of pillows against the wall to make it more comfortable.

"How are you holding up?" asks Grams. Now that Ariel and Ash aren't listening in, she cuts right to the chase. I give her a quick summary of our meeting with Trip and the setup in the tunnels. I leave out the part about our injuries or the psychotic enforcer firing squad. I don't want to worry her any more than I already have.

"I'll talk to Trip tomorrow. We should get some credit for escaping the enforcers. I don't think even their most experienced runners would be able to do that."

Grams sighs. "This needs to stop. You're going to get yourself killed, Wren."

"I can't. I'm doing this for Miles, remember?"

"I don't think Miles would want you to die trying to help him."

"That's not fair," I whisper.

"It's the truth. I'm sorry, Wren. I know he means a lot to you, but this is too dangerous. Tell Ash you can't be a part of this anymore and let it go. We'll keep looking for a lawyer. There has to be someone who can represent Miles within our price range."

We both know there isn't one. If there was, that would have been my first choice before joining the enforcers. Besides, the lawyers are elites. The good ones, anyway. They don't represent grunts, because there's no point defending someone in a rigged system. Sure, they would take the paycheck, but I doubt they would put in any effort.

"Miles wouldn't let it go if our places were reversed," I say.

"Are you sure about that?" Grams asks. I scowl at her.

"What's that supposed to mean?"

"Nothing," she says, but she clearly had something in mind when she made her comment.

"No, I want to know. If there's something you know about my best friend that I don't, then tell me."

"It's not my place," sighs Grams.

What is that supposed to mean? She changes the subject and starts talking about the food Don has been bringing to the apartment. I have a hard time following the conversation. My mind is still churning over her comment regarding Miles. There's something going on she's not willing to tell me and when I asked, she shut it down with the same tone she's used on me since the *incident*.

It's the same tone Miles uses, like I woke up in the hospital after a terrible accident and they're preparing to deliver my prognosis. It's the tone they use when they're sugarcoating or concealing the truth, because they don't think I'm strong enough to handle it. I almost push back. Before Ash, I wouldn't have thought twice about it. I guess at some point I normalized it in my mind. Something bad happened to me, so logically my loved ones should bubble wrap the world to keep me from getting hurt again. Maybe I wanted that before, but I don't now.

Regardless, I don't want to spend my time arguing with Grams on the phone. So, I bite my tongue and comment on

Gram's story like I would have done a month ago. After half an hour has passed, I tell Grams and Ariel I love them and we hang up. I sit on the bed for a few more minutes, thoughts pinging around my head like flies trapped between a window and the blinds. Eventually, I open the door and go back into the living room.

Ash is gone.

The couch is empty. The bathroom door is wide open, so I know Ash isn't in there. Then, I spot a piece of paper on the kitchen table and a ball of unease settles in my stomach. I recognize Ash's handwriting from the note he left at my door when we were at the Academy.

Wren,

I'm sorry to leave without saying goodbye. I know I wouldn't have had the willpower to walk away if I said this to your face. It's a terrible excuse and I'm a coward, but it's the truth.

Today, I realized something I should have figured out sooner. I'm willing to risk everything to take down the Syndicate. My life. My sanity. My career. But not you.

I guess I finally found my line.

Your family can use my apartment for as long as they want. I'll text you when we arrest Trip, so you know it's safe. I'll make sure Miles is released. He should be home in a few hours. You once told me Miles is built into your foundation. That your house fell apart when we took him from you. I hope returning your missing piece will let you rebuild.

The truth is, I care about you, Wren. More than I thought possible. More than I've ever cared about anyone. I couldn't admit that to myself until recently.

I'm done being the villain in your story. Let me try to make this right.

I grip the paper so tightly it crinkles around my fingers. So, that's it then? He just packs up and leaves? I wad up the paper and throw it against the wall. It doesn't escape me that I'm a hypocrite. Not two minutes ago I was thinking about how Ash is the root of all my problems. He just gave me everything I wanted and walked away. I could move Grams and Ariel back home tonight. I could have my family back.

So why do I feel like I lost something?

I shove back from the table, the chair toppling over behind me. I throw open my apartment door and take the stairs faster than I should with a sprained ankle. I'm not wearing shoes or a coat and I left the apartment unlocked. I can't find it in myself to care. I don't stop until I'm standing in the middle of the street in front of my building.

Ash is long gone.

There aren't any cars or pedestrians. Just the burnt-out shell of my neighborhood and my empty husk of a heart.

I scream. Why? No clue, but it feels good.

I yell and yell until my voice is hoarse and there's nothing left. Then, I sit on the curb and watch the sun sink below the horizon. Lights turn on in the building across the street. I see the outlines of people moving in their apartments behind closed curtains.

I start fifty different texts to Ash, but delete them all. What can I say? He's right. We belong to two different worlds. He did me a favor by drawing the line and staying on his side. I should go back inside. I should call Grams back and tell her it's time to come home. There are a million things I should be doing and none of them involve sitting on a curb waiting for someone who isn't coming back. At some point, I go inside. I collapse on the couch and stare at the ceiling. A few hours later, there's a knock on the door. I don't bother looking through the peephole. I just open it.

Miles is standing in the hall. He looks good aside from being a bit thinner than the last time I saw him. His blond beard is long and unruly. His hair is out of control. He's wearing the same clothes he was arrested in, but his eyes are the same.

The same cerulean eyes I've looked in and been reassured by since we were kids.

"Hey there, Chickadee." He barely gets the words out before I body slam him, the force of my hug causing him to backpedal a few steps. I feel like sobbing, but I won't. I don't cry.

The little voice in my head whispers, "You cried in front of Ash."

It doesn't matter. That version of Wren was an enforcer recruit who moved mountains to get her best friend back and put her family in danger.

The version of me who started to fall for an enforcer.

It wasn't the crazy head over heels infatuation you see in old movies. It wasn't even a traditional crush. It was just the seed of a feeling that grew over time until it was too tall to ignore, then it was cut down before it had a chance to bloom.

This is the Wren who puts her family first. The Wren who doesn't get the luxury of falling apart.

It was freeing to be someone else for a few weeks. To lean on another person without feeling guilty, like I was breaking a set of unwritten rules created by the people who saw me at my worst. I was...free.

I should be more excited that Miles is home, but I just feel gutted.

Confused and gutted.

Ash told me he returned the missing part of my foundation.

So why do I feel like my house is still falling down?

Chapter 16

Ash

I'm an absolute piece of shit.

The scum of the Earth.

The worst person in this city and that's saying something considering Jace lives here.

Why? Pick your poison.

Kissing Wren and walking away. Holding Miles over her head. Putting Wren and her family in danger.

They're all valid reasons. I don't deserve her affection. I don't even know if it's real or some angle Wren's playing to get me to release her friend. I honestly wouldn't blame her if it was. I couldn't just sit there and pretend like everything is fine. It's not. I'm done. I pull out my phone to order a Pod and curse when I remember I have zero credits to my name. I shove a piece of gum in my mouth and text Elle.

Ash: Can I borrow twenty credits?

Elle: I'm doing fine, thanks for asking.

Ash: Please. It's important.

Elle: Why? You're rich.

Ash: Not when my last name is Laghari.

Elle: The all-powerful successor is broke. Never thought I'd see the day.

Ash: Are you going to help me or not?

Elle: What do I get in return?

Ash: My endless gratitude. You know I'm good for twenty credits.

Elle: How about a coffee instead?

Ash: I can do that.

Elle: No you can't, because you're broke. *laughing emoji*

A notification comes through with twenty credits despite Elle's comments. I'll repay her and buy her a coffee for good measure. We both know I owe her more than that. I direct the Pod to an address a few blocks from here. I'm already a mile or so away from Wren's apartment and I haven't noticed a tail. Maybe Trip thinks his setup was successful. It doesn't hurt to be cautious. I won't let him catch me with my guard down a second time.

The sun is starting to set behind the buildings, casting shadows across the sidewalk and road. It's the perfect venue to host my internal pity party. I should probably feel out of my element or, at the very least, a bit scared. The truth is, it took me less than a day to readjust to this life. My childhood home wasn't much different from this neighborhood. Sure, it was across the city, but it was still a slum. The Syndicate was still running rampant. You still had to watch your back. I certainly didn't have anyone to watch it for me.

I noticed the way I talked and walked changed while I was working at Jimmy's Auto. I guess you can take the kid out of the gutter, but you can't take the gutter out of the kid. It makes me second guess some of the Syndicate arrests and raids I've led or been involved in while I've worked with the enforcers. I wonder if Byron feels the same? I find my mind wandering to some dangerous questions. I stop that line of thought and pop another stick of gum in my mouth. After walking away from Wren, I don't have the emotional energy for anything else today.

I scrub a hand over my face and sigh. A few weeks ago, I had a purpose.

A goal.

Something to wake up for.

Then, Wren came along and screwed everything up. Even now, I can't bring myself to hate her for it. If anything, I made the first move by upending her life when I led the raid on Jimmy's Auto. I hit her first and she hit back twice as hard.

No. That's not right.

Wren went right for my soul and decimated me.

She makes me question things I haven't questioned before.

Things maybe I should have been questioning all along.

Two blocks ahead, I see a Pod parked beside the road. I haven't noticed anyone tailing me. Maybe Trip and the surge crew still think we were arrested by the enforcers. I jog the last few blocks suddenly eager to escape my thoughts. Like running back to the Academy is going to solve my problems, but I can dream. The Pod drifts away from the curb, carrying me back downtown.

It's strange to see the lavish high rises, clean streets, and well-dressed elite citizens milling about. Belatedly, I realize this must have been a fraction of what Wren was feeling. Eating canned beans on the floor in a dirty auto shop is a far cry from the restaurants I'm passing now. I never realized how unobtainable it all is.

A plastic lifestyle for plastic people in a plastic town filled with plastic ideals surrounded by a fence too tall to climb.

The only way in is to be born at the top.

I stick another piece of gum in my mouth as the Pod pulls into the Academy parking garage. Elle is standing outside waiting for me. I sigh. I was hoping to avoid talking to anyone until I could stop by my compartment to grab a uniform.

At least that's what I was telling myself on the way here.

In reality, I could use a few minutes to collect my thoughts before becoming Asher Axton again. I sort of liked being

Ash Laghari - the mediocre mechanic. No one had high expectations for that guy. He didn't have anything anyone else wanted. It was refreshing not to wear the Axton last name for once. I wonder if the director feels the same way?

I snort at the thought, getting out of the Pod. I doubt the director would know how to live without the power and respect his name warrants. He might have been born in a grunt neighborhood, but those days are long behind him. I'm not looking forward to seeing him again. I've ignored every call and text he has sent while I was away from the Academy. He's eager to announce me as his successor and, possibly, even more eager to set a wedding date with Elle. It's a conversation I'm not in the mood to deal with now or ever.

Elle is wearing her enforcer uniform with two cups of coffee in her hands. Her long blond hair is pulled back in a tight ponytail. She offers me one of the coffees. I accept it and take a long sip, almost groaning aloud. After a week of sub-par coffee at Wren's shop, this is absolute heaven.

"You look like trash," she says, taking another sip.

"It's nice to see you too."

Elle snickers. "I didn't think you'd be back so soon."

"Something came up. I need to talk to you and Liam. Where is he?"

Elle rolls her eyes. "He's been holed up on the operations floor since you left, trying to get as much information as he can on the surge crew members."

"How pissed is he?" I ask.

"Not pissed enough to stop worrying about you."

I wince. Liam has steered clear of any operation regarding the surge crew since his rescue. I'm sure it's more than a little triggering to monitor the people responsible for putting you through hell. Elle summons the elevator. When we get inside, she hesitates before selecting a floor.

"You should go to medical," she says.

"Not until after I talk to Liam."

"Stubborn idiot," mutters Elle. She hits the button for the operations floor. I catch her glancing at me out of the corner of her eye. She opens her mouth as if to say something then takes a sip of coffee instead.

"What?" I ask. She makes a sweeping gesture from my shoes to my face.

"I don't remember the last time I saw you dressed so casually."

"It's not like I brought a uniform with me. That would kind of counteract the whole 'undercover' thing."

"It suits you," she says. "Is that a tattoo?"

I look down. Sure enough, the tip of the bird's wing is visible in the opening of the v-neck. I shift the material to hide it.

"Yeah."

"Didn't know you had one."

I shrug. "I make it a point to hide my ink. In a way, tattoos are just beautiful scars and you don't see me showing those off. They tell a story only I can read." I give her a pointed look. "I prefer to keep it that way."

"Fair enough," Elle shrugs and takes another sip of coffee as the doors open. Two techs are waiting for the elevator. They startle when they see us, stepping aside and saluting. Elle waves them off. Liam's office is in the middle of the hall nested between group workspaces. It's practically a glorified closet with no windows and monitors lining the walls. I don't bother knocking.

Liam is sitting behind his desk, typing on his keyboard. He glances over the top of the monitor with a scowl, irritated at the interruption. When he sees it's us, his frown deepens and his eyes go back to the screen.

"Go away," he says. I ignore him and step further into the room. Elle closes the door behind us.

"I need a favor," I say.

"Why are you still here?" asks Liam, continuing to type without looking up.

"I don't have time for this," says Elle. She strides into the room and sits in the seat across from Liam. She rests her left foot on her right knee, settling in for a long conversation. "You two need to kiss and make up. Something tells me we have bigger problems to worry about."

Liam lets out an exasperated sigh. He removes the thick, black-framed glasses he only uses when he's at the computer and tosses them on the desk without folding them. It's one of those minimalist electronic desks that convert from sitting to standing with the press of a button. He has dark circles under his eyes and his hair is slightly greasy. For the first time, I notice the food containers piled on the floor beside the desk.

"I'm not speaking to him," Liam says.

"Too bad." I sit beside Elle and lean forward, bracing my forearms on his desk. Liam presses a button under the desk and the surface starts rising. He holds the button down until the angle is uncomfortable. I remove my arms and sit back. Dick.

What are we, twelve?

I bite back my comment, because I need his help. He has a right to be pissed at me. I know that. Now is not the time to pick a fight. I take a sip of the coffee Elle gave me earlier. Liam eyes it until I set it on the desk and scoot it towards him. He snatches it and chugs it in one go.

"Thank you for looking into the surge crew," I say. Liam stares at his hands, spinning the now empty coffee cup on its' edge.

"It isn't a big deal," he mutters. It is, but I don't push it. I start from the beginning. I tell Liam and Elle about working at Jimmy's Auto. I talk about Trip, citing the location of the surge den for Liam's files, and end with the ambush in the tunnels.

"I never authorized a mission to the tunnels," says Liam. "I especially would have remembered if I signed off on live rounds." He puts his glasses back on and searches for something on his computer. "I can't find a record of it anywhere."

"What about you?" I ask Elle.

"No," she says. "Are you sure they were enforcers?"

"They had the right uniforms and equipment."

"I'll keep looking. If nothing else, there has to be an entry for when the weapons and bikes were signed out. I'll let you know what I find."

"There should also be a record of Trip's call tipping the enforcers off on our location," I say.

"You're right," Liam agrees.

Elle leans back in her seat, a contemplative expression on her face. "No offense Ash, but you could have just called us and told us to look into this. Why risk blowing your cover by making a trip to the Academy?" Liam stops typing, clearly curious about my answer as well. I sigh and run my hands through my hair.

"I need to have a prisoner released from custody - Miles O'Reilly."

"The Syndicate mechanic?" Liam asks. "Wren's guy?"

"He's not her guy," I growl.

"Why?" asks Elle. "Wren didn't deliver on the bargain you made. You have no obligation to release him. In fact, it's illegal."

"I know," I say.

"Then wait until Wren helps you deliver surge-"

"She's done," I cut her off. "She can't help us anymore."

Elle crosses her arms. "Explain."

I turn my attention to Liam. "I'm sorry about the way we left things at Intrepid. I should have listened to you when you were warning me about the surge crew. The truth is, they have more pull than I thought they did. That doesn't mean I'm going to stop going after them, but I'm not dragging Wren down with me. She could have been killed in that tunnel today."

"She's an enforcer. She knows what she signed up for," scoffs Elle.

"You care about her," says Liam. It's not a question so much as a statement. I nod.

"The only reason she agreed to take on the surge crew was to get Miles back. I know what it feels like to have the people you cared about used against you. I can't do that to her anymore or I'm just as bad as Byron."

Liam nods slowly. "I'll arrange for Miles to be released under Ash's orders. We'll need to come up with a plan to find this Trip guy soon. If we do that, we can justify his release as a fair exchange for the information Wren helped you gather as part of your operation."

"What happens if someone discovers you released the prisoner before you find Trip?" asks Elle. "Ash would be arrested."

Liam nods. "Ash's name will be on the release form. If this goes sideways, he's the only one that can be tied to it." He directs his next question at me. "Are you still willing to attach your name to this?"

"Yes," I answer without hesitation.

Liam studies my face. Whatever he sees in my expression must satisfy him. He grunts and goes back to work. "I'll get things moving. You should be able to pick Miles up in half an hour or so."

"Great," says Elle. She nudges my arm and gets up. "That gives us plenty of time to stop by medical."

"I told you, I'm fine," I groan.

"Good, then it'll be a quick visit."

Elle and I leave the operations floor and take the elevator to the medical floor. We make a couple of turns and continue down the same whitewashed corridors with faded floral paintings. I wonder if the staff put them up to give patients hope? Instead, they look like still lives of funeral flowers. I sign in with the nurse at the counter and they direct me to a room down the hall. Elle follows.

"You can leave now," I say.

Elle shrugs. "I have nowhere else I need to be. Besides, if I go now you'll wait five minutes and leave without getting a check-up."

I curse internally, because that's exactly what I was planning to do. Elle smirks as if she can hear my thoughts. She leans against the wall outside the examination room making it clear she's not leaving. The nurse comes in and does a full body checkup that takes longer than I'd like. He takes some x-rays to see if I have any broken bones. When he finally releases me, I go outside. Elle is still standing by the door typing something on her phone. She clicks the screen off and tucks it in her back pocket before picking up a bag at her feet that wasn't there before.

"Well?" she asks.

"I have a couple of cuts and bruises. Some road rash. Nothing to be worried about."

"You're lucky."

She's right. I kind of wish Wren was here right now so they could take a look at her ankle. I don't think it was broken, but it would be a good idea to confirm it.

"Here," says Elle, shoving the bag at me. "I had someone find the clothes Miles was wearing when we brought him in. It'll draw less attention if he's not walking around the city in a prison jumpsuit."

I accept the bag and start walking toward the elevator. "Thanks."

The elevator dings and the doors slide open before I can press the button, revealing Jace. He's wearing a white enforcer uniform. It's similar to mine, but I wasn't aware we stocked a size large enough to fit his ego. He steps out of the elevator, blocking my path. He smirks at me.

"What, did you get sick of that grunt already-"

I sucker punch him.

Again.

Jace howls, doubling over clutching his nose. It was probably unnecessary, but screw it. I've had a long day. Besides, Byron didn't exactly bust my balls over hitting him the first time and it's not like he didn't deserve it.

"I think you broke my nose," says Jace.

"Good thing you're on the medical floor. Go talk to someone who cares."

I give him a two-finger wave as I pass. A nursing bot zooms in front of me.

"Blood detected. Please stop and wait for assistance." I send a kick into the side of the machine, toppling it over. The tracks spin in the air, but it can't right itself. "Assistance needed," the bot intones.

I get into the waiting elevator with Elle.

As soon as the doors close, she cackles. "The director isn't going to like that."

"The director can kiss my ass," I growl, choosing the button for the lower level holding cells. The scanner lights up requiring an access code, so I press my chip implant against it. "Access Denied" flashes in big letters. I curse. I should have asked Liam to get my chip switched back. I make a mental note to text him about it later. Elle scans her chip and presses the button for me. She selects the floor her compartment is on.

"I hope you know what you're doing," she says, getting off on her floor.

Yeah, you and me both.

I haven't spent much time in the basement of the Academy. It's where the holding cells and interrogation rooms are located. There's a kid behind the desk. He can't be much older than my recruits. Maybe eighteen or nineteen. He has a pimple on his chin and patchy facial hair like he's trying to grow a beard, but can't. He's reading something on his phone with his feet kicked up on the desk.

I clear my throat.

The kid's eyes shoot up. When he recognizes me, he removes his feet so quickly he almost topples out of the chair. His cheeks flush bright red. He sets his phone face down on the counter.

"I'm here for a prisoner transport. Miles O'Reilly," I say, ignoring his obvious discomfort. The kid types something into the computer. He backspaces more characters than he types, clearly frazzled.

"Looks like all the paperwork is here. I just need you to sign the screen and I can bring him out for you." He swivels the tablet around so I can sign.

"That won't be necessary. I can get him myself."

The kid freezes. "That's against protocol," he squeaks.

"I'm sure the director won't mind," I say. The kid looks scared, so I lean into it. I stand tall, towering over the desk and give him my best glare. I probably just look constipated, but whatever. It's worth a shot. I made Wren a promise and I intend to keep it. Miles will be leaving the Academy today one way or another.

The kid actually gulps. I'm betting on the fact that he doesn't know what my relationship with Byron is truly like. Byron has gone to enormous lengths to portray himself, Jace, and me as the perfect example of an elite family. I guess the ruse is believable, because the kid turns the screen back around without a signature. He tells me where Miles' cell is located and hands me a temporary key fob to unlock the door. I take a few deep breaths.

I'm nervous.

The realization shocks me. I'm not sure why. The first time I met Miles, he leveled a gun at my chest. Maybe that's it. It's just the adrenaline kicking in. My body preparing itself for a fight based on our shared past. I know I'm lying to myself the second the thought crosses my mind. Miles is Wren's best friend. Releasing Miles breaks the last thread binding us together. This is where our paths converge. I hate everything about this. I force myself into the hall lined with holding cells.

The air conditioning is on full blast. Most of the prisoners are curled up on their bunks, wrapped under thin blankets. Everything about this space is meant to keep prisoners uncomfortable. On edge. Willing to negotiate. When I get to the cell number the kid gave me, Miles is laying in his bunk tossing his shoe at the ceiling and catching it before it hits his face. He couldn't look more at ease if he tried. It rubs me the wrong way.

"Miles O'Reilly?" I ask with more venom than I intended.

He glances up. "Who's asking?"

"A friend of Wren's."

That gets his attention.

"What does this have to do with Wren?"

He sits up abruptly and slips on his shoes before standing in front of me. Miles looks different from the last time I saw him. Thinner maybe. His cheekbones and jaw are more prominent like he hasn't been getting enough to eat. There are dark circles under his eyes and his lips are chapped. His shoulder-length, blond hair is greasy and unkempt. He's about my height and I know from his file he's the same age as Wren. He would look like a dead man walking if it weren't for the glint of determination in his eyes.

That's not the look of a man who has given up.

He scowls. "Wait a minute, you're the enforcer from the raid. What did you do to Wren?"

He snakes an arm through the bars so quickly it catches me by surprise. His hand wraps around my neck, but his grip is too weak to choke me. I swat his hand away.

"Wren is fine. She negotiated your release."

Miles looks suspicious, but he allows his hands to fall to his sides.

"Where is she?" he asks.

"Home. At her apartment."

"Take me to her," he orders.

This guy.

I bite my tongue, silently re-committing to not being a jerk. I just wish he would make it easier for me. I tap the key fob against the lock. Miles is swinging at me before the cell door finishes opening. I catch his wrist, redirecting his punch and sending him off balance. He falls on his back, the air whooshing out of him with a huff.

"Are you done trying to beat up your rescuer?" I sigh. "Look, I'm risking a lot by getting you out of here. I need you to put these on." I shove the bag of clothes Elle gave me between the bars. I toss the handcuffs at his feet. He eyes the handcuffs with apprehension. "They're just for appearances. I'll take them off when we're outside."

Miles gives me a look that could be interpreted as something like "eat shit and die." I turn around to give him some privacy to change. He clears his throat when he's finished and I turn around. I reach for his elbow and he balks.

"I have to escort you outside. People will ask questions if a prisoner is walking around freely." Miles' jaw clenches. "Do it for her," I say, adding it as an afterthought. Miles' eyes flicker to mine. For a moment, they soften. I reach for him again and, this time, he lets me take his arm.

I keep expecting someone to stop me, but no one does. Not the kid at the desk. Not the officers I pass in the hall. It's almost too easy to walk Miles out to the parking garage. I find a spot without cameras before releasing his arm. I pause with the key above his cuffs.

"Before you were brought to the Academy, you were being held at a black site. Why is that?"

Miles shrugs. "Guess I pissed someone off when I was arrested."

Right. We're still playing this game.

"Whatever you're involved in, will it put Wren in danger?" I ask.

"No," he growls. This time, he doesn't seem to be lying. I'm tempted to drag him back down to an interrogation room, but I remove the cuffs instead. I doubt Wren would be pleased to discover I beat up her best friend before releasing him. I'll just have to trust he has her best interests at heart. As soon as I remove the restraints, Miles bolts. I watch him disappear around the corner. He'll probably take the train back to his apartment. I could have offered him a ride, but screw that.

He can walk home.

Chapter 17

Wren

"**W**hat are you doing?"

I glance up from the stack of invoices I'm sorting through. Miles is standing in the door of Dad's office. He has a brown paper sack in his hand, his face flushed red from the wind. Miles and I started back at Jimmy's Auto the day after he got home. Ash returned most of Miles' equipment when we reopened the shop, so we didn't have much to replace. Business is slow today. Miles went for a walk to kill some time. I could have gone with him, but there's an awkwardness surrounding our relationship that wasn't there before he was arrested. So, I decided to stay behind and clean.

In some ways, it still feels like I'm betraying Dad by going through his stuff. There's a finality in it, as if I'm saying goodbye all over again. I'm beginning to think it's okay to let go. The truth is, this shop has never felt like my own and it won't until I can find the courage to move on. To permit myself to heal and to stop feeling guilty for living.

"Cleaning Dad's office," I say, stating the obvious. I pick up the picture frame I unearthed and offer it to him. It's a photo of my parents, grandparents, and me standing in front of Jimmy's Auto. I don't remember taking it. I'm maybe five years old in the picture. It was the day my grandfather officially retired and signed the shop over to Dad, continuing the legacy. In the picture, Grams is smiling up at my grandfather. My mom and dad are holding me, kissing me on either cheek. I'm laughing.

We look like a family.

It was hidden under a stack of papers on the desk, turned glass down, as if Dad couldn't bear to look at it. It makes sense. After losing grandpa and mom, I could see how that picture would bring more sorrow than happiness. After losing Dad, you would think it would be outright depressing. I still feel a twinge of sadness because you never stop grieving those you've lost. At least, not entirely. But the sadness isn't as soul-crushing as it once was. It's accompanied by warmth and joy, a sense of gratitude that they were a part of my life at all, and a desire to remember them the way they were.

In love. Together. A family.

My family.

Miles glances at the picture, but he doesn't take it from me. I see the exact moment his expression morphs from curiosity to pity. I try to keep myself from wincing, setting the picture up in a corner of the desk I've already cleared.

"You don't have to do this, Wren," he says gently like he's trying to placate a cornered animal.

"Yes, I do," I sigh. "This is me trying to move on. I would appreciate it if you didn't look at me like a kicked puppy while I do it."

Miles stares at me, completely taken off guard. I can't say I blame him. This is the first time I've pushed back. I'm just so fed up with him and Grams babying me. I didn't realize how bad it had gotten until Ash showed me what it could be like to talk to someone as an equal. Someone who didn't expect me to shatter into a million pieces when they gave me their honest opinion. Someone who didn't see me as a victim.

"What crawled up your ass?" Miles asks. He tosses the bag of food on the desk and crosses his arms. "Are you still pouting about that pansy prick leaving?"

What in the world.

Now, I'm pissed.

"Absolutely not. This is me telling you I'm tired of being treated like a casualty of something that happened two years ago. Two *years*, Miles. That's how long you and Grams have been tiptoeing around me and I'm sick of it. If the enforcers need more protection fees, you don't tell me. You take on some side work and pay them before I find out." Miles' eyes widen. "Yeah, I knew about that. You need to stop shielding me from the world. I know you care about me and I appreciate what you're trying to do, but it has to stop. I want my best friend back."

The truth is, this argument has been a long time coming. Miles has had a chip on his shoulder ever since he got back from the Academy. I couldn't blame him at first. He looked rough like he hadn't had enough food or sleep for far too long. He was also angry.

Is angry.

Angry at me. Angry at Ash. Angry at the whole world.

He told me he thought I'd gone soft. That all it took was a few "fancy meals" and some "special attention from the pansies" to make me switch sides. His words, not mine. Like somehow I was a terrible person for winning the lottery and trying to save his sorry ass.

"I'm right here, Wren. What more do you want from me?" Miles asks, his voice low.

"I want you to treat me like your partner."

"I do treat you like my partner-"

"No, you don't. You're still lying to me about something. You feel guilty. We've known each other since we were five. I can tell when something is eating at you-"

Miles kisses me. Hard.

I kiss him back.

It's like a continuation of our argument, both of us trying to get the last word in. It's not bad. It's everything a kiss should be - spontaneous and passionate with an underlying hunger - but it's also strange. Like coming home to find someone has rearranged all the furniture.

It's not bad, but it's not good either.

I break the kiss, knowing it was a mistake.

I take a few steps back. We're both breathing heavily. Miles' eyes look like the sky after a thunderstorm at sea.

"I love you, Wren," he whispers. "I feel guilty because you tried to rescue me. You joined the enforcers and put yourself in danger trying to take down the surge crew. You had to deal with *that pansy* living in your apartment for a week. I love you and I let that happen to you. What kind of a partner does that make me? Of course, I feel guilty."

I love you.

The words bounce around inside of my head. Of course, he loves me. I love him too. He's my family. Always has been. Always will be. But this is different. This is Miles saying he's *in* love with me and I'm not sure that's something I can deal with.

A few months ago, I probably would have been ecstatic. I had a crush on Miles for years. A borderline unhealthy obsession that I wished would turn into something more. I think we might have been headed towards a relationship at some point, but then the *incident* happened and derailed my life. I couldn't blame the guy for keeping his distance after that. He knew I was hurting. He isn't heartless - he didn't want to push me towards something I wasn't ready for.

It took me a long time to start to trust people again. It took me even longer to want to be with someone intimately. Eventually, I got over that too. My flings lasted about as long as an ice cream cone in the summer sun. They never met my family, I never introduced them to Ariel, but that was never the point. I wasn't with them to find a life partner. I was with them to prove to myself that I was okay.

Step by step I pulled myself out of the deep dark throes of depression and took back control of my life. I was ready to give it a shot with Miles, but he didn't seem interested. I just assumed he moved on and that our moment had passed. Then, Ash crashed into my life with the subtlety of a wrecking ball through a glass window and changed everything, including the feelings I thought I had for my best friend.

You shouldn't have kissed him back.

"I love you too," I say slowly, "but not in the way I think you want me to." Miles releases my arms and steps away, a distant look in his eyes. "I'm sorry. Just...give me some time?"

"Sure, Wren. Whatever." He goes into the shop, leaving me alone in Dad's office.

I should go after him, but I'm just so tired. Tired of hiding how I feel because I'm worried about how it will impact others. Tired of smoothing over relationships like it's my job to be the salve that heals our wounds. Just so damn tired of taking care of everyone else but myself and my daughter. My phone vibrates. It's sitting face-up on the desk, so I can see the screen. It's an unknown number. I ignore it, but then it buzzes again with a second message from the same anonymous sender. It's probably a client. I sigh and unlock the screen. I could use a distraction right now, so I might as well get back to work.

I drop the phone, letting it clatter to the desk when I read the text.

"Miles," I croak. He jogs back into the office, something in my tone alerting him that something is wrong. He picks up my phone and reads the messages, his expression darkening. It's a picture of Robbie. He's tied to a chair with a gag in his mouth. There's blood running down his face from a gash near his hairline. His pupils are blown out with fear.

"The surge crew has Robbie. They want us to meet them in thirty minutes or they will kill him." My voice cracks. I have a client's car in the shop waiting for them to pick it up. We'll have to take that. I haven't had a chance to replace Indy. My mind is already charging ahead, trying to figure out how to get Robbie back unharmed. The picture is so zoomed in I can't make out his surroundings. I don't recognize the address. Just like the setup with Trip, we're going in blind. I stop in the middle of the shop and dial Grams.

I don't know how they got to Robbie. They were all still staying at Ash's apartment despite Miles' complaints. Ash said he would contact me when Trip and the surge crew were no longer a problem. I didn't hear from him, so I told them to stay put. What if they have Grams and Ariel too?

"Hello," says Grams.

"Where are you? Are you safe? Is Ariel with you?"

"What's going on? I'm at the pansy's apartment with Ariel. Don is at work. Robbie went for a walk around the building."

"You let him leave the apartment?" I practically yell.

"He's going stir crazy in here. I thought he could use the exercise. The building is secure, so I didn't think it would be an issue. He should have been back by now."

"The surge crew has him," I choke out. "Stay in the apartment with Ariel. Don't open the door for anyone but me, Miles, or Ash. I'm going after Robbie."

"Wren-"

I hang up on her and take a deep breath. They're safe. I open the driver-side door. Miles stops me with a hand on my arm.

"They'll kill us if we go," he says, his voice calmer than I feel.

"It's Robbie," I say, throwing his hand off. "We have to go."

"I know. Jesus, don't you think I know that." Miles kicks the trash can by his desk sending it flying across the room, its contents littering the shop floor. "We need a plan"

"We don't have time."

I put on my jacket, snatching the keys from a hook by the door. I wish we had a gun. Miles' shotgun was confiscated during the raid and I haven't replaced it. Stupid. That should have been the first thing I bought when I returned to the shop. Miles opens the garage door and I back the car out. He shuts the door and, a few seconds later, he jogs around the side of the building. I didn't even think about locking up the shop. That's how desperate I am to get to Robbie.

Miles just manages to get the passenger door closed before I floor it. He puts his seatbelt on as I take the first turn on two wheels. This is a terrible idea. I know that. Miles knows it too, but this is Robbie. We don't have a choice. Keeping one hand on the wheel, I pull out my phone and call Ash, putting it on speaker. I still have his number saved in my contacts. I couldn't bring myself to delete it. The line connects on the second ring.

"The surge crew has Robbie. They're going to kill him if Miles and I don't meet them now. We're on our way. I'll text you the address. Just promise me you'll get Robbie out of there." I rush everything out in a single breath. My voice is shaking. My hand is shaking.

The whole world is shaking.

"Miles is with you? Wren, he's with-"

"Promise me," I say, cutting Ash off.

Ash sighs. "Yeah, I promise. But he's-"

I end the call and toss my phone in Miles' lap.

"Text Ash the address." Miles stares at my phone. I glance back at the road and narrowly avoid a washing machine sitting in the middle of the street, because this neighborhood has it out for me.

"Miles! Focus. I need you to text Ash the address."

"We don't need his help," Miles yells, as if raising his voice increases the validity of his opinion.

"Do it for Robbie," I say. It's a low blow, but we don't have time to argue. Miles looks like it pains him, but he copies the address from the surge crew text and forwards it to Ash. He pulls out his phone and starts typing. I don't know what Ash can do. According to the GPS, we'll be at the address in fifteen minutes. Sooner with the way I'm driving. That's not enough time for him to organize a team and get across town. I'll just have to stall them to give Ash as much time as I can to get Robbie out of there.

I don't think I've ever driven this fast or this recklessly. That includes the surge run Trip sent us on. The GPS notifies us when we arrive, but it isn't necessary. I count at least five guards lined up in front of the entrance. They're not even trying to be discreet, armed with semi-automatic rifles and standing in the open. It's meant as a deterrent, an open threat to anyone who thinks about crossing the surge crew. I kill the engine and get out with my hands up.

I'm not an idiot. I don't have a death wish despite my decision to come here.

"I'm Wren Parker. We're here for Robbie," I say, proud that my voice doesn't waver. Miles gets out of the car with his hands raised, mimicking my stance. The guards surround us. One of them produces a chip scanner he uses to confirm our identities.

"It's them," he says. "Take them inside."

Someone pats me down, searching for weapons. They're giving us more credit than they should. I would have shown up in my pajamas if that's what I was wearing when I got their text. Miles' guard finishes searching him, then we're led inside. There are two guards assigned to each of us. That leaves only one guy protecting the entrance.

I hope that makes it easier for Ash and the enforcers to raid the place.

Inside, there's a small front office with a few desks. The walls are bare, the paint peeling and faded with age. A few more guards are sitting around looking bored out of their minds. I do a quick count. I hope there aren't a ton of people on the roof or stationed in the surrounding buildings for Ash's sake. They lead us through a door at the back of the office and into the warehouse.

I don't know what I was expecting. I guess part of me was picturing a scene similar to the surge den Ash and I met Trip at. It certainly wasn't this. There are pallet racks pushed up against the walls on both sides. Instead of boxes, there are hammocks strung between the beams - each compartment a unique living space decorated by the owner. It's almost like an apartment complex. I see colorful rugs and pillows occupying some platforms. There are flat screens and string lights fed by a cluster of extension cords that screams "fire hazard." Surge crew members are draped over the platforms, sitting on the edge with their feet dangling off or simply lounging with their friends. They're talking, the buzz of fifty different conversations filling the room. I almost question if we're in the right place.

Then, I see him.

Robbie is tied to a chair flanked by a handful of guards. I don't think they've moved him at all since they sent the picture. The cut on his head looks worse in person. I don't know why they bother guarding him at all. It's not like he can move. Robbie tries to say something, but it's muffled by his gag. One of the guards slams the butt of his rifle into Robbie's face. He cries out.

I lose it.

I tug against the guards holding me back, but they're too strong.

"You got what you wanted. We're here. Let him go," snarls Miles.

"I could, but I'm not going to." It's a woman's voice that sounds like honey flowing over rust. She steps out from behind the wall of guards. Her blond hair, cut short, is spiked to give it some volume. She's wearing a familiar torn canvas jacket with patches on the arms and across the front. Her team ambushed Ash and me at the dive bar during my first patrol. She's the woman Robbie worked for.

"What are you doing here?" I ask.

She quirks one perfectly sculpted eyebrow. "This is my crew." She pulls something out of her breast pocket and lets it drop between her fingers.

My locket.

Ash hadn't contacted me about it, so I assumed it was lost. She smirks at my stricken expression.

"Imagine my surprise when I saw a picture of my latest prospect, an enforcer mole, and a kingpin inside." She sets her hands on Robbie's shoulders, making him flinch. There are a few murmurs in the crowd, surprise evident on their faces. The conversation has died down, our audience hanging on to every word the woman is saying.

"Don't touch him," I say. The woman smirks. She removes her hands from Robbie's shoulders and walks around the chair, stopping in front of Miles. She runs her finger down his face. I'm surprised he doesn't try to bite it off, he looks practically rabid with anger. It's the kind of pissed off that overrides reason and makes you do something stupid. I pray he keeps his cool for Robbie's sake.

"I'm not a mole," I say, trying to distract her to give Miles time to compose himself. The woman rolls her eyes, but she stops touching Miles and stands in front of me instead.

"Please, I saw you and pretty boy at the bar in your uniforms."

"If you knew who we were, then why arrange the setup in the tunnel? Why not kill us? It would have been easier." I'm stalling. The longer I keep her talking, the more time I give Ash to get here. I wonder if he's on his way or if he decided not to come. It's not like he owes me anything. If he won't do this for me or Robbie, I hope he'll at least do it to hurt the surge crew.

"Because killing Asher Axton would bring a storm down on my crew I don't need or want." She gives me a curious smile. "No, it would be easier if he was gunned down by his own people."

The massacre in the tunnel was an assassination attempt. Which means, she has at least one contact inside the enforcers. There had to be at least a dozen enforcers who went against protocol when they fired on us. Which means she either has a lot of loyal enforcers reporting to her or someone powerful enough to give the order.

"Sorry, we ruined your plans," I mutter.

"Don't worry, I'm glad you escaped. If you hadn't dropped your locket, I wouldn't have linked you to him." She inclines her chin at Miles. I glance at my friend. She referred to him as a kingpin. What does that mean? Why is Miles so important to her? Aside from our run-in at the bar, I don't remember seeing the woman before. I don't think she's one of my customers. I'm usually pretty good at keeping track of who comes in the shop.

"What do you want?" Miles asks.

She stops pacing in front of him. "Nation-wide exclusivity on surge distribution."

Miles snorts. "I don't have the power to authorize that."

"You do if you want your friends to walk out of here." The light playful tone in her voice drops to something more threatening. Miles glares at her. I've never seen that look on his face. Like he would kill her without a second thought if the guards released him. It's terrifying.

"I need my phone," growls Miles. "It's in the car."

I have no idea what she thinks he can do for her. We run an auto body shop. I have no idea what that has to do with surge distribution, but going to the car will buy us a few more minutes so I'm all for it.

Let the crazy lady think she won.

I look at Robbie. His face streaked with tears. He looks younger than he is. Dwarfed by the guards standing around him, made smaller by our circumstances. I want to tell him that it's going to be alright, but I don't want the guard to hit him again if he responds.

This is all my fault.

The thought keeps repeating in my head over and over again. I put Robbie on a collision course with the Syndicate when I left for the enforcers. I blew his cover when I lost my locket. That's on me. I should have been more careful. Even as I think it, I'm not sure how I could've been. If I hadn't joined the enforcers, Miles would still be locked up.

"Search the car," the woman orders. Two of the guards standing watch behind Robbie leave. I tense when I realize I left my phone in the car. What if they see the text message we sent to Ash? I should have asked him to delete it. The woman paces in front of us looking thoroughly in her element while I have a silent panic attack. I scan the room, searching for an exit I might have missed the first time. The door at the back of the building has been boarded over. There are windows near the ceiling. I might be able to reach them if I scale the pallet racks, but then what? Jump a few stories and break my leg? Yeah, no thanks. There are crew members everywhere. The only way out of the building appears to be the door we came in through. The guards haven't relaxed their hold and Robbie isn't in any condition to walk, let alone run.

In summary, we're stuck.

There are a few shouts and gunfire. It's coming from the entrance behind us. I try to look around my guards to see what's going on, but they won't move.

Then, there's a loud bang.

Surge crew members scream and start scrambling down the pallet racks. A few of them manage to pry the barrier off the back door, escaping outside. Crowd control bots speed into view, creating a perimeter around our group. The woman frantically fishes something out of her pocket. It looks like a small gray remote. She pushes a button and the bots stop.

"You shouldn't have called your friends," she says. "I was willing to make a deal."

"Go to hell." Miles spits on the floor at her feet.

It occurs to me that this was probably why she wanted to capture the lead bot - to develop something that could stop them. The indicator lights on the bot weapons change from red to blue. I think back to my training classes at the Academy. Red is live rounds. Blue is for tranquilizer darts. The woman's face pales. She frantically hits the button on the remote.

The lead bot shoots Robbie in the head.

Chapter 18

Ash

I didn't know the successor title came with a dose of pheromones that only attracts dipshits.

I might have reconsidered taking the position. You know, if I had actually had a choice.

"Can't talk now, busy," I say, shoving past the third Council member to stand outside of my compartment in as many days. The man stutters out an apology, but I ignore him. The other squad leaders chatting in the hall fall silent when I pass. I'm surprised word of my promotion hasn't gotten around. It hasn't been announced, but since I returned to the Academy the Council members have been relentless. They all want something.

A favor.

Additional funding.

More protection from the enforcers for their assets.

You name it, they've pitched it.

It's not the norm for Council members to hang out on the enforcer leadership floors. If they did, we would probably have wood paneling and golden toilet seats for their pompous asses. They usually wouldn't be caught dead slumming with us peasants, so you'd have to be an idiot not to realize something is going on.

I wonder if Jace received the same onslaught of requests from the Council, but I doubt it. Jace doesn't do favors. If he offers you something, you have to ask yourself what he's getting in return. He doesn't do anything for free. Despite Byron's comments about Jace's impulsiveness, I've seen the ruthless side of him. The side that is more similar to Byron than either of them would care to admit. Jace is a master manipulator when he wants to be, but he buries it under an in-your-face personality.

I'd go so far as to say many of the Council members would approach Byron with a proposal before going to Jace. At least Byron would listen to what they have to say before kicking them out. I tilt my neck from side to side, trying to get it to pop. There's a massive knot in my right shoulder that keeps growing larger by the day, sending waves of pain into the base of my skull. I've been pulling insane hours since I got back to the Academy, sleeping an average of four hours a night and spending the rest of it behind a computer with Liam. Not to mention, I still have recruits to train and my daily duties as an enforcer squad leader to fulfill.

I can't count the number of times I've almost caved and asked Glitch if she has heard from Wren. I don't know if they're still talking, but they seemed to be friends. She's definitely on better terms with Wren than I am. At least, I assume that's the case.

You don't ditch a girl after kissing her with a hastily written excuse and expect her to be happy about it.

I had a good reason, but...still. I could have told her in person. We could have had a conversation like adults, but I just had to get out of there.

Her daughter asked for a stuffed T-Rex.

That detail would be insignificant to anyone else - a cute gesture from a little kid just trying to make a new friend. I know better, because I've been in her shoes. I know what it's like to grow up poor. I was just like her. The kid with a single mom who didn't have enough money to put food on the table, let alone buy toys. Ariel could have asked for anything in the world, but she chose a stuffed T-Rex.

Why? She thought it was my favorite.

I'm pretty sure she could ask me for my heart and I would rip it out of my chest to make her happy, because I love Wren Parker. And you can't love Wren Parker without loving her daughter too.

Some part of me hoped she would come back to the Academy, but then what? I apologize, tell her how I feel, and we ride off into the sunset? Yeah, right. Technically, she still has a job here. I asked Liam to make sure no one would come after her for leaving. The other recruits asked about her, but I gave them the same excuse I gave everyone: Wren is still out on assignment. She'll be back when it's over.

If only that were true.

Wren has everything she needs: her family, Jimmy's Auto, and Miles. I'm not on that list. Even thinking Miles' name makes me grit my teeth. There's something about him that puts me on edge, but I have no idea what it is. Liam dug into his background before authorizing his release, but he didn't find anything alarming.

Worse than that, we haven't been able to find any documented reason for why he was being held at a black site. Liam chalked it up to some kind of clerical error, but I don't buy it. A clerical error is when you assign a prisoner to the wrong cell in the same block. A clerical error isn't transferring a prisoner from the Academy to a black site without solid documentation. Unfortunately, I haven't had time to do a thorough investigation. My focus has been on finding Trip and fending off Byron.

No joke, the man has been hounding me since I got back.

About the successor announcement. About planning the wedding.

I really need to tell him the engagement is off. Maybe Elle and I can stage a blow-up fight in the cafeteria or something. I groan, taking the stairs two at a time to the basement. It's just one more thing I don't have time to deal with right now. I convinced Byron to wait a few more weeks before making a televised statement. I told him I wanted to take down the surge crew to have something to talk about on my broadcast.

My gift to the people, because I'm a regular humanitarian.

In reality, I needed a few more days to bring Trip in to ensure Wren's safety. Thankfully, Byron bought it. So, I'm working around the clock trying to meet an impossible deadline with limited resources and no sleep.

Elle arrested Trip this morning. Liam managed to find the two or three places he could be staying. We decided to send teams to all of them. I would have liked to be more discreet, but we don't have the time. I was in Council meetings the entire day. Elle sent me a text when they picked up Trip. I almost walked out while Byron was talking, but that would have landed me in his office for another lecture and it would have taken me even longer to get out of there.

Today, they approved funding for the bot expansion. Jace wasn't there. Maybe he was worried I would punch him a third time. It's a valid fear. I can't imagine a time when seeing him won't make me think about what he did to Wren. For his sake, it's better if we aren't in the same room for a while.

When the meeting adjourned, I texted Elle and Liam to get Trip set up in an interrogation room. Then, I stopped by my compartment to swap out my dress clothes for my uniform, because there's no world in which I interrogate a Syndicate drug runner dressed as a news anchor. I dealt with the Council member who followed me home and headed straight for the basement. Elle and Liam are waiting for me in the lobby. The seat behind the front desk is empty. Elle must have dismissed whoever was on duty.

"Cameras?" I ask.

"Already turned off," says Liam.

"Elle, you're with me. Liam, you're in the viewing room."

Elle leads the way to the interrogation block. Liam gives us a nod, disappearing into the room next door to monitor. Neither one of them comment on the orders I'm doling out or my lack of manners. They know how much this means to me and what's riding on this interrogation being successful. I take a deep breath. I know exactly how I'm going to start this conversation, already imagining Trip's responses in my head and figuring out how to reply.

When I open the door, my plan ceases to exist.

Trip is sitting behind the desk with his hands chained in front of him. He has his feet kicked up on the chair looking completely at ease.

Sometimes going on a rampage is exactly what you need.

Sure, your closest friends will look at you like you're some kind of sociopath who needs psychological help.

Sometimes it's worth it.

Elle pulls me off of Trip with more force than I would have thought she was capable of. His face is a bloody mess. I'm not even sure how many times I hit him.

"Cool it," she yells. Trip cackles like a lunatic. "Sit your ass down or you're out of this interrogation."

That gets through to me. I tug out the chair and sink into it. Elle takes the seat beside me.

"Why did you turn us into the enforcers?" I ask.

He shrugs. "I don't know. Bosses orders."

"Not good enough."

"It's all I got."

"You don't seem surprised to see me here in an enforcer uniform," I press.

"What can I say, I don't surprise easy."

Trip knows he's pushing my buttons. Either he has a death wish or he's more afraid of what the surge crew will do to him if he talks to us. That's fine. I just have to make sure I'm scarier than his boss. Elle steps in before I can.

"Do you like TV, Trip?" she asks sweetly. Trip smirks at her, his eyes dropping to her chest. I sit back, allowing Elle to take the lead. She clearly has a plan.

"Yeah, sweetheart. Maybe we can watch a show together." He winks.

He's a waste of oxygen.

"That's good," says Elle. "You know, I think you could have a show of your own. We'll give it a snappy title like *Evan Murphy Tells All*." He pales when Elle drops his real name. Liam must have hacked his chip implant to get his real identity. Elle pulls out her phone and takes a picture of him. She turns it around so he can see it.

"I think this can be the thumbnail." Evan pales. "What do you think, Ash?"

I pretend to look at his picture, contemplating her question. "Yeah, we could start with an emergency Council broadcast. Those end up on personal media devices."

"That means every television, tablet, and phone will get a notification," Elle continues, picking up where I left off. "Your picture will be on the public viewing screens downtown. That means your face is projected four stories tall on the side of every building. Have you ever wondered what it's like to be famous, Evan?"

"I'm not talking," he says. Trip leans back in his chair, trying to appear unphased by what Elle is saying, but I'm not buying it. He knows he's in trouble.

"It doesn't matter. Do you really think the surge crew will risk it after seeing a broadcast like that?" She turns to me and shrugs. "Guess we can let Evan go. He's not going to tell us anything."

"Wait, you can't do that," he cries, dropping the tough-guy persona. Elle glances at me, I can see the smile in her eyes.

She's in her element. She turns back to Trip, keeping her expression neutral.

"Then give me a reason not to," she says.

"Why did you turn us in?" I repeat my question from earlier. Trip takes a deep breath and sighs.

"We knew you and Wren were with the enforcers."

"Then why didn't you kill us?"

He scoffs, crossing his arms. "Kill the director's son? Yeah, no thanks. The surge crew doesn't need that kind of heat. Our leader thought it would be easier if you were killed by your own people. We could make it look like an accident."

I raise an eyebrow. Not only did the surge crew know we were enforcers, but they knew exactly who I was from the beginning. I watch Trip carefully, but there's no indication he's lying to me. It makes sense in a twisted way. They needed to stop Wren and me from poking around, but they didn't want Byron to wage a personal war against their operations. Byron wouldn't think twice about me getting gunned down on the job. I'm sure he'd make a half-assed attempt to find the enforcers involved, but I doubt he would connect the dots between the surge crew and the attack.

I'm not sure anyone could.

Liam has been trying to locate the enforcers who orchestrated the attack for days with no results. Someone knew how to cover their tracks. Of course they did - they were being backed by the Syndicate. A few weeks ago, Byron told me he was beginning to suspect the enforcers had a mole. He was right, but it's worse than he thought. We have more than one.

"How did you know we were enforcers?" I ask. I've been on broadcasts in the past, but I've always managed to stay out of the spotlight. People are generally more interested in hearing from Byron and Jace. Byron excludes me whenever possible. Even my proposal was recorded at a distance.

"Our leader saw you at the bar," says Trip.

"What bar?" I ask.

"The Iron Maiden."

I think back over the last few weeks. The only bar Wren and I went to together was Intrepid. It takes me a moment to realize that isn't entirely true.

"The Iron Maiden," I repeat. Trip nods. "Does it have a faded red awning?"

"Yeah, that's the one."

That's when it dawns on me.

The hijacked bot. The blond woman who held Wren at gunpoint.

I describe the woman to Trip.

"Yeah, that sounds like Rook."

"Rook?"

"She's the leader of the surge crew," he says.

Shit. We came face to face with the leader of the surge crew and didn't know it. Did Wren know who she was? No. She couldn't have. She definitely would have told me, especially when she found out Robbie was working for her.

"What would it take for the surge crew to leave Wren and Jimmy's Auto alone? She's not with the enforcers anymore. There's no reason to go after her."

Trip laughs. "Yeah, right." I give him a look that makes his Adam's apple bob in discomfort. He clears his throat. "Our people found your girlfriend's necklace in the tunnel. It had a picture of her with one of our new crew members. I think his name is Richie? Ricardo?"

"Robbie?"

"Yeah, that sounds right. There was another guy in the picture our leader recognized."

"Longish blond hair, blue eyes, about six feet tall?"

"Maybe. Your girl was a kid in the picture. The guy could be taller now."

He's *family*. Wren told me that herself. It's not unreasonable that he would be included in a family photo.

"How did your leader...Rook... recognize him?" I ask.

"The dude is a Syndicate kingpin." He must see my confusion, because he clarifies. "A higher up. Someone at the very top."

"Are you sure?" Elle asks. I'm glad she jumped in. My mouth is the consistency of sandpaper.

"Rook seemed sure. She had seen him before. Said he's in charge of national operations after a recent...reorganization." Trip shrugs.

That's when his words start to sink in.

Not only did I meet the leader of the surge crew and let her escape, I let the leader of the entire Syndicate operation walk out the back door. I slam my fist on the table making Trip and Elle jump. Did Wren know about Miles' affiliation with the Syndicate this whole time? Was she playing me?

My phone buzzes in my pocket. I pull it out, but I'm not in the right headspace to talk to anyone right now.

It's Wren.

I swipe to answer the call before I can convince myself it's a bad idea.

"The surge crew has Robbie," she says. There's a rumble underlying her words like she's in a car. I get out of my seat, taking a few steps away from Trip and Elle. "They're going to kill him if Miles and I don't meet them now. We're on our way. I'll text you the address. Just promise me you'll get Robbie out of there."

"Miles is with you? Wren, he's with-"

"Promise me," she says, cutting me off. The fear in her voice cuts deep.

I let out a breath. "Yeah, I promise. But he's-" Wren ends the call. A few seconds later a text comes through with an address.

That's when I realize I don't care if she played me. It doesn't erase my feelings for her. She's knowingly walking into a trap to save Robbie, putting herself on the line to keep her family together. Again. I may not know her history, but I know *her*.

"What's at this address?" I show Trip my screen. He blanches, his face turning pale.

"It's...uh," he swallows. "It's the slaughterhouse."

"The what?"

"It's not an actual slaughterhouse. Just some old warehouse deep in surge crew territory. We use it as housing for newer members, interrogations, and getting rid of people," Trip rushes out. I want to break a few of his teeth out of his skull, but I fight the urge. I storm out of the interrogation room, Elle jogging to keep pace.

"Who was that?" she asks.

Liam joins us in the hall.

"The surge crew took Wren's kid brother. She's going after him. We have to send as many squads as we can to this address right now." I toss my phone to Liam who catches it against his chest. "She's with Miles, the Syndicate mechanic I released. He's the leader of the Syndicate." I watch the expression on Elle's face as it all comes together. She looks at me with a mixture of pity and fear, on my behalf.

My name was on the release form. If anyone finds out I let the leader of the Syndicate walk, I'll be arrested for treason.

"I'm going after them," I say. Liam gives me my phone back.

"I'll head to the operations floor to get things set up. You two go to the garage," Liam says, typing away on his phone. I stop in the stairwell.

"You don't have to help me. You should be putting as much distance between us as possible."

"Not a chance," says Liam. He thumps my back, before heading up the stairs. I look at Elle.

"We've got you," she says. This operation is already botched. Elle has to know that. I search her expression for any hesitation, but there isn't any.

I guess we're doing this.

Ten minutes later, I'm sitting in an enforcer Pod with a squad of riot bots. Liam managed to get four Pods in total. Elle is in one. Liam managed to pull two squad leaders he trusts for the other two bringing us to four humans and twenty-four crowd control bots. I would have liked more units. Actually, I would have liked to have any semblance of a plan at all. When we arrive at the address, I hammer the button to open the Pod door. The virtual assistant screeches out a warning.

Wait for the bots to leave first.

You're in danger.

Blah, blah, blah.

I ignore it.

Two guys are tossing a car parked in front of the warehouse and a guard on the door. I take out the guard at the entrance. The bots catch up, shooting the other two with tranquilizer darts. That's when Liam takes control of the bots. They crash through the front door. I go in behind them, sweeping the room for assailants. The room is clear, four unconscious guards laying on the floor.

"Breach the warehouse," I say.

"The others aren't in a position-" Liam starts.

"Do it now," I bark.

Liam directs the bots forward so they crash through the door leading into the warehouse. I follow them, bile rising in my throat as I take in the scene. Robbie is tied to a chair in the center of the room with a gag in his mouth and blood running down his face. He's in bad shape. Rook, the surge crew leader, has a gun pressed to Robbie's head. Wren and Miles are standing in front of Robbie, held in place by two guards each. Surge crew members are scrambling down pallet racks, escaping through the back door.

Where is Elle?

My bots speed into the room. They take out a few of the surge crew members trying to escape before forming a circle around the group in the middle. Then, they freeze. That's when I notice the gray remote Rook is holding. I curse. The lead bot they stole. We recovered it a few days later and everything appeared to be in place, but they must have figured out how to create a tool to control them. I've never seen anything like this. Axton AI security is impenetrable. We've never had a breach.

Correction - we haven't had a breach, until now.

Elle finally arrives, crashing through the back door. I have a moment to hope that her bots won't be impacted before they freeze too, caught up in whatever signal Rook is broadcasting.

"Rook is overriding the bots," I say. There's silence on the line. "Liam, can you do something?"

I'm greeted with more silence.

Something is wrong.

Then, the bots start moving again. The lights on the bots turn from blue to red, indicating they're using live rounds instead of tranquilizer darts. Rook pounds on the remote, but the machines won't respond to her. If she isn't in control and Liam isn't answering, who is directing the bots?

"Liam, they switched to live rounds. Do something!"

That's when the lead bot shoots Robbie.

"No," I yell, sprinting towards them. Robbie is blown backwards from the impact, the chair toppling over. Wren screams in anguish. She pulls against the guards and, this time, they let her go. She races forward, collapsing over Robbie. Miles rushes after her. Rook and the rest of her people run for the exit. The bots manage to take out a few of them, but I see Rook slip out the back door. Elle tries to follow them, but someone starts shooting and she's forced to take cover.

There are few times in my life I have felt completely helpless. I didn't know the meaning of the word until this moment.

Wren is sobbing, cradling Robbie's head. Miles is trying to get her to leave. His eyes are scanning the bots wildly. He knows what's happening, but Wren won't leave Robbie and Miles refuses to leave her. They're going to be killed.

I don't think. I run faster, skidding to a stop between the bots and Wren. I wave my arms, trying to make myself the target. The bots remain immobile, the red lights still on.

I panic. I thought this was going to work. I don't have a backup plan.

Then, the bots power down.

I let out a breath, dropping my arms.

"You're an idiot! Are you trying to get yourself killed?" Elle asks, jogging towards us.

"Most bots are programmed not to shoot an Axton or a Council member. I took a chance. It paid off," I say, still in awe that it worked.

"You didn't know for sure?"

"No."

"Jesus, Ash." Elle's phone rings. It's probably Liam, wondering what is going on. He lost control of the bots and our comms went down. I can't imagine what he's going through right now. Panicking that Wren and Miles were going to be gunned down, while sitting uselessly behind the controls. Elle takes the call, giving me a look that says our conversation is far from over.

I turn around. Wren is still laying over Robbie's body, shielding him with her own. Her chest is heaving with sobs. Miles is still tugging on her arm.

"He's gone, Wren. We have to get out of here," Miles begs, his voice choked with emotion. Tears are streaming down his face. Wren ignores him, completely lost in her grief. I squat down beside them.

"Wren," I start, gently. She looks up, her green eyes shining with a pain that completely guts me. I loop my arms around her, hugging her against my chest. She hits me with closed fists, trying to get me to let go so she can go back to Robbie. There's some power behind them. It hurts, but I don't let go. She tires herself out after a moment and falls against me, sobbing into my shirt. Her fists ball into the fabric of my uniform.

"I'm so sorry, Wren," I say. Tears running down my face and falling off my chin. "I'm so, so, sorry."

There's nothing else to say.

Chapter 19

Wren

My link to reality has been severed.

I hear people talking, but I can't make out their words. That's a good thing. If I can distance myself from this situation, I can pretend this isn't happening to me. That this is someone else's life and I'm just a passenger inside their head.

"Wren," Ash shakes me again. I wonder how many times he has said my name. I blink. His brown eyes are like melted chocolate, warm and inviting. The kind of eyes you could spend a lifetime getting lost in. I wish I was the kind of girl who could.

"Ash," I whisper, trailing my fingers down his face to confirm he's real. He captures my fingers and gives my hand a reaffirming squeeze.

"That was Liam," says Elle, rejoining us. "An emergency broadcast just went out naming Wren Parker and Miles O'Reilly fugitives. Congratulations, you're famous."

I glance at Miles. He's sitting cross-legged behind us staring at the ground beside Robbie's body. I've never seen him look so dejected. Broken. Empty. I untangle myself from Ash and scoot closer to my best friend. I don't touch him. I don't even try to comfort him. When Miles is like this, he prefers to withdraw. He did the same thing when his mom walked out.

He stayed in his room for days without talking to anyone. He rarely ate and barely slept. He came out a few days later and pretended like nothing happened. Miles copes with loss by going into social hibernation, shutting everyone out so he can focus on staying alive. He processes his grief and moves on quietly, preferring not to dwell. I can't judge him. I'm not exactly a sharer when it comes to working through my problems. Miles just takes it a step further.

"What do you want to do?" Elle asks Ash.

I know what she's really asking him: Should she arrest us or let us go?

I'm not sure why the Council put out a call for us. Maybe they figured out we work for the Syndicate or that I betrayed the enforcers? If Ash lets us walk, he would be ignoring a Council order. He would also be releasing two confirmed Syndicate members, something I know he would never do.

So, you can imagine my surprise when Ash says, "Let them go." His lips are pressed in a grim expression, his fists clenching at his sides like he wants to beat up the person who put him in this situation.

"You'll be arrested," warns Elle. She gives him a look that says she'll be the first in line to haul him into the Academy.

"Whatever happens, happens," says Ash. They have a silent conversation that ends in Elle shrugging and Ash nodding at her. I don't believe for a second he's as apathetic as he sounds. This is his career. Actually, it's more than that. It's his whole life. Letting us go means letting the Syndicate win. Albeit, in a small way. We're just mechanics, it's not like we're that important in the grand scheme of things.

"I know who you are," Ash addresses Miles. Miles glances up at him, still sitting on the ground. Tears run off his chin, splattering on the tops of his thighs. He tugs his shirt up, using the inside of the collar to wipe his face. Of course, Ash knows who Miles is. He was the one who released him from the Academy. Ash sighs when Miles stands with his arms crossed, failing to acknowledge his comment. "You need to leave town tonight. I'll talk to the director about the bots. If they can be hacked, they need to be decommissioned."

"Leave town? We don't have travel permits," I say, logic catching up to me.

"I'll handle it," grunts Miles. We don't have enough credits for travel permits. I'm not sure how he's going to arrange that unless he has a bunch of cash stashed somewhere I don't know about. Miles clears his throat. "Can you make sure Robbie gets a proper burial?" His voice catches on his brother's name and my heart breaks for him.

"I'll do everything in my power to ensure it," says Ash. He turns to me. "I'm sorry for how I left things between us. I hope you have a good life, Wren. You deserve it."

"That sounds an awful lot like a goodbye."

"That's because it is." Ash scrubs a hand through his hair.

"Come with us," I hear myself say. I have no idea where we're going, but I know I want him at my side.

"I can't," he sighs. "I'm done running. From Byron. The successor title. All of it. It's hard to bury your head in the sand when you've seen how people live outside of the elite sectors. I'll probably screw it up, but I figured taking my seat at the table is the first step." He gives me a shy smile. I try to remember the man I met a few months ago - the cocky pansy with a holier-than-thou attitude and a one-size-fits-all morality construct. It's hard to believe they're the same person.

"I'm proud of you," I say, wrapping my arms around his waist. Ash tugs me against his chest, resting his chin on my head.

"I love-," he whispers, too low for Miles or Elle to hear.

"No," I groan. Ash tenses up. "Don't you dare finish that sentence. You don't get to tell me that when you're saying goodbye. Tell me when you see me again."

"What if I don't?"

"Then you'll never know if I'll say it back."

Ash chuckles. "You are the most stubborn person I've ever met." He kisses my brow and takes a few steps back, putting space between us. "Goodbye, Wren."

"Goodbye," I mouth, backing towards the door. I already miss him. It's pathetic, but it's true. I've been missing him for the last week. His warm, reassuring eyes. His chewing gum addiction. Even his irritating drive to climb the walls I've built just to get a peek inside at what makes me tick. Telling him how I feel will only open us up for more pain and we've both had enough to last a lifetime.

Miles nudges my shoulder and I nod, letting him know I'm ready to go. I don't want to leave, but there's nothing left to say. I force my feet to move, refusing to look over my shoulder. We jog out the back door and down the street. My heart is heavy in my chest, my breath rattling my ribs. There are unconscious surge crew members sprawled out across the sidewalk. No one tries to stop us. Everyone must have bailed when the doors were breached. Miles tugs out his phone and makes a call. He tells the person on the other end to meet us a few blocks away and hangs up.

"Who was that?" I ask.

"A friend. You know her," he says.

That wasn't sketchy at all.

I'm too out of breath to argue. I keep pace with Miles until we see a beat-up station wagon idling under an old gas station awning. Glitch is behind the wheel and Roy is in the passenger seat. Miles tugs open the back door and scoots across the seat to leave room for me to get in.

"What...? How...?" I ask. Glitch pulls out of the gas station, heading in the opposite direction of the warehouse. She quirks an eyebrow in the rearview mirror.

"I'm not touching that with a ten-foot pole. Ask lover boy," she says. Miles scowls, sinking lower into the seat.

"Glitch works for me," he grumbles.

"Doing what?" Jesus, it's like pulling teeth to get any information from him.

"I'm a hacker," Glitch offers. It makes sense considering the woman's nickname. She couldn't have been less discreet. It's so overt it's covert? Something like that. It's fitting. The woman isn't passive about the persona she puts out to the world. She owns who she is and doesn't pretend to be anyone but herself. Why would her nickname be any different?

"What do you...hack?" I ask, unsure of the correct phrasing.

"The Ascent Day lottery, for one. How do you think you got a winning ticket?"

"Glitch," Miles admonishes.

"What? She's going to find out sooner or later."

Everyone knows the lotteries are rigged by the Council, but it's not unheard of for grunts to win. They have to let just enough of us in to make it seem like a fair system. I was so desperate for a way to save Miles I thought winning might be a sign from the universe that I've been through enough and karma was sending a win my way. I should have known better.

"Wait a minute, you knew you were giving me a winning lottery ticket?" I ask Miles.

"Yes," Glitch responds for him.

"Glitch, can you shut up?"

She rolls her eyes, returning her focus to the road.

"Did you know there was going to be a raid on Jimmy's Auto?" I ask, putting two and two together. Miles was on edge when he gave me the ticket. If he knew it was a winner, that makes sense. He was handing me a free pass out of the grunt sectors. Miles glances at me. The guilt etched into his expression tells me everything I need to know. "How? Why didn't you try to stop it?"

"That's a long story," he says.

"And that's a cop-out," I counter.

Miles turns in his seat so he can meet my eyes. "This isn't something I can explain in the two-minute car ride. Just...trust me for a few more hours and I'll tell you everything. Deal?"

There's that word again. It doesn't matter what I say. I know Miles won't reveal anything until he's ready.

"What about Roy, does he work for you too?" I ask. Roy is sitting quietly in the front seat. He didn't even acknowledge us when we got in the car.

"Absolutely not," Roy growls, sounding about as pissed as I feel. He glares at Glitch and she shrinks under his scrutiny. I saw them dancing together at Intrepid, but I'm not sure how their relationship progressed while I was away from the Academy. Roy has to feel betrayed. I know I do. It's the natural response when you find out someone has been lying to you. I have never seen Glitch so uncomfortable. "Apparently, I'm in danger. Glitch asked me to come with her," says Roy.

It makes sense. Regardless of labels, anyone with eyes can see there's some kind of relationship between the two of them. If it came out that Glitch is involved with the Syndicate, I could see how that would pose a problem for Roy.

"I'm assuming you gave yourself a winning ticket too. Why?" I ask. Glitch glances at Miles. He nods, indicating it's alright to respond. Since when did Miles become the gatekeeper to what information I'm given?

"I needed to find a way to bust Miles out, so I decided to join the enforcers. I shouldn't have approached you at all, but I was curious. He has talked about you for years. I wanted to meet the person that has him all tied up in knots."

"She doesn't have me 'tied up in knots,'" says Miles.

"Could've fooled me. Anyways, I talked to you when I shouldn't have. Then you joined the enforcers. That was unexpected. That being said, our friendship was genuine." She gives Roy a meaningful look. "Ours too."

Roy snorts. I feel like this is a continuation of an earlier conversation between them. Glitch takes another turn and I realize we're heading to Ash's apartment. Sure enough, a few minutes later we pull into the underground parking garage. Glitch slams the car in park and rushes to get out of the car, like spending any more time with Roy's hostility will make her implode. She punches in the access code on the panel next to the elevator.

I should be surprised she knew where Ash's apartment is. I should be even more shocked she could get access. If she's capable of hacking the lottery, I'm sure finding a secret apartment is child's play. We pile into the elevator in uncomfortable silence. Light music plays in the background, the overture of the shit show. Roy and I stand off to the side, united on the front that we have no idea what's going on and are mutually pissed off at being kept in the dark.

When we get to Ash's unit, Grams is standing in the kitchen with sandwich fixings spread out on the counter. She frowns at us when we walk in, wiping her hands and coming out from behind the counter. Ash's apartment is different from the last time I saw it. There are blankets left rumbled on the couch, a tablet laying on the coffee table, and toys littering the floor of the living room. It looks more lived-in than it did before. It's a good change. Max leaps off the couch and practically tackles me trying to lick my face. I pet his head until he drops back to all fours. His tail is wagging so fiercely that his back legs are swaying side to side.

"Where's Robbie?" Grams asks. I wince. She takes in my expression, her hand going to her mouth. Her eyes fill with tears.

"He isn't?"

"He's dead," says Miles, brushing past her. He plops down on the couch, kicking his dirty boots up on the white leather upholstery. Grams bursts into tears. I wrap my arms around her, shooting Miles a dirty look he promptly ignores. I know he lost his baby brother, but we're all hurting. That doesn't mean he can treat people like garbage. Glitch and Roy stand in the foyer, unsure of how to proceed. Grams sniffles and wipes her eyes.

"Who are your friends?" I break our hug so I can introduce them, but Glitch beats me to it.

"I'm Glitch, this is Roy." Grams hugs them both, taking them off guard.

"I'll make a few more sandwiches for everyone," says Grams.

"You don't need to do that, ma'am," says Roy. The poor guy looks like he'd rather gnaw off his arm than take another step into the apartment.

"I need to stay busy," chokes Grams. "I'm sorry." The tears won't stop falling. She wipes her eyes again and hustles to the kitchen. "Ariel just went down for a nap," she says. I'm excited to see my daughter, but I think we all need a few minutes to process our new reality.

"When does Don get here?" Miles asks. Grams drops something in the kitchen.

"He should be here soon. He usually picks up groceries after work," she says. Roy and Glitch take a seat at the bar so they can talk to Grams while she's making sandwiches. I pick up Miles' feet and drop them off the couch, making room for myself. I sit beside him.

"I'm sorry," I say. Miles grunts.

"Yeah. Me too." He grabs the remote off the coffee table and turns on the Council news channel. Sure enough, there are side-by-side pictures of Miles and me on the screen. They're asking citizens for their help to find us and there's a sizable reward for any information leading to our arrest.

"Well, this is nothing short of a catastrophe."

"Yep, that sums it up," Miles sighs. The front door opens and Don appears, his arms laden with grocery bags. He pauses in the entryway when he sees us.

"Sup, pops," says Miles. He crosses his arms behind his head, sinking further into the couch.

"What are you doing here?" Don asks. To my knowledge, this is the first time Don has seen Miles since he was released. Don's eyes go from Miles to the TV, still showing our pictures. He drops the bags. "You need to leave."

Miles rolls his eyes. "Yeah, that's the plan. Are you coming with us?"

"Why?" asks Don.

"I don't know," says Miles, sounding bored. "As of today, I'm the only son you have left. I thought you might want to be a part of my life."

Don leans against the wall for support. "What happened to Robbie?"

"His head met a bullet."

"Miles!" I snap. Miles crosses his arms.

"Are you coming with us or what?" Miles asks again. His voice is unnaturally cold. I've seen Miles threaten Syndicate brawlers at our shop. I've watched him haggle in the marketplace. I've seen him get into a few scuffles. I have never heard him sound like he does now.

Miles and Don have had a strained relationship since his mom walked out. According to Miles, Don never tried to find her. He didn't seem depressed or even particularly upset that she left. He simply pretended nothing was wrong and went on with his life. He checked out of being a parent, leaving Miles to look after Robbie. Still. They both lost Robbie today. You'd think they could put aside their differences for a while to be there for each other.

"No, I'm staying," says Don. Miles gets off the couch. He offers me his hand.

"Time to go then. Do you want to wake up Ariel or should I?"

"I will," I say. I get up, ignoring Miles' hand. I don't accept help from strangers and, at the rate we're going, I have no idea who my best friend is anymore. I go to the bedroom, opening the door softly. Ariel is asleep in the center of a queen-sized bed. It dwarfs her, making her appear even younger than she is. Her brown hair is strewn across the pillow, her lips parted with sleep. She looks like sleeping beauty. Her arms are wrapped around the stuffed T-Rex she showed me in the video. It's purple and orange with fuzzy fur that's already starting to look a bit dirty from being dragged across the floor.

There are two suitcases open on the floor with clothes spilling out of them. I check the dresser drawers, but it looks like Grams didn't unpack anything. I guess she wasn't expecting to be here for as long as she was. The familiar wave of guilt gnaws at my insides. I'm asking them to move again. They haven't been home in weeks. I hate uprooting my family. I hate being away from them. Most of all? I hate that I can't give them the life that they deserve. That I'm hopelessly inadequate when it comes to taking care of the people who mean the most to me.

I pile the clothes back in the suitcases and zip them up. I'll have to check the bathroom for toiletries, but I can do that in a few minutes. Kneeling next to the bed, I push Ariel's hair back from her face. Her nose crinkles and her eyes blink open slowly.

"Hi, baby girl," I smile.

"Mommy!" She scrambles over to me, throwing her arms around my neck. I hug her against me, rocking side to side.

"I love you," I say.

"Love you too."

"Grams is making sandwiches. Do you want one?"

"Okay," she says with an adorable yawn. I scoop her up, grabbing the T-Rex before rejoining the others in the living room.

Miles is sitting on the couch where I left him. He's trying to watch the TV around Don who continues to yell at him. Grams is setting plates on the bar in front of Glitch and Roy. I carry Ariel to the island, setting her down on a barstool.

"These are my friends, Glitch and Roy," I tell her. "This is Ariel."

Glitch uses the back of her hand to wipe mustard from her mouth. She beams at Ariel. "It's nice to meet you. Miles has told me a lot about you." I raise an eyebrow. I'm not comfortable with Miles talking about Ariel to people I don't know. Glitch seems alright. There's a lot I don't know about her, but I don't think she's a serial killer or anything like that. That doesn't mean he should be talking about Ariel. Especially, without running it by me first.

"Does Miles make it a habit to tell random people about my daughter?" I ask, sounding as accusatory and on guard as I feel. Glitch draws back.

"I don't think so. Miles and I are close. He trusts me and I trust him. I only knew enough about his family to help keep them safe. You have my word." Her eyes shine with determination to make me believe her. It isn't necessary. I know she's telling the truth.

"Your word doesn't mean anything," mutters Roy.

"Language," says Grams. She smacks her spatula on the counter making us all flinch.

"Sorry, Ms. Parker," says Roy. He gets up and takes his plate to the other side of the room by the windows.

"He said a bad word," says Ariel. She has more sandwich on her face than in her mouth. I grab a paper towel to clean her up.

"He did and you should never ever say that word," I tell her. After I finish cleaning her face, I crinkle up the paper towel and throw it away. A heavy hand falls on my shoulder. I flinch.

"Sorry," says Don, removing his hand. "You don't have to go with him, you know. You and Ash must have gotten close. I've known him since he was a kid. He doesn't go in to the field with people he doesn't trust and you made the cut. You could talk to him. If you explain that you had no idea what Miles was involved in, he could probably get you pardoned."

"And what exactly is Miles wrapped up in?" I ask, crossing my arms. "If you know, please tell me. From where I'm standing, I don't have a choice. Let's say I ask Ash for help. I would still have to answer to the Council. I would still be put on trial and they would question me about Miles. Even if everything went my way, I can't go back to work at Jimmy's Auto and I doubt they would let me rejoin the enforcers. I would have no way to provide for Grams and Ariel. That's not an option."

"Miles is Syndicate leadership."

I take a deep breath, my mind working overtime to process what he's saying. I don't want to believe him. I assume you don't rise to power in the Syndicate overnight. That means Miles has been working with them for years without me noticing. That either makes me a horrible friend or him an excellent liar. Maybe both.

Sadly, I still trust him to do the right thing. He wouldn't be taking Grams, Ariel, and me with him if he didn't care about our wellbeing. If he's a leader in the Syndicate? So be it.

"I'm going with him," I say.

"Then, you're not as smart as I thought you were." Don's words hit me like a slap to the face. He has always been nasty to Miles and Robbie, but his anger has not once been directed at me.

"Enough," says Miles, laying a heavy hand on Don's shoulder. "Stop giving Wren a hard time. You're coming with us."

Don's look turns murderous. "No, I'm not."

Miles quirks an eyebrow. "Do you think the elites will accept you when it comes out that not one, but two of your sons were working with the Syndicate?"

"Of course, Director Axton knows I'm loyal."

Miles laughs. It's a callous, haunted sound. "You sure about that?" I watch the doubt slowly creep into Don's expression. Miles shrugs and snatches a piece of cheese off the counter.

He folds it and shoves the whole thing in his mouth. "Come with us or stay behind and die. I don't care," he says while chewing his food.

"I'll pack a bag," Don mutters.

Chapter 20

Ash

I watch Wren and Miles leave the warehouse. It takes every ounce of restraint I have to keep my feet rooted in place. She asked me to come with them, but I couldn't because I made a promise.

Two promises, actually.

The first was to eliminate the Syndicate. I could have arrested Miles. He would have been put on trial and interrogated. We probably could have dismantled the whole organization if he truly is as high ranking as Trip thinks he is, but what would that solve? Wren once told me that the Syndicate gave people like her a way to breathe when the Council watched them drown.

She has a point.

I got to know the people who fell through the cracks while I was working at Jimmy's Auto. People like Wren and her family. Hardworking people who couldn't find a place in the new world, so they were left behind. They didn't join the Syndicate because they're inherently evil. Maybe some do, but you could say the same thing about enforcers. Any organization that offers money and power draws both crowds - the innocents and the corrupt. Wren forced me to see the system as it truly is, beneficial to a select few and detrimental to the masses.

Which leads me to my second promise. I told Wren I didn't want to be the villain in her story. I could cross that one off after letting her escape, but that wasn't the intent of my promise. If I want to make things right, then I need to stop pretending to be someone I'm not.

When Byron named me his successor, I balked at the idea. I threw a tantrum of epic proportions, but it doesn't change the fact that I'm still next in line to lead the Council. I didn't want to be a part of a broken system. Now, I'm beginning to think the only way I can change the Council is from the inside. It won't be overnight. The elites are slow to accept change. It could be years before Byron is ready to step down and longer still for the Council to warm to my ideas, but it's a start.

I owe it to Robbie to try.

"You know I have to arrest you," Elle sighs, breaking our silence.

I can't say I'm surprised. She told me as much before I made my decision. Elle is an elite through and through. She's willing to break some of the rules and she'll lie to protect the people she cares about, but she will never do anything that could be considered treason. Elle believes in the system. She might complain about Jace and the Council, but fundamentally she thinks they make our city a better place. I just let a Syndicate leader walk. That's treason.

"Yeah," I reply, holding out my hands so she can cuff me.

"You aren't going to fight me on it?"

"You joined the enforcers to put an end to the Syndicate. You can't pretend like what I just did is alright." Elle snaps the cuffs on my wrists, securing them a little tighter than necessary. I wince and pull away from her.

"Ow, what was that for?"

"For being an idiot," she seethes. Her eyebrows are drawn together, creating the crease on her forehead that only appears when she's truly annoyed. "You joined the enforcers to take down the Syndicate. I joined, because I wanted to help people like my best friend." She pokes her finger into my chest.

She joined the enforcers for me? I had no idea.

"You could have stopped them from running," I say.

Elle sighs. "You love her."

"Yeah." I don't even try to deny it.

"If they were arrested, they would have gone to trial. You know how that works - grunts are guilty until proven innocent. I don't think our friendship would survive that. It's not a risk I'm willing to take."

"Elle-"

"You're the director's son. He'll be pissed, but you won't be executed for treason."

"I'm sorry you picked a terrible best friend," I mutter. She gives me a sad smile before pulling out her phone and trying someone. I hear it roll over to voicemail.

"Where is Liam?" Elle asks.

"I thought he called you a few minutes ago," I say.

Elle shakes her head. "That was headquarters. They wanted to know why we're out without authorization. I fed them some excuses to buy us some time, but I need to talk to Liam so we can get our story straight.

Her call rings out and the voicemail clicks on. Elle curses. Liam always answers his phone. Elle starts another call and puts it on speaker. An enforcer on duty under Liam answers. Elle recites her ID number. She gives the enforcer the address and asks for a prisoner transport.

"There's already a transport routed to that location," he says. Elle shoots me a look.

"Where is Liam?" Elle asks.

There's silence on the other end. "Oh, you mean Lieutenant Richards? He was arrested a few minutes ago. Not sure why-" Elle ends the call. Her eyes come to mine, a blue that could freeze the arctic. I hear Pods pulling up outside. The Syndicate moles must be responsible for this. They're going to pin this on Liam and me. I'm fine with taking the fall. I expected to do just that, but Liam isn't an Axton. They'll kill him for letting two fugitives walk. What do we do?

"We stick to the plan," says Elle, reading my mind. "They already know Miles escaped. I need you to buy me some time so I can get Liam released, then we'll figure out what we're going to do about you. Let's meet them outside, we don't have anything to hide." She's right. It's our best play until we can find out more.

"If I'm detained, can you make arrangements for Robbie?" I ask. Elle nods. She takes my arm, leading me to the exit. When we get to the office, she raises her weapon so it's pointing into my ribs. It's all for show. She has to sell this as a legitimate arrest. Her freedom and Liam's life may depend on it. When we get outside, there are no fewer than twenty Pods parked in the street. Enforcers train their weapons on us. Where were all of these squads when we needed to rescue Robbie?

"Don't shoot!" Elle calls. "I have a prisoner."

"Hey, that's Asher Axton," one of the soldiers mutters. He lowers his rifle. Whispers spread through the crowd as others do the same. Jace exits one of the rear Pods. He's wearing his gaudy lieutenant dress uniform with the gold epaulets. I've never seen an enforcer wear one of those outside of the Ascent Day celebration.

"You've got to be kidding me," I grumble. Jace tsks.

"Your time with the grunts managed to erase a decade of elite schooling in a matter of days. What a waste," he scoffs.

"I'm sorry, would my foot up your ass be a more appropriate greeting?" I ask with a smirk I know will drive Jace crazy. He inclines his chin at an enforcer to his right. I recognize the guy, he was in my training class at the Academy. I think his name is Joel. He doesn't move.

"Rough him up," Jace growls. "That's an order."

Joel gives me an apologetic look before punching me in the stomach. It's hard enough to make me fold over, but I can tell he pulled his punch. Joel steps back. I take a few breaths, playing it up, before straightening back to my full height. Elle tenses up beside me. I know she doesn't approve of unnecessary force, but getting herself arrested with me isn't going to help anyone.

"I need to talk to the director," I say.

"Do you think I would take a traitor to the Axton mansion?" Jace laughs.

"No, but as designated successor I command it." Elle inhales sharply beside me and a few of the enforcers gasp. After the Council voted to remove Jace, Byron kept my new position under wraps. There would have been broadcasts, pictures, and a ton of publicity surrounding an announcement of that magnitude, all of which would have been terrible for an undercover operative. Until now, only Council members were privy to the change in command.

"He's right," says Elle, trying to hide her amusement. "According to Council law, a successor can request a trial with the director himself when accused of a crime before a hearing."

"I know what the law says," Jace seethes. His face is red and he keeps clenching his fists like he's thinking about ordering Joel to hit me again.

"Careful, Jace. You're beginning to sound like a grunt." I smirk. A few of the enforcers laugh, turning Jace's face impossibly redder. They try to hide it with coughs, but the damage is done.

"Fine. We're taking him to the Axton mansion. Inform the director we want an audience." Jace stalks away with his hands clasped behind his back, his posture ramrod straight from the years of scolding. Elle leads me to another Pod. Four other enforcers get in with us, including Commander Harper. He doesn't bother to hide his open disdain for me with a scowl etched across his face and a glare that could bore a hole to the center of the Earth. I try to ignore him. The Pod leaves the outer districts and carries us to my childhood neighborhood. Immaculate lawns filled with maintained flower beds and fountains are hidden behind gates. I watch a drone drop off a parcel on someone's front porch. I wish Wren could see the antique cars our neighbors park outdoors like lawn ornaments.

Lamborghini. Ferrari. Rolls Royce.

I check them off in my mind like an elite version of bingo. It's something I wouldn't have noticed before spending time in Wren's neighborhood. I guess I had become desensitized to it over the years without realizing it. I needed the wake-up call, the stark reminder of where I came from. The Pod stops in front of the Axton mansion, the gate gliding open automatically when we approach. Armed security guards patrol the circle drive. The building itself is extraordinary and oddly out of place. The rest of the homes are newer, taking on modern trends with massive floor-to-ceiling windows, white walls, and crisp lines. The Axton mansion reeks of old money. It looks like it belongs in a travel brochure for Western Europe. What's the word I'm looking for? Villa? Chateau? Whatever.

It's fancy.

Tall towers on either side of the building end in turrets. The front entrance showcases two massive wooden doors framed by a pair of seven-foot-tall dragon statues. The building looks like it's going to devour me. I know from experience the people are worse. I get out of the Pod unprompted and walk with Elle and the other enforcers to the door. They have their weapons trained on me, but it doesn't matter. I'm not going to run. Two servants open the double mahogany doors when we approach.

"The director will receive you in his study," one of them says quietly. Jace comes in behind us, a spring in his step as he enters the foyer. He's not even bothering to hide his smugness at my predicament.

"You two, come with us. Elle, you're dismissed," says Jace. Elle presses her lips together. She doesn't like being ordered around, especially by Jace. She gives my good arm a reassuring squeeze before she releases it and steps back.

"Yes, sir," she grates out. Commander Harper and another senior enforcer flank me, leading me through the halls of the Axton mansion. Jace picked them for a reason. Commander Harper is a die-hard loyalist to the Council cause. I'm assuming his other pick is the same. Regardless of what happens, the two men beside me will remain loyal to the Council. Right now, I'm a criminal of the state. They are definitely not on my side. We take a staircase to the second level where the private rooms are. Jace knocks on the door to the study.

"You may enter," my stepfather says. Jace opens the door. The director is sitting behind a massive wood desk. It's the kind of thing you expect to see in movies from the 1800s about important political figures. You know the type. Well-groomed, rich white men in tailored suits with a Jace-sized ego. It's the kind of desk where decisions that impact entire nations are made. The walls are lined with books that are dust-free despite being antiques. Even though he runs a technology company, Byron has always preferred to read physical books. He shies away from tablets and phones where possible.

Byron himself is in his usual black suit, white shirt, and a red tie. The tie hasn't been loosened at all. It looks like he's getting ready to start his day, not winding down for the evening. There are two seats positioned in front of the desk. Jace takes one, slouching and propping his left ankle on his right knee. The guards still have their weapons trained on me. I didn't make it this far to get shot, so I remain standing.

"Guards, you can wait outside," Byron says. Commander Harper salutes and leaves the room with the other enforcer.

He closes the door behind them to give us some privacy. Goody. "Ash, take a seat."

"No thanks, I'd rather stand," I say. I take a few steps forward and hold the back of the chair with my good hand. It's hard to appear confident and intimidating when you're wearing handcuffs, but I do my best. Byron glares at me, steepling his fingers under his chin. He's not used to being told no, but I've never been one to follow social convention. He should know that by now.

"The penalty for treason is death. I should have you killed where you stand," he growls.

I should *have* you killed, not "I *will* kill you." Figures.

My stepfather refuses to take an active part in my life even when it comes to ending it. I committed my life to a cause I no longer believe in to get approval from a parent who is ultimately indifferent. That was my choice, I own that, but I didn't expect it to feel this terrible.

"You won't," I counter. "You'll sit there and listen. You told me once you respected me for my opinions and my honesty, so here it is: I didn't let two fugitives escape. Wren Parker helped us infiltrate the Syndicate crew responsible for the distribution and sale of surge. As compensation for her help, she negotiated the release of Miles O'Reilly."

"You stopped the bots from killing two known Syndicate sympathizers," says Byron.

"I stopped the bots from killing an enforcer and an unarmed civilian after murdering an innocent kid." My grip tightens on the back of the chair until my knuckles whiten.

"That kid," scoffs Jace, "was a Syndicate mechanic. He was hardly innocent."

"He was a child," I say, raising my voice. I meet Byron's eyes, refusing to back down. "Unmonitored bots should not be used in combat for obvious reasons. They can be hacked. They don't have a conscience. You said the reason you created the Council and Axton AI was to prevent the same loss of life you experienced firsthand. Can you seriously say you're making the world a better place for that boy's family?"

I let my words hang between us. Byron looks...shaken. A crack is starting to form in his confidence, so I keep hammering. "You asked me to be your successor. I accept, but it will be on my terms and I will get a say in the Council policy. I won't be content standing by your side as a fat, dumb, and happy puppet like Jace has done for years." Jace crosses his arms and scowls. "I will not let actions like this stand. Taking down the Syndicate isn't worth the life of an innocent."

"That's-" Jace starts, but Byron holds up a hand to silence him. He interlocks his fingers together as if he's praying. He rests his lips against his knuckles. I don't lower my gaze. I don't even breathe.

"I'm sorry," he says, letting his hands fall to the desk with a thud. It takes me a minute to pick my jaw up off the floor. Byron never apologizes. I didn't think he knew the word. "I have failed you and I have failed the people. I'll call a Council meeting tomorrow and we'll decommission the bots. I want you to lead the discussion as my successor." I don't know what to say. For the first time in my life, I don't have a witty comeback or a snide remark.

"This is bullshit!" Jace yells. He stands up so fast, that his chair topples backward and crashes to the floor. "He betrayed you and you're still making him your successor? You're an idiot."

"That's enough," snaps Byron. "I told you six months ago and my opinion hasn't changed. Get on board with your new role or you're out." Jace laughs. It's a terrible sound lilted by pain, like a wounded wolf trying to dodge cars on an expressway. Jace pulls a gun out of his waistband, aiming it at my stepfather's chest. He doesn't hesitate. His hands are completely steady when he pulls the trigger.

The shot is deafening in the small space, punctuating a scene that plays like a stop motion film. Byron slumping in his seat. A red hole in his shirt above his heart. The bloom of blood the same color as his tie. The scenes assault me one by one until I'm sure I will remember them in vivid detail for the rest of my life.

At that moment, two things become abundantly clear.

One, I drastically underestimated how far Jace was willing to go to seize power. And two, I don't know my stepbrother at all. Jace tosses the gun on the floor and tackles me at the same time the door flies open. Commander Harper and the other guard rush in, staring in wide-mouthed horror at my stepfather's body.

"Ash shot the director," Jace screams. He scrambles off of me, pointing his finger in accusation. Vaguely, my mind starts to piece together the facts of the evening. Jace was planning this from the beginning. He sent Elle away for a reason. This wasn't a crime of passion, it was premeditated. The facts run through my mind in a jumbled mess, but they don't pass my lips.

"It was Jace," I mumble, but Commander Harper ignores me. While the other guard is still staring, he grabs my arm and hauls me to my feet with a bruising grip. I don't know why I bothered. It's my word against Jace's. I'm the enforcer that went rogue and sided with the Syndicate. Who are they going to believe?

"I can call a prisoner transport to take him to the Academy. Where do you want us to hold him in the interim?" Commander Harper asks. Jace leans against my stepfather's desk with a look bordering on triumph. I can't believe I'm the only one who sees it.

"Take him to the kennel in the courtyard. I don't want my father's murderer under the same roof." Jace dismisses us with a wave of his hand. The guards hook me under the arms and haul me out the door. I can't tear my eyes away from my stepfather. We've had our differences over the years, but that doesn't mean I wanted him dead.

A memory drips over my eyes like paint on a canvas beginning to take form. My mother in a white wedding gown at the courthouse. Byron in a suit. She had a smile so radiant it could power the city. A look of utter devotion on Byron's face. They were...happy. In love. It was easy for me to forget that after mom died, but it was evident to anyone who spent more than a few minutes in the same room. They loved each other. He deserved better than to die at his son's hands.

I don't fight the guards as they lead me through my childhood home, but they keep their grip strong. We pass the door that led to my childhood bedroom and the wall of Axton family members immortalized in oil paintings. When we get to the end, I trip and barely manage to catch myself.

There's a portrait of me.

Byron must have had it painted and hung since the last time I was here. Unlike the other Axton's, I'm not wearing a suit. He took my enforcer Academy graduation photo and had it recreated. The simple fatigues stand out against a sea of dark tuxedos and evening gowns - a black sheep dressed in white.

"He treated you better than you deserved," growls Commander Harper, tugging my arm so I'm forced to continue.

"I didn't kill the director," I repeat, hollowly.

"I'll handle this. Call the Academy and have them organize a prisoner transport," orders Commander Harper. The other guard nods and leaves us. The commander leads me to the courtyard. I contemplate trying to overpower him. I could probably do it, but where would I go? The Syndicate? I almost laugh aloud at the thought.

When we get outside, the commander half drags me across the courtyard to the dog kennels tucked in the corner where Byron used to keep his Great Danes. The enclosure is plain compared to the rest of the courtyard, a chain link box built for utility rather than appearance. I'm not sure why Byron didn't tear them down. Maybe he thought he would get another dog one day. The commander drags open the door and shoves me inside, slamming the gate behind me. He snaps the lock in place.

"Did you consider her at all when you decided to kill the director?" asks the commander.

"Who?"

"Elle," he booms. "As your fiancé, her reputation is on the line. She'll be questioned. She could even be arrested for treason. I'll never understand why she chose a grunt. She could have done so much better." On that, we can agree. He spits on the ground at my feet. "A kennel for a Syndicate dog. Seems fitting."

He gestures for two enforcers I don't recognize to guard me. They stand outside of the gate to make sure there's no chance I can escape. I shuck my pride and sit in the dirt. The sky outside is an angry gray. It looks like it's going to storm. What will happen to Elle? She has powerful friends, the commander included. I know they will do everything they can to clear her name. A traitorous grunt killing the director makes sense, but the elite golden girl? No way. She'll have to make them believe I deceived her. That she's heartbroken over my betrayal. Elle's a good actress, she'll make it work.

One of the guards lights a cigarette. The smell brings out the cravings I've worked so hard to stave off. I dig in my pocket for my pack of gum, but I don't have any on me. The sky opens up and it starts to pour, because the universe has it out for me today. The guards curse.

"Do you think the commander will notice if we guard the prisoner from inside?" One of them asks.

"I don't care. I'm not standing here getting wet." The guard tosses his cigarette on the ground and they step inside. I pick it up, the end still smoldering despite the rain.

Chapter 21

Wren

"Are you going to tell me where we're going?" I ask Miles. He's driving the station wagon with the demeanor of an eighty-year-old, going five miles under the speed limit and obeying all traffic signs with diligence bordering on obsession. I keep glancing out the back window expecting a horde of enforcers to appear. So far, we've been lucky. I just wish he'd speed up.

"Don't worry," says Glitch. She's sitting in the passenger seat next to Miles. I'm in the back seat with Grams, Don, and Ariel. It's a tight fit, but we made it work. Roy and Max are sitting in the trunk with our luggage. I dip my hand over the backseat to stroke Max's fur. He shifts under my touch before settling down again. Glitch turns around, leaning over the center console so she can look at me. "They won't be able to track us. I'm also monitoring the enforcer frequencies. If they're following us, I'd know about it."

"Thanks for the update, but I was asking Miles," I say.

"How long are you going to make me suffer before we can talk like normal people again?" asks Glitch.

"Until the Friday after hell freezes over," I say.

"That's mature."

"Bite me." I stick out my tongue. Glitch rolls her eyes and turns back around. I'm being a jerk. I know that, but she lied to me. It's going to take me some time to get over her betrayal, if I ever can. Miles taps his fingers on the steering wheel. I can't make out a song. I think it's just a pattern born out of anxiety or nerves.

"Are you going to answer my question?" I ask.

Miles sighs. "The Syndicate is going to help us escape the city." My stomach heaves. I've never been outside of the city before. I don't know what to expect. I know there's more to the world than our city. We're not Neanderthals, we have a TV. It's just that everything outside of the city seems like an exotic place that's cool to hear about, but you would never want to visit.

"I don't have enough credits for fake travel permits," I say.

"We don't need credits," says Miles.

"Why not? Please, explain what I'm missing here. You've been avoiding my questions like a seasoned politician. What gives?"

Miles slams his hand against the steering wheel. "For once in your life, can you just fucking trust me?"

"Language," Don and Grams interject at the same time.

I cross my arms and sink further into my seat. "I think a single f-bomb is warranted. It's more than Miles gave when he got involved with the Syndicate outside of Jimmy's Auto."

Miles glares at me in the rearview mirror. "You work for the Syndicate too, in case you've forgotten. We all do. Or are you too good for us after shacking up with the director's son and joining the enforcers?"

That's it. I see red. "I joined the enforcers to bust you out."

Miles snorts. "Screwing around with the director's son doesn't count as joining the enforcers."

I throw up my hands. "For f-," I swallow the curse word when Grams gives me a sharp look. "For fudge sake," I finish lamely. Ariel looks at me with wide eyes.

I take a few deep breaths and try to keep it together for the sake of my toddler. She has been through enough over the last few months. She doesn't need more disruption in her life.

"Sorry sweetie, just a bit of traffic. Nothing to worry about," I say. We haven't seen another car in five minutes. Thankfully, Ariel accepts my answer and goes back to playing with her doll.

"We'll talk about this later. Right now, I just need you to trust me," says Miles.

There's that word again. Trust.

It's quickly rising to the top of my least favorite words of all time. I don't trust what people say. I trust how they act and, right now, Miles is acting shady. I wish I could tell him exactly what I think about that, but I don't need Ariel to pick up any curse words from listening to the adults speak.

"Can you at least tell me what you do for the Syndicate?" I ask, trying to keep my anger in check. "Arranging travel permits and an untraceable car at a moments notice are more than a Syndicate mechanic can do. Clearly you have another job."

Miles flicks on his turning indicator, making a full stop at the light before he proceeds. "I'm a hacker."

"Like Glitch?" I ask.

"Better," says Glitch. She doesn't sound upset, rather her tone borders on admiration. Miles and Glitch share a look, an unspoken conversation passing between them. Something tugs at my stomach. I'm not jealous of Miles' friendship with Glitch. That would be petty. It's more a recognition of the grief I feel for the friendship Miles and I once shared. The realization that my best friend is a stranger. Part of me wishes we could rewind to the night before the enforcers stormed the auto shop. Back to when everything was simple.

But is that really what I want?

I get the feeling Miles has been lying to me for some time. Do I really want to go back to being ignorant? Miles turns off the main road, passing through an open gate. The hair on the back of my neck stands on end. We're driving through an empty rail yard that could be the set for a late-night horror movie.

We're near the city border, I can see the perimeter wall looming ominously in the distance. Intermodal shipping containers are stacked four high along a gravel access road. I don't see any people and the only source of light comes from our car. The digital display on the dash shows that it's two in the morning. I've been so jacked on adrenaline since the warehouse, I don't feel tired. Rage is better than any energy drink. If I could bottle this moment and sell it, I would make a fortune.

Miles pulls off the access road and parks beside a truck that is already loaded with a container. The container makes up most of the truck - there isn't a cab for a driver, it's completely autonomous. It looks like a steel box on wheels, but I'm guessing it's more complicated than that with sensors and a GPS guidance system for navigation. Miles flashes his headlights twice and two figures in dark clothing step out from the shadows into the beam. I tense and pull the gun out of my waistband. Grams gave it back to me when we left Ash's apartment.

"Don't worry," says Miles. "They're mine."

He's high enough up in the Syndicate to have his own people? My uneasiness grows.

"Stay here." Miles gets out of the car.

"I don't trust them," I say, making no move to put my gun away.

"Do we have a choice?" asks Roy. He has been quiet the whole drive. Where I've been poking Miles for answers since we got in the car, Roy seems resigned to our fate.

"Probably not," I mutter. I put my arm around Ariel, tugging her into my side, "but that doesn't mean I have to like it."

"Wren," says Glitch. She doesn't bother turning around this time. "I know this is a lot to process, but Miles would never do anything to hurt you. You know that."

Don scoffs. I glare at him, but he doesn't elaborate.

"I thought I knew a lot of things, but now I'm not so sure," I say. After a few minutes, Miles gestures for us to join him. Glitch opens the door and goes to meet him.

"Stay behind me. If anything goes wrong, I want you and Ariel to take the car while I hold them off," I say.

"Wren..." I look at Grams. It's difficult to make out her face in the dimly lit car, but I can tell she's worried.

"Promise me," I say.

Her shoulders slump in defeat. "I promise."

I get out of the car and approach the group, leading with my gun. The gravel crunches underfoot, punctuating each step. Miles' contacts are wearing masks to conceal their features. I don't miss the handguns strapped to their waists, but none of them have their weapons drawn. I guess that's something to be thankful for.

"Want to tell your girl to stash her piece?" says one of the men.

"I'm not his girl."

He laughs. "Yeah, whatever."

Miles takes a few steps toward me. He raises his hands in a placating motion that's bordering on condescending. "I told you," he says. "They're with me."

"And I told you I'm not in a trusting mood today," I say.

"So I've noticed," says Miles.

I don't lower the gun.

"This container is programmed to take us out of the city," says Miles. "This is the only way out." The open container behind him has a few crates inside, but it's mostly empty. That's when it dawns on me.

"Wait a minute, your friends are going to lock us in a metal box we have zero control over and ship us off to who knows where? That's your brilliant plan?" I ask.

Miles scowls. "I told you, these are my men. We can trust them."

"Trust me. Trust them. You've been saying that a lot lately, but you haven't said one thing tonight that makes me want to."

Miles drops his arms to his side. He doesn't try to come closer. He just stands there and gives me a sad smile.

"When we were kids, I told you that we would take care of each other. That you didn't need to worry about anything, because I was in your corner. This is me keeping that promise."

For just a moment, I get a glimpse of the old Miles. The boy with the missing front tooth who moved into the apartment down the hall. The friend who helped me with my homework. The guy who held my hand at my mother's funeral. The man who stood by me when I was pregnant with Ariel. The business partner who helped me take over Jimmy's Auto when I was depressed and overwhelmed.

I lower the gun.

"Okay," I say. I climb in the back of the container, helping Grams and Ariel up after me. Max hops in after us. I grab his body and haul him forward until his back feet can gain purchase. I know this is our best option. I could go back to an apartment the enforcers know about or spend my days in hiding, but that's no way to live. I can't raise Ariel like that and it's not fair to ask Grams to go on the run. They have both been through so much already.

I situate us near the back of the container behind some boxes. Don and Grams sit beside me. Ariel lays down and puts her head on my lap and Max curls up next to her. Glitch takes a seat against the wall across from us. She pulls out her tablet and studiously avoids eye contact. Roy sits next to Grams, putting as much physical distance between himself and Glitch as he can. Miles spends a few more minutes talking with his men outside before joining us. He sits next to Glitch and leans his head against the wall. The doors slam shut and I hear the deadbolt slide into place. We're trapped. I have a vague picture of us getting stuck in here for days until we slowly starve to death, but I cut off that line of thinking. It's not productive. I can't afford to have a panic attack right now.

"It's going to be okay, Chickadee," says Miles, sensing my impending breakdown.

"Don't call me that," I snap. Max growls at Miles, baring his teeth. Miles blanches. I rest my hand on Max's back gently to calm him down. It's the first time Max has ever growled at him.

The truck lurches forward.

"Do you have any lights?" asks Grams. I'm sure she's thinking about Ariel. She's asleep now, but I know when she wakes up she'll be scared.

"I do, but we can't risk the border patrols seeing them," Miles whispers. "We have to be quiet until we get out of the city, then I can turn on a light and we can talk."

I swear the truck hits every pothole on the street. Combine that with the frequent stops that accompany city driving and I'm ready to hurl. I don't usually get carsick, but it's a rough ride and I can't exactly crack a window. I focus on my breathing and pray I don't puke in a confined space. That would be less than ideal.

Finally, the truck rolls to a stop. I hear people talking outside, but their voices are muffled and I can't understand what they're saying. There's some scuffling near the back door. I assume they're checking the deadbolt lock and our permits to make sure this is a legal shipment.

After the longest two minutes of my life, the truck starts moving again. Miles waits another ten minutes or so before he turns on a flashlight. It's small, no bigger than his palm, but it provides a surprising amount of light in the enclosed space.

Ariel is still asleep on my lap. I'm glad she wasn't awake for the border crossing. She's usually pretty good about listening to me, but she's still a kid and this is a foreign situation.

"Where are we going?" I ask again, not expecting a response.

"A Syndicate stronghold in the country where big brother turns a blind eye."

There are a few more turns and then the truck picks up speed. It's loud inside the container without insulation. There's wind and tire noise that makes it difficult to talk. I assume we merged onto a highway. Thankfully, there aren't any potholes and the turns are more gentle. It gives me a minute to get my nausea under control. I lean my head against the wall and try to sleep, but it's impossible. I'm too worked up to relax and steel doesn't make for a great pillow.

After about an hour, Miles turns the light back on.

"Everyone wake up, we're almost at the drop point." Miles raises his voice to be heard over the road noise. I gently shake Ariel to wake her. I'm amazed she managed to sleep through the ride. It's a skill I wish I had.

"Wake up, honey," I say. Ariel rubs her eyes and gives an adorable yawn. Max stirs beside her. He licks her face and she bats him away with a sleepy smile. Her eyes pop open and she frowns.

"Where are we? I'm hungry. I have to go potty."

"Miles is taking us somewhere safe," I say, hoping it's the truth. "Just hold on for a few more minutes and we'll get you some food and a bathroom."

"I'm going to turn off the light for a bit. We're almost there," Miles says. He turns off the flashlight and the space returns to darkness. I feel the truck turn and we start to slow down. I drape my arm around Ariel as the truck brakes. When it stops completely, I get up and stretch my arms over my head. I'm stiff after sitting on the hard floor. There's some noise at the container doors before they swing open. The sun is just starting to come up, painting the sky pink. We're parked under a highway overpass. Miles and Glitch exit the truck first. Roy helps Grams down while I help Ariel.

Above us, I hear the traffic racing by. I hate to admit Miles picked a good location. We're hidden from the drivers above. If we parked beside the road and got out of the container, it would have drawn some attention. There's a gas station by the off-ramp, but it looks abandoned. There are panels missing from the canopy and the shop windows are broken. If there was anything valuable inside, it's long gone. There's a two-lane road leading to a town in the distance. It's hard to make out the details, but I can see a handful of houses. The container door closes with a bang, making me jump. A man I don't recognize locks the container. He's tall and skinny with straight, shoulder-length black hair he pushes behind his ear while he taps on his tablet. The truck pulls away and disappears up the on-ramp.

"Thanks for picking us up," says Miles.

"Yeah, sure," says the man. He glances up long enough for me to see he has a narrow face with severe cheekbones and heavy eyebrows. He crosses the street and gets in the driver's seat of an ancient minivan.

"Seems like a great conversationalist," I mutter.

Glitch snickers. "Don't mind Viper. He's a lot better with computers than people."

Viper. Glitch. I'm beginning to wonder if everyone in the Syndicate, aside from Miles, uses an alias. It has to be exhausting after a while. I take Ariel's hand and follow Miles to the car. He takes the passenger seat and the rest of us pile in the back. Viper makes a u-turn and drives towards the town.

"Won't the enforcers know the truck stopped here?" I ask.

"No," says Miles. "Viper covered our tracks. He hacked the container, so the logs reflect a nonstop trip. If anyone looks at the records, everything will check out. Besides, the infrastructure out here is dated compared to the city. There are dead zones and some areas with poor reception."

As we drive through the town, I see the truth in his words. The houses are dilapidated with weather battered siding and shingles that needed to be replaced twenty years ago. What landscaping there once was has gone feral, the grass sitting at waist height with wildflowers interspersed. Some of the houses have ivy crawling up them, abandoning their trellises in favor of the taller structures. There are indicators that this place was alive once. A forgotten tricycle lying in a driveway overtaken by weeds. A movie theater with a crooked sign. A diner trimmed with neon tubes sitting dormant. The world moved on and left this place behind.

We leave town, the houses instantly turning to cornfields. The crop has turned brown in the fields, dried out by the autumn sun. A huge machine chugs along, harvesting the crop and spitting out plant debris.

"Don't worry about the combines. They're autonomous," says Miles. "A huge commercial farm bought up the land thirty years ago or so. There's no one here to report us."

"I'm surprised they got the families to sell," says Grams. She came from a small farming community. I wonder if this looks anything like where she grew up?

"Most of them didn't have a choice," says Miles. Viper keeps driving. He takes a few turns until the road slopes down and the cornfields turn into a forest. The leaves are just starting to change color. I try to imagine what this road will look like in a week or so. I'm certain it's breathtaking. Viper brakes, turning down a gravel driveway that's barely visible between the trees.

About twenty feet into the forest, we stop in front of a tall chain-link fence with armed guards blocking our path. Up ahead, the gravel road slopes up to a two-story house with a wrap-around porch. It's boxy with white siding and black shutters. Unlike the houses in town, someone has been maintaining this one. The paint looks fresh and I even spot a garden out back. I feel like the only thing missing is a white picket fence. Grams sniffles. Silent tears are streaming down her face.

"What's wrong?" I ask in alarm.

"This was my house," says Grams. I open my mouth to ask what we're doing here, but Viper rolls down the window to talk to the guards.

"Open the gate," he says. The guards hustle to obey. They aren't like any guards I've ever seen. One of them is wearing a tank top and blue jeans. The other guy has a t-shirt and cargo shorts. After being around the enforcers for a few months, it's strange to me that they aren't wearing uniforms. Viper drives into the compound and stops in front of the house. He opens the door and leaves without so much as a goodbye.

"Wren, will you come inside with me? We need to talk."

"Why not? I'm already in a cult compound. What could go wrong?" I mutter. Miles glances at me. I shrug. Maybe he'll finally tell me what's going on.

"Are you okay?" I ask Grams. She takes Ariel's hand.

"I'll be fine," I tell Max to stay with them and I hand Grams my gun. I'm not letting them go unarmed, especially when I'm not with them. Some part of me knows Miles wouldn't let anything bad happen to them. I wouldn't be leaving them at all if I didn't believe that on some fundamental level. Still, the added protection makes me feel better.

"I'll stay with them," says Roy.

"Thanks."

"I'll check in with the team and come back with an update," says Glitch. Miles nods.

"This way." He gestures to the front porch with open arms. The front door opens into a large foyer with hardwood floors and a stained glass window I didn't notice from the outside. To the right is a grand staircase and to the left is a sitting room with large windows overlooking the forest. Miles leads us into the living room and plops down in an armchair.

"I didn't expect a Syndicate stronghold to look like this," I say, trailing my fingers along the wall.

"Most of them don't," says Miles. He guides me into the living room and takes a seat in an armchair. I take the couch across from him.

"Start talking," I say.

"I don't know where to start."

"What do you do for the Syndicate?"

"I told you, I'm a hacker," says Miles.

"Too vague. Try again."

"I created the 8-Bit app."

I snort. "Sure and I'm a millionaire."

Miles doesn't crack a smile. He keeps watching me as if expecting a bomb to drop.

"You're serious?" I ask. Miles nods. "But the app is only a few years old. That means you created it when we were...thirteen?"

"Fourteen," he mutters.

I knew Miles was a genius with computers, but I never pegged him as being capable of developing a technology that could impact millions. I think back to the conversations Miles and I have had over the past few years regarding the 8-Bit app. We talked about how it could be improved and fantasized about who created it. Miles played along with the conversation so well that I never pegged him as the creator, but, now that I think about it, every feature I ever wished for was eventually added. I was an unknowing sounding board for the largest employer in my neighborhood.

"Let me start over," says Miles. He leans forward and props his forearms on his knees. "When we were fourteen, your dad had just died. We were trying to get Jimmy's Auto up and running, but it was a mess. We couldn't drum up enough business. That's how I came up with the idea for the app. I pitched it to the leader of the Syndicate and she agreed."

"She?" I ask. Miles gives me a look that tells me I'm not going to like what comes out of his mouth.

"The leader of the Syndicate was Marcia Navarro."

Marcia Navarro. My mom.

"That doesn't make sense. Mom was a police officer. How could she be the mastermind behind the criminal organization she was fighting against? Not to mention she died when we were twelve. You were at the funeral, Miles!"

"Yeah, a funeral that was a closed casket." Miles scrubs his hands over his face, looking as if he has aged a decade in the last few hours. "That's what she wanted you to think. It's what she wanted the whole world to think. Marcia was the founder of the Syndicate. You have to remember what the world looked like a decade ago. Axton AI and companies like it eliminated most of the jobs overnight. The Council had just come to power. Marcia saw that happening in her neighborhood. She saw what was happening to Jimmy's Auto. She saw it in the riots she had to break up and the people she had to evict. It wasn't just something that was happening in the news. It was happening to people she knew."

"Thanks for the history lesson."

"I've seen the restricted footage and news articles from before the Council came to power, Wren," Miles says, a bit more forcefully. "The police force couldn't do anything. They were almost exclusively breaking up protests against the tech. companies. People hated them for it. You know your mom. Do you think she would have sat by and let everything go up in flames?" He gives me a pointed look. "Could you?"

"That's impossible," I say even though everything he's saying makes sense. I know neither one of us could sit back and watch the destruction in our homes and our families, but I refuse to believe it. Because if I do, that means mom chose to fake her death.

It means she left my dad and me behind.

It means she was aware she had a grandchild she didn't bother to meet.

It means I didn't know my mom at all.

Chapter 22

Wren

Miles gets up and opens a door into an adjacent room. The lights are off, but I can see the dull illumination of a few computer screens. He comes back with a worn piece of paper and hands it to me. It's a photo of Miles and my mom. She has her arm around his shoulders and they're smiling at the camera. It must have been taken a long time ago. Miles is shorter than her, barely coming up to her shoulders. He was still in that awkward lanky phase before he grew into his body.

"We took this the day the 8-Bit app launched," says Miles.

Mom is just as beautiful as I remember. She's smiling, a big toothy grin. There's a pink scar running along her jawline on the left side of her face that I don't remember her having. I try to ignore the differences between my memory of Mom and the photo, but it's impossible. This picture was taken after the funeral. If she didn't die six years ago, does that mean she's still alive? My shock transforms into anger the longer I stare at her image. My fingers press into the edges, crinkling it.

"Where is she?" I growl. I can't believe she had Miles break the news to me. I'm simultaneously elated by the idea she could still be alive and pissed off at her for remaining distant.

"I'm sorry," Miles says. He might as well have stabbed me in the chest. It would have been less painful than those two words. He takes the picture from my fingers gently, so I stop putting wrinkles in it.

"When?" I choke.

"She died a little over a month ago and left me in charge."

"Why didn't you tell me? About mom. About joining the Syndicate. All of it. I thought we were friends. We've spent every day together for as long as I can remember. You couldn't take two seconds to say 'Yo Wren, your mom is still alive and guess what? I built the 8-Bit app, you're welcome,'" I yell. Miles winces.

"She made me promise that I wouldn't. Running the Syndicate is dangerous. She kept her family a secret to keep you safe. The Syndicate needed a hacker to protect them against the growing influence of Axton AI and the Council. We had to find a way to connect people left behind by society. When I pitched the 8-Bit app, it was easy to get Marcia on board. She started a team to manage the app and put me in charge. Eventually, I became her second in command."

"Why you?" Miles gives me a pitying look. He knows what I'm really asking: Why didn't she ask me?

"You've always treated me like family, but I'm not. I was expendable, her daughter wasn't. She wanted me to break ties with you, but I couldn't do it. So, I kept one foot in both worlds. I helped you run Jimmy's Auto and I helped the Syndicate on the side."

I think back to the early days. Miles would disappear for hours at a time. I sometimes wondered about it, but I was too overcome with grief to care. I'd lost both my parents. Grams had just moved in. I was trying to keep a failing business afloat. I was depressed, anxious, and borderline apathetic.

"Can you let me at least try to explain without interruption? I promise I'll answer any questions you have, but I need to get everything out in the open first," says Miles.

I nod. He sits down and studies his hands for a few moments as if organizing his thoughts.

"Six years ago, we went to your mom's funeral. I was the first person to get to the church. When I walked inside, I heard voices. I got a bad feeling, so I hid in a coat closet and waited for them to leave. I saw your mom through the crack. I wasn't thinking, but I was so relieved to see her that I ran out and gave her a hug. She wasn't alone."

I try to think back to my mom's funeral. It was a small service held at a local church, a small brick building nestled between a grocery store and a gas station. Dad sprung for some white lilies, because they were mom's favorite flower. I wore a bubblegum pink dress - my only dress - made by our next-door neighbor. That was before Dad started drinking. I went to school that day. He said it was better to stay busy. Now, I wonder if it was because he needed some time to pull himself together. I wouldn't have held it against him, but Dad was always private like that. Incapable of sharing emotions with anything other than the bottom of a bottle.

"There were a few scary-looking guys with her. They were going to kill me and Marcia was going to let them. I know that's not how you remember your mom, but it's the truth. She was different with you and Jimmy than she was with other people. Softer. I told her I could keep my mouth shut. I offered to keep an eye on you for her, to be a link between her and her family."

A memory hits me. When we got to the church, Miles was sitting in the first row. Other people were just starting to arrive. He had his forearms resting on his knees, his head tucked between them like he was dizzy or about to be sick. I remember letting go of Dad's hand so I could run to him. I asked if he was alright. There was something in his eyes when he looked at me. Almost like guilt. I remember thinking it was strange, but Dad made me stand by the casket to talk to people before I could question him. I forgot to bring it up after the ceremony.

"Thankfully, Marcia agreed to let me live. I kept in touch with her at a distance for the next two years. I'd always been good with computers, so she gave me a job. It started small. Creating fake travel permits for runners. Things like that. When you took over Jimmy's Auto and we struggled to find customers, I started developing what would become the 8-Bit app. It didn't come to me all at once. I showed the prototype to Marcia and she saw the value instantly. It was a discreet way to connect Syndicate members and grunts with our services. It would make us very rich, very quickly. It would also give us a way to push back against the Council and the enforcers. I started coding the app when I was fourteen. For me, it was a fun after-school project. It was a challenging problem I liked working on. I had no idea how big it would get. It also brought me closer to Marcia. I felt like it was my duty to keep an eye on her, because you couldn't be there."

"I would have been if you had told me," I say.

"She would have disappeared and shut us both out," he replies evenly. "The 8-Bit app kept evolving and we needed more people to support our business. I started bringing on other hackers, like Glitch and Viper, to help with some of the workload. Things were going well. Over four years we grew the reach of the app and our services. Then, Jace Axton contacted me six months ago. He knew who I was. He knew who your mom was. He made Marcia an offer. She could continue to run the Syndicate and he wouldn't interfere if she helped him take ownership of Axton AI and the Council.

"We still don't know how Jace was able to identify us. Marcia agreed to meet with him to buy us some time. I wanted to go with her, but she asked me to stay behind as her second in command. I was going to ignore her orders. That's why I gave you the lottery ticket," says Miles, throwing me a sad smile. "I wanted to make sure you were taken care of if things went south. Marcia lied to me about the meeting time. It was a setup. Jace had her killed." White, hot anger courses through me. He's a dead man.

"Jace planned the raid on Jimmy's Auto," I say, connecting the dots. Ash arrested one of my customers after a tip was phoned in. It would have been easy for Jace to organize that if he was having us watched. My stomach sinks. "And the enforcer attack in the tunnels," I add. When the director named Ash his successor, Ash became another roadblock for Jace to remove. I wonder if the director told Jace what his plans were before he announced them to the Council? That would explain Jace's desire to take immediate ownership of the Council and Axton AI. I'm worried about Ash. He has no idea what Jace is involved in. I have to warn him.

"We suspect Jace has been gathering a following among the Council, the enforcers, and the Syndicate crew leaders," sighs Miles. "The crew leaders have been unhappy for years. Rook, the blond woman who leads the surge crew, has been the loudest. She has threatened us before, but the surge crew has never had the power to pose a real threat. We control the 8-Bit app which is the primary source of their business. We know who every member of the surge crew is and where they're located at all times. When Marcia died and I was arrested, it created a power vacuum. The crews are fighting amongst themselves to identify a new leader."

"But you're back now."

"It doesn't matter," Miles sighs. "There's no loyalty in the Syndicate without strength. If I want to stay in power, I need to put the surge crew in their place. That means starting a war. You should have taken the lottery ticket and found a comfortable job for yourself. You should have forgotten I existed at all. You would have been safer."

I stare at him. "Miles, you're my best friend. Did you really think I was going to leave you rotting away in an enforcer prison?"

Miles shrugged. "I expected you to make a smart move. To think about Ariel and Grams. My people would have gotten me out eventually."

"That's what families do, Miles. We protect each other. If you don't understand that, then you're a moron."

"Grow up!" Miles snaps. "It's time to take the training wheels off. If you put everyone before yourself, you're going to end up dead or worse."

"You're right. Maybe I care too much, but someone has to look out for this family."

"I am looking out for this family!"

"Oh yeah? Tell that to Robbie." I regret the words as soon as they leave my lips. My eyes are welling with tears and Miles shuts down.

"Get the out of this house," Miles seethes pointing at the door.

"With pleasure." If I stay any longer, I'm going to do something stupid like torch the farmhouse or forgive him for the last six years. I sprint around the house and head for the trees. but I don't make it more than twenty feet into the foliage before I'm confronted by a chain-link fence topped in barbed wire. It has to be at least ten feet tall, so there's no way I'm climbing it. My mom created a fortress, but all I see is a prison. I sit on the ground cross-legged.

For the first time in my life, I don't know what my next step is.

I'm not exactly a planner, but I've always been quick to make a decision. My life has been a constant stream of yes or no questions. I don't do gray areas. I don't do what-ifs or regrets. Life happens, but I always kept trudging forward.

I was able to make fast decisions, because I always had a solid foundation to fall back on. My family. My friendship with Miles. My job. None of that matters anymore, because it was all a lie. The people around me have changed...or maybe they're all the same, but I'm seeing them without a filter for the first time.

Or maybe people don't change at all. They just get worse at hiding who they are.

Maybe their masks wear down over time, just like the oil filter in a car. They filter out all the garbage until they're completely clogged and do more harm than good. The sounds of leaves rustling underfoot draws my attention. Grams pushes aside a branch, her eyes coming to rest on me. I turn back around, making no move to get up.

"Did you know about mom?" I ask. Right now, it's the only question that matters. Grams is silent. That's the only answer I need. "Why didn't you tell me?"

"Would it have made a difference?"

I glare at her. "Dad might still be alive if he knew mom was out there."

"He knew too, Wren."

"What?"

Grams sighs. She sits down beside me, taking a moment to lower herself to the ground. She's getting older and I know the hard dirt can't be good for her aching hips, but I'm not following her anywhere until I get an explanation.

"Marcia told Jimmy what her plan was. He knew the funeral was fake. He knew she was leaving us behind to run the Syndicate. He didn't want to force you into that life when you were too young to decide for yourself, so they decided to split up. They thought it would be easier on you if you thought she was dead. That way, you wouldn't go looking for her in the future."

"So, everyone knew but me."

"We did it to protect you."

"Why do you and Miles do that?" I groan. "You sugarcoat life like you think that'll make it sweeter for me, but it just makes it harder for me to be honest with you. It's okay for me to be in pain. It's okay for me to have explosive feelings and meltdowns and heartbreak. Life sucks sometimes! It's dirty. It's hard. It's complicated. It's a nuclear explosion of shit day in and day out, but instead of protecting me from it you made me feel like I was alone. You and Miles tiptoe around me like I'm some sort of plague victim. I thought it was my fault. I thought you pictured me as weak and fragile - someone who couldn't be trusted with reality because they might shatter under the weight of the truth. Now I know you avoided me because you felt guilty about lying to me."

"Wren-"

"I can't do this right now." I tear through the trees putting as much space between Grams and I as I can, because I know I'll say something I regret. When someone kicks me, I kick back twice as hard. I don't just get even. I obliterate the opposition. No matter what happens, I love Grams. I love Miles. I just can't be around them right now. They're the only family I have left. As much as it pains me to admit it when they hurt me so badly, it's the truth.

When I emerge from the trees, Glitch and Roy are playing with Ariel in the grass in front of the old red barn. They have a soccer ball they're kicking around. I can't remember the last time I played with Ariel outside. For just a moment, I can imagine a different life, but it's just a fantasy.

No matter how secluded this house is, we're still fugitives. The Syndicate is on the brink of war and Jace knows Miles' identity. The best decision I can make is to leave with Ariel and settle down in a new city. Maybe somewhere across the country where they will be less likely to know my face. It's a long shot. I know that. I have zero experience traveling outside of the city without drawing unwanted attention.

I have never felt so exposed and vulnerable and weak in my life.

Viper runs out of the barn waving at Glitch. She stops kicking the ball to speak with him, an alarmed expression on her face. It's the most animated I've seen Viper since I met him. I get the feeling it takes a lot to rattle the guy. I jog over to them.

"What's going on?" I ask.

"The director was assassinated," says Glitch. My legs go weak.

No. No, No, No, this can't be happening. Ash was going to talk to the director, get him to see reason. I have to warn him about Jace.

"Jace Axton just made an emergency announcement," explains Viper. "He named Asher Axton as the murderer."

"He's lying," I say, glancing from Glitch to Viper and back again. Glitch gives me a sympathetic look. I don't know if she believes that Ash is innocent, but she has an idea of how I feel about him.

"They named Jace as the new director," he says.

"But Ash was the designated successor," I say.

Viper blinks. "No, he wasn't."

"Yes, he was. He told me he was."

Viper shrugs. "There was never a public announcement. If the Council is aware, they're keeping quiet. It makes sense if you think about it. They can't have an assassin take the director seat."

"Ash wouldn't kill Byron," I say. "Jace probably killed him and pinned it on Ash."

Glitch frowns. "Even if that's true, there's nothing we can do about it. There's no proof."

"They're planning a trial for later this week," says Viper. "If Ash is the true successor, they'll probably opt for execution to silence him."

"No." My knees give out and I sink to the ground. Roy crouches down next to me. I know he's saying something, but I can't focus. His lips are moving, but the words aren't registering.

I made the wrong choice.

I should have taken Don's offer. I should have stayed with Ash.

Ariel sits beside me. "Are you okay, mommy?"

I pull her into my lap and let the tears fall down my face. "No, baby girl. I'm not."

I'm shaking. Or Ariel's shaking. I can't tell. All I know is holding Ariel is the only thing keeping me together while my world falls apart.

Epilogue

Ash

I roll the cigarette between my fingers. It's strange how time can change your perception, taking an action once familiar and making it feel foreign. Even the smell is different. Or maybe I just built the experience up in my mind, putting it on a pedestal that reality could never measure up to. It's hard to tell.

The rain has slowed to a steady drizzle. I've always loved the rain. The stillness. The quiet. The moment of peace when everyone else runs inside and you're left alone. My clothes are soaked through, my shirt plastered against my chest. Water droplets gather on the bars until they grow large enough to fall in my hair. They trickle down my face, emulating tears that never came.

"Can you give me a minute with the traitor?" I straighten up when I recognize Elle's voice just inside the door. The guards scramble to their feet from where they were sitting in the doorway, protected from the rain. They give her a sloppy salute and straighten their clothes. They're probably embarrassed Elle caught them discussing video games, bored out of their minds.

"We're not supposed to let anyone talk to him," says one of the guards.

"I'll be quick." Elle gives him a smile so warm it could thaw a glacier. I'm amazed he doesn't see through it, but he blushes. She trails her fingers along his arm. "Please? I have something I'd like to give him before they transport him to the Academy." She opens her palm to show him something and the guards chuckle.

"Just be fast, okay? I don't want the commander to find out about this. I'll get in trouble."

"Sure," says Elle. She winks at him. I roll my eyes.

"Here's an umbrella," says the younger guard. He fumbles it, but Elle catches it before it hits the ground.

"Thank you." She opens the umbrella and walks toward my cage. The older guard elbows his buddy giving him a what-was-that look. He shrugs, continuing to watch Elle. I guess we won't be afforded any privacy. Not that I expected her wishes to be honored. The guards may be a bit starstruck, but they're not complete idiots. Bending the rules to let Elle talk to me is one thing. Abandoning their post is another. I stand up and wrap my hands around the bars. Elle eyes the cigarette protruding between my fingers.

"It's amazing how something so small can be so dangerous," I say.

"You didn't-"

"No," I scoff. "I didn't smoke it, if that's what you're wondering." I flick the butt between the bars so it lands on the brick path behind Elle. She shoots a discreet glance at the guards. They're trying to act nonchalant, but I can tell they're hanging on to every word we say.

"I wanted to give this back." She holds up the Axton seal ring and steps closer so I can take it from her. She gives me a meaningful look. I grab her wrist and yank her towards the cage. Elle yelps, but I know it's because we're being watched. I was careful not to hurt her.

"I know you didn't kill the director," she whispers. The guards are already rushing toward us. "I'll find a way to bust you and Liam out before your trial. Don't trust Don, he's working for Jace." The guard that gave Elle the umbrella punches me in the side through the bars. It's an awkward hit. It doesn't particularly hurt, but I release Elle's wrist and stumble back, feigning injury.

Don't trust Don.

Don with his kind smile and friendly words. Don, the man who was practically a father to me.

He's working for Jace.

Don, the man who disowned both of his sons when he found out they worked for the Syndicate.

How did I miss that? I start making connections I should have made a long time ago. The raid on Jimmy's Auto, Jace showing up at Wren's apartment, the leaked patrol routes and the stolen bot, the enforcers in the tunnel, and the squad that arrested me at the warehouse. Jace has been executing a plan six months in the making. I have no doubt he has been working on this since Byron told him he was giving me the successor title.

Don was a match dropped in a puddle of gasoline. He gave Jace the Syndicate leader and Jace leveraged that to create an army.

The older guard raises his rifle. "I should kill you, traitor."

I shrug. "Go for it. It's not like I'll live past my trial."

Elle pushes the barrel down and gives me a scathing look. "That's quite unnecessary. He's just a little upset, that's all." She turns to leave with the guards.

"If you find Wren, can you tell her I'm sorry?" I ask. Elle freezes, the guards stopping beside her.

She frowns. "I'll see what I can do." Elle and the guards disappear inside.

Byron was going to call a Council meeting tomorrow to cancel the bot expansion. Jace doesn't have the same moral dilemma when it comes to using machines. I won't be surprised if he has the grunt sectors under martial law within the week. I think of Wren and her family and all the people I've met over the last month. They're going to suffer, because I didn't anticipate how far Jace would go to secure the director title.

I can't let that happen. I won't let that happen.

I have no idea where Wren is or if she can help, but if Elle is planning to bust Liam and me out of the Academy we'll need somewhere safe to lie low. There isn't anyone in this city who would take me in after today. I'm sure Jace is broadcasting my betrayal to the public. I grind my teeth. My only option is the Syndicate.

If Elle can get in touch with Wren, she might be able to convince Miles to smuggle Liam and me out of the city. Then, I have to convince him to go to war against the Council. I almost laugh. The irony isn't lost on me. I spent my entire life trying to dismantle the Syndicate only to turn around and ask them to do the very thing I was trying to prevent.

I pick up the seal ring and wipe off the mud, revealing the cursive 'A.' In the end, Byron was right. Having something to lose makes you easy to control, but he forgot the second part. Having something to lose gives you a reason to fight. I slip the ring on my finger and smile. I'm an Axton.

Axton's don't fight fair. We fight to win.

Acknowledgments

This book almost killed me.

Joking aside, I never would have been able to finish the story that has been rattling around inside my head without a lot of help and coffee.

Don't forget coffee.

I have to start by thanking my husband, Michael, for putting up with my near fanatic writing bouts and hermit-like tendencies. I wouldn't have been able to do this without your love and support.

Thank you to the strong women in my life who are my inspirations in all things. A very special thanks to my mom who encouraged me to follow my dreams. My readers have you to thank for realistic injuries and treatments from your time as a surgical tech. You're probably the only reason I haven't ended up on an FBI watch list for my Internet browsing history.

To my grandma Gena who once went out and got a job simply because she was told she couldn't do it. Thank you for showing me early on that you are the only person who can limit your potential.

To my beta readers: Meri, Taylor, Erica, and Katelyn. Thank you for suffering through my crappy first drafts and for being the voice of reason in all my endeavors. You're the Glitch(s) to my Wren, the good friends to my bad choices. Life would be boring without you.

To my mentors and teachers - Linda, Amelia, Joanne, and Cassy - thank you for your feedback and guidance. I wouldn't be where I am today without you.

To my readers - thank you for taking a chance on Ash and Wren.

About the Author

April Orion loves to write about near-future worlds and the technologies that will impact how we live and love. She is a data scientist by trade and a sommelier at heart. She is a lover of coffee, all things science fiction, and annoying her husband by singing off-key (and very loudly) to punk rock anthems. Visit aprilorion.com for the latest book news and giveaways.

f facebook.com/aprilorionauthor/

⊙ instagram.com/aprilorionauthor/

Also By